Between the Alpha's War

S. E. Dymek

Warning: book contains scenes of sexual content, violence, adult content, and foul language. Some scenes may be triggers to some and are not appropriate for all ages. Thank you for reading- S.E Dymek

Dedication

To Aaralyn, Ivy, and Caiden. My biggest inspirations for everything I do. To my husband, Aaron, who is my biggest support.

Acknowledgements

I'd like to thank my parents, close family, and all my inner, dearest friends who listened to me babble about ideas and were willing to read them. I love you all. Thank you to all my readers!

About the Author

S.E. Dymek is an upcoming author who has published **The Star Saga:** Including The Morning Star, The Evening Star, and The North Star available with Barnes and Nobles, Amazon, Kindle, and other book selling sites. She is also published on several ebook platforms. She has a passion for writing romance novels including paranormal romance novels and fantasy. All of her works include twists and turns, keeping her readers on their toes. She is a mother of three and loving wife. When she is not writing; she is working as a veterinary technician. Born and raised in Rhode Island, she has found her second home in Texas.

Chapter One
Shattered

Something was wrong. She knew it the instant she pushed the door open to her home. The door; she stared at the yellow door as it swung back to her. Her mother had been going on about painting the door for days now and finally, just had finished it. The door swung back open, creaking as it did. Her breath caught in her throat as she pushed herself. She stepped inside the dark house. Her house was always warm and comforting. It was cold, and the chill gave her instant goosebumps. She could hear the TV static coming from the living room as she stepped inside.

"Mom?" She called into the darkness, her voice shaking.

Her mother spent most nights passed out on the couch watching TV after working her shifts at the hospital. Why did this not feel like most nights? Her feet hit the soft beige carpet of the living room, and as she did, she was hit with the strangest smell. She put her hand up to her nose. Iron? But… sweet? Maybe metallic? There was so much of it. She gagged as it overwhelmed her. She put her hand over her nose to stop the smell from invading her nose.

"Mom? Dad?" She called into the living room; Her voice bounced off the walls of the silent home, echoing back to her..

Her stomach twisted, she didn't want to go in the room. She had to force herself to go further into the room. She took a deep breath and rounded the brown sofa that sat directly in front of the TV. Her feet stepped onto something wet and sticky. Her eyes shot down, staring at the red in confusion. Her body began to shake as it recognized what the red substance was before her mind could. A wave of nausea hit her as she looked from the floor to the couch.

Sitting side by side, with their heads tilted back, were both her parents. They had gaping holes in their necks. Blood flowed down the front of their chest like a waterfall and onto the floor, causing a river of blood that came down from the couch and ended where her feet began. Her mother's eyes staring vacantly at the TV, as if she didn't see anything coming. Her father's head was turned slightly, looking at her mother. His eyes were wide open with horror as if he had seen what happened to his wife before it happened to him. She fell to her knees, doubling over as her body began to shake. She put her hands over her head as a bloodcurdling scream erupted from her chest. She looked back up at her parents. Shaking, she fell backward onto her bottom and scooted herself away from them. She got to her feet, shaking as she almost stumbled forward into the pond of blood. She fumbled in her back pocket, choking down another wave of nausea. She tried to get her hands to work as she dialed 911. The operator came over the phone.

"911. What's your emergency?"

"Help! My parents…there's so much blood." Her voice broke as she spoke, forcing the words out of herself.

"Ma'am, can you tell me your name?"

"Nora. Please, I don't think…they can't still be alive," she choked out through the falling tears.

"Nora, is there anyone else in the home with you? I've pulled up your address and help is on the way."

Is anyone else in the home? Nora's stomach flipped inward on itself. James. Her phone fell from her hand, smashing into the blood as she rushed up the stairs.

"James!" She screamed as she raced up the stairs.

She rounded the banister of the stairs as her feet hit the hardwood floor of the upper landing. She ran to his room, tripping and falling in front of the batman poster on his door. As she fell, her fingertips brushed the door, and it slowly creaked open.

Another wave of sweet metal hit her nostrils, and she cringed. Her mind screamed; this can't be real. She pulled herself up to her feet and went into the room. Please god. She yelled in her mind as she begged for James to be ok. The room was dark, except for his batman light projecting the bat symbol onto the ceiling of his room. She saw his twin-size bed and it looked like he was curled up in his batman bedspread, sleeping. She paused, praying that he was sleeping. She walked in what felt like slow motion. As she approached the bed, she could see his little dark curls peeking out from under the blankets.

"James." Nora whispered, her hand shaking as she reached for her ten-year-old brother.

He didn't respond. Her hand shakenly grabbed the blanket, and she slowly pulled on it. As the blanket came back, blood poured out of the bed. She raced to him and rolled him over. His throat looked the same as their parents. She scooped her brother into her arms as she crashed to the floor, cradling him.

"Jamie!" She cried, calling him by his nickname.

"Please, no! Jamie! No, you're fine, you're ok! Stop." She cried as she tried shaking him lightly.

She wrapped her arms around him, cradling him close to her chest. Scooping him into her arms, she carried him down the stairs, hoping there was still a chance. Reaching the bottom step, she caught a glimpse of something. She could hear the sirens outside from the police. She was almost at the door.

Something very large stepped out from the living room. Deep, dark red brown fur approached her from the side. Nora froze, looking over her shoulder, stopping just in front of the yellow front door, which hung wide open. Red glowing eyes, teeth, and dark red brown fur were all she saw before searing pain hit her, and she crashed to the ground. She could feel her own blood leaving her as coldness enveloped her.

"Nora?" A voice called to her.

"Hang on." Another voice said as she felt something touch her face.

"James." Nora whispered, trying hard to come back.

The officers knew from the amount of blood on the floor that there was no way the young boy was still alive. Nora jumped as the officer touched her.

"Please help him." She cried, holding her brother out to him.

The officer didn't have the heart to tell her that there was no helping the boy. He took the boy in his arms and motioned for the other officer to get Nora. The EMTs arrived and took over. They quickly got Nora onto a stretcher and carried her out. She was in and out of consciousness.

"Animal attack?" One officer said to another.

"How? An animal forced entry into the home and then killed them all without them noticing?" The other whispered back.

"The wounds look animalistic." The first officer whispered back.

Nora's head began to spin. Animal? All? James? Dead? The world began to blur, and her vision tunneled. She woke up in a hospital bed with monitors strapped to her and an IV in her arm. She was confused about the IV, but she knew from her mom that if someone came into the ER, more than likely they were getting an IV, everyone would get an IV. She smiled, thinking about her mom making jokes about it. Mom…The word echoed in her head, and then everything came rushing back to her. The monitor started to alarm as her heart rate skyrocketed.

A nurse came rushing in. The side of Nora's throat felt stiff. She touched it lightly as she looked at the nurse. She felt the prickles of sutures. The nurse coming to her side and touching her arm got her attention.

"My mom? James? My Dad?" She blurted out in between heavy breaths.

She could feel her airway starting to constrict as panic set in her. She wanted someone to just tell her this was a dream. That she had fallen and, while she was out she had made up a horrible nightmare. Another nurse came in.

"She's having a panic attack. We need to give her something to calm her down. She is going to hyperventilate." The nurse said to the one that just walked in. With a nod, the other nurse disappeared.

"Nora, honey, I need you to try to take deep breaths. In through your nose, out your mouth. Air through your nose, and push it out your mouth." The nurse said, using her hands while she talked.

"My….fam..ily.." Nora stuttered out between gasps.

The nurse tried to hide the emotions on her face, but Nora saw it. That small look of pity the nurse let escape was all Nora needed to know this wasn't a dream. Her chest constricted more, she couldn't breathe, and her throat felt like it was caving in. Her lungs were on fire, screaming for air. The second nurse ran back into the room with something in a syringe. They put it into the IV port and flushed whatever drug into her bloodstream. She began to breathe slowly, her body began to relax, but as it did, darkness took over, and she was back asleep.

Jace heard about the family being attacked. He was sitting seven houses away in his car, listening. He thought it was a simple attack by Kip's pack again, but from what he heard being described, it seemed almost planned. Yes, it was brutal but it was thought out, which was not like Kip at all. All of the previous attacks were mindless. Jace was on his way to cover up the scene but the police got there so quickly.

"All dead." He heard one officer say.

Jace frowned, but at least he didn't have to keep checking in on this one now. He usually had to follow up on the ones Kip missed, just in case they began remembering the attack or would expose them.

"Everything ok, Alpha?" Dante's voice chimed *in his head.*

"Everything's good. Head back home, nothing to do here." He mind-linked back.

Jace switched his car into gear and took off back to the community

Chapter Two
Broken

"Damn it, Nora! Wake up!" The sound of beer bottles being tripped over echoed through the room as they were kicked about.

"Look at this mess! Nora! Wake the hell up!" A hand shook her awake.

She rolled over, groaning. Her head was killing her, and as she rolled over, she knocked over a beer bottle. The bottle crashed to the floor, spilling the remaining liquid everywhere.

"You need to get up. God, you need a shower, and we need to get going." A strong voice said as Nora was yanked up.

Nora growled and yanked her arm away but stumbled. She was still drunk. The hand came back and steadied her.

"Damn it, sweetheart. You need to do better." The voice said, calming down.

"I know life fucking sucks, but you can't keep trying to drown yourself. Come on, let's get you cleaned up."

"Joel?" Nora said, slurring as she focused her eyes on the person she was holding onto for dear life.

"Yeah, hun. It's me. Come on, a warm shower will do you good." Joel said with a smile.

"Ok." Nora said as she stumbled through more cans and bottles.

Joel was Nora's best friend since they were kids. After her parents and little brother were killed with no leads, Joel made it his job to make sure Nora stayed alive. The house and everything were paid off with her parents' death benefits. She was all alone, with no grandparents, aunts, or uncles. Just her and… Joel.

Joel helped a very drunk wobbly Nora to the bathroom. He sat her down on the toilet and yanked her vomited stain shirt over her head. She heard him mumbling something about how he could never leave her alone, not even for one night. She giggled slightly.

"It's not funny, Nora! You could have killed yourself." Joel said angrily at her.

Nora shrugged and began to slip off her socks. She almost fell over as she did so. Joel steadied her, his eyes scolding her as he did.

"Don't fucking shrug your shoulders at me." Joel yelled at her again as he turned around and turned on the shower.

"You don't have to keep doing this, Joel. I am fine on my own." Nora said, pulling her bra off.

"Yeah. One fine mess." Joel muttered as he tested the water.

"Can you even stand in the shower or should I turn this into a bath?" Joel said, looking about the bathroom for something.

"I can stand." Nora said, rolling her eyes.

She stood and started undoing her pants. She felt like she was on a ship at sea. Everything was so unstable. She smirked at her own thoughts. She was unstable, that was sure. She dropped her jeans and underwear to the floor, kicking them away from her as she stumbled to the shower. She yanked back the curtain and climbed in. The warm water felt good on her body; she let it hit the base of her neck, hoping it would chase away her horrible headache.

"Where do you keep going? Who's letting you buy all this booze?" Joel questioned her as he walked back into the bathroom carrying clean towels.

"I'm a girl. I've learned that, if I flirt and bat my eyes, I can pretty much get what I want. You should try it." Nora chuckled.

"Are you coming to school today?" Joel asked, leaning over and looking at himself in the mirror.

"Not sure, why should I?" Nora said carelessly.

"Because we're like two weeks from graduating and before everything happened, your GPA was so high that you probably could get your degree if you would just come." Joel said, plucking out a straggler eyebrow hair.

"Will you stop being mad at me if I go?" Nora asked like a child in trouble.

"I guess so." Joel said, now moving on to checking his complexion.

"Fine. I'll go, but I can't promise I'll make it through the whole day." Nora said, pushing the shower curtain open and holding her hand out for a towel.

Joel turned and handed her a towel but paused, holding out the towel and seeing bruises on her ribs. Joel immediately scooted off the counter.

"Nora, what the hell are those?" He yelled at her, pointing at the very purple rib.

"Bruises, Joel." Nora said, wrapping the towel around her.

"Duh. I'm not blind. Where did they come from?" Joel said, putting his hands on his hips.

"I think from some railings. Yeah, railings. Some brute pushed me into them trying to be a little too friendly. So I shoved my knee into his pair of friends, the ones he wanted to show me, and knocked his ass down the stairs." Nora said, walking out of the bathroom.

"For fuck's sake Nora!" Joel said, following her.

"Joel, I can defend myself. Besides the bruises, I am perfectly fine." Nora said, grabbing a black t-shirt and jeans from her closet.

"I'm moving in." Joel announced.

"Excuse me?" Nora asked from under her black t-shirt.

"Yup, you heard me. I'll bring my things over tonight, so you better pick which side of the room you like bestie, because the other side is mine. You apparently need a live-in babysitter, with your stupid ass." Joel said, walking to her bedroom door.

Nora laughed at her friend as he very dramatically exited the room. Joel loved her in a way no friend had ever loved her. He stepped up when her world crashed, and he was still trying to put out the fires she was starting. She sighed; she hated that she was causing him so much trouble but was secretly grateful she still had someone left in this world.

Walking out of her bedroom, she froze; her heart sank as she looked across the hall. She hadn't touched anything since that night. The Batman poster was still perfectly in place, like it was just waiting for James to come home. She didn't even know if the bat symbol night-light ever got turned off. She couldn't bring herself to go in there. She thought about moving. She still couldn't go into the living room. She hung sheets in front of the living room entrance so she wouldn't have to look into it anymore. She couldn't live on her own, with no job and no income. She was stuck here because she could survive here. 'Survive' was a funny word to call it. She existed in the sorrow and madness that became her world. Part of her felt like she needed to stay in the dark place. Whenever she felt the slightest bit of happiness, she felt that she was betraying them. How dare she be happy when they're not here... when they're dead. She didn't realize it, but she was shaking, hot tears fell silently from her eyes as she stood unmoving, staring down James' door.

She didn't even hear Joel come back up the stairs. She felt his strong arm slip around her shoulders as he pulled her into him.

"Come on doll, let's get out of here." Joel said, leading her away from James's door and down the stairwell.

Joel made sure to block the living room with his body even though the sheets were doing that. He pulled open the front door and held it open for Nora. She walked out of it almost like a lost puppy that wasn't really sure what she should be doing. The yellow door caught her eye, and the image of it swaying back and forth that night crept into her mind. Joel pretended not to see the look in her eyes. He didn't want to help her go down memory lane. He closed the door and pressed the clicker on his keys to unlock his Honda Civic car. He nudged Nora forward as he started walking to his car. He opened the passenger side door for her and waited for her to finish slow motion walking to his car.

"Come on Nora, I promise today won't be so bad." He smiled at her.

She hated school. She hated the looks she got, the small whispers about how she was a shell of a person. The sad pitiful looks, pitying stares she got. You would think a college campus would be too busy for all of that, but welcome to living in a small town. She sighed, sitting down in the passenger seat; she watched Joel close her door and jog over to the driver's side. He opened the door and was in the car in no time. Joel placed the key in ignition, he was driving them to their horrible destination.

"Maybe you should move in with me?" Joel said softly.

Nora was silent, Joel still lived at home, and she loved Joel's parents. Joel's father had passed away a few years ago but they kept to themselves for the most part and loved Joel with their whole heart. Even when he came out as gay. They were actually upset that he felt he needed to tell them, like why he thought it would have made a difference for them in loving him or not. Nora was there that day, Joel clung to her hand as if she was his only support. It was one of the most beautiful things she had ever witnessed, too. The way his parents loved him made her miss hers so much more.

"There's that spare room, and it has its own bathroom. The tub even has jets in it." Joel said to her as if he was trying to sell her a timeshare.

She chuckled at his selling point of the tub. She wanted to say, yes; she wanted to be anywhere that didn't still smell like blood, somewhere she didn't see their hollow vacant stares of her parents when she left her room to go to the bathroom or get a drink from the kitchen. She wanted to be away from it so badly, yet it was the only thing keeping her with them. Grief was the craziest thing she has ever experienced.

"Maybe." She managed to say.

"Well, either way, you're not staying alone anymore." Joel said firmly.

"If you say so," Nora said, giving him a weak smile as Joel turned the car into the campus parking lot.

He pulled his black two door Honda Civic car with its shiny spoiler into the student parking spot. She chuckled as he closed the sunroof. She remembered going car shopping with him. There were only three items on his list. It had to be black, it had to have a sunroof, and he wanted it to have a spoiler. It was like he was some type of racing fan. She smiled, still laughing at the memory. He glanced over at her; his eyebrow was raised, asking her what she was thinking about. She shook her head.

"Well, we've reached our destination. How are you feeling? There's Tylenol in the glove box if you need it," Joel nodded to the glove box as he spoke.

"I'm good. Does the car ride count as me going to school? I mean technically, I am here," Nora smiled brightly at him, batting her eyes as she did.

"Doll, this look might get you free booze, but it doesn't work on me. Get your ass out of my car, and let's do this," Joel said, rolling his eyes as he pushed his car door open.

"Ugh, fine!" Nora groaned, going to shove her shoulder into his door but didn't realize Joel had already opened it.

Joel frowned at how upset she was, but offered her his arm. She sighed, giving in as she wrapped her arm into his, cuddling into his upper arm as they walked. She truly was so grateful that he was in her life. She didn't know where she would be right now without Joel.

Chapter Three
Nightmare

Dread pitted in her stomach as they made their way up the walkway to the school. While entering the gym, her stomach knotted. She saw the hard stares of the cheerleaders. As she walked by, they leaned in and whispered to each other. She used to be one of them. She was even going to college on a scholarship from cheerleading. She would go to practice every Monday, Wednesday, and Friday with them. She and Laura would be in constant contact about new routines. She was one of the lead cheerleaders; they looked up to her. Cheerleading had been her life. She thought the squad was her friend, but when her world crashed and burned, they were the first to let her fall and drift away.

"Let's see how long she makes it today. Anyone wants to place bets?" Laura giggled as Nora walked past.

"Wanna place bets on how many football players smashed you…does the whole team count? You know what a cheerleader is, right? You weren't supposed to cheer for the whole team….by yourself." Joel said, stopping short and giving Laura a death stare.

Laura gasped as she tried to think of something clever to say back, but Joel didn't have time to waste. He left her with her mouth hanging open as he pulled Nora along. He glanced down at Nora, who was staring straight ahead. She was pretending she didn't hear any of what just took place. They left the gym and started down the hall. She didn't want to do this. She could already feel each person's eyes on her as she walked. She cringed, seeing the guidance counselor up ahead, Mrs. Jone. She tried to shrink away behind Joel, but it was too late.

"Nora! Nora sweetheart. Oh, it is so good to see you at school!" Mrs. Jones said, rushing over to her.

"Hi, Mrs. Jones." Nora smiled weakly at her.

"Do you need anything? I have plenty of spots open today. Why don't you come by my office around eleven, and we can catch up." Mrs. Jones said to her casually, like they were meeting up for drinks.

"Ok," Nora said, thinking she was not going.

"All right, you run along." Mrs. Jone said excitedly, clasping her hands together as she spoke.

Joel was trying his hardest not to laugh. Nora saw him and elbowed him in the stomach. She shot him a look as if to tell him that was enough. He chuckled but moved through the hall silently. Nora saw her first class coming up and frowned. She would need to leave Joel. She closed her eyes and told herself she could do this. She straightened herself out as they reached the door. Joel squeezed her arm slightly, and she glanced over at him.

"You got this, babe," Joel said, leaning forward and kissing her forehead lightly.

Nora sighed and nodded. She wanted to. Deep down inside, she did want a way out of the darkness, but it felt wrong sometimes. She watched Joel walk away in the perfect white t-shirt that he had probably ironed this morning until he was gone. She dragged herself into the room; the room went silent as she walked in. She rolled her eyes as she made her way to the back corner and sat. The professor came in and began his lecture. His monotone voice echoed off the walls in the room as she zoned out. The professor's voice was making her eyelids heavy. She rubbed her hand over her face trying to stay awake. She couldn't even focus on what he was teaching; his voice was so low and just sounded like a constant dull noise. She felt her head drop forward.

"Nora." A faint whisper called to her. It was haunting but beautiful.

Nora lifted her head at the sound of the voice. It was familiar and warm. She rubbed her face trying to get herself to wake up.

"Nora." The voice called to her again.

"Hello?" Nora answered and forced her eyes open as she looked around.

She was leaning on her kitchen counter. She ran her hand over the granite. How? Did she lie about going to school? Did Joel even come over? She thought as she began drumming her fingers on the counter.

"Nora." The voice said urgently.

"Where are you? Who are you?" She called out in her kitchen.

"Nora, it's coming. You have to be prepared. When you turn twenty-one, you will learn everything.

You need to be ready. The world is not what it seems," the voice whispered.

"What?" Nora asked, turning around and looking at where the sound was coming from.

"Mom?" Nora asked the woman standing inches from her.

The woman looked just like her. There was no way she was here. She wanted to reach out and touch her. Her long raven black hair flowed down around her and perfect waves. Her porcelain skin made her perfect gray eyes stand out. She wanted to wrap her arms around her. She missed her so much.

"Nora, you need to be ready, or they will find you." She said as she stepped away.

"Mom, wait, who? Don't go. Please," Nora said, reaching out to her and starting to follow her.

"Nora, they'll find you and kill you if you're not careful." Nora's mother turned around.

As she turned and finished her sentence, her neck flayed open. Nora gasped, backing away as a river of blood began pouring down the front of her. Images of that night began flashing in front of Nora's eyes. The yellow door, the smell of blood, the TV static. Nora clutched her chest as she began to have trouble breathing.

"Nora, you need to make it to your birthday. Stop being so reckless." Her mother said through the river of blood.

"Hey." "Hey, girl!" "Hey, wake up!"

Nora bolted upright, her hand coming up swinging, trying to push whatever was touching her away.

Something caught her hand. Her cheeks were wet with tears; she was shaking and breathing uncontrollably. She looked around wide-eyed. The room came into focus. Some boy was shaking her. She had never seen him before; she tried to calm herself by looking at him. She frantically looked around the room. It was empty, and everyone had cleared out. Nora tried to slow her breathing. She began to panic more, realizing she had drifted off to sleep in class and had one of her nightmares. She pulled her hand away from the stranger and stood up slowly.

"Hey, are you ok?" He asked, concerned. His hand was still holding onto her shoulder.

"Yes." She got out in between breaths.

"Are you sure?" He asked again, his dark brown eyes full of concern for her.

Nora shook her head, backing away from him. He had been kneeling next to her, his blond hair hanging down into his eyes. He stood up, looking at her confused. Nora didn't say anything else but turned and left as quickly as she could.

"Hey, let me walk you-" Nora could hear him attempt to say as her slow backing away turned into fleeing.

She found the bathroom as quickly as she could, praying no one was in there as she pushed open the door. She paused as she entered. Thank god, she thought as she walked over to the sink. She turned on the water, cupping her hands, and watched the water fill them. She splashed it over her face. Closing her eyes as the water dripped down them. She let out a long breath as she opened her eyes and looked into the mirror. She looked at herself. She studied her face. She looked very much like her mother. Long raven-colored hair that flowed past her shoulders in perfect waves, she had the same almond eye shape, but she had her father's honeycomb colored eyes. Unlike her pure, almost snow- white skin, her skin was sun-kissed like her father's. It made the honey color in her eyes stand out even more. She hated looking in the mirror because she could see both of them in her, and her heart ached.

     She grabbed paper towels and patted her face dry. She thought about her nightmare. It was different. Normally it was just scenes from the night. She never had her mother come to her and speak to her like that. Why was she warning her? Why was her birthday so important? She sighed. Why was she giving any thought to her crazy dream? Dreams don't have answers in them. She thought, grumbling as she threw the paper towel away. She glanced down at her watch. It was noon. How did she miss the whole day? Thank god she was halfway through the day. She glanced at the mirror and told herself she could do this. At least now she could meet up with Joel. She turned away from the mirror and began walking out of the bathroom.

Chapter Four
Struggle

Jace leaned over his desk, his eyes shut, squeezing his hands into it. He could feel the wood giving under his hands. A map was laid out in front of him. All little red markers on it, a total of ten now. He was trying to focus on his anger. The office door creaked open, and Dante walked in. Jace knew who it was before the door was even opened. There were only two people who would just walk into his office without waiting to be approved. Dante and Wyatt. Jace's ice blue snapped open, staring down whoever walked in. Dante threw his hands up, a smirk on his face.

"I come in peace." Dante said, trying to lighten the very heavy mood.

Jace grunted but didn't respond. He looked back over the map, trying to find a pattern or something that would make sense. All he saw was Kip's madness.

"How many now?" Dante asked quietly, coming to Jace's side.

"Ten. Ten mindless attacks." Jace said, letting go of the sides of the desk Dante's eyes scanned over the map.

Next to the map were newspaper articles stacked on top of each other. The top page headline was "Animal attacks on the rise." Dante frowned. He looked over the desk and raised an eyebrow at Jace. Jace saw him scan the desk and sighed.

"If I can't stop this, I will have to go to the council. I am building my case." Jace explained, walking to the window and looking out it.

"The council?" Dante repeated, distaste in his mouth.

"Yes." Jace said, gritting his teeth.

Dante was quiet. He hated the council. They were a bunch of power-hungry wolves who thought they were better than everyone else. Dante let out a small sigh as he wondered why Jace was trying to figure out a pattern to this, Kip was insane, and everyone knew it. His own pack knew it, but they either enjoyed it or were too terrified to do anything about it.

"Set up a meeting with Kip, neutral territory." Jace said; the word sounded exhausting, coming out of his mouth as if it was one of the hardest things for him to say.

"What?" Dante asked. His ears had to be hearing wrong.

"Don't make me repeat myself." Jace growled.

"Yes, Alpha." Dante answered quietly.

He was going to argue about how it was useless, that Kip was never going to listen to reason, but he wasn't going to question his Alpha any further. Jace didn't say anything else, and Dante quietly left the room.

Jace paced back and forth in front of the window for a moment. He was restless. His wolf was restless. He needs to escape. He glanced down at his watch, debating. He could go for a quick run. It would relax his mind and relax his wolf.

The hallway began to fill with people. Nora shuddered as she tried to make it through the crowd. She felt like a ping pong ball as she bounced from one person to the next. Each one made some rude comment as she tried to hold her own. She pushed her way through until she was finally out of the hall. She leaned up against the wall, panic setting in as she looked around. She felt like a cornered animal looking for a way out. She pressed her back further into the wall, trying to stay far away from everyone passing. She glanced in the direction of the lunch room. It was so close but so far away. She inhaled deeply and shut her eyes, tuning the noise out. The world around her went silent as she focused on her breathing. Her breathing slowed, and she felt better. As she opened her eyes, the halls were empty. She let out a sigh of relief as she stepped away from the wall.

The school was quiet, with the only noise coming from the cafeteria. Shaking, she put her brave face on and walked to the cafeteria. She took a deep breath pausing in the doorway of it. She never used to be like this. She didn't feel overwhelmed in any situation. She used to live for the thrill of competing in front of thousands of people for cheer, but now she panics at a handful of kids her own age. I should just leave. She thought, as she began withdrawing her foot from the entrance.

"Nora!" Joel's voice called to her as he began making his way over to her.

Nora relaxed a little bit even though every inch of her wanted to run and flee the school. She watched Joel walk to her. She forced a small smile on her face to let him know she was fine. Joel frowned at the smile as he got closer.

"So, I know that's fake, but we're going to ignore it. You're still here and making it through the day, so you need to be proud of yourself right now." Joel said, nudging her.

"If you say so," Nora shrugged. She wasn't proud of anything lately.

"Shut up. Let's go get food. I am starving." Joel smiled, looping his arm into hers and pulling her into the cafeteria.

She wasn't hungry. She was fighting the urge to nervously vomit off and on all day, but she followed Joel. He escorted her over to the line and handed her a red tray. Nora grasped the red tray in her hands, probably holding onto it more tightly than she should have. Joel moved into the lunch line and began placing his food on his tray. Nora was up next, and the lunch aide gave her a look. Nora looked over the food. Her stomach grumbled, but she still felt nauseous. Her eyes settled on the grilled cheese and fries. Without saying anything, she pointed to it. The lunch aide nodded and took her tray. In a few seconds, Nora had her tray back, her sandwich, and fries. Joel swiped his card at the checkout spot twice. Nora already knew before she could get up there to stop him that he was paying for her food. She sighed, giving him a look as she reached him. He flashed her a smile and began walking. Nora followed him. He paused, scanning the lunch room. It was still very much like high school.

The cheerleaders sat together, eyeing the football players that were literally the next table over. The smart kids all sat towards the front of the lunchroom. The rebels are in the very back corner. Nora looked around the room and realized she didn't fit in anywhere anymore. Joel nudged her, telling her to follow him. She slowly began walking after him. He made his way toward the left side of the cafeteria, Nora following slowly behind him. She kept her eyes locked on the ground as she made her way over. She saw Joel settle by the window, and she smiled. Just as she was about to reach the table, someone bumped into her. The grilled cheese toppled into her. The fries scattered to the ground, and a loud smash was heard. The ketchup bottle smashed to the ground. The ketchup spilled all over the ground, a large red puddle pouring out of the bottle. Nora froze, staring at the ketchup on the ground. It looked like Blood. The tray fell out of her hands as an image of her parents sitting on the couch flashed through her mind. Then James. She began to shake, backing away from the ketchup.

"Nora?" The person that bumped into her said quietly.

Nora's eyes flashed up to Brad. The last person she needed to see right now. Brad was the captain of the football team and her ex-boyfriend. The first thing he did after her parents died was break up with her. He said he couldn't handle the rollercoaster of emotions she had turned into. Her eyes filled up with tears as she looked back down at the ketchup spill. She let the red tray fall from her hands as she backed away from the mess. James's vacant eyes stared back at her from the red puddle.

"I can't do this." She whispered before she turned and ran out.

"Nora!" Brad called after her.

"Shut up, Brad." Joel said, rushing by him, throwing his shoulder into Brad as she went by.

"What the Fuck!" Brad yelled angrily at Joel's back.

Nora ran out into the hall heading to the closest exit. Her lungs burned as she raced down the hall, her eyes locked on the door to the outside. She needed air. She needed outside. She needed to be anywhere but here.

"Nora! No, not that door!" Joel yelled at her back. It was too late.

Nora crashed into the door and pushed it open. As soon as she pushed the door open, a siren began to sound. Nora didn't realize it, but she busted through the fire exit. The fire alarms began to sound. Nora cringed, but it was too late for her to do anything about it. She didn't care at that point anymore. She ran down the steps of the school, looking around for someplace to disappear. She spotted the woods just beyond the parking lot. She didn't know why it sounded like the best place to be right now, but it did. She took off running as the students and teachers began exiting the school. She raced towards the woods like her life depended on it. She just wanted to disappear

Chapter Five
Space

Jace walked out of his office, deciding running would be the best thing for both him and his wolf. He walked through the den, and several men who were there stood seeing their Alpha walk in; they bowed their heads respectfully. Jace nodded back, walking to the door.

"Dante, I'm going out" Jace's mind linked him, *not seeing him anywhere close by.*

"Want company?" Dante replied back, his voice playful.

" No. Let me know when you hear back from Kip's pack." Jace said back, his voice not thrilled.

"Yes, Alpha." Dante replied back.

Jace pulled open the door, the warm sunlight hitting him felt good on his flesh. He could feel his wolf become excited, as if it couldn't hold back any longer. Jace smirked a little bit and walked to the woods. Stepping far enough away from his eyes, he shifted. His wolf took off running. Jace sat back and let his wolf do his thing. He enjoyed not being in control for once. All the pressure of making sure everything was together and right and perfect slipped away when he was his wolf. His wolf took off in full gear, running playfully about. Then in a split second, everything changed. His wolf's ears went up and his nose went to the sky. Jace watched curiously. Was he hunting? He didn't notice a deer or anything around. What was he doing? After several sniffs. His wolf took off, running towards the pond.

Hey, what are we doing? Jace asked, trying to regain control.

His wolf ignored him, resisting the hold Jace was trying to place on him.

Hey! Jace tried to gain its attention.

Jace quickly realized he was going from co-pilot to passenger and tried to gain control.

His wolf resisted, and the world around Jace went black.

Nora raced into the woods, panic and anxiety driving her. She needed to be away. She ran until her lungs burned deep in her chest. A raised tree branch caught her foot, and she crashed forward into the ground. Her chest pressed into the soil; the fall knocked the wind out of her. She rolled over and begged for air to return to her lungs as she tried desperately to breathe in. Getting to her knees and leaning over, she dug her hands into the soil. Finally, air rushed into her, and she inhaled deeply. Sitting back on her heels, she brought her head up and she started to breathe calmer. As she raised her head up, her eyes locked eyes with a pair of ice-blue ones. Ice-blue eyes and jet black fur. Nora froze as she was face to face with a very large wolf. The wolf leaned forward and pressed its nose into her hair. The wolf inhaled deeply, closing its eyes as it did. Nora stayed still, closing her eyes and praying she was making this up. She felt another rush of hot air and knew the wolf was real. She shifted further back. She locked eyes with the wolf, and the fear she had was gone. She decided she was going to be brave and gently put her hand on the wolf's head. Electricity ran through her when she touched the wolf. The wolf must have felt it, too, because it jumped back. Confusion flashed in its cold eyes.

"Hey, it's ok," Nora whispered, holding her hand out to him again.

The wolf narrowed its eyes at her but slowly approached her again. It nudged her hand with its nose and then pushed it up onto its head. Once her hand touched his coal-black fur, the electricity filtered through both of them. The wolf made a weird noise and jumped back. The wolf began pacing in front of her. Nora watched as it seemed to be trying to work out the feeling.

"Hey, hey, come here." She whispered and then realized how insane she must be right now.

This wolf could snap any minute and destroy her. The wolf whimpered. It wanted to, but it was fighting with itself. The wolf would step towards her but then turn the other way. It continued pacing, looking at her. One minute he looked like he wanted to kill her. The next moment, he looked like a lost puppy. Nora sat down on the ground watching the wolf. Even though it would throw an angry glare at her, she didn't feel threatened. She thought she had officially lost it, but she couldn't bring herself to leave.

"Do you have a name?" She asked for some reason, and then once she heard her question, she laughed.

"Of course, you don't. You're a wild wolf, not a pet." She laughed.

At the sound of her laughter, the wolf tilted its head and sat. It acted like it liked the sound of her laughter. She smiled as she sat there studying it.

"How about Shadow?" Nora asked.

The wolf blew hot air out of its nose at her and flipped its tail. She laughed again. The wolf's tail seemed to almost wag when she laughed once more.

"Blacky." She said, laughing again at the silly name when the wolf shook its head fiercely.

She laughed harder. She calmed herself down as a tear rolled down her cheek from laughing so hard. She hadn't laughed in weeks now. The realization felt good. She took a deep breath in as the wolf inched closer to her.

"What about Cole? I kinda like Cole. Your fur is as dark as it is." She said softly, holding her hand out to the massive wolf.

The Wolf seemed to debate with the name and almost shrugged like a person would as he approached her again. As he reached her, the wolf pressed its nose into her hand and inhaled. It then began smelling up her arm. She stood still, letting the wolf smell her. She wanted it to know she wasn't going to hurt it. This very dangerous animal could literally kill her, but she was worried about not scaring it. She smiled at the thought. The wolf pushed its nose into her hair and inhaled. She reached up and scratched behind the wolf's ear. The wolf flinched slightly, and more sparks followed as they touched. A hollow erupted through the silence off in the distance. The wolf picked its head up away from her and looked towards the woods. If the wolf could have frowned, he would have. He stepped away from Nora and nudged her with his nose. He nudged her again, almost as if he was telling her to go. He pushed her again hard. She stumbled back as he shoved her. He then took off running toward the woods.

Nora watched the black wolf disappear into the woods. She felt sad that the wolf was leaving her. She sat still a little longer, almost as if she was waiting to see if he would come back. After several minutes the sting in her knee brought her attention to it. Her jeans had a blood stain and were ripped from the fall. She sighed as she stood. She didn't notice that the woods were getting dark. She hadn't been gone for more than fifteen minutes. How? She stood and began walking out of the woods.

As she exited the woods, she noticed the sky was dark and the moon was out. She looked at the school. It had been closed for hours now. She needed to go home. She didn't want to go home. Her stomach felt sick as she didn't have anywhere else to go. She followed the walkway around to the front of the school, limping slightly at the pain in her knee. She stopped in front of the bright spotlight near the school sign. She reached into her pocket, looking for her phone. Twelve missed calls and twenty three text messages, all from Joel. How did she not hear any of these? She flipped open her phone just as it started to ring again.

"Hello?" Nora answered.

"In the name of all that is holy! Where the hell have you been? I've been to your house several times, that sleazy-ass bar that lets anyone in. Where the hell are you?" Joel said, clearly upset.

"Joel, I am so sorry. I don't know how I didn't hear the phone. It's been a weird night. I am still at school." Nora said, leaning against the spotlight pole.

"School! You're still at the freaking school?" Joel said angrily.

"Yeah, after I accidentally set the fire alarm off, I kinda ran into the woods and, I guess, fell asleep," Nora said quietly.

"You're a psycho. Don't freaking move. I'm literally five minutes away." Joel said she could hear the eye roll in his voice as he spoke to her.

"I won't go anywhere. Love you, Joel." Nora said sweetly to him.

"I know you do. Love you too, babes. See you in five," Joel said, clicking the phone.

Psycho, she definitely felt like a psycho. Losing track of time and petting wild animals. She suddenly got a weird feeling, like she was being watched. She looked about, trying to find the source of the feeling.

"Cole?" She felt funny calling out the made-up name she gave the black wolf.

There was no response. She sighed. She was definitely losing it. She saw headlights and watched the black Honda Civic whip into the parking lot. Joel flung around the circle drive, stopping right next to the sidewalk where she was leaning against the spotlight pole. Nora knew she was going to have a lecture the whole ride home. She smiled, thankful at how much Joel cared. She opened the car door and got in. As she did, she swore she could feel a pair of eyes on her. She closed the door and clicked her seatbelt in.

"I swear, Nora, you're going to be the death of me," Joel said, sighing and looking at her.

She swallowed hard, trying not to be sensitive to him talking about her being the cause of his death. She knew whatever killed her parents had nothing to do with her, but sometimes she wondered why, whatever or whoever didn't wait for her to get home. Why was she alive? Joel saw her thoughts spiraling. He reached over and tapped her hand softly. He put the car into drive with one hand and began leaving the school.

"Where to, doll?" Joel asked.

"I don't want to go home tonight," Nora said, her voice full of sadness.

"Not to worry, I wasn't going to let you anyways. You can crash at my house." Joel smiled at her as he changed direction and started towards his house.

Chapter Six
Ready

Jace stared down at the mirror, his ice-blue eyes staring back at him. What just happened? He had never disconnected from his wolf before. He couldn't recall anything that had happened. He was angry with his wolf. His wolf blocked him out. He didn't even know that was possible. They were supposed to be one. He let out a long breath looking at himself as he tried to control his temper. He was frustrated and angry and felt like he had lost control. He never lost control. He felt like his wolf was keeping something from him. He looked harder at the mirror as if it held some type of answer.

"Alpha." Dante's voice chimed in his head.

"Go ahead." Jace answered quickly, his patience growing thin.

"I spoke with Kip's beta. They will meet at the local theater. " Dante reported.

"The theater?" Jace repeated.

"That's what they said," Jace could hear the frown in Dante's voice.

"It doesn't sit right with me," Jace said, not comfortable with being in a very crowded area with Kip.

"I agree." Dante spoke back.

"Get in touch with Adam and make sure his connections are in place in case anything goes down," Jace ordered

"Yes, Alpha." Dante replied, and the mind link ended.

Jace turned on the sink and splashed cold water over his face. He let the water run off his face staring down into the sink. He grabbed the side of the sink, the porcelain cracking beneath his hands. He could feel the porcelain splintering into his palms, blood dripping down it. Knock, Knock. The sound came from the bedroom door. He growled, letting go of the sink and walking to the door. Who the hell was bothering him? Pulling open the door, ready to yell at someone, he paused. Rosie. Jace sighed. She was standing in his doorway with a long coat covering her body. Her dyed maroon hair spiraled down in curls matching her lips in color.

"Evening, Alpha." She smiled through her very pouty lips.

"Can I help you-" As Jace was about to ask her what she needed, she pulled open the coat, exposing a very lacey bra and matching panties.

"I was thinking I could help you." Rosie had a seductive smile playing on her lips as she spoke.

Jace's eyes wandered down her perfectly placed curves and breasts. He gritted his teeth. Any other time this may have been the perfect stress reliever, but for some reason, he just got annoyed.

"Not tonight, Rosie," Jace said in a stern voice.

"But Alpha, you look..so..so tense." Rosie said, stepping into him, her hands going to his shoulder, her breast brushing against him.

"Rose, I said not tonight." Jace growled as he pushed her back away from him.

"Jace-"

"Alpha! Go!" Jace corrected her using his alpha tone on her.

Rosie cowered and wrapped the coat around her. She looked at him, her eyes a mix of hurt and fear as she took off down the hall. Jace groaned, running his hand through his jet-black hair before stepping back into his room. He shut the door, and the power he used vibrated the door frame. He looked down at his hands, which were already healing but still had dried blood smeared on them. He sat down on his bed. What was wrong with him? Was something off? He reached out to his wolf and got the cold shoulder. He gritted his jaw, his teeth crunching into the*m.*

"Drinks?" Dante's voice popped into his head. Jace somewhat smiled, hearing Dante. He could sure use a drink.

"Yes."

"Here or out?" Dante asked him back.

"Out. I need to get away from here." Jace said back to him.

"Roger, see you in ten by your car," Dante said back.

"Just you. I don't want to deal with anyone else tonight," Jace ordered back.

"Sounds good, Alpha," Dante replied back.

Dante and Jace were best friends growing up, and when Dante was marked to be his Beta, Jace couldn't think of anyone better. He was grateful they were in this together.

"Hey, get up." Joel's voice yelled at Nora.

"No." Nora groaned, rolling over.

"Get up. It's been like a whole day. And I have plans tonight," Joel laughed.

"Almost a day? What time is it?" Nora asked Joel while looking out the window.

"Hurry! Up! Up! I have plans." Joel said, leaning over and shaking the covers.

She could see the sun was setting through the blinds. She really did sleep way too long. She really needed it, though. She looked back at Joel.

"Plans?" Nora asked him.

Part of herself was worried that it might be something where he asked her to leave. She really didn't want to be alone anymore. She was just starting to realize that she needed someone to fill the void, to fill the emptiness and silence in her. Joel smiled at her softly.

"Your birthday is tomorrow, so we're going out tonight! I already got VIP at Luna. So we're gonna go, we're gonna dance, we're gonna have fun, and we're gonna escape this world for a little bit," He said, coming and sitting down next to her on the bed.

"Are you really sure that is a good idea?" She asked quietly.

"Babe, you need to quit punishing yourself. You haven't had one ounce of fun since…well, since." Joel said, wrapping his arm around her and pulling her in close.

"I don't know if fun is what I need, Joel." She said, her voice just above a whisper.

"Well, maybe not in the long run but for right now and tonight. It's not going to hurt anything." Joel said, pushing his shoulder into her playfully.

Nora shrugged slightly, her stomach getting upset. How can she be happy or have fun when they can't? Joel saw her starting to go to her dark place, and he shoved a bag in her lap.

"Stop. Here, go try these on." Joel said firmly, shoving a black bag in her face.

Nora took the bag from him, still wrapped up in her thoughts. She held the bag like it was a foreign object.

"Nora, you need to remember your amazingness. You may be a little broken right now, but everyone at some point is. You need to know people love you. I love you." He whispered to her.

As he said the words to her, she began to shake slightly, fighting back the tears. He held her tightly for several minutes, just letting her give into her emotion and not bury them like she normally did. The tears began to flow pretty quickly as she silently cried in his arms. He placed another kiss on top of her head. Joel wasn't letting her hurt herself anymore, he promised himself. After a few more minutes, he felt her breathing slowed and her body loosened up. He placed a hand under her chin and wiped her tears.

"Go on. Go get dressed. It will be ok." Joel said, squeezing her shoulder.

Nora took a deep breath and crossed the room, holding the black bag in her hand. She glanced down, not recognizing it. Joel must have gone shopping while she was asleep. She was sure glad she missed that. Stepping into the bathroom, she looked inside the bag. She pulled out two black dresses. One was very dramatic, with a deep plunge and full of shimmer. The other was a simple black dress. It had a heart-shaped neckline. She quickly shoved the dramatic one back into the black bag. The words hell no echo in her mind as she tosses it aside. She disgraded her oversized hoodie and blue jeans aside. Slipping the black dress over her head. She smoothed it out before looking into the mirror. The simple black dress hugged her hourglass figure perfectly but left just enough up to the imagination.

"Will you come out already!" Joel yelled into the bathroom door.

She had been staring at herself for a few minutes before Joel's impatient voice came through the door. Nora sighed and reached over, and unlocked the door. Pushing it open, she let Joel in.

"Damn, girl! You are stunning, and we haven't even done hair and makeup." Joel said excitedly.

"Joel, I think we should take baby steps and keep the rest pretty simple. You got me out of the hoody. You should be happy." Nora said, putting her hand up as if trying to halt some attack.

"What, no curls?" Joel said, holding up the curling iron.

Nora chuckled, shaking her head. She reached up and undid her messy bun. Her hair fell down in soft waves. It framed her face perfectly, and because it had been up in a bun for so long, the hair almost did look like it was curled.

"Fine, your hair is amazing, but can I please do your makeup!" Joel said, his voice whiny, as he held up a makeup bag.

"Um, no." Nora laughed, holding her hand out for the bag.

"Ugh, fine. I guess I will count my blessings." Joel said, giving up.

Nora laughed, taking the bag from Joel and ducking back into the bathroom. She emptied the bag onto the counter. Glitter eyeshadows spilled out from the bag, along with every other makeup item you could think of. Nora shook her head and found the black eyeliner and mascara. She outlined the top and bottom lid of her eyes. The black eyeliner made her honey eyes stand out even more. She then applied a gracious amount of mascara. She was shocked at how much of a difference that little bit made. She looked down at the makeup Joel had put out for her. She saw all sorts of lip colors. She found a simple, almost nude pink color and placed it on her lips. She glanced up at the mirror. She almost didn't recognize herself. Her eyes looked like they had life in them, like they were brighter. The way the simple lip color looked against her sun-kissed skin made her lips look like they were set up for the perfect kiss, all plumped and ready.

"Well, I take back my groans. You look stunning, Babe." Joel said, coming back into the bathroom.

Nora smiled weakly at him. She still felt weird. She missed the comfort of the big oversize hoodie, and showing her legs off was a little different lately. She spent most of the time lately trying to hide. She didn't want to draw any attention to herself. She glanced at Joel, who came in and started doing his hair. He wore a black button-down shirt and dark blue jeans. It was just enough, not too fancy but not comfortable. He wore his silver chain around his neck. Nora could see it shimmer from underneath the shirt as he left the very top bottom undone.

"All right... heels... and we're good to go," Joel said, pointing to Nora's feet.

"Heels." Nora groaned.

"Aa yeah, your tennis shoes aren't going to go with that dress." Joel said, holding out two pairs of heels.

One set had a strap that would crisscross up her leg. The others were just simple black high heel shoes. She debated wondering if the crisscross strap might make her feel like she was wearing pants. She decided against it and settled on the simple ones. She took them from Joel and slipped them on.

"Ready?" Joel smiled at her.

"Ready as I'll ever be." She smirked back at him.

"Then let's get going!" Joel said, super excited, grabbing ahold of her hand and leading her out of the room.

Chapter Seven
Damage Control

Jace walked outside to find Dante leaning against his cobalt blue Audie R8. Jace growled slightly, and Dante quickly got out of the car with a silly smirk on his lips.

"Where to, boss?" Dante chuckled as Jace approached them.

"I don't care. After dealing with Rosie and the stress of Kip, anywhere that has hard liquor," Jace grumbled, going around to the driver's side.

"Rosie? How did you handle her?" Dante said, busting a smile as he spoke.

"I didn't." Jace groaned.

"You know she wants to be your Luna, right?" Dante said to his back.

"Dante, do I need to go by myself?" Jace said sternly.

"No, no, I'll stop." Dante said quickly.

"Place?" Jace said. He unlocked the car and got it.

Dante followed suit. He could see what Dante was thinking, and he smiled. He was thinking a little too hard.

"Seriously?" Jace said, a small chuckle escaping his mouth.

"Well, there's Luna if you want to do more of a club vibe. There's Temple which is still more of a club than a bar. Seven, which is a bar. And if you want a hole in the wall, the Crow's nest…or do we want a bar with a show?" Dante said, wiggling his eyebrows at the last comment.

"Dante, you are becoming as annoying as everyone else," Jace growled as his car revived to life.

"No, let's just go to Seven." Dante smiled.

"Alpha." The mindlink buzzed inside Jace's head.

Jace shut his eyes, a headache forming as he at the sound of the mind link. He knew by the way the word Alpha was said it was not good.

"Go ahead." Dante looked at Jace confused, but when he saw his glossed-over look, he knew someone was paging him.

He frowned slightly, watching his Alpha and friend's face grow dark.

"We have another problem," Matthew said carefully to his Alpha.

"Ok…" Jace said with a long breath.

"Alpha Kip's pack. They laid havoc on a small theater just south of here on the outskirts of our town. He has no intent on cleaning it up or covering his tracks." Mathew said anxiously.

Jace looked over to Dante, his face angry.

"When was the meeting with Kip?" Jace managed to ask through his anger to Dante.

"Tomorrow evening," Dante replied, confused. Jace's eyes glossed over again.

"Get Adam to start the cover-up, Dante and I will meet you at the theater. Bring Wyatt as well." Jace mind-linked Matt.

"Yes, Alpha." Jace threw the car into gear as the mind link ended.

Reversing out of his parking spot as quickly as possible. Throwing the car into drive, the tire screeched as he took off.

"So.." Dante asked carefully.

"Kip attacked the theater we were supposed to meet at tomorrow. I'm taking it as a message to us." Jace said through his teeth.

"Are you fucking serious," Dante said, becoming just as upset.

"The rest of the team is on the way there," Jace said quietly.

The rest of the car ride was quiet as Jace did far over the speed limit to get there. Jace's hands gripped the steering wheel till his knuckles were white. They weren't sure what they were walking into, and the only plan they had was to get there, keep it from the public, and clean up any damage Kips pack had done. His dark blue Audi skidded into the first available parking lot. Jace recognized the faded black van sitting in the back parking spot. Once Jace's car was settled into the parking spot, the van pulled up next to it. They emptied out of the vehicles, all ready for what could possibly await them, looking like something out of a movie. Each one of them was dressed in a black T-shirt and dark jeans. Dante's sleeves had been ripped off of his shirt, exposing his very large biceps.

Jace nodded to his crew and started to make his way to the movie theater. Jace walked up the concrete stairs making it to the top with long strides. He opened the large glass door and stepped inside. As he stepped inside, the men walked in behind him. They all stopped and glanced at each other. The smell invaded their nostrils, even from the lobby. Blood and lots of it. Jace looked at Matt, and he nodded. Matt didn't need anything to be said. He knew what he needed to do.

Matt walked up to the ticket counter and flashed a badge. Each high-ranking member of his pack had taken a job in their society that would benefit the pack. Matt was a police officer, Wyatt was a doctor, and Adam worked at the city hall. They weren't sure what Adam did, but he knew all the ins and outs of the town and everything that was going to happen. The girl at the front eyes grew wide seeing the badge. Matt began to tell her about a potential gas leak in the area, and he needed the theater cleared out. The girl quickly nodded and rushed to the loudspeaker.

"Attention to all patrons, please proceed to the nearest exit and evacuate the building immediately," The girl sent the announcement.

A manager came out from the back, looking at the confused girl. Jace could hear the whole conversation. The manager was upset that the girl didn't check with her first and then became concerned when she told her about the gas leak.

"We will help evacuate the rest of the theater. Please stay up front and help guide everyone out." Matt said to the girl and the manager.

The manager nodded and then left to inform the staff. Jace walked past Matt with the rest of his men following. They walked through the crowd of people rushing out of the cinema rooms. Jace's eyes locked on the room he knew the smell was coming from. They paused in front of the doorway. Jace's eyes flicker to the movie poster next to the door. A horror movie.

"Well, at least he did us a flavor there. No one probably knew the screams were actual screams and not from the movie." Dante said next to Jace.

"Matt, you stay in front of the door in case anyone comes looking. The rest of you are with me." Jace ordered them.

He stepped forward and pushed the closed door open. The wave of blood hit him. He was hoping it was only one or two people watching a movie, but from the smell of the blood, he knew there were at least five. He felt Adam go a little stiff as they rounded the corner. The scene unfolded in front of them. The dark maroon carpet of the theater was soaked with blood. A woman was flung over the front row seat, and blood was pouring out of a single neck wound. Next to her, her date was mauled. His face was scratched and torn up so that there was little left to it. Flesh dangled off his jaw. His final undoing was a neck wound. Another couple suffered the same neck wounds. Jace was counting in his head so far four. He scanned the room. There had to be an exit in the actual room. His eyes fell on the red emergency exit sign. He walked over to it. Tracing the wires that would sound the alarm if the door was opened. He yanked them out from the source.

"Adam, bring the van around to this exit here. We will take the body's from here. Get hold of your connections and get a cleaning crew out here. Tell them there's hush money involved." Jace said to Adam.

"Yes, Alpha." Adam said, ducking out the exit and leaving. He seemed like he was more than happy to get out of there.

"How many?" Jace called Dante and Wyatt.

"Seven so far." Dante answered.

"Eight….we have one still alive." Wyatt called from the back room.

He was on the ground, almost underneath the seat. You could tell from his position he was trying to hide. Wyatt had his hand pressed to a neck wound, trying to stop the bleeding. Jace was up the stairs and by Wyatt's side in no time. Jace overlooked the young man. He was probably not older than twenty. He had lost enough blood and was unconscious.

"What do you think?" Jace asked Wyatt.

"I don't know, If I can get him back to the pack house, I might be able to do something. I don't know if he will make it." Wyatt said quietly.

"What do you need?" Jace asked.

"Something to wrap around his neck to apply pressure and slow the bleeding," Wyatt said.

"Adam, bring something from the van to wrap a wound." Jace's mind is linked to Adam.

Jace ran his hand through his hair, frustrated. They had to do everything they could to try and save the boy, but it would be easier if he was dead. If he survived, then they would need to come up with a vicious animal story and leave evidence linking it to a rabid dog or something. He was trying to come up with a story if the boy lived. He was praying the boy didn't get a good look at Kip's pack or if he saw anyone shift. That would be harder to explain.

"Matt, I need you to come up with something to tell the manager to lock this theater room down for the next day or so. We have one alive, and depending on how it goes, a simple cleaning crew will do, or we might need to stage a wild animal attack." Jace's mind is linked to Matt.

"Got it, Alpha. Gas leaks are funny things and can need to keep certain areas shut down for a while and need special cleaning crews." Matt said Jace could hear the smirk in the mind link that he knew was plastered on his face.

"This really needs to stop," Dante said, a course of anger flowing through him.

He let a body fall to the floor that he was carrying as he turned to meet Jace's eyes. Jace felt his anger and watched Dante carefully. Waiting to see if he was going to explode.

"Someone needs to get Kip to get a handle on his pack. Look at this. This is against all laws. We all know he feels we shouldn't have to hide. That humans are beneath us, and we should wipe them out. This is all done on purpose. Someone needs to take him out." Dante said, clenching his fist as he closed his eyes, trying to get the anger he was feeling to creep back down into his gut.

"He's going to bring hunters here." Wyatt whispered.

Jace's eyes flickered to Dante at the hunter's statement. The veins in Dante's arms were starting to bulge outward. Jace nudged Wyatt as if to say "what the fuck" to him as he quickly raced down the stairway to Dante. At this point, Dante's fangs had already descended. He was hunched over and shaking, trying to control and stop himself from turning. Jace grabbed hold of him by the shoulders, making him stand upright. Dante's eyes locked with Jace's.

"Stop. You are in control. You will not turn." Jace said, his eyes glowing a lighter shade of blue as he spoke to Dante.

"Yes, Alpha." Dante managed to get out through the course of shaking.

"You will not shift. Look at me. I command you not to shift." Jace said in his alpha tone.

The waves of authority coming off of Jace were calming Dante. Dante slowly returned back to normal, and his fangs rescinded. He stood tall and was shaking. He looked at Jace, his eyes apologetic, but Jace shook his head.

"Get the last two bodies to the door and when Adam gets here, load them into the van." Jace said to him as he looked back up at Wyatt.

A knock came from the front door of the theater room. Jace stiffened as he began walking to it.

His senses didn't tell him that anyone else was there besides Matt, but he was still nervous. He didn't need any more people involved. He cracked the door open, and Matt handed him a first aid kit.

"Don't fucking do that again." Jace growled at him, snatching the first aid kit, and slammed the door in his face.

"What?" Matt's mind linked him back, but Jace chose to ignore it.

Jace came back into the room, walking up the stairs to Wyatt. He handed Wyatt the first aid kit and glanced down to where Dante was. Adam had come, and they had begun loading the bodies into the van. He looked down at Wyatt.

"I am going to need help, Alpha. I can't hold pressure and open the kit up." Wyatt explained softly.

Jace nodded. He was so wrapped up in everything happening that he wasn't thinking about helping Wyatt. Part of him wanted to tell Wyatt to just let the boy die, but he couldn't. If the boy was dead, it would be less of a problem. Jace cracked open the first aid kit and found some gauze. He handed the gauze to Wyatt. Wyatt grasped the gauze in one-hand and switched out hands, quickly reapplying pressure holding gauze to his neck. Jace grabbed the ace bandage that was in the kit and kneeled down. He picked the boy upright while Wyatt was still holding pressure on the wound. It would be easier to wrap the wound with him sitting up.

"Ok, wrapped the bandage around his neck tight but not too tight we don't want to choke him.

Start here where my hand is. I'll lift and reapply pressure each time you go around." Wyatt said, explaining to Jace.

Jace nodded, and they began wrapping the bandage around the boy's neck. On the last wrap, the boy opened his eyes and groaned. Jace stood still for a second, not sure what to do or say.

"You're ok. We got you." Wyatt said calmly.

He was used to working with people and traumatic injuries. The boy's eyes rolled back in his head, and he went back unconscious. Once they were done wrapping his neck, Wyatt double-checked it. He looked to Jace, who was studying the boy. His heartbeat was strong, but his breathing was shallow. He could tell the boy could go either way. Jace nodded to Wyatt to tell him to get the boy and let go. As he walked down to the space in front of the screen, Adam came up to him.

"The cleaning crew will be here in less than three minutes." Adam reported to Jace.

"Matt, cleaning crew here in three minutes. Hang out till they are done. We have one still alive that we need to get back to the pack house and get these bodies out of here. Link us when it's all cleaned up. Once finished, take my car back." He minded link Matt.

"Will do, Alpha," Matt responded.

"Load up." Jace said to the others in the room and ducked out the fire exit door.

The cleaning crew pulled up next to the van as Jace got into the driver's seat. He watched Adam tell them what was expected and handed the man in charge of the cleaning crew money. Adam smiled, but not the heartwarming smile. It was a threat as he began telling them how they were not to speak of this to anyone. The men looked at each and looked like they were going to ask questions, but Adam handed him another stack of money. The men grinned and nodded their heads without any questions as the cleaning crew went into the theater. Adam was the last in the van. Dante jumped into the passenger seat as Adam got into the back. The bodies were stacked on top of each other in the very back. Their eyes stared at Adam as he turned his back on them. Wyatt was busy attending to the boy, the little that he could do in the moving van.

"You ok?" Jace mind linked with Dante.

Dante was staring out the window and just nodded. Dante almost lost it back there. The anger he had built up for Kip and his pack was just the edge of it. When Wyatt brought up hunters, he almost completely lost control. He hated hunters. He wanted to rid the world of them. Hunters killed his whole family in front of him before he came to Jace's pack. He was a young teenager at the time and didn't know why they left him alive. He could still see his mother's eye's as they went wide in horror as she tried to save his sister from the hunter. Then he watched her eyes gloss over as life left hers. He fidgeted in his seat, trying to chase the memory from his mind. Telling his wolf to calm down.

"Dante." Jace's voice broke through to him, the warning in it sent his wolf into obedience, and the anger resided.

Dante gave him a small smile and focused on the trees passing out the window. Jace eyed him worried but saw that he had got himself back under control. He looked at his men in the back of the van. Wyatt trying his hardest to save the boy, and Adam zones out slightly. He gripped the steering wheel tighter. They were almost back home.

Chapter Eight
Luna

Joel turned up the radio, already blasting dance music, and was jamming out by the time they pulled into the parking lot of the club. The blue neon lights of the sign beamed down into the parking lot, giving everything a hazy blue glow. Nora looked up at the sign. The word Luna was hanging off a crescent-shaped moon. Typical nightclub with some moon name. Nora thought, rolling her eyes. Joel was a perfect gentleman and beat her to open her own door. She smiled as the door opened, and Joel offered her his hand to get out.

"Why, thank you, kind sir." Nora chuckled while getting out of the car.

"You're welcome, milady. Now the fun begins." Joel said to her, making a funny face.

"Joel, I-

"I know, I know this all a lot, and you might not make it the whole night. And you don't want to ruin it for me, so you're going to try to tell me something, so I might let you out of this. Doll. I know. We will try to have fun. If anything happens. I will scoop you out of here and will go order pizza at my house and watch Pretty in Pink." Joel said, grabbing her by the shoulders.

"I love you," Nora said, grabbing him into a hug.

"I love you too. Now let's go try to get some drinks out of a hot bartender." Joel said, squeezing her back.

"Dante, take the bodies to the infirmary and dispose of them. Adam, help Wyatt get the boy to our hospital." He said, giving out commands as he pulled into his parking spot.

He left the van running and stepped out.

"Yes, Alpha." They all said as Dante switched over to the driver seat.

The dark van pulled quickly out of sight. Jace let out a long breath he had been holding in as he looked up at the cold night sky. He sighed, running his hand over his face. Dante was right that something needed to be done about Kip.

"Everything is all set and squared up here. Heading back now." Matthew's mind linked him.

"Don't wreck my car," Jace replied.

"Wouldn't dream of it, Alpha." Matt replied back, lightness in his voice.

Jace cracked a small smile, which quickly darkened as he paced the driveway. He would need to reach out to the council. He would have to get them involved if he were to do this the legal way. Kip was clearly sending Jace a message, his anger wanted him to respond, but he had to remain calm and do what was best.

"Lockdown for the next forty-eight hours. Stay in the community. We had some issues with the Alpha Kips pack tonight. If you need to leave the community, get my permission first." Jace sent a mind link out to the member of his pack.

Jace could feel the pack's feelings, disappointment and frustration at having to remain in lockdown, scared at what was happening. He himself was agitated and frustrated. If Kip could just reel in his wolves, there would be fewer problems for everyone. Instead of keeping everyone safe, he now felt like he was Kip's personal cleaning crew. The thought enraged him. As Alpha, you are supposed to be watching out for your pack, making sure nothing is done to expose the wolf kind, but Kip was out there " accidentally" risking everything. The aggravation quickly was becoming anger the more he thought. He could feel his wolf snarling at the thought of Kip and his pack. His wolf wanted to fight, to get rid of Kip. His wolf was begging to come out. He needed to let him out to run. His restlessness was getting to Jace. Over the last few months, his pack, his home, and everything he loved was becoming a prison.

"Wyatt, how's the boy?" Jace's mind linked him.

"I don't know, Alpha. He's still holding on. I guess only time will tell." Wyatt mind linked him back.

"Keep me posted if anything begins to change, and report to me right away." Jace gave an order.

"Yes, Alpha." Wyatt replied. Jace's wolf was clawing at him from the inside.

Jace winced as he began to get a headache and felt nauseous. His wolf had never tried to get out like this before.

What was going on? Stop it! Jace growls inside his own head, hoping to silence his wolf.

The wolf began howling back. What was going on with him? Jace thought, trying to get himself together. He needed to go for a run. The last time his wolf was acting like this, somewhere along the lines, Jace blacked out, and it was just his wolf. He was nervous. Being Alpha ment being the one in control at all times, and it made him anxious that his own wolf was trying to hide something from him. Sweat beaded across his forehead as he tried to make sense of it all. He needs to let his wolf out. His vision started to blur.

"Dante. I am going for a run. You're in charge till I get back. Everyone is still on lockdown." Jace Mindlinked his beta.

"Understood, Alpha." Dante replied back.

"Listen to me if I let you go for a run. You do not hide anything from me. If you do what you did last time, I'll lock you away for a whole month." Jace said sternly, looking up at the sky.

The wolf inside him began to dance happily. Jace rolled his eyes as he grabbed a change of clothes from the garage. The mirror hanging in it caught his eye. He paused in front of the mirror, the glow was settling down, and his wolf was behaving, knowing that he was going to get a chance to come out. The headache Jace was starting to get subsided.

"Fine." Jace grumbled, walking into the forest line.

Entering the forest line, Jace stripped. He tied a small bag holding his clothing in it to his leg. He felt his skin immediately goosebumps as the night air hit it. He then began to tingle as he allowed his wolf to come forward. The tingle turned into a ripping, burning sensation that spread through out him. Before he knew it, his bones were twisting and turning. Each time it got easier, but the pain was still surprising each time. He arched his back as he morphed into his wolf. Jace's wolf was the largest in his pack. He had jet-black fur as dark as the night sky. He looked like something made from nightmares. His wolf seemed to look around and stuck his nose up in his ear, sniffed it, and took off as fast as he could. He was going after something.

Nora held Joel's hand tightly as they made their way through the dark club. Joel was vibing. This was his type of scene. He loved music, dancing, and just being around people. Nora could have done without the people part. Nora squeezed Joel's hand, letting him know he was moving too fast for her. She was beginning to pin pong off of people.

"Joel!" She shouted forward to him.

He didn't hear her. He turned to make a beeline for the dance floor. Hell no, Nora thought. She was not ready for the dance floor. She found her breath starting to catch in her lungs. She yanked back on Joel's hand, pulling her hand away from him. Joel stopped turning around, looking at her, confused. Nora was trying her best to keep herself from freaking out. She didn't want to ruin this for Joel. She forced a smile and pointed to the bar. She pulled on his shirt, and he leaned forward.

"I need a drink. You can go dancing. I'll find you." She smiled brightly.

Joel made a face trying to figure out if Nora was ok or not. She playfully shoved him, turning her back on him and making her way to one of the bars. Nora made it to the bar that looked less crowded. She managed to get a seat. She sat, trying to breathe. She felt like the walls were closing in on her.

"Hey, Darling." A warm voice came across the bar. Nora looked up, seeing warm coffee-colored eyes. The man's eyes matched his hair color as a warm smile spread across his lips. He could tell she was struggling.

"What do you need?" He asked her softly.

"Um, something strong." Nora choked on her voice cracking, she didn't realize it, but she was digging her nails into the bar.

The bartender reached across and patted her clenched hand. Nora dropped her hand away from the bar as instinct. He threw his hands up as if to say he didn't mean anything.

"Ok. something strong, coming up." He said with a smile and threw her a wink.

Jace let his wolf take control. He sat back and enjoyed the ride, happy that his wolf wasn't cutting him out. He was hunting something. He could tell by the way he was tracking and moving. He just didn't know what. Jace quickly realized his wolf was getting close to the city. He was ok with his wolf taking off and tracking something, but now that he had tracked whatever it was into the city, he was about to take back over. Jace's wolf stepped out of the woods and started heading across the parking lot. The parking lot was illuminated by a hazy blue light. Jace began to quickly put the brakes on. He pulled his wolf back into the woods. Trying to get it to change course. His wolf did not want to give up. Whatever it was after, it was intent on going for it and was not backing down. Jace tried to figure out what was going on, but his wolf wouldn't communicate. All he was getting was an overwhelming need to go. Jace yanked control from his wolf and fought with him to turn back. It took an overwhelming amount of power, but his wolf finally gave, and Jace was able to shift back to human form.

Coming back into human form, Jace was out of breath like he had been actually fighting someone. He was angry with his wolf as he began getting himself dressed. He slipped his t-shirt over his head and pulled up his dark jeans. He then lanced up his boots

"What the hell was that?" He growled at his wolf, who was now not responding to him.

"Fine, be that way." He muttered. He looked about the woods.

He was a long way from the community. He would need to call for a ride back. He could mind link but he was trying to put distance between his wolf and himself right now. He stepped out into the parking lot and began making his way toward the building. As he approached the building, he read the sign. Luna. He rolled his eyes at the name of the small nightclub. He walked over to the entrance of the club, cutting the line. The bouncer was about to say something but then recognized him.

"Oh, it's you, Mr. Knight. You go right ahead in. Are any of your members coming with you tonight?" The bounce said, unhooking the rope and stepping aside.

"No, just me." Jace muttered, walking past him.

The town didn't know much about Jace and his community. All sorts of rumors flew about ranging from mafia to drug dealers. They didn't know what went on, but they knew they had money, and money meant power. Jace didn't mind the rumors; as long as they kept people away, he didn't care. Entering the club, the wave of heat from the bodies in there hit him like a train. His senses were still heightened from his recent shift. He tried to ignore the hormones the people were giving off. He spotted a small bar and quickly made his way there. People stepped away from him as he cut across the room. Some of the girls began to ogle at him. He could feel the lust pouring off them as they eyed him. He ignored it and dodged as many of them as he could. He took a seat at the bar and waited for the bartender. A girl in her early twenties was behind the bar tending it. Her hair was dyed a bright blue, and her eye shadow and makeup matched it. She saw him sit and approached him with a big smile.

"What can I get you, handsome?" She asked him. Her voice was overwhelmingly sweet.

"I need to make a phone call." Jace said, his voice flat as he spoke.

"Ok, no problem. Anything to drink while you make your phone call?" She smiled charmingly.

"Bourbon on the rocks." Jace said, being short with her.

"Ok, I'll grab the cordless and your drink, cutie." She smiled again and disappeared.

It was a small club with one dance floor, a DJ booth, and the v.i.p section was a small area off to the right of the DJ with coaches. They had their own bartender, but other than that and the couch, the v.i.p section wasn't so grand. The theme of the club followed the name. Everything was shades of dark blues. The lights were all star-and-moon shaped and seemed to glow. The DJ booth was in a half-moon shape. Even the bar he was sitting at was a crescent moon. Along the walls, there were different scenes of the night sky. He had been there before a few times when things were easier. He and the men would go grab a few drinks every so often. Maybe pick up a few girls. But everything was different now. With the pressure and constant damage control for Kip and his pack, there hadn't been much free time. He sighed as the bartender brought him his drink and the cordless phone. As she handed it to him, her hand casually rubbed his hand. She shot him a sexy smile.

"You let me know if there's anything else I can do for you." She was very flirtatious with him.

He didn't say anything but clicked on the phone and dialed Dante's phone. He looked out over the dance floor. The lights were doing a weird shimmer effect. As the phone rang, he began looking at the people. A flash of jet blue- black hair caught his eye. A girl in the middle of the floor dances by herself. The dress she was wearing matched her hair. She spun in a circle as she moved her hips to the music, throwing her head back. His eyes locked in on her. As he did, he caught her scent. The wolf inside of him began to go crazy. Jace tilted his head, trying to figure out his wolf's excitement. He stood, moving closer to the dance floor. It took Jace a second to realize that she was the thing his wolf was hunting. Jace inhaled her scent once, and it hit him. Hunter. Jace kicked off the phone. Fucking great, he thought. He began watching her movement more intensely. Killing a hunter wasn't on his to-do list tonight, but the rules were the rules.

Chapter Nine
Hunting

He stalked her from the outside of the dance floor. Did she know he was here? Was she hunting? He watched her giggle as she bumped into someone and made her way back to the bar. The bartender leaned over, whispering softly to her. Jace's wolf inside growled. He had been pacing on the inside of him and now was angry. Jace was confused, trying to connect the dots.

Listen, I need you to get yourself in check. He thought to his wolf.

The bartender rubbed her hand softly as he handed her another shot. Jace stepped forward, the anger from his wolf affecting him now. A shot girl walked by him, and he scooped one off the tray in her hand, downing it. What the hell was going on with him?

How do you not know? His wolf growled inside of him.

There was something more than her being a hunter, he couldn't put his finger on it, and his wolf was so excited. He loved hunting, but this was more than that. He couldn't figure it out because again, his wolf was concealing something from him. He had been silent this whole time. Jace was angry with him, with this hunter, and with the world. He clenched his fist, the shot glass giving in to his strength and breaking into tiny pieces. He needed to get this over with and go home.

Nora laughed as the bartender told her how beautiful she looked. He slid another drink towards her, which she didn't mind. The drinks were the only thing keeping her from surviving this night. She looked up at the clock, 11 pm. She had sixty minutes before she turned twenty-one. She sighed; the alcohol made her body feel warm. She was starting to feel everything she had just drank. Her eyes began searching for the bathroom. She spotted Joel, he had caught the eye of a young man with fabulous hair, and the two of them were off dancing in the corner. Nora basically had to shove Joel at the man a few moments ago. She could tell he wanted to go but didn't want to leave her alone. Joel was laughing as the man he was dancing with Joel pulled him close. Nora saw him lean in and whisper into Joel's ear.

"How about I take you home, gorgeous? I could show you all sorts of things and treat you real nice." Nora's eyes widened; there was no way she had heard that.

She tore her eyes away, not wanting to hear anything else. She glanced back to the bar; the bartender was talking to another worker.

"So you've been chatting up that dark hair beauty all night." The other bartender said, shoving the one that had been serving Nora all night.

"Yeah, I think I'm going to take her home tonight. She seems like she'll be easy and damaged." He laughed, shoving him back.

"Are you fucking kidding me," Nora said out loud, not connecting that again she heard something too far away to hear.

Nora made her way away from the bar; she needed to get some space. There was something wrong with her vision; she could see the tiniest details of things. It was overwhelming. She walked through the crowd. She slammed into someone. The person fell over like they hit a brick wall. She needed out; she needed to air. This was all crazy; she shouldn't be able to see tiny details across the room. She shouldn't be able to hear whispered conversations across the room over loud blasting dance music. She certainly wasn't strong enough that people bumping into her would make them fall over. She started to try to make her way out of the fog, trying not to bump or touch anyone.

She placed her hands over her ears as all the conversations of the club came rushing in. She could feel her body shaking. As she reached the edge of the dance floor, she walked into something hard and solid. The person didn't move or fall over, thankfully. When she looked up, she saw a man staring at her with his ice-blue eyes. She blinked, feeling confused by his gaze. She then caught a whiff of his scent, which was amazing. It wasn't the smell of cologne but rather a familiar scent that made her want to curl into him. It felt like he was hers. As the strange feelings overwhelmed her, Nora took a step back, feeling a sense of panic.

"Hey, calm down; why don't we go get some air." The pleasant-smelling stranger said to her.

Normally she was all about stranger danger, but she needed out, and he was offering to help her. She nodded. He went to reach for her hand, but a static shock caught him by surprise. They both pulled back from each other. He nodded to her, holding his hand oddly, almost cautiously to her. She watched him drop his hand, and he began leading the way out of the club. Jace knew what was happening. She was about to shift; she must be turning twenty-one, he thought as the girl followed him outside. He glanced back as she paused as the cold air hit her. He needed to get it over with soon. Before she completely turned into a hunter.

On a Hunter's twenty-first birthday, they are completely shifted into the world of the unknown. Up until their birthday, they have no powers; they are just an average human. As the hour of their birthday approaches, they start getting their abilities. They are suddenly able to see sharper, hear things better, and get the strength that they never had before. Not only do all their senses heighten, but they get all the knowledge of their ancestors. It can be pretty brutal if the upcoming hunter is not prepared or has anyone to guide them through it. Jace didn't know why he was thinking about that. He began to walk down an alleyway. He glanced back at her; she held her head slightly. She's acting like she has no clue. He thought.

She doesn't. His wolf said, his tone annoyed.

Jace made a face hearing his absent wolf chime in.

"Hey, wait." The girl said as she started following him.

This was easy. He thought about waiting for her. He leaned against the wall waiting for the girl to catch up. The wolf inside him was going crazy with anticipation. Jace was getting mixed vibes from his wolf. He was excited, but it was different. The girl stumbled into the alleyway after him. He took one look at her and grabbed her by the throat, pinning her against the wall. The bricks slammed into her back; she didn't even whimper. He needed it to look like a regular murder, so strangling was the only thing he could think of at the moment. A shocked look of surprise passed through her eyes but then acceptance. She didn't even fight. It threw him off. He stopped applying pressure just by being confused. He narrowed his eyes at her trying to figure this out.

"Do it." She whispered as she grabbed his hand and pressed on it.

As her hand touched his, a spark was sent through him; his wolf began to whimper as if he could sense her pain. The wolf inside began to howl as her pain began to cause him pain. He looked at her honeycomb eyes, and his stomach knotted up. Why was she in so much pain? He loosened his grip on her, and his free hand went to her cheek.

"Why?" He whispered. A single tear fell from her eye and trailed down her cheek hitting his thumb.

She closed her eyes, leaning back into the brick wall.

"Just do it." She begged.

Why the hell did he care so much? This should be the easiest thing in the world. A hunter wants to die. Done deal. Why did it hurt him to see her in pain? The world seemed to slow down as he looked at her. He felt something in the pit of his stomach, longing. He felt like she was the answer to the ache in him. His body wanted to be close to hers. He needed to be near her. He tried to suppress this feeling.

His wolf began whimpering more and then finally whispered, "Mate."

The word fell out of his mouth. Jace backed away from her. She can't be. He thought about looking at her. A hunter of all things! He was angry, but looking at her, he couldn't help but want to be close to her. Everything in him was pulling him to her. He wanted to make all her pain disappear. He looked at her flawless face and tear-stained cheeks. Her perfect pouty mouth begged for him. He fought hard with himself.

You are the alpha; your pack depends on you. Hunters are a threat, and she is a threat. You need to do this. His wolf whimpered inside, and he tried turning it off. His wolf howled as he closed the gap between them. His skin crawled, his body shaking as he was trying everything possible to make himself kill her. As he stepped near her, her eyes shot open, and she looked at him. He was expecting to see more sadness or for her to be scared, but she was looking at him as if she was threatening him.

"Do it." She demanded, stepping towards him.

He was taken back as he stared, confused, at her. She reached forward, grabbed his hand, placing it on her throat.

"I said fucking do it!" She screamed at his face.

"What the hell is wrong with you?" Jace growled at her, ripping his hand away from her throat.

She was angry with him. As she stared him down, her eyes locked into his as if she could command him with her eyes.

"You have no idea." She whispered with a hint of laughter in her voice.

His mate was a psychopath. He looked at her, studying her. He saw past the anger and the craziness. She was hurt, wounded, and broken. His wolf whimpered inside of him, feeling the pain radiating off of her. Jace stepped away from her. He couldn't. His wolf was already so locked into her and the way he was feeling. His body, his heart, all of it wouldn't let him do it anyways. He let out a long sigh as he stepped back.

"Chicken!" She chuckled, leaning against the brick wall.

"Shut up!" He sneered at her as he began pacing in the alley.

He needed a plan. She would turn any minute, and who knows what that would lead to. He needed to make sure his pack would be safe. He also needed to find a way to protect her. If someone found out she was his mate, there would be a bigger target on her back. Kip would make it his personal mission to slaughter her. Then there was the whole smelling like a hunter. He didn't know how he was going to hide that. He groaned, leaning against the wall across from her and looking at her.

"Why don't you just leave?" She said to him; her tone was snotty.

"Do you not know what shut up means?" He growled at her again.

"Bye, Douche." She said to him rolling her eyes and began trying to stumble her way out of the alley.

His hand caught her wrist and spun her back towards him, crashing her into his chest. She glared at him and shoved his shoulder. He was surprised at how his shoulder went back; he wasn't ready for her to have strength like that yet. She balled her hands up into a fist and began pounding on his chest. He let her hit him several times before he shoved her back into the wall.

"Alright, that's enough." Jace said, stopping her.

Her chest was heaving up and down as she tried to catch her breath. She wasn't sure why she was so angry with this complete stranger. She stopped hitting him and tried to calm herself.

"Just leave me alone." she said, trying to control her emotions.

"I wish." he muttered while stepping away from her.

As he did, she let out a loud painful moan. His eyes studied her closely. He quickly stole a glance at the watch on his wrist, and he shut his eyes, frustrated. 12 am.

Chapter Ten
Shifting

The pain rushing through her was mind-numbing. She felt like her skin was going to melt off. She grabbed onto the stranger in front of her. Sweat poured down her back as her body began to convulse. Everything hurt. It even hurt to breathe. Something invisible was attacking her. She squeezed her eyes shut as she gritted her teeth. She could taste blood in her mouth. Then everything stopped. She opened her eyes slowly, and all she could see was darkness. Everything was pure black, and a haunting light appeared off in the distance. Then a rush of wind. Nora shielded her eyes. A metal smell flooded her nose. Her stomach curled in on itself. She knew the smell right away. It was a smell that haunted her. Blood. Images began to flash through her head.

A family slaughtered in a small cabin. Wolf tracks on the floor, covered in blood. A woman comes home to find her family dead. The image hurt; she knew how it felt. The next flash was the same woman wearing a gray veil over her face in mourning. She stood over a candle burning something. She was mumbling words in a foreign language. Images of several women dressed in hunting gear passed through her mind; the next was one of the women in gear hunting something. She watched her chase down a large wolf and end it. As she ended it, the wolf's figure turned human.

Nora was horrified as she watched several more hunting scenes. Several of them were wolves mauling these hunters. Nora's mind began to fill with all the knowledge. It was like the knowledge was coming from these past hunters. She instantly knew about werewolves. She knew how to hunt them, how to track them, and their weakness; she felt this overwhelming feeling of duty. That she needed to honor these women and men that came and died before her. She felt all the overwhelming pain, and it shook her to the core.

"Breathe. Focus on your breathing. In through your nose and blow it slowly out your mouth. Focus on one breath at a time," Jace whispered calmly to her. His voice cut through the images.

She focused on his voice, trying to pull herself back.

"It's ok. It's going to be ok. I got you," his voice whispered to her.

She felt his warmth wrap around her as the pain began to subside. She felt like she had been running for her life. Her body and limbs felt like jello. The strange thing was she felt better, stronger, and quicker. She looked up, her eyes locking with the ice-blue ones that were kneeling next to her.

"Are you ok?" Jace whispered to her, not sure what to expect next.

She was about to thank him, but the more she looked at him. She knew something was off. She looked him over and immediately knew. She moved away from him. He let her and watched her carefully.

His guard was up, but he wanted to help her as much as he could. He also needed to keep her close. When she was away from him, she narrowed her eyes at him, hate flashing in them.

"Wolf." She spat at him and grimaced as if it was the worst word to say.

Jace sighed deeply. His wolf inside whimpered again, hearing the hate in her voice. He wanted to comfort her. Jace fought against the urge himself. He tried to ignore what she had just said.

"Are you ok?" He asked again.

"I am, but if you stay anywhere near me, you won't be." She sneered at him.

Jace studied her face cautiously, not sure what she was about to do. He didn't confirm nor deny what he was. She looked at him, and her face curled with disgust. She shoved him with both hands away from her. The urge to hit him harder and more powerfully coursed through her. Jace was taken back by the shove, but he didn't budge. She clenched her jaw shut and balled her hands into a fist. She was still drunk, but her newly found power was making her able to focus more. She slammed both of her fists into his chest. It caused him to shift back but not completely move. He stepped into her, backing her up against the wall. A growl erupted from his chest that sent vibrations through her. Her honey eyes glared at him, not backing down. The heat radiating from his skin sent shivers through her. Her body received too many mixed messages. Everything was way too overwhelming at the moment.

She leaned back into the brick wall behind her, staring at him. His arms captured her between the wall and him but not touching her. Her eyes ran over every muscular forearm that blocked the exit. She was pinned, his arms on either side of her head. She shifted her eyes back to his sharp, ice-blue, and almost glowing eyes.

"Well, what are you waiting for, wolf?" She asked, her eyes burning into him.

Jace didn't answer. He was having too many emotions and was trying to stay calm. His wolf was going crazy, wanting to be as close as possible to her. Wanting to claim what was his. His head was telling him to kill her now. He growled again in response to the fight between his mind and wolf. It was all becoming too much. With a fierce glare, she challenged the wolf to do what he had come to do.

"Go ahead." She spat, her voice laced with bitterness.

"Just like your kind slaughtered my family. You better do it now, or I'll find a way to put an end to your kind, just like you ended mine." Her chest heaved with anger as she spoke, her teeth gritted in determination.

Jace narrowed his eyebrows at her, half confused, half hearing her threat.

His wolf whimpered at the pain coming off of his mate. Jace narrowed his eyes at her, letting out a breath as he tried to calm himself. He was ignoring how perfect her skin was, how perfect her mouth was, and the way her hair moved around her face. His eyes couldn't help but find her neck. His wolf whimpered. He inhaled, closing his eyes for a second.

STOP. He yelled inward at his wolf.

His eyes opened and locked back with hers.

"I wouldn't throw threats around, little hunter," he said, his hand going into her hair and yanking her head back.

"Now, I need you to hear me and listen. This may be your only shot. You need to get away from here. You need to go. My pack didn't kill your family, but you are probably right that wolves did. Now that you've turned, they will be able to smell you. They will be able to find you, and they won't be as nice as me. You need to leave. Stay away from the redwood. I won't help you again." Jace growled, letting go of her hair and stepping away from her.

"And if I don't?" She spat back.

"Well, it will be your funeral, hunter," Jace said, keeping his distance.

He could feel his fangs coming down due to the heightened emotion. She glared at him; she wanted to hurt him. Everything in her body was telling her to fight him, to kill him, but there was this other pull. A weird sense of wanting to be close to him. She shook her head, trying to chase the sense of longing away from her. A door slamming in the distance caught her ears.

"Nora!" Joel was yelling for her out the back door of the club.

She sighed, rolling her eyes. She looked Jace up and down before walking past him. She was memorizing what he looked like. His jet-black hair seems to shimmer blue in the moonlight. His very chiseled jaw and perfect cheekbones, his ice blue eyes that burned into her. He was tall and had very broad shoulders. She could tell by the way his t-shirt hugged him that his abs and chest were much like his jaw, chiseled and perfect. She shook her head, shaking the thoughts of him from her mind.

As she walked past him, he reached out and grabbed her hand, stopping her. The electricity that shot through her at his touch made her almost jump. The way her stomach flipped when he touched her was like butterflies on steroids. She gave him a dirty look for touching her.

"Mountain ash, wolfsbane, and mistletoe. Get some and figure out how to use it." He said through his teeth.

Nora looked at him confused but took note of what he told her. Her eyes lingered on his long fangs that appeared when he talked. She almost wanted to reach out and touch them to ensure that this was all real. She yanked her arm away from him.

"Bye, wolf." She growled as she walked away from him.

"Stay away, little hunter." He said to her back.

He heard her groan in disgust as he watched her walk away.

His eyes lingered on her as she grew out of sight. Even the way she walked, the way her hips moved. It was getting to him. His wolf was going crazy. He wanted to be near her.

"How dare you let her leave us!" His wolf growled inside him.

"That's enough!" Jace commanded him.

His wolf growled angrily inside of him but went silent. Jace shut his eyes and focused on the sounds around him. He could hear that she had met up with the boy looking for her. He felt strange. Why would he be mated to a hunter? It can't be right, and it must have been the sensation of being too close to a hunter when they turned that made everything haywire. Why did he tell her about the plants? Giving a hunter information about plants that could harm wolves was a bad idea, but the words just fell out of his mouth. He felt the need to protect her.

"Where the heck did you go?" Joel began lecturing her as she got to him.

"For air." Nora said a little too short.

Joel raised an eyebrow at her, looking over her shoulder. Was there someone with her? He looked back at her, his face full of questions.

"Doll, are you ok?" Joel asked worriedly.

"I'm actually feeling ok. Did you want to go back inside? I saw you with that handsome fellow." Nora said with a playful smile on her lips.

"Are you sure?" Joel asked her, a little worried about her shift in attitude.

There was something different. The Nora that he knew lately shied away and would take any opportunity to not be out in public. He was worried but excited that he saw a glimpse of his old friend.

"Yeah, let's do this," Nora said and playfully shoved him.

Joel fell back into the club's door as Nora shoved him. He bounced off the door and looked with wide eyes at Nora.

"Dude, calm down there, she-hulk." He said, regaining himself.

"Sorry, I was excited. I didn't mean to shove you that hard." Nora said, making a note that her strength was definitely different now.

"It's ok. Let's get back inside." Joel laughed, opening the club door, and the two of them disappeared.

Chapter Eleven
Wolf

Jace had been listening and growled. His body vibrated as he tried to control himself and make himself walk away. Go home. He wanted her to go home! Why was she going back into the public? She has no clue what just happened to her or what signals she was sending out, he thought, slamming his fist into the brick wall. The wall cracked instantly, and his knuckles were bloodied. He clenched his jaw so hard he thought he was going to break a tooth. He groaned as he began walking to the club. He was going to have to drag her home.

Home with us. His wolf said excitedly.
Her home. Jace growled at him.
She belongs with us. His wolf howled.

Jace blocked him out as he walked up the cement ramp to the club's door. Grabbing the handle, he pulled the door back. The door flung back, and the handle popped off of it. He dropped the doorknob to the ground stepping inside. He took several deep breaths as he searched for her. He could smell her; her scent was intoxicating and enveloped him. His eyes searched through the crowd, following her scent.

She didn't take any time. She was smack dab in the middle of the dance floor. Her arm draped across some man's shoulder as they danced. Jace felt his blood boil. The word mine echoed in his head. Jace crossed the floor in long strides. People literally hurried out of his way. Reaching them, he grabbed her hand off the man's shoulder and pulled her towards him. She landed in his chest.

"Hey!" She yelled, crashing to his chest.

"Hey buddy, she was dancing with me." The man with dusty brown hair grabbed Jace's shoulder.

"And now she's not," Jace said, throwing his shoulder back into the man.

The man crashed to the floor and skidded backward. The man blinked several times before standing up and walking quickly away. Nora hit him hard in his chest. He winced but didn't budge.

"Hey-"

"You were supposed to go home," Jace said, looking down at her.

"Well, you're not my father. I am a big girl, so I'm staying." Nora said, giving up on physically fighting him at that moment.

"No, you need to go. I already told you what could happen." He said, grabbing her wrist and starting to lead her off the dance floor.

She yanked her arm hardback, and Jace stumbled backward. He had never met someone who had strength as close to his. She might be as strong, if not stronger, than his top wolves. He blinked at her.

"I said I'm staying, Wolf." she said, taking her stance.

"If you do not leave now, you will regret making me do what comes next." Jace said, stepping towards her.

"Do it." Nora said, stepping closer to him and squaring up with him.

Jace growled, his hand going for her waist. He was about to throw her over his shoulder and walk out of place.

"Nora, what is going on?" Joel asked her to stand next to her and eyeball Jace.

"Nothing," Nora said, glaring at Jace.

"Who is this?" Joel asked, pointing to a very pissed-off and scary-looking Jace.

"Wolf." Nora said with a grin.

"Wolf…ok, um Wolf. I'm not sure what's going on with you and my friend here, but I think you should go," Joel said, being as polite as possible.

"Alpha, we have a problem." Wyatt mind linked him.

"Fuck." Jace said out loud.

Nora and Joel looked at him, confused, as Jace's eyes seemed to gloss over.

"What is it? I got some of my own right now," Jace answered Wyatt.

"The boy, he's shifting." Wyatt responded, sounding worried.

"He's what?" Jace responded.

"Turning into a wolf." Wyatt said cautiously.

"Are you sure?" Jace said, frustrated.

"Yes." Wyatt answered shortly.

Jace could tell he was holding back some smart-ass comment.

"Get him in the holding cell. I will be there as soon as I can." Jace said shortly back to Wyatt.

"Yes, Alpha." Wyatt said as the mind link was cut off.

"Um, dude, are you ok?" Joel asked him.

"Look, if you care about her, get her ass home. She is about to cause a whole bunch of trouble," Jace said shortly.

He glanced at Nora.

"If you care about your friend, I would lie low until you figure out your shit." Jace said, still glaring at her.

"Nora, what the hell is he talking about?" Joel asked her, super worried.

Jace turned away from them, his wolf panicking, torn between his Alpha's duty and protecting his mate. Jace exited the club as quickly as he could. His mind processed what Wyatt had said. The only way the boy would be turning was, if Kip purposely gave him some of his blood. You need the blood of an Alpha to make wolves that were not born into it. It was risky, and most of the time did not work. They caused massive amounts of destruction and, in the end, killed themselves. They are pure emotion and deadly.

Jace walked over to a dark blue charger sitting nestled in the corner of a parking lot. He looked around, trying to see if there were any cameras. None. He broke the window, and the alarm began to ring. He flew open the door and found the alarm mechanism, and with one light touch, it was ripped out. He quickly hotwired the car and took off. He did not trust himself shifting right now and running home. He knew that his wolf would just lead him back to her. He needed to be far away from her.

The ground screamed against the tires, dirt and dust kicking up around the car. The gate flew open, seeing him coming. He barely missed it as two men manually moved it out of the way. He didn't slow down until he could see his home in his view. He turned slightly as he got to the driveway. Smoke from the tires rubbing against the ground puffed up as he slid into his parking spot. He was out of the car and at the door in seconds, throwing it open. He crossed the room with several long strides reaching the stairs. As he reached them, he could hear it happening.

The screaming, the animalistic sounds, the pain. It echoed into the stairwell. The sounds wrapped around him as he began walking down the stairs. With his sharp hearing, he could hear the boy's bones crunching and popping as he came down the stairs. The basement was dark, with no windows and only one way in or out. They kept it like this so that if anything ever got out of hand, there would be fewer chances for someone to escape.

All the members of his pack have their first shift here. Most of them went smoothly, but this was different. This boy was not meant to shift. He didn't have wolf blood. He was being forced into this. He wouldn't survive this. Jace's feet hit the cement floor of the holding cell. The boy was behind bars, shackled down the best they could. The smell of blood hit him; the boy was bleeding from his mouth as his fangs busted through his gums. His nose was bleeding as well. His body was hunched over, cracking and bending. Wyatt was at the door of the cell, watching intently. Dante, Adam, and Matt were in the back of the room. Dante was prepared; he was holding the silver sword in his hand, waiting with dread. Jace walked over to the group as the boy continued to shift. The screams slowly became howls. Claws emerging and then fur. The boy had shifted, but there was something wrong. The wolf's face was distorted. His eyes were sunk back and hollow. They were completely black, with no white or pupils. The rage kicked in, and he began wrestling with the shackles. They watched as the wolf began to realize what was keeping him in place. He pulled hard on one of the chains, and it slowly began to break. He looked down at the other one and then at his arm. In one swift motion, the wolf bit through his arm. The piece of his arm that would have been his hand flopped down onto the floor. The hand turned human as it did.

"What the fuck!" Matt screamed, seeing the act.

The wolf's eyes flickered to Matt. He started showing teeth. Matt growled back at the wolf, his own wolf becoming angry at the stare-down. The wolf seemed to smile sadistically and began pulling endlessly on the chain, keeping him in place. The links were beginning to move as he pulled. Dante was ready; he shifted his stance with the sword waiting for the go-ahead.

"Wyatt, don't you have anything to sedate him?" Jace said as he stepped towards the cell, his eyes glued to the wolf.

"I don't know if we have anything with a high enough dose, and then how the hell are we going to get it in him?" Wyatt asked as he began searching through his medical supplies.

"Just come up with something," Jace said, stepping forward to the cell.

"Calm down," Jace called into the cell, using his Alpha tone.

The wolf paused, his soulless eyes looking for the source. His eyes locked with Jace; Jace allowed his wolf to come forward, and his eyes glowed slightly.

"That's enough." Jace said, trying to use his Alpha status to control this newly feral wolf.

The wolf seemed to snicker, and then a hacking noise emerged as if the wolf was laughing. Jace was taken back by this. He glanced over to Wyatt, who was drawing up and injecting. Wyatt nodded to Jace, coming next to him. The wolf began pulling on the chain more. The blood from his hanging limb created a puddle on the ground below him. He pulled hard and slipped on the blood. Jace saw an opportunity.

"How the hell are we going to do this?" Wyatt asked, his voice just above a whisper.

"It has trouble getting up without its limbs. If we can get it to fall again, I will get the injection in him." Jace said.

"Alpha, let's just end it." Dante said, moving forward with the sword.

"We need to see what will happen at the end of this." Jace said, holding up a hand to Dante.

Dante grumbled. "I don't think going in there is a good idea."

"Well, we don't have many options right now. Ready?" Jace said, grasping the cell door.

Wyatt nodded. Matt and Adam were on standby waiting for the call. They both stopped off the side, their wolves just behind the veil waiting to be called on. Dante was fidgeting nervously with the sword. He just wanted the threat gone.

"Wyatt, stay by the door as soon as he's down. Chuck me the injection." Jace said, pulling open the heavy door.

The wolf saw the door open, it's hollow eyes fixed eyes on it. Seeing Jace enter the cell, its fur stood up. Jace eyed Dante, who nodded, letting him know he wouldn't be too far behind him if it went south. The wolf smiled. Its long fangs hang out of its mouth with long strands of drool dripping from them. It jerked its arm forward, and the sound of metal breaking echoed throughout the cell. Jace saw the chain drop that was holding the beast back. He narrowed his eyes, readying himself. He heard Wyatt opening the door.

"Lock it!" He yelled as he grabbed hold of the door and slammed it.

Wyatt looked at him like he was crazy, Jace growled, and Wyatt did as he said. The wolf ran at him, his jaw chomping open and closed as it ran towards him.

"Shot!" Jace yelled to Wyatt, holding his ground.

Wyatt tossed the shot through the bars of the cell. Jace caught it in his hand, taking the cap off it as the wolf reached him. He lunged at Jace. Jace stepped to the side just in time as the wolf flung passed him. Jace slammed the injection down into the muscle of it's back. The wolf whimpered, turning as quickly as it could. Regaining direction, it ran at Jace again. It slammed into Jace, pushing him up against the wall. Jace held It's head back as it chomped and snarled at him. It wanted his throat as he tried pushing closer to Jace. Jace's arms were holding its shoulders. It used it's one good paw to snake its way around to Jace's abdomen and pressed it's claws into his stomach. Jace winced as he felt the nails pierced his skin.

"How long does this take?" Jace growled.

"I don't really know. I'm not even sure it's going to work." Wyatt yelled.

"Move!" Dante yelled to Wyatt.

"No, don't!" Jace yelled.

He felt the wolf shift its attention. It wanted out. They couldn't risk this thing getting out. Its strength almost matched Jace's. This thing would be on the warpath, destroying whoever and whatever it could if it got out.

"Jace!" Dante yelled as he tried to go against his command.

"Dante, don't." Jace growled, throwing his head back and then smashing it into the wolf's face.

One of the fangs grazed Jace's forehead, but the impact he gave the creature retracted it's claws from his stomach and caused it to stumble. Jace took the opportunity and swept it's leg out from under him. The wolf fell onto the floor. It tried to get its balance to get up, but Jace was on top of it, pinning it to the floor. It faced the cold cement, still chomping and biting. Jace held it to the ground waiting for the medicine to kick in. The wolf's body began to twitch, and blood began to pour out of its nose. Jace did not relax his hold but watched carefully. The wolf's legs turned back into human legs and it's abdomen. It's head and front leg remained in wolf form. The wolf's human legs began to kick as he let out a horrible sounding howl. The howl then turned into a gurgling, blood began to pour out of its mouth. The body was starting to give out.

"Dante!" Jace called to him.

Dante didn't even hesitate. He almost broke the door of the cell off as he stepped inside. Sword over his head as he walked towards the dying creature. Jace was holding on still; even though it was clearly dying, it was like it didn't care and was still trying to find a way to escape. Jace looked up to Dante, who was holding the sword ready.

"On three," Jace said, and Dante nodded.

"One…Two… Three!" Jace yelled, letting go and moving his hands out of his way.

As soon as Jace let go of the wolf, it lunged it's head forward, trying to attack; Dante brought the sword down. The wolf's teeth managed to sink into Dante's legs. Dante let out a scream as he pushed the sword through the wolf's neck, severing the head from the body. Blood sprayed upwards and out like a fountain. The two of them were covered in blood. Jace stood up, wiping the blood from his face.

"What the hell!" Dante screamed, pointing down at his leg.

Jace looked over and saw the wolf's head still attached to his leg. Its teeth sank. Jace cracked a smile, trying not to laugh. Dante leaned over, trying to pull it off. He tugged on it and winced, he then tried to pry its jaw open, and it wouldn't open.

"Hey, Wyatt, can you, um..fix that?" Jace asked, trying not to laugh.

"It's not funny." Dante growled.

"I didn't say it was." Jace said, his voice cracking with laughter.

Dante rolled his eyes, walking out of the cell, dragging the leg with the wolf's head still attached. Jace thought it was odd that the body hadn't transformed back into its human form. There was something very wrong about this whole thing. Jace walked out of the cell, Adam and Matt looking at the bloody scene, their faces concerned as well.

"He didn't shift back." Adam said out loud. Wyatt looked up from studying Dante's leg.

He frowned deeply, realizing it, too, as Adam said it out loud. His crew exchanged glances.

“We can figure that out later. Wyatt, get that off of Dante. Matt and Adam clean up duty. Not a word of this to anyone until we know for sure what's going on.” Jace ordered as he walked out of the holding room.

Chapter Twelve
Encounters

"Nora. Come on, let's go home." Joel said, pulling her arm.

Nora was standing on the sidewalk, looking around. She thought she heard or felt something. She glanced at the crowd coming out of the nightclub. As Joel tugged on her, she turned to look over his shoulder. A man was watching her. He had dark blond hair that looked like he had just rolled out of bed. He was leaning against the brick wall in the alley across the street, just staring at her.

"Earth to Nora!" Joel said, shaking her.

"What?" She asked a little annoyed, her eyes going from the stranger to Joel.

"Geesh, calm down, girl. I was saying we should leave," Joel said defensively.

Nora sighed, looking back to the alleyway to see the man gone. She looked back at Joel and smiled. She was sorry for the attitude she gave him. The man Joel had been dancing with all night came up behind him and put his arm around his shoulder.

"Where are you off to?" He asked into Joel's ear. Joel blushed deeply and giggled slightly.

"Home."

"Ahh, but whose home." He said with a playful smile hanging on his lips.

"Nora, this is Nick. Nick, Nora." Joel said, introducing them.

"Pleasure." Nick said, holding out his hand.

"Nice to meet you," Nora said, looking him over.

"So home?" Nick smiled.

"Yeah, I was telling Nora we should get going." Joel said as Nick entwined his hand in Joel's.

Joel blushed again and closed his fingers around Nick's. Nora rolled her eyes and looked around. A flash of messy blond hair caught her attention. He was across the street, walking down it.

"Joel, why don't you and Nick head back to your place, and I'll meet you there in a few. I need some air. Ok?" Nora said as she took a few steps wanting to hurry and follow this guy.

"Nora, what?" Joel said, surprised.

"It's fine. I'll see you later." Nora said, pecking a kiss on his cheek, and took off.

"Nora, you don't even have a car! Nora!" Joel yelled, letting go of Nick's hand.

Joel attempted to go after her, but before he could even catch up to her, she was gone. He couldn't find her anywhere. He looked around and through the crowds. Where could she have gone so quickly?

"Joel, your friend is a little off.' Nick said, coming up behind him.

"Ah, she's had a rough time lately. I don't know where she went. Did you see?" Joel asked, still looking around.

"No, she's fast." Nick said, scanning the crowd.

"Damn it. I don't even know what to do now."
Joel grumbled.

"Well, you have two options, we can keep
searching, or we can go wait for her at your place."
Nick shrugged.

Joel debated with himself. Nora said she would
meet him back at home, but what if she had really lost
it and was now running the streets?

Nora cursed that she was wearing the dress as
she tried to catch up to the guy. He walked further
away from the city, and he walked fast. The nightlife
was fading away as she tracked him. She could tell
he was in pretty good shape, and even though he
didn't seem like he noticed her, something was telling
her that he knew she was following him. He made a
sharp right down an alleyway. Nora's guard was up as
she quickly turned it down. She slammed into his
back. In a swift movement, she was pinned up against
the wall.

"Why are you following me?" He asked, his
hands on her shoulder, shoving her back into the wall.

In one swift movement, Nora placed her hands
on his shoulders and used his own weight against
him. She yanked him towards her and then spun. The
man ended up being shoved up against the wall by
Nora.

"Why were you watching me?" Nora asked
him, applying pressure to his shoulders.

The man blinked; confused by her strength, he
studied her. Nora was doing the same, she wasn't

sure how she knew the man with ice-blue eyes was a wolf, but she wasn't getting any reading on this one.

"Are you one of them?" She asked vaguely.

"One of them?" He asked back.

"Great, so we're going to go back and forth like this all night?" Nora said, digging her thumb into his collarbone.

The man smirked, and his brown eyes showed amusement. He made almost the same move and pulled Nora towards him, but as he did, he swept her leg. She landed on her back and was pinned to the ground beneath him.

"Well, you're not a wolf." The man said with a grin on his face.

Nora struggled beneath him, her mind calculating ways out.

"Wolf." She said in breathless suspense as she fidgeted under him.

"Yeah, as in the big bad ones." He smirked, pushing her hard into the ground.

Nora smiled sweetly at him and moved her head like she was going to tell him a secret. He grinned and leaned forward. As he did, she smashed her forehead into his face. As he let go of her shoulders to grab ahold of his nose, she shoved her knees into his stomach and pushed him back and off of her. She quickly got to her feet, ready to fight.

"Shit!" He groaned, getting to his feet.

"Are you one?" Nora asked her feet apart and hands in a fist.

"No, but if I was one, I would probably be killing you right now." He said, touching his nose.

"So then, what are you?" Nora demanded.

"I'm thinking the same as you, but I think you're new." He said, rubbing his head.

"Your …what did he call me…. A hunter?" Nora said, remembering.

"Yes, and who called you that?" He asked, looking over his shoulder.

"Some stranger. So what does this mean? Are we enemies too?" Nora asked.

"Only if you hit me like that again." He said, straightening the bridge of his nose.

A loud pop echoed in the alleyway as he reset his nose, blood dripping out of it. Nora watched him carefully as he pulled a tissue out of his pocket and jammed it up his nose.

"Logan." He said to her.

"Logan?" Nora asked back.

"Oh god, love, did turning fry your brain, or were you like this before? Honestly, we don't need any airheads on our side, and you won't last long." Logan said, going into a rant.

"Nora and the answer is no to both options. Also, who says ``I want to join you." She said sharply to him.

"Well, there's safety in numbers," Logan said with a wink.

"Can you teach me how to find them?" Nora asked quickly, the thought of revenging her family popping into her mind.

"I can teach you a whole lot more than that, but I got to get approval. We just don't let anyone in." Logan said, searching around in his pocket.

He pulled out a card and walked over to her. He held it out to her.

Nora looked at him suspiciously but slowly took it. The word 'Vanator' was written on it, and on the back of the card was an address. Nora raised an eyebrow at him.

"Be there tomorrow at seven." Logan said to her.

"Or?" Nora called after him.

"Or it's your funeral doll." Logan shrugged his shoulders, walking away.

"Jokes on you." She muttered to his back.

Why does everyone keep telling me I'm going to die? Nora groaned to herself annoyingly.

"Name?" Logan stopped at the end of the alley.

"Nora." She said after him.

"Seven. Nora." Logan said, disappearing.

Nora sighed deeply before turning on her heels and walking out of the alleyway. She gripped the card tightly in her hand. She needed to do research. She needed to know everything she could know about this new world. Nora thought about going back to Joel's, but she didn't want to interrupt anything that may be happening. She would go home.

The image of her face flashed before his eyes. Her haunting honey eyes burned into him. Do it! She shouted. Why did she want to die? He felt his wolf wince in pain. Jace tossed over in his bed, his damp hair flopping to the side as he turned. Why was she in so much pain? Wolf, she said with disgust. She instantly hated him. He felt the acid in his stomach building up. The thought of her eating away at him.

He sat up, the blanket falling away from his bare chest. He ran his hand over his face as he kicked the blanket away, his feet touching the floor. His wolf stirred inside him; he was just as restless and aggravated as he was.

Run. His wolf summoned him.

Run, really, you think after everything you've been doing lately, I should let you go for a run?

Run! Jace felt his body shudder as his wolf tried to force his way through.

Stop, he growled at him.

His wolf was becoming uncontrollable. He finally gave in, and his wolf whimpered.

Mate.

At least you're being honest now. Jace grumbled.

He wanted to see her too. The nagging thought of her not being ok was irritating him.

"Fine, Run." Jace groaned out loud.

Jace wasn't going to sleep much anyways, so there was no point. He knew his wolf would be leading them right back to the girl, but he didn't care. He needed to see her. His footsteps were soundless as he made his way down from the top floor. The packed house was silent. Normally it was just Dante, Matt, Adam, and Wyatt besides himself staying. He walked to the door and stepped out into the night air. He smelt the air and allowed his wolf to take over.

Within seconds his wolf had her scent and was rushing after it. The night sky shone down as he took off running. He used the night mask as his presence as he turned down a suburban street. His wolf was searching as he ran past several houses. His wolf slowed down at a two-story house, the yellow door of it standing out. Why did he know this house? Jace thought behind his wolf's eyes. His wolf walked up the concrete steps to the home, nudging the door. It swung open slowly. Stepping in, the old smell of blood hit him. It was faint and almost gone, but seeing how there wasn't any blood, he could see. He knew it was from the past; there must have been a lot of it for it to still linger. Stepping in further, he got a shiver, and he remembered. All dead. The words rang in his mind. This home was hit several weeks ago by Kip's pack. He said it was home to an up-and- coming hunter. He murdered everyone brutally. His wolf ears perked up as he heard small muffled cries coming from upstairs.

Mate. His wolf thought, rushing up the stairs.

He cleared the stairs and was at the top of the landing in no time. His wolf nudged open the door. She was sprawled across her bed. A loose hanging t-shirt that was bunched up around her exposing her stomach. Her shorts rode up as well, and her black hair draped out around her. His wolf sat looking at her. She's beautiful, Jace thought to himself.

Mine.

Stop. She doesn't even know us. You need to chill. Remember, she's a hunter. Jace growled at him, his wolf starting to pace the bedroom floor, annoyed with Jace.

She let out a cry, it was full of pain, and she curled into herself. Her body was shaking. His wolf hopped up onto the bed, trying to see what was hurting her. He whimpered softly and pressed his cold nose into her stomach.

Nightmares. Jace told him as he whimpered again.

His wolf laid down next to her, trying to comfort her. As his nose hit her stomach once more, her eyes shot open. She sat up, her eyes scanning the room, and then widened, seeing the enormous black wolf lying next to her.

"Wolf." She whispered, sweat beading across her forehead.

She pushed herself into her headboard, trying to scan the room for a weapon. His wolf whimpered, putting his head down, trying to tell her he meant no harm. Nora looked at the wolf, confused.

"Cole?" She whispered.

The wolf whimpered happily and nuzzled closer to her.

Since when did you become a pet? And how does she know your name? Jace said, teasing him.

His wolf ignored him as Nora reached out and patted his head.

"What are you doing here? How did you find me?" Nora asked as the wolf pushed his face into her neck, rubbing his head against hers.

"Hey, easy there, you'll knock me off the bed." Nora chuckled as the wolf licked the side of her face.

"You know tonight has been insane. Why wouldn't a wolf be in my bed acting like an oversized dog." Nora laughed, trying to push Cole's head away from her face.

"You know someone said I should be afraid of wolves," Nora said, rubbing his ears.

Cole all but climbed on top of her, nuzzling his face into hers. Nora shoved his head away from hers, and he let her. He whimpered as she pushed him away from her.

"Ugh, fine, you can stay, but no more licking me, and be careful." Nora said, sighing as she rolled over onto her side.

Cole seemed to purr as he snuggled up next to her. She chuckled lightly and patted his side.

"I might need to go check myself into a hospital. This shit is crazy." She laughed, closing her eyes.

You really are acting like an oversized dog. Jace smirked at Cole.

Dont care. I'm close to her. We need her. Cole responded back, placing his head on her side and closing her eyes.

Jace was silent at Cole's statement; the internal battle going on inside him was raging. He felt Cole relax, and her scent invaded him. She smelt amazing and instantly pushed his turmoil aside. Her scent makes them both relax and grow tired. He gave in to it all.

Chapter Thirteen
Cole

Nora stretched into something warm. She curled into the heavy heat. It felt amazing. A scent invaded her nostrils. She nuzzled her head into the smell. It was amazing, like how it smelled after it rained. She felt something strong wrap around her, and a deep hum came from it. Nora froze, realizing something had her. Her hand traveled over a very chiseled bare chest. Alarms went off in her head as she slowly opened her eyes, finding a strong pair of arms had her captured. The person pressed his face into her neck. Another soft hum escaped them as he inhaled. She pulled back slightly, trying to see her capture's face. She spotted the jet-black tousled hair first. A piece of it fell onto his brow bone, she couldn't help it, and before she could stop herself, she found her hand betraying her and brushing it softly away from his eye. His eyes opened slowly at her touch. The bright, ice-blue eyes stared down at her. For a minute, she had forgotten he was a stranger in her bed with his arms locked around her. The way her body fit perfectly with his, the way his warmth and arms made her feel safe. She had forgotten the world for a minute. Just a minute.

She blinked and pushed her hands into his chest, pushing herself away from him. She nearly fell off the bed. He caught her, pulling her back. She swiftly landed on top of him. Her legs straddled his waist, which was barely covered by the blanket. She looked down and felt her face grow warm.

"Naked." She breathed out.

Jace eyebrows came together at her word, and then a smirk came across his face. Naked…he was naked. He shifted during his sleep back to his human form. She was now flopping around like a fish, trying to get away from him.

"Woah, Woah. Listen, if you keep doing that, you're going to touch something that's going to make you really blush." Jace laughed, capturing her by her waist.

She was frozen hearing his words. She could feel him beneath her, her heart racing in her chest when she realized what he meant. She stopped moving all together. She looked down at him, the blush from her cheeks going away and fire crossing into her eyes.

"Why the hell are you naked in my bed!" She said angrily at him.

He smirked at her anger, it made her even more appealing. She saw his smirk, and her brows narrowed. She grabbed ahold of his hand on her and bent his fingers back. The sharp pain she sent through him made him pull his hand away from her. It gave her enough time to scoot off of him. She backed away from her bed. Still watching him. He gripped the blanket around him as he stood up.

"You did not answer my question." She said, her hands in a fist.

He just smiled, standing up. As he stood up, her eyes traveled over him. He had the most board perfect shoulders she had ever seen. The muscles rippling off him were insane. He looked like some god out of a book. There were countless scars across his body, all shapes and sizes, but that didn't take away from his perfectness. She glanced back up at his face; a grin was plastered on it.

"Enjoying the view?" He smirked.

"No." She said, her eyes shot down as her face flushed.

"So are you going to explain-wait, Cole?" Nora said, confused, looking around.

"Cole." Jace repeated, pulling up his pants.

"Yes, how did you get past the big black wolf?" Nora asked, confused.

"Wolf?" Jace smirked.

Tell her. Cole growled.

"Oh god, I'm hallucinating now," Nora said, her hand going to her face.

"What's your name, little hunter." Jace asked, looking around for his shirt.

"Nora." She muttered.

"Nora." Jace repeated it, liking the sound of her name.

"Wait, Wolf…" Nora said, taking her hands off her face and pointing at him.

"You're a lot smarter than I thought, little hunter. Jace smirked as she connected the dots.

"You're Cole?" Nora said, squinting at him.

Before he could answer, she crossed the room and grabbed his face. She squished it, looking into his eyes. He had never had someone grab him before. No one would even dare to try.

"How does this even work?" She said, squishing his cheeks.

Her closeness to him was overwhelming. He grabbed her around her waist and pulled her closer to him. Little tiny electric tingles went through her; as she was pressed against his chest. He leaned down, pressing his face into her neck, inhaling. Nora shivered. He made his way up to her ear.

"Cole is my wolf." He whispered into her ear.

His hot breath against her ear caused goosebumps to run down her arms. She softened her hands that were squashing his face. One hand moved to his neck, and the other held his face gently. He moved away from her ear and looked down at her. His eyes seemed like they were glowing. She cleared her throat. His eyes lingered on her lips. He leaned down, his nose brushing against her. She closed her eyes, waiting for it but then felt cold. She opened her eyes and realized he had stepped away from her. He was throwing on his black T- shirt. She watched him finish getting dressed, not meaning to stare, but she was trying to process everything. She couldn't help but feel this strange pull to him and this strong want to be near him, but then there was this gut-wrenching hate in her stomach when she thought of what he was. He changes into an enormous black wolf who acts like a dog. She was a hunter. Hunter, that's right. She looked over at her nightstand. The business card was sitting on it. Seven tonight. Did she want to continue walking into this world? She was trying to get a hold of her thoughts.

"Hungry?" Jace asked her as he tied up his shoe.

"Maybe." Nora answered.

"You don't know if you're hungry?" Jace asked her, giving her a funny look.

"No, I don't know about you. Everything in me says to hate and fight you, but there's another side. And it all doesn't seem real." She blurted out.

She has to come with us. Cole ordered.

Jace rolled his eyes at Cole. His possessiveness was stirring his own. He wanted her to come too. He didn't know how this would play out, but he couldn't deal with her being too far. Cole wouldn't let him rest if she wasn't close.

"Well, it's real, and I'm not sure what to do with you yet, either. So let's start with breakfast." Jace said, shrugging as he walked to her bedroom door.

"Breakfast." Nora nodded and then looked down.

"I'll meet you downstairs; go wait." Nora said, walking to her closet.

Jace nodded and continued out of her room. Her home was empty. You could feel there was once warmth and love here, but now it was enveloped with cold sadness. He looked at the pictures on the stairwell as he walked down them. Camping trips, and family photos, he spotted a young Nora holding on to her father's fingers, trying to walk. He walked the rest of the way down the stairs. The memories made him sad for her. He spotted a room to the left with a large curtain in the doorway. He paused. He looked at it strangely and then walked to the curtain, pulling it open. This was where the old blood smell was coming from. Walking into the room, he saw a large stain on the carpet floor and a blood-stained couch. He knew right away it was Kip's work.

Kip! Must hurt Kip. Cole growled.

Before Jace could calm Cole down, he heard the curtain snap open. He looked to the entrance of the room seeing a furious Nora standing in the doorway. Her chest heaved up and down as she looked at him.

"What do you think you're doing in here, Wolf?" Nora spat, seeing him standing near the spot her parents were murdered.

Jace studied her face, hurt and anger all twisted together. His stomach turned, seeing her pain.

"I smelt blood." The words fell out of his mouth before he could stop himself.

"Yeah, because of your kind." Nora said, her body shaking.

She had not stepped foot in that room since it happened. She was so angry at him that she didn't realize it till it was too late. She felt her legs starting to give out, her stomach twisting wanting her to vomit. She looked behind him and saw their faces. Their neck's wide open, the blood, and their emotionless eyes. She stepped back, tripping on the curtain. It wrapped around her foot, making her fall backward. She heard the curtain ripping down from the walls. She braced for the brutal impact of the title floor, shutting her eyes. She had smashed into something, but it wasn't the cold tile floor. It was warm. She opened her eyes and found herself once again in his arms.

"Are you alright?" He whispered, moving the hair out of her face.

"I uh...I no yes, but no!" Nora said, still struggling to be mad at him.

"I'm so sorry." Jace said softly, cupping her face with his hand.

The pain she was feeling was making him hurt. He stepped back from her, allowing her space. She looked at him, confused. The apology was genuine, and he looked like he felt her pain. She shut her eyes and took a deep breath in. She let it out slowly, trying to focus. Her hearing picked up the sound of scraping. She opened her eyes, seeing him replacing the curtain. He fixed it and closed it so the room couldn't be seen. She sighed; she should be mad at him. Her mind was screaming. He's a wolf. He's a killer, and everything is horrible. As she watched him try to right his wrong, she found herself with a small smile. She shook her head at herself and walked to the front door.

"Coming wolf?" She asked him as he was still straightening out the curtain.

He nodded and walked over to her. He looked her up and down. He shook his head slightly as if fighting with himself as well. Nora smiled more, seeing the same conversation play out in his head that she had just had. Things were going to be interesting.

"You need to lock that when you are here," Jace said, walking past her and nodding to the door.

"Why couldn't the big bad wolf kick it in if he wanted to?" She smirked behind his back.

"There's more than one bad wolf, and it would give you more time to escape if it was locked," Jace said, not paying attention to the playfulness in her voice.

She sighed as he stopped at the driveway. He glanced at her, and she looked back, confused.

"Car?" He said shortly.

"Oh, you don't have one? I guess make sense. Why would you when you can just wolf out." Nora said, rolling her eyes as she walked over to her car.

She unlocked the door and went to sit in the driver's seat, but Jace came over holding his hand out for the keys. She looked at him, baffled.

"Um, excuse me? My car I drive. You're welcome to run behind the car chasing it." She smirked at her joke.

"I don't chase cars, and you don't know where I'm taking you." He groaned.

"Does Cole chase cars?" Nora chuckled.

No chase cars! We'll go in Car with her! Cole growled at Jace.

"Keys?" Jace smirked at how upset Cole was getting.

She groaned, dropping the keys into his open hand before walking to the passenger side and getting in. She clicked her seat belt into place as she watched Jace get settled.

"What's your name? Or should I keep calling you wolf?" Nora asked, looking at him.

"Jace." He answered shortly before throwing the car into reserve and backing out.

"Jace….why are you here?" She asked, her eyes studying him intensely.

"Cole likes you." Jace answers truthfully with a shrug.

"Uh…. Well, I like him too." Nora said with a slight chuckle.

"Good." Jace answered shortly as he turned onto the busy road.

Cole flipped around happily inside of him at the comment. Nora chuckled again at the response before turning on her cell phone. She had thirty text messages from Joel. She shook her head and began to reply. She glanced over at Jace. There was more to him than what she knew. She leaned her head back, enjoying the silence.

Chapter Fourteen
Plotting

Kip sat back in his office, his feet on his desk, a drink in his hand. It had been hours since the attack, yet there was no retaliation. He sat up frustrated, pulling his dark red-brown hair back into a ponytail. No phone call. He drummed his fingers on his desk. What was Jace doing?

Taylor, has Dante reached out to you at all? Kip mind- linked his beta.

No, Alpha, everything is quiet. Taylor responded.

How are things going in the lab? Kip asked You should probably come down.

I didn't want to disturb you earlier, but things have shifted slightly. You will see what I mean when you come down. Taylor said hesitantly.

On my way. Kip responded, down the last of his scotch.

Kip made his way down a winding stairwell. Reaching a vault door, he punched the password on a key panel, and the door released open. He walked down another short tunnel and entered a different code on another door before it swung open. He stepped inside his lab. There were cells upon cells, with humans locked inside. He had his own wing for his test subjects. He made his way there, ignoring the cries of the humans he walked past. He reached the center of the room, where he had cameras set up. He came up behind Taylor, tapping him on the shoulder. Taylor scooted aside so Kip could see. Kip looked at the monitors. He narrowed his brown eyes looking at every human he attempted to change. They were all the same. Dead. They laid on the floor blood pooling out of their mouth and noses. Their bodies contoured in exorcist-looking ways. The rooms were torn apart. The nurses and doctors that were in the room were mutilated. Pieces of them everywhere. Kip sighed.

"How long?" Kip asked, frustrated.

"Fifteen minutes," Taylor shrugged.

"How much of my blood?" Kip asked.

"Were up to 10 mls." Taylor answered.

"Is the next round almost ready?" Kip asked, annoyed.

"If that's what you want, Alpha," Taylor answered.

"Yes, it's what I want!" Kip growled, slamming his fist down on the desk.

"Do you have enough blood left?" Kip asked.

"We are getting low, but I'm afraid about taking much more from you, Alpha. We do not need you jeopardizing your health." Taylor said respectfully.

"Up the milliliters to 30, and I will worry about the blood. You're right, though; I do not need to be weak. Maybe there's another alternative." Kip said, thinking out loud.

"The blood has to be from an Alpha…Alpha." Taylor said, slightly confused.

"Exactly, Taylor. Exactly." Kip smirked.

"Alpha?" Taylor said, starting to become worried.

Kip pressed the intercom button for the lab.

"Next round of test subjects. Up the blood to 30 milliliters." Kip announced before turning to leave.

Taylor hurried after him. The last statement he said made him nervous. He would follow his Alpha to the ends of the earth, but he didn't want him to get hurt. Kip was unstable, and Taylor, for the most part, enjoyed it. He followed Kip back to the office. Kip walked over to the wall and ripped a hanging map off it. He threw it on top of his desk.

"Now, let's see." Kip said, amusement sparkling on his face.

Taylor came over to the desk, curious. Kip had pulled a map of territories off the wall. Kip traced his pack's territory. His pack was the second largest. He found Jace's pack and begrudgingly looked it over. He couldn't take Jace on yet. His eyes scanned the map. He needs a small territory. A vulnerable pack. An outcast pack that has no alliances. The Black Sand pack. His finger tapped it, and he looked up at Taylor. A wide grin spread across his face. Taylor looked at him, confused, but the grin gave him chills.

"I found a solution to the blood issue." Kip chuckled, tapping the Black Sand Pack's territory.

Everything clicked into Taylor's mind as he looked from Kip to the map.

Nora chased her egg yolk around her plate, glancing up at Jace. His face was buried in the paper as he scanned through it. He had ordered black coffee and an English muffin. For someone who wanted to eat breakfast, he sure didn't eat much. She studied him and watched as his eyes seemed to glaze over. She watched as he seemed to disappear.

"Alpha, where are you?" Dante's mind linked him.

"In town, is everything ok?" Jace answered.

"Just worried; I knew you left last night but haven't returned," Dante replied.

"Border patrol going?" Jace asked.

He was worried about Kip and his pack. He had not contacted Kip about not meeting with him and leaving havoc instead.

"Adam is leading it now, later Matt, and then Myself. Wyatt will take the later shift. We've doubled up precautions in the events of the other night." Dante responded.

"I need to set up a meeting with the council. When Adam gets back, have him reach out to them. He's more political." Jace ordered and added the political part so Dante wouldn't get his feelings hurt.

"Yes, Alpha."

"To keep things normal, call Taylor, so they think we're not up to something. Threaten him or something. Do not make another time to meet. I do not need them setting up another attack." Jace said, gritting his teeth as he thought of Kip.

"Yes Alpha. How long till you're back?" Dante asked curiously.

"Taking care of something in town, and then I will return." Jace responded, cutting the mind link off before Dante could ask any more questions.

His vision returned to focus, and he found Nora staring at him. Her eyebrows were brought together, and her eyes studied him intensely. He made a face at her.

"What was that?' Nora asked.

"What?" Jace asked with a coy smile on his lips.

"Whatever you just did." Nora said, pointing her fork at his face.

"You don't need to make up excuses to stare at me. You can look; it's no bother to me." Jace smirked, throwing her a wink.

"No, you were doing something. Is it a wolf thing?' Nora asked, getting annoyed with him.

"Are you going to eat or just play with your food?" Jace asked her in return.

"Do you eat?" She nodded at him, pointing to the black coffee and the untouched muffin.

"Do you want to know what a wolf eats?" He asked as he moved his coffee aside.

He smirked, looking at her. The smirk and the way his eyes turned dark made her shift in her seat. She could feel her ears getting warm as a blush crept across her cheeks. It wasn't so much what he said but how he said it. He said it as if he had whispered the most intimate thing, not asking but saying it with promise.

"I've read red riding hood....maybe you should. It doesn't turn out so well for the wolf." She winked at him trying to regain herself.

A smile broke across his face, a small laugh escaping his lips. The more time he spent with her, the more he liked her. She was embarrassed quickly but was quick enough with her wit. She chuckled softly, seeing him laugh. She shook her head, taking a long sip of orange juice.

"Mr. Knight, it's on the house. So you go on whenever you're ready. It was great seeing you." The owner of the breakfast nook came over.

Jace nodded his thanks, and the owner ducked away as quickly as he came over. Jace pulled out his wallet and still left money on the table. Nora eyeballed the amount, too much for what they had ordered. She looked at him for a second. He folded up the paper. Took a sip of his coffee.

"Ready?" Jace asked her as he stood up.

"Um, sure," Nora said, uncertain.

She stood up, and they walked out to her car. He took the driver's seat again. She rolled her eyes, sighed, and went into the passenger seat. Getting in the car, she looked at him as he started the car.

"Questions." Nora announced.

Jace started laughing at her strange way of announcing she had questions. Jace nodded to her, waiting for them.

"Ok, one, what the heck was that? Are you like a drug dealer or something, as well as a wolf? Two, where the hell are we going? And why are you being friendly to me?" Nora asked, turning sideways in her seat to see him.

"No, I'm not a drug dealer, Mafia, or anything you could think of. My family has always been well-connected; money makes being a wolf easier. I'm not sure yet, I have a few places in mind, and I already told you Cole likes you." Jace said, putting the car in reserve and pulling out of the parking lot.

Nora clenched her jaw; she liked that every time he spoke, it was honest. She could tell for some reason he wasn't lying. Her phone began to buzz. She glanced down at it and bit her lip. Joel, she had ghosted him and felt terrible.

"Hey." She said, answering it.

"Where the hell are you? You didn't come back last night. You're not at your house; your car is gone. What the hell, Nor." Joel blurted out the instant she answered the phone.

"Woah, woah, calmed down. I'm sorry. I should have called you. I'm out with a …friend." Nora said awkwardly and glanced at Jace as she told her friend.

"Friend. I'm your friend and have had a panic attack since you took off last night. This friend is the guy you were chasing," Joel yelled.

Jace was hearing the whole conversation and gripped the steering wheel a little hard when he heard she had disappeared on her friend last night chasing someone. He looked over at her and studied her as she responded.

"No. No. This is someone else. We went to breakfast." Nora said awkwardly.

"Breakfast, so you spent the night with him," Joel said, switching gears.

"Kind of." Nora responded.

"Girl, what does he look like? Is he cute? When can I meet him? Did you get some?" Joel rambled on.

"Joel, I love you, but not now, ok. I'll talk to you later, ok. I promise I'm ok." Nora said, glancing at Jace, the same smirk returning from earlier on his face.

She knew he could hear the conversation. She quickly clicked the phone off before pretending she didn't see Jace's responses.

"Who were you chasing last night?" Jace asked, pulling the car down the road.

"His name is Logan." Nora said, unsure why she was answering him.

"Logan." Jace said, a growl coming from his chest.

"Yeah, that's what he said his name was. He was staring at me, and I wanted to know why." Nora said, shrugging.

"Matt." Jace's mind linked him.

"Yes, Alpha." Matt said back.

"I need you to find something to mask a hunter's scent. Don't tell anyone. I need something by the end of the day. I want you to do only this today." Jace ordered him.

"Ok," Matt responded.

"Got it, tell no one," Jace growled through mind link.

"Yes, Alpha."

"You did it again!" Nora said, shoving him in the arm.

"What the hell is that?" She asked, pushing his arm for the second time.

Jace looked at her funny as she shoved him. He shook his head at her, and when she went to push him once more for not answering, he caught her hand in his and held onto it. The tingles made their way up her hand from his touch.

"Keep shoving me and you'll be sorry." Jace said with a wink, still holding onto her hand.

"Fine, but it's a wolf thing, isn't it." Nora said, trying to take her hand away.

Jace shrugged. Nora struggled, trying to pry her hand from his. Jace wasn't letting go; he liked the way it felt touching her. Cole stirred in him happily. She threw her hand down, giving into holding his hand. Jace pulled into a small old shop parking lot. Nora read the sign—Tim's antiques. Nora threw him a glance. Jace didn't say anything as he put the car into park.

Chapter Fifteen
Research

"What are we doing here?" Nora asked as they stepped into the dusty old shop.

"Research." Jace answered as he approached the counter.

Nora looked around; the store was filled with items she could have sworn came from her grandmother's home: old tea sets, dollies, vintage vase, and glasses. A large mirror hung next to an old grandfather clock. The clock began to ring out as the hour struck. Nora stepped away from Jace, who was busy talking to the store owner. The dongs from the clock memorized her. She stood in front of watching the pendulum bob swing back and forth. She glanced up at the time and tried to focus on it. It was fuzzy, and she couldn't make it out. Dong. The clock rang again as her head began to sway. Dong. The world around her went black.

She was standing in the middle of a forest. In the center of a clearing. She hushed whispers but couldn't navigate where they were coming from. The moon light hit a woman whispering to three children. She removed something around her neck and placed it on the youngest daughter. She whispered something into her ear and pushed them towards the forest. Go! She heard her say. She saw the young girl didn't want to leave, but the two older boys dragged her off. She saw the little one-mouth mama. Nora's heart broke for her. What was happening?

Then Nora heard it. She could hear the pounding of feet, the earth vibrating as the train-like noise came from the opposite direction. The woman stood tall. Sword drew at her side with her other hand on a crossbow. She was ready for war. A rush of air and teeth and red glowing eyes surrounded them. Wolfs. Nora backed herself into the middle of the clearing with the woman. They were surrounded. Why didn't she run? An image of the children crossing a river flashed before her eyes. She stayed to protect her children. The woman began firing into the circle of wolves around her. The first shot she fired landed neatly in one of the wolf's necks. It fell over to its side. Arrows were being let go as quickly as she could. The wolves began to charge. Dropping the crossbow, she went to her sword. She slayed down as many as she could. Wolves and blood covered the forest floor. Just when Nora had gained hope for her, a large black wolf stepped out from the shadows, running at her. She was tossed forward, and just like that, it was over. The massive wolf sunk its teeth into her throat. Her blood mixed into the forest with the rest of the dead. Nora hit the floor, her body shaking. She was having trouble finding air. Her head began to throb instantly as her stomach felt sick. She curled into herself, trying to let the pain pass.

"Nora? Nora?" Jace's voice came through the haze of pain.

She opened her eyes, confused, looking up at him. Tears were staining the sides of her face. Jace scooped her into his arms, holding her against his chest. His warmth seemed to help, and she focused on his heart beating. Within seconds her own heart found its rhythm again, and breathing became easier. She relaxed slightly and went to move away from Jace, but he held on to her tightly.

"What happened?" He asked.

She shook her head. She didn't want to talk about it or think about the poor woman and her family. She didn't want to see their eyes or fangs anymore. She curled further into Jace, gaining comfort from him.

"Miss, here's some water." A soft, kind voice said.

Nora moved her face away from Jace's chest to see the shop owner holding out a bottle of water. She smiled gratefully and took it. She took slow, steady sips and began to feel normal again. She went to move away from Jace, but he wouldn't let her go. She suddenly felt angry with him. She shoved him hard, making him stumble back. She got up to her feet quickly and stepped away. Jace looked at her, confused, and saw anger on her face. Cole growled inside, angry that she was upset and mad that she was putting distance between them and her.

"Give me a second." She snapped, realizing she was being too angry with him, but she couldn't help it.

She had just watched a wolf rip apart another woman who looked like all she was trying to do was save her family. Family. She shut her eyes, trying hard not to think of hers. Nora heard Jace step towards her, and she shifted back, opening her eyes.

"I said give me a second wolf." Nora said. The anger spurring from her words made Jace tense up.

"Fine hunter." Jace said, just as insulting back to her.

He walked away, going back to his conversation with the store owner. Nora took several deep breaths, trying to calm herself. She glanced at Jace, who was busy conversing with the shop owner. The owner fidgeted a little bit but then nodded. He pulled out a key and nodded to Jace before walking out from behind the desk.

"Follow me." The man said softly.

"Coming." Jace said sharp and short.

He didn't even turn to look at Nora, knowing he was being observed. He didn't wait for her to answer as he followed after the shop owner. Nora groaned; she wanted to tell him to fuck off, but her curiosity got the best of her. She sighed, staring down the hall after them. Jace was waiting for her holding an old-looking door open. Nora stopped just outside the door. Jace rolled his eyes at her stepping into the room. Following them Nora found that the antique shop turned into an old library. Jace made his way to the middle before shifting through old books. He muttered something to the owner, who then disappeared and shortly returned with more books. Nora wanders over to the table.

"What are you looking for?" She asked, sitting down at the opposite side of the table.

"Answers." He muttered.

"Same." Nora sighed, looking over the books.

Jace kinda smirked at the answer she gave. He picked up a book and passed it to her. She looked at it carefully before taking it.

"Here, it's all about werewolves and hunters. You might get some answers while I try to figure out my own problems." Jace said softly.

Nora took the book eagerly and started reading. The room faded out as she dived in, becoming lost. She quickly learned all of their weaknesses. She was shocked. Jace told her that the plants, wolfbane, mountain ash, and mistletoe were poisonous and could be deadly to wolves. There was the rumor of silver. The book added it in but wasn't sure about it. She also learned that the wolf and human forms were two different entities. They had their own personalities, but we're connected. Two souls, one body. The moon and their emotions control them. The book described them as raw and sometimes uncontrollable beings. She glanced up at Jace. He seemed like he was in control of himself at all times. She wondered how accurate all this was. She turned the page and got lost in its words again. Jace cleared his throat and caught Nora's attention. She looked up at him, wondering what he needed.

"Time to go, little hunter." Jace said, trying to stand up.

She frowned slightly because she wasn't done reading. She looked down at the book in her hands, trying to remember it. Maybe she could find it online.

"Take it." Jace said, waiting on her.

"Can I?" Nora asked delightfully.

"Yes." He smiled at her excitement.

She smiled brightly and brought the book to her chest. Jace shook his head slightly, gathering up two scrolls. The owner of the shop came back to check on them.

"These scrolls and the book." Jace said, seeing him.

"Mr. Knight, we can't sell these." The owner began.

"Tim, I will return them, but I'm taking them with me now," Jace said sternly.

Tim bit his tongue, wanting to argue, but he knew better. Jace walked past him, holding the scrolls. Nora awkwardly walked by, nodding slightly to Tim as she did.

"Alpha." Matt's voice came through mind-link.

Jace was heading to the car, Nora walking quickly behind him. He froze upon hearing the mind-link. Nora stopped short, bumping into his back. She went to fall backwards. Jace turned quickly and grabbed her waist in time.

"Yes?" Jace responded, holding Nora close to him.

Nora shifted in his arms, watching his eyes gloss over.

"You ok?" She asked him, looking at his face.

"I don't know how true it is, but a black onyx is supposed to disguise hunters from wolves. Is

everything ok? You've been gone almost all day." Matt
asked him worriedly.

"Perfect, be home shortly. Everything is fine."
Jace responded.

"Hey. You're doing it again." Nora said, her
hand touching his cheek.

Her hand touching his face sent a shiver,
pulling him from the mind-link. He instinctively pulled
her closer.

"I'm fine." He said, looking down at her, his
face inches from hers.

"Oh, ok." Nora managed to get out, her heart
racing as his mouth seemed to move closer to hers.

"Come on, little hunter." He said, letting go of
her waist and stepping away.

He needed distance from her. The way she
made him feel. He needed to get used to it so he
could control himself better. Everything about her
made him want her more and to touch her.

"Now where are we going?" Nora said, almost
disappointed, that he wasn't next to her.

"Somewhere." Jace smirked, opening the
passenger side door.

Chapter Sixteen
Plans

Nora groaned as she got into the car. Jace got in quietly and turned the car on. Before she could think of anything to say, they were driving off. She glanced over at him.

"You know this might work for other girls, but this, getting in the car, we're going where I want, it doesn't really work for me," Nora said firmly.

"It doesn't?" Jace said with a playful smile on his lips.

"No," Nora said, annoyed.

"Right." Jace said, his smile turning into a smirk.

"Right?" Nora asked, her annoyance growing.

"Well, where are you now, and what are we doing?" Jace asked, not looking over at her.

"I-

"Exactly." Jace grinned.

"You are annoying," Nora said, tuning to looking out the window. For the first time, she realized that it was growing dark. She glanced at the dashboard. It was 6 pm. She jumped slightly, digging in her pocket to find the card. It said 7 pm. She was going to be late. She glanced at Jace. She shouldn't bring him with her; if this was really a group of hunters, then she couldn't bring him. He could get hurt. She thought about looking at the card.

"Is there somewhere I could drop you off? I have plans soon." Nora said, sitting up straight.

Jace glanced at her sideways and ignored the statement. He kept driving, coming to the older part of town. He ignored her question, and he pulled into a parking spot.

"So, is this where you're going? Do you work here?" Nora asked, looking out the window.

It was an old jewelry store. The building was old brick, and a dim light was peeking out from the doorway. She looked at him, confused. He sighed, shaking his head. He turned off the engine and got out of the car.

"Wait here." He said to her without even giving her a minute to speak and shut the door behind.

What the hell am I doing? Nora thought. She had spent the day with a very strange man who she didn't even know at all. He was also a werewolf, and she was letting him drag her all around town. She sank back into the chair, trying to decide what to do. She, for some strange reason, liked being with Jace. There was this strange pull to him, and she couldn't resist the intense feelings she got whenever he touched her. She groaned, shutting her eyes. She needed to meet this Logan person and know more about her hunter side. The car door opening made her jump as Jace got back inside. Nora looked at him, confused, as he handed her a golden bag. She stared at the bag in her lap and looked at him with questions.

"Just open it and put it on." Jace said, starting the car.

"You know, this whole do what I say act is getting old." Nora mumbled, opening the bag.

Inside was a soft velvet black box. She instantly knew it was jewelry, and she closed the bag. Nope, no way. She wasn't doing this. She thought, shaking her head and handing the bag back to him. A growl rolled out of Jace's chest as he pushed the bag back.

"Open it." Jace said, his voice short and snappy.

Nora sighed, opening the bag and then grabbing the box. She paused a minute, trying to find a way out of opening it. Jace made another noise as she was just staring at the black box. She sighed and opened the box. Inside the box layed a small black onyx necklace. It was a simple square onyx stone that hung on a silver chain and was very beautiful.

"What? I can't take this. Why would you-

"Black onyx can disguise hunters from wolves. Put it on." Jace ordered as he cut her off.

Nora looked at him, confused. Why would he help hide her? She carefully undid the necklace from the box. She let it dangle in front of her as it spun. It was beautiful. She slipped it over her head, and the necklace settled between her collarbone and throat. She glanced over to Jace.

"Does it work?" She asked curiously.

Jace shrugged. He couldn't tell; he was so in touch with her now that he wasn't sure if anything could block him from her. Cole was connected with her, his bond growing with each moment they spent together. Nora shrugged back, playing with it. She was trying to come up with something to say or ask.

"So where are you going? Can I drop you off at your home?" Nora said, glancing at the clock.

"Why are you trying to get rid of me?" Jace looked at her side-eye, and Cole began to get upset inside him.

"I have plans," Nora said quietly.

"Plans?" Jace asked, his jaw shut tight.

"Yes, plans. Unlike what I've been doing all day with you. Things planned ahead of time." Nora rolled her eyes at him.

"What are you doing? He asked, looking at her as he drove.

"Robbing a bank, why?" Nora said sarcastically to him.

Jace was getting annoyed, and he knew it was just because Cole was becoming pathetic and wanted to know everything about her and stay with her.

"Really." Jace said, his tone showing his annoyance.

"No, not really, but first, you're not my father, second I don't know you, and I don't need to be explaining anything to you or keeping you in the loop and third, I think we're supposed to be enemies so thanks for today, but I think we should go our separate ways," Nora said, glancing out the window Jace gripped the steering wheel tighter.

He was about to go off on her.

"Alpha." Adam mind linked him.

"For fuck sake!" Jace said out loud, hearing the mind- link.

"Well, sorry to upset you, but it's all true. So where can I drop you off?" Nora said, shifting in her seat to look at him.

"What," Jace replied, ignoring Nora.

"There are reports of bodies on the outer part of our territory." Adam said shortly.

"Bodies?" Jace asked.

"Yes, some are half-transformed," Adam said almost carefully.

"Kip." Jace responded.

Kip had the bodies he experimented on dumped on his land. He was going to lose it. The attack at the theater was enough, but now this. He didn't need anyone finding the bodies. He yanked the car over to the side.

"What the hell." Nora yelled at him as she was tossed about by how quickly he jerked the car over.

She glanced at him and saw the look on his face. He wasn't there right now. She observed him trying to figure out what this thing was that kept happening.

"Dante." He connected Dante to the link he was sharing with Adam.

"Yes, Alpha." Dante came through.

"The bodies," Jace said point blank.

"In the woods outside a baseball field, just waiting to be found. Matt and Wyatt are on it." Dante replied quickly.

"Don't dispose of them. Save them. I want proof of what Kip is doing. Call the council. I want a meeting now. If they refuse or start bullshitting, let

them know I will take matters into my own hands."
Jace growled.

"Yes, Alpha." Adam and Dante said at the
same time.

Jace was growling out loud. Nora could see how tightly he was squeezing the steering wheel. It looked like it was going to give any second. She could see his chest vibrating, and his eyes were dilated. Nora didn't know why, but she reached over and placed her hand gently on his arm. Jace was frozen at her touch, and the growling stopped as his eyes returned to normal. He looked at her, confused.

"Are you ok?" She asked quietly, unknowingly rubbing his arm.

Her touch softened him for a brief moment, but then he remembered what they were talking about. He frowned deeply.

"Dante, pick me up at the corner of Main and
Jefferson." Jace's mind linked him.

"You ok? Can you shift? Do you not have your
car?" Dante asked worriedly.

"I am fine. If I shift now, Cole will be ripping out
Kip's throat as soon as he can, and no. Come get
me!" Jace ordered, ending the mind link.

"Hey," Nora said softly again.

"No, I need to leave. Have fun with your plans." Jace said, opening the drive-side door and stepping out of the car.

Nora stared at Jace's back as she watched him walk away from the car. She could see the anger vibrating off of him. Something was very wrong. She was confused. Confused about what just happened to him but even more about how part of her wanted to chase after him. She shook her head, the clock catching her eye. 6:45 glowed out from the dashboard. She had fifteen minutes. She sighed deeply, trying to figure out what she wanted more. The urge to find out more about herself or chasing after Jace. She climbed over to the driver seat and put the car into drive. She needed to know more about being a hunter. She needed to understand why she was seeing things from the past. She needed to find out who killed her family. She needed revenge. She turned the car away from Jace and drove off.

Chapter Seventeen
Societatea Vânătorului

Jace was facing the opposite way when he heard the car pull away. He turned, watching the car pull aw*ay from the sidewalk and down the road.*

Cole's voice came through. "We don't chase cars, remember?"

The comment was smug, and Jace's lip twitched as he heard even his own wolf sassing him. His body pulled him towards chasing after her.

Shut up your about to start whimpering like some sad puppy dog. So there. Cole whimpered in response; the car no longer had any insight.

Nora pulled up to the old warehouse-looking building. She grabbed hold of the card as she double-checked the address. She shrugged slightly, and she guessed it fit the whole mysterious vibe. She turned the car off and got out walking slowly to the big brass doors. She clutched the card in her fist as she reached the door, squeezing it in her hands. The nerves she was feeling right now made her stomach knot. Her brain screamed at her that this was crazy.

"Get a hold of yourself." She whispered as she stuck her hand out and knocked on the door.

Her knock echoed back to her like the building was empty. She shifted uncomfortably as if this was not what it was supposed to be. She thought about stepping back away from the door. Just as she was about to leave and go home, she heard shuffling. The sound of several locks moving, the clinks and clanks. The door slowly creaked open. She looked at it, and no one was standing in the doorway. This was starting to look like the beginning of a horror movie.

"Hello?" Nora called out and then shook her head.

That's exactly what girls do right before they die in horror movies, shout hello into the darkness. She thought.

"Name." Was shouted back to her from the darkness.

Nora tried to peer into the building without moving from her spot. She had enough space between her and the door that she could if she needed to bolt.

"I'm looking for Logan." She called back, her hands in a fist as she waited for anything to happen.

"Name." Was the response she got again.

"Logan." Nora smirked to herself.

"Your name." echoed to her from the darkness.

"This is absolutely ridiculous. If I was any type of threat, it would have been over and done with while you were trying to get my name. Nora. It's Nora, a 7 pm appointment." Nora yelled back, rolling her eyes.

"Enter."

Nora rolled her eyes again, stepping into the building. The door was shut rapidly behind her. Someone came behind her grabbing her wrist. She felt movement around her feet. Nope, this wasn't about to happen, she thought. She could tell someone was standing right directly behind her. She shut her eyes while listening. She could hear them breathe in and exhale softly. She pulled them into her by jerking her wrist towards her back. She threw her head into their face as they approached her back. She heard a pop and a loud groan. They let go of her, and she could tell they went to lean forward as they did; Nora elbowed who or whatever was behind her. Her elbow made contact as she heard the air rush out of the person. She heard the person slump to the floor. She couldn't tell what was around her feet. She could listen to more people around her, almost forming a circle. Great, she thought. She kept her eyes close so she could focus on what she heard. There were not many of them but enough to form a small circle around her. She waited, listening to their heartbeat. Nothing happened.

The lights quickly went on. Nora opened her eyes to see what was going on. There were three women and three men on each side of her. She looked at them, looking for Logan. She felt someone grab her ankle, whatever was around it was tugged. Her feet gave out from under her. She crashed onto the floor. She was then pinned to the floor. Blond hair and dark eyes were staring back at her. Blood dripped from his nose as he held her to the floor.

"Logan?" She asked, confused.

"You broke my nose." He smirked down at her, blood was stained under his nose.

"You attacked me in the dark and now are pinning me to the floor. Also, you have five seconds to let me up, or it's all done." Nora said, narrowing her eyes at him.

"Really?" Logan smirked. Nora didn't say anything but locked her eyes with him.

She slowly counted in her head, bringing her leg slowly up. She would launch him forward and smash his nose again if he didn't get off her. Just as she was ready, someone cleared their throat.

"Logan let her up. She's clearly not a wolf. She has mountain ash all over her." A woman with dark maroon hair said with a sigh.

"Yeah, let her up before she hurts you." Another girl chuckled, realizing Nora's plan.

Logan winked at her before getting off of her. He offered her his hand, but Nora pushed it away and stood up.

"So this was all to see if I was a wolf. You realize they can probably see much better in the dark than us. A wolf would have killed you all if I could break his nose and knock him to the ground." Nora said, beyond annoyed.

These were the people she was supposed to get answers from, and they couldn't even make an attack right. She could feel her blood boil as she thought she wasted her time. She stared them all down angrily.

"I like her, and she's right." A girl with dark pink highlights said.

"Yeah, she does have a point; we need to think this over better." A bald man with an earring second the girl's statement.

"So what is this?" Nora asked, looking at Logan.

"This is Societatea Vânătorului, also known as The Hunter's Society or I like to call it the society. The girl with the maroon hair is Mina, the pink highlight is Lilly, and the blond girl is Kat. Then baldy is Drake, and lastly, tall, dark, and broody over there is Phil." Logan said, introducing Nora to everyone.

"Have any of you killed a wolf?" Nora asked, cutting to the chase.

They all nodded; Lilly smiled at her. Kat stepped forward, looking at her. She looked Nora up and down with a frown.

"Why does it feel like you're interviewing us when it should be the other way around." Kat sneered at her.

"Why does it feel like this is some weird dungeon and dragons club and not a group of hunters that are badass wolf killers?" Nora asked back.

Logan smirked, enjoying someone standing up to Kat. He watched Kat's expression go from confident and changed to fluster. Kat's eyes snapped to Logan.

"I vote no." Kat announced, walking off to the side.

"I vote yes." Logan called after her, his smirk turning into a grin.

"I vote yes too. I like her. She's on fire." Drake said to the side of Logan.

"Me too, I'm a yes." Lilly called, her voice excited.

"Fine, I'll go yes too." Mina said.

"No." Phil said short.

"Well, the majority wins. It's a yes." Logan announced, placing his arm across Nora's shoulder.

"What's a yes?" Nora asked, picking up his arm off her shoulder.

"Yes, let you try being part of our society." Logan said brightly.

Kat stormed off quickly, Lilly squeaked excitedly, and the rest just left. Logan tapped her arm as Lilly came over to greet her.

"I can show you around," Logan said, wiping blood from his nose.

"Hi, I'm Lilly! If you need anything, let me know. I love new people!" Lilly said excitedly.

"Ok thanks, I will," Nora said, looking at Lilly.

She was so happy and bubbly. Thinking of Lilly fighting or killing anything didn't seem like it could happen.

"Hey, Lilly," Logan called after her before she left.

"Yeah, bud?" Lilly asked.

"Could you straighten my nose?" Logan asked her with a sad look.

Lilly laughed. She walked over to Logan, quickly grabbed his nose, and snapped it into place. She did it so effortlessly and without any hesitation. Logan grunted as his nose went back into place, his hand going to it as Lilly stepped away.

"Thanks, Lilly." He said, touching the bridge of his nose slightly.

"Anytime. See you around, Nora." Lilly said and skipped off.

Nora blinked as the girl quickly went from happy and bubbly to precise and almost deadly in how she moved to fix his nose. Nora glanced at Logan; that hurt, but he acted like it was just a discomfort. Maybe there was more to this group than she thought.

"Ready for the tour?" Logan asked with a goofy grin on his face.

"I guess lead the way," Nora said with a shrug.

Logan offered his arm to her, and Nora shook her head at him. He did make her smile, though. He sighed deeply and flapped his arms at her.

"Alright, let's go." He said, leading her towards a stairwell.

"You did break my nose. The least you could do is hold my hand." Logan smirked.

Nora chuckled but shook her head again. He sighed before walking in front of her. He was a little forward, she thought, but He made her smile. She could tell he was just a fun, goofy person.

"Alright, let's go." He said, leading her towards a stairwell.

Chapter Eighteen
Tour

Jace leaned against the wall of a store that was on the corner of Jefferson and Main. His eyes shut as he focused on his breathing. He was trying to calm down Cole, who was crawling beneath his skin; the car screeched in front of him. Dante always drove too fast and even faster when he thought something was wrong. Jace sighed, pulling open the passenger side door. Jace sat down in the car like he was carrying the weight of the world.

"Hey, are you alright?" Dante said, pulling the car away from the sidewalk.

"I'm fine. Just take us there." Jace said, rubbing his forehead.

"What were you doing in town?" Dante asked curiously.

"Wrapping up a few things." Jace answered vaguely.

"Ok then." Dante responded, focusing back on driving.

With how Dante drove, they were there in what felt like a matter of seconds. Jace had closed his eyes and seemed asleep, but he was trying to keep Cole in check the whole time. He was doing nothing but talking about how he needed his mate. The endlessness of it was causing Jace to have a headache. Dante looked over at Jace. He didn't look good; he was pale. He could tell something was wrong with him.

"Jace, I can handle this. Why Don't you go get some rest." Dante said, reaching out and touching Jace's shoulder.

Jace shook his head and got out of the car. He walked over to the spot; he knew right away by the smell of it. The smell of blood hung in the air. Matt and Adam were there picking up the last two bodies.

"This is freaking insane." Matt said to Adam as he picked up one of the bodies.

"Yeah, tell me about it." Adam said as he got a mixture of blood and body secretions over his shirt.

Jace walked over to the dark utility van and looked inside. Six bodies were inside the van, and two more were coming as Adam and Matt carried them to the van. Three of the bodies were half transformed. One still had a wolf head, another a wolf arm, and the last one lower half was still in wolf form. The bodies were contoured and twisted into shapes that were impossible to make with a human body. Blood ran out of their noses and mouths. Most of them looked like they died screaming. Matt and Adam squeezed by Jace to place the last two bodies in.

"What do you think, Alpha?" Matt asked, standing next to them.

"I think war is coming." Jace said out loud, looking at the bodies.

"Matt, up the training. I want everyone who can train to start training now." Jace ordered him.

"Take the bodies to Wyatt to see if he can make any sense of what is happening here. Try to get the blood smell gone. It will attract unwanted attention." Jace said, shaking his head, and began walking away from the van.

He heard the murmur of Yes, Alpha as he got into the car. Dante followed quickly after them. As he got into the car, Dante looked over at him.

"Yes, I really think war is coming. Yes, I think Kip is planning something much bigger and darker than we can think. No, I'm not sure what yet." Jace smiled slightly, being able to answer Dante's questions without him asking.

Dante shook his head, Putting the car into drive and pulling away from the small wooded ditch in which the bodies had been lying.

"And this is the bathroom we all have to share, but there's more than one stall for showers, and we got curtains." Logan said to Nora as he held a curtain out to her.

The bathroom was set up like her school gym. It had several small shower stalls with flimsy curtains over them. There were three stalls for toilets, and then on the far side, a mirror covered a wall with a countertop sink

"Um, nice." Nora smirked a little as Logan flapped a fish shower curtain at her.

"Next stop on the tour, your potential room." Logan announced, walking out of the bathroom.

"Potential?" Nora called to his back as she followed him back into the hall.

"Yes, potential. You don't have to move in, but it's easier. Training is early, and most of us don't have family, so we all live here." Logan said, turning down another corridor.

Nora followed him down the hall. He stopped short in front of a metal door. Logan walked over and fumbled around in his pocket of a key. He opened the door and swung the door open.

"After you." Logan smiled, stepping aside.

Nora walked into the room; the carpet was a dark blue, the walls were plain white, and a full size bed was smack dab in the middle of the room. A lonely dresser sat on the wall by an old paneled window. It was simple but would do if she thought about staying.

"Not bad uh?" Logan asked quietly, leaning against the wall and watching Nora check it out.

"Nope, not bad." Nora said, going over to the small closet and looking inside it.

"Best news, we are hall mates." Logan said with a wink.

"Hall mates?" Nora said with a smile cracking across her face.

"Yup, yours truly lives right there." Logan said, pointing across the hall.

"Wonderful." Nora laughed.

"Yeah, if you want you can paint the room or decorate however you want," Logan said enthusiastically.

"Thanks, I'll keep that in mind." Nora said, shutting the closet door.

"What's your favorite color?" Logan asked.

"Umm…I guess blue." Nora replied with a shrug.

"Yeah, but like, what blue? There are so many kinds of blues out there, midnight blue, sky blue, turquoise, um, robin egg blue-

"Ice blue," Nora repeated aloud, not picking the color but saying it because she instantly thought of Jace's eyes.

"Hmm, ice blue, that's different," Logan said quietly.

"I might be able to find that color." He said, looking around.

"It's ok." Nora said with a chuckle, shaking the image of Jace's face and his eyes that made her shiver out of her mind.

"So, are you gonna stay?" Logan asked bluntly.

"When's training?" Nora asked.

"We start at six in the morning." A voice came from behind Logan.

"Ok, I guess I can run home, pick some things, and come back." Nora said quietly.

"I have something if you wanna borrow something to sleep in." Lilly said, stepping out from behind Logan.

"Um, it's ok. I need to grab-

"Phone charge got you covered. I have a drawer of them." Logan chimed in.

"You guys are starting to make me feel like I'm joining a cult and can't leave." Nora laughed.

"By all means, feel free to leave and not come back." Kat's voice echoed into the room.

"Ignore her; she's a bitch. You will get used to her," Logan told Nora, elbowing her slightly.

"Fine, I'll stay one night to try this out. I'm not joining your club just yet." Nora said, looking at Lily and Logan.

"Yay!" Lilly shouted, and before Nora could respond, she was gone.

"Let me see your phone," Logan said, holding out his hand.

"Um, hard pass. I'm keeping that." Nora said, stepping away from him.

"No, I don't want to take it weirdo. I wanted to see what kind of charger it took. Geez." Logan said, shaking his head.

"Oh, it takes a USB C charger. Sorry." Nora said quietly.

"Got it. Be right back." Logan said, going across the hall to his room.

Nora stood in the middle of the room looking around, it was not home, but then again, home had not felt like home in a long time. Maybe this will not be bad.

"Hey, I bought a T-shirt, tank top, shorts, and PJ pants. I don't know what you like to sleep in but feel free to pick whatever out." Lilly smiled happily, dropping the clothing on her bed.

Nora laughed at how excited Lilly was about all of this. Nora looked at the clothes grabbing the shorts and tank top. Lilly nodded, and Nora raised an eyebrow at her nod.

"I figured you were a shorts and tank top person. You can keep the other ones in here, in case you get a cold or something. Well, if you need anything, I am two doors down." Lilly smiled, leaving the room.

Nora watched her go, confused. By how excited she was that Nora was spending the night here, she thought Lilly would ask her to watch a movie or girl talk or something. The sleepover reminded her that she needed to call Joel. She felt terrible leaving him in the dark.

"Ok, here you go." Logan announced, holding the charger up in the air as he walked into the room.

He held the light blue charge out to Nora, who took it, and a small smile came across her face. She raised her eyebrow at Logan, and he shrugged.

"I had blue and pink figured you wanted the blue," Logan said with a wink as he started to open the door.

"Let me know if you need anything or if you're hungry. I can take you down to the kitchen. Oh, here." He chuckled the key to the room at her.

"That's the only one, so don't lose it.' Logan said as Nora caught it in her hands.

"Got it," Nora said with a nod.

"Night," Logan said, leaving the room and closing the door behind him.

Nora looked outside the window at the stars as she typed a text to Joel, letting him know that she was still out and would come by tomorrow to see him. She shut her phone, staring about the room. Realizing she was really doing this. The last few days didn't seem real. She grabbed the clothes Lilly let her borrow and changed quickly. She put the key on the dresser, shrugging about locking the door. She plopped down on the bed, scrolling threw her phone till her eyes got heavy. She thought that maybe she should have gotten Jace's phone number, closing her eyes.

<h2 style="text-align:center">Chapter Nineteen
Training</h2>

Soft cries across the hall crept under his doorway. Logan sat up in bed, trying to figure out what he was hearing. Was someone hurt? He got up quickly, not bothering to throw a shirt on, and opened his bedroom door. He heard the soft muffled cries again. It registered that they were coming from Nora's room. He crossed the hall and knocked on the door. He waited a few seconds, and when no answer came, he started pushing the door. Then a sound like someone was in trouble emerged from inside. He opened the door.

"Nora?" He called into the dark.

She didn't answer, he ventured into her room. She was tossing and turning in her bed. Tears were leaking out of her eyes. She was acting like she was in pain. Logan walked over and shook her lightly.

"Nora. Hey Nora." He said softly, trying to wake her.

"Jaime." She cried out; the sound was heartbreaking, her whole body shaking like it had broken her too.

Logan climbed into the bed next to her and pulled her into him. He recognized trauma. He didn't know what hers was, but there was something. She struggled slightly against him, but as he began to rub the side of her face, she relaxed in his arms. He cradled her until she stopped and the nightmare passed. Logan frowned; something horrible had happened to her. He brushed the long strand of dark hair out from her face. She was beautiful, he thought, and then a yawn escaped him. He went to move away from her, but she snuggled into him. He laid his head down, not wanting her to return to whatever she was dreaming about, his arm still cradling her as she drifted asleep.

She jumped upright. Her hand coming in a fist to attack whatever was getting her. Her hand was caught by something powerful. Another hand pulled her into a warm chest. The other hand cradled her head.

"Hey, it's ok. Calm down." Nora pulled back and looked into warm brown eyes.

Logan's blond hair was frazzled about, and he was cradling her. She looked at him, confused. Thinking, why was he in her room? She moved away from him slightly, and he let her go.

"What are you doing here?" She asked, confused, realizing that he was topless in her bed.

"You were crying. I tried waking you up, but I couldn't get you to. Then you started shaking. The only thing that worked was holding you, and then I got tired." Logan said, stretching.

Logan looked over to the window, the sky barely starting to get light. He stretched again, sitting up in her bed. As the covers fell away, exposing more of him. He swung his legs off the bed and stood. Nora's cheeks flushed red seeing he was only in boxer briefs that hugged everything. Her eyes couldn't help but look at a very large bulge. Logan caught her looking and laughed.

"What, it's the morning, it's got a mind of its own. It doesn't help that you're beautiful." Logan laughed, walking to the doorway.

"Training in like 15 minutes. See you downstairs." Logan said, winking at her before he walked out the door.

Nora sat in her bed, playing out everything that just happened. She knew she must have been dreaming about the attack. This waking up next to strangers was becoming a little odd. Lock the door next time, Nora told herself. She stood up, stretching. New clothes were sitting on her dresser. A sports bra, workout pants, and another T-shirt was sitting there. She smiled, knowing it had to be Lilly. She then wondered if Lilly saw Logan cuddling her. This might be awkward. She thought as she was throwing on the clothing. She grabbed her sneakers and laced them up. The last thing she did was throw her hair up into a ponytail. She was ready and excited about training. She wanted to learn everything she could. Jamie's eyes flashed in her head, and she shut hers tightly. She vowed to herself that the wolf that ruined her life would regret it.

"What do you mean? He's not doing anything wrong!" Jace's voice bellowed off the walls in his office.

"They are humans turned wolves. That is against the law. How can you say he's not doing anything wrong." Jace growled, Cole, flashing in his eyes.

"The fucking bodies, Walter! I have the fucking bodies! That's how I know!" Jace yelled as the corded phone in his hand started to snap as he got angry.

"Who else would it be?" Jace growled.

"Well, that's the council's job. Look into it. Search his territory. Do something. What is the point of having a council to help keep packs in line if you're not going to do something." Jace said as the phone cracked more in his hand.

"You know what, Walter, you let them know I am handling it myself the next time something happens on my territory. So they better get on this now." Jace threatened as the phone cracked into pieces.

"Good talk?' Dante smirked from the doorway.

"God, they are useless." Jace groaned.

"I heard; the whole pack might have heard." Dante smirked again.

"Did you get a hold of Taylor?" Jace said through his teeth.

"I did. We basically had the same conversation. Although I went into detail about how I would rip his spine out and strangle Kip with it, but hey, we all can't be beautiful speakers." Dante said, throwing a wink at Jace.

"We need better proof, although it sounds like the council is on his side or afraid of him now." Jace said.

"Dante gets a call into the Moonlight pack's second in command. Let them know your Alpha needs to talk to theirs. If everything goes south, we might need more than just our pack." Jace said, rubbing his forehead.

His head was hurting again; he didn't know if it was Kip or being away from Nora. Cole was furious with Kip, and his killer instincts were going into overdrive as well as his desire for Nora. He took a deep breath. Dante shook his shoulder lightly.

"You should talk to Wyatt, he's got info on the bodies, and maybe he can take a look at you. You don't look great." Dante said, concerned.

"Ok." Jace answered, not wanting to argue with Dante.

He knew why he was feeling like crap, and there was nothing Wyatt could do to make him better. Only one person right now could calm his mind, and he couldn't bring her into this. It was too dangerous. He can't risk her life; Kip would target her.

"I'm going to go to the other office since this one now needs a phone." Dante laughed, walking out the door.

"Hey, when's the last time you ate?" Dante asked, hanging in the doorway.

"Go, Dante." Jace grumbled.

"Fine, don't say I didn't care." Dante called from the hall.

Nora came down the stairs to the lower floor. She could hear a commotion coming from the far room. Nora walked towards the noise. As she pushed open the door, she saw Mina and Drake fighting. Mina ran at Drake's back and scaled it. She now had her legs wrapped around his neck and was hitting him repeatedly in the head. Drake backed into the wall slamming her. She was about to step in when her elbow was caught.

"Their sparring." Logan's voice said as he pulled her back.

He nodded across the room at Kat and Lily. They were actually using real weapons. Kat had two swords that she swung towards Lilly. Lilly was blocking with a long wooden staff. Nora watched Kat's movement and waited for Lilly to see the mistake Kat kept making. As if Nora told her, Lilly found and pushed the staff into Kat's stomach, causing her to fall back. Lilly used the staff to pin Kat to the floor as she kicked the swords away from her. Nora smiled at Lilly winning. Logan wasn't watching the crew spar. He was watching Nora. He saw the way she was taking everything in, watching everyone's moves. He wondered if she had any training before.

"You ready?" Logan said, nudging her.

"Ready for?" Nora said, looking at him confused.

"Training princess." Kat's voice said from the floor.

"You wanna be with us? You need to be able to fight. If you can't fight, you're dead." Kat finished getting up off the ground.

Nora nodded, and it made sense. She hadn't ever been in a fight before but was good on her feet and could throw a punch. Kat got up, looking her over. With a very snotty look all over her face, Nora matched her stare.

"Can you even fight?" Kat said her words sounded like they were coated in venom as she spoke.

Nora shrugged, not really responding to her. She glanced at Logan.

"All right, I'm in the game; how does this work?" Nora said to Logan.

"Well, we fight till someone gives up." He nodded towards Mina and Drake.

Mina now had Drake on the floor. He was turning blue, her legs still wrapped around him. Drake began vigorously tapping her leg. A smile plastered across Mina's face as she let go. Drake inhaled a big gulp of air as Mina rolled away from him. She chuckled lightly as she stood, offering him a hand up. He laughed, shaking his head as he took her hand, standing up. He clapped her on the back as they went for water. Nora watched and understood. She didn't know if she was ready but knew she needed to be. She walked out onto the mat, a little nervous but ready. Logan started to walk out, but Kat was too quick and stood in front of Nora. Great, Nora thought as she watched Kat eagerly take her stance. Lilly came over and stood next to Logan.

"This is gonna be good." Lilly whispered to Logan.

Logan shoved him lightly; he was a little worried. Phil reached over and rang the bell. Nora looked at him, confused, and Kat didn't waste a minute. She flung her fist towards Nora's face. The world seemed to slow down as Kat's fist approached Nora's face. Nora saw it coming but was unsure why everything was going in slow motion. She moved her head out of the way of the fist. As soon as Kat's fist passed her face, the world sped up again. Kat stumbled forward, not connecting with anything. Nora shoved her back away from her. The confusion on her face made Nora smile. Kat came back at her, throwing two more punches. As Kat first made its way towards her face again, the world slowed. She dodged the first fist and then grabbed a hold of the second fist. Nora twisted Kat's arm and swung her around forward. As she turned her, the world sped up, sending Kat flying forward on the ground. Kat hit the mat. As her chest hit the mat, she let out a long nose, the air getting knocked out. Kat slammed her fist into the mat, getting angry. She was back up on her feet in no time. This time, running at Nora. As Kat approached her, the world slowed down again. Nora smirked and stepped aside; putting her foot out, she tripped Kat. She smashed into the mat again. Kat's face planted, and her peers around her made an "O" sound. She stood up, ripping a staff off the wall and coming at Nora.

"Kat!" Logan yelled at her, but she ignored him.

"Nora!" Lilly yelled, throwing her another staff.

Nora turned to catch it but couldn't turn back around in time to block Kat. Kat swung the staff whacking Nora across her back. Nora fell to her knees in pain, and a small yell escaped her mouth as she did. Kat backed up about hitting her again.

"Kat, don't fucking do it." Logan said, walking quickly towards them.

Kat smirked and swung. Nora ducked to the floor, the staff going just above her head. She swung her staff at Kat's leg, swiping them out from under. As Kat fell backwards Nora got to her feet. She took her staff and smacked Kat's hand with it. Kat's hand released her staff, and Nora kicked it away. Kat went to get up, and Nora slammed her back down with her foot. Stepping on her shoulder, pinning her to the mat. She then brought her staff to Kat's throat and froze there. Kat went to move, and Nora pressed her staff into her throat.

"Give." Nora growled.

Kat looked at her, angry and confused, and went to move again. Nora pressed hard; this time Kat began to cough.

"I said give." Nora said, her voice chilling.

"I give." Kat coughed. Nora let her go and stepped back.

Logan reached her side as Kat got to her feet. Kat kicked the staff and stormed out of the training room.

"You ok?" Logan asked Nora.

"I'm fine." Nora told Logan, watching Kat leave.

"That was awesome! Good job Nora," Lilly said, smiling brightly beside her.

She saw Phil watching her, and then he left after Kat. She wondered if they were a thing. She also wondered who was in charge here. She thought Phil was just because of how quiet and standoffish he was.

"Come, let's go shower, and I can take a look at your back. She swung like she was playing baseball. That had to hurt." Lilly said with a smile on her face.

"Yeah, just a little bit." Nora chuckled.

"Ok well, let's go." Lilly said, walking out of the training room.

"Hey Lilly, I am actually gonna head home for a little bit." She called after.

"Ok, we will see you later." Lilly called back to her.

"Are you leaving?" Logan asked, a little concerned.

"Well yeah, if I'm going to commit to this, I need to get some of my things. I can't keep borrowing Lilly's clothing. Besides, I need to call my friend Joel and maybe see him. He might think I've become an episode on Dateline if I don't talk to him soon." Nora chuckled.

"Are you sure you're ok?" Logan asked her to reach out and touched her cheek.

"Yeah, it hurts like hell, but life hurts right." Nora laughed awkwardly as she shrugged, trying to politely step away from his hand.

"Ok. See you tonight?" Logan asked her.

"Yeah, I'll be back." Nora said; for some reason, she squeezed his shoulder.

Logan smiled at her and motioned to follow him. He held onto her hand as he walked her to the door. Nora was confused, part of her didn't mind holding his hand, but the other part of her felt like it was wrong. Like she was doing something wrong. She shook her head, and as they got to the outside door, she took her hand back.

"Ok, see you in a little bit." Logan said, opening the door for her.

"See you soon." Nora said, stepping outside and closing the door behind her.

Chapter Twenty
Pizza

Nora got into her car as she sat back, and she winced. Her back hurt like hell. All she could think of was how badly she wanted a hot shower. She turned her car on and took off towards her house. She fumbled around, looking for her cell phone. Finding it, she dialed Joel.

"Hi-

"For the love of everything, where the hell have you been?" Joel started as soon as he answered the phone.

"Um, it's a long story. Lunch?" Nora asked, hoping he didn't go on his rampage right now.

"Long story, Nora, I swear you will be the reason why I don't have children. Where and when for lunch?"Joel asked if she could hear him rolling his eyes at her.

"About an hour? I'll come to get you. You home?" Nora asked.

"Yeah, just don't go disappearing ok." Joel said softly.

Nora felt instantly bad. Joel probably had been worrying about her nonstop. She frowned deeply; she needed to tell him something so he would stop worrying, especially if she was going to start staying with the other hunters.

"I won't. I'll pick you up shortly." Nora said, hanging up.

Wyatt, what did you find? I don't have the energy right now to come down there if there's nothing worth looking at. Jace mind linked to Wyatt.

Honestly Alpha, it's pretty much what we were guessing already. I can tell you that they were given blood from an Alpha, and then their bodies couldn't handle it. Some died in the transformation others completed their transformation but still died. The blood leaking from their nose and mouth is from their brain. It is fried, as well as other internal organs. I don't know why they did not turn back to human form after they died, though. Wyatt responded.

Keep the bodies in the morgue to keep them from decomposing. We may need them for proof. I am waiting to hear back from Dante. I am requesting a meeting with the Moonlight pack. We may need extra support if war does happen. I may need to show their Alpha what we're dealing with. From there, I may contact the other Alphas to see if we can, strong arm the council into doing something about Kip. We just need to know why. Why is he trying to turn humans? I don't see anything beneficial about it. Jace replied back to Wyatt as he processed.

I'm not sure about Alpha. Take it easy. You sound drained. Wyatt responded.

Jace cut the mind-link off; he didn't need anyone else telling him how he looked or sounded. A shower was the first thing on his to-do list. He made his way to his room as quickly as possible, avoiding other pack members as best as possible. He just wanted some peace. His head was throbbing as he made his way into the shower. He let the hot water hit the back of his neck. It relieves the pain slightly. Cole whimpered.

Cole, I know I need her too, but the pack needs us right now. We will go check on her soon. Can you please tone it down before you give me an aneurysm. Jace pleaded with Cole.

There was silence for the first time from Cole since they left Nora.

Thank you. Jace thought, grateful for it.

He finished showering and came out in a towel. He saw his bed and laid back on it. He was exhausted. He was drained. He shut his eyes, thoughts of Nora creeping into his mind. He exhaled softly, calming himself and drifting to sleep. Even in his sleep, he dreamed of her. He was holding her, his arms wrapped around her perfect body. He inhaled her scent, and it instantly calmed and excited him. Her long black hair spread across his chest. She began placing soft kisses over it. The trail of kisses ended at his waist, and his hands moved into her hair. She glanced up at him innocently before pulling his towel off. She placed a teasing kiss right above his member. He let out a soft growl as he anticipates her next move.

"You like that, Alpha." The voice was wrong.

He realized that the hair he had felt was wrong. His eyes shot open. Was he dreaming? He sat slightly up and felt pressure on his thighs. His eyebrows narrowed as his hand pulled the red hair upwards. Hovering over him was Rosie.

"What are you doing?" Jace growled at her.

"Taking care of you." She said with a smile, not catching his tone.

"Get off of me now." Jace said, warning her.

She went to protest. He pulled up on her hair and tossed her off of him with his hand. She landed on the ground, looking up at him, shocked and confused. He grabbed the towel and wrapped it around his waist.

"Out." He said to her sternly.

"Alpha, I don't understand." Rosie said, pouting.

"Get out!" Jace bellowed Cole, flashing in his eyes.

Rosie hung her head and submitted as she quickly exited the room. She almost fell as she rushed out the door. She left it slightly open as she made her escape. Jace rubbed the back of his neck. He hadn't meant to nod out. He stretched slightly, looking out the window of his room. There was a knock on his door, and he grumbled. What now, he thought, looking at the door.

"What?" He asked sharply.

"Knock, Knock. Thought I come to check on you." Dante said, walking in.

"I'm fine." Jace said, rolling his eyes.

"Saw Rosie….you sure you're fine?" Dante said, leaning against the door frame.

"For fuck sake, yes, I'm fine. Just because I don't want her doesn't mean I am not fine. Ask me again if I'm fine, and I swear I'll forget we're friends." Jace retorted.

"Ayy easy killer. You should be happy. I love you." Dante said, throwing a wink at him.

Jace shook his head, walking over to his walk-in closet and going inside of it. Dante walked over to a chair, sat, and propped his feet up. Jace came out wearing jeans and holding a shirt in his hand. He made a face seeing Dante making himself comfortable.

"Didn't I give you things to do?" Jace said, finishing pulling the navy blue t-shirt over his head.

"Yup, all done. Alpha of the moonlight pack is coming Friday." Dante said, wiggling his legs.

"You check on Wyatt?" Jace said, rolling his eyes.

"Power of delegation! Adam is helping Wyatt." Dante grinned.

"Why don't you go check on Rosie," Jace smirked.

"Maybe but you seem bored today." Dante made a face at him.

"Have you eaten yet?" Dante asked him, kiddings aside.

"I will." Jace sighed softly.

"K, if you promise to, I'll leave you alone. Order you pizza?" Dante said with a goofy grin.

"I will eat; just quit pestering me." Jace groaned.

"Alright, alright. Love you big guy." Dante said, standing up

. "How's training?" Jace asked Dante's back as he was walking out the door.

"The men are ready for whatever. You know they would follow you to the end of the earth if needed." Dante said over his shoulder.

"Good, increase the border patrol now that we've contacted another pack and the council. If Kip gets wind of it, I won't put it past him to do something foolish." Jace said.

"Yeah, like leaving dead bodies on our front lawn." Dante huffed.

"Something like that," Jace said softly.

"Ordering you a pizza, you better eat it!" Dante said from down the hall. Jace rolled his eyes.

He needed more than a pizza.

"One chicken bacon ranch pizza." The waitress said, placing the pizza down on the table.

"Thank you. Nora smiled at her.

"Can I get yall anything else?" The waitress asked with a bright smile.

"No, we are good. Thank you." Joel responded as he stared Nora down from the other side of the table.

The waitress nodded and left quietly. Nora grabbed a slice of pizza, her belly growling loudly as she did. Joel sighed, raising an eyebrow at her. She made a face at him and pushed the pizza towards him. He grunted, taking a piece.

"Start talking." Joel said, biting into the pizza.

"Ok, but you have to promise one, not to say anything, and two, to believe me." Nora said with her mouth full, her eyes already eyeing the next pizza she was going to devour.

"You can't just request that I don't even know what we'll discuss." Joel said, putting his pizza down and staring at her.

"Fine, but I swear if you don't believe me or try to admit me somewhere, we will never be friends ever again!" Nora said firmly.

"Ok, that's dramatic, but I guess it's fair. It's really not, but heck, I need to know. So fine." Joel said, processing out loud.

"Ok, so werewolves are real." Nora said quietly, looking around as she said it and pausing so Joel could process.

Joel stared at her hardcore. He sat there waiting for her to laugh or smile. When none of that came, his expression turned concerned, and he looked at her crazy.

"Doll, did you just say what I thought you said?" Joel said, putting down his piece of pizza.

"Ok, so just listen. On my birthday, everything got weird. I am stronger, I can hear and see better. All my senses have heightened. My family came from a descent of what they call hunters. So when all that happened, I bumped into this guy; he could turn into an actual wolf. Oh wait, look, I have a book." Nora said, grabbing the book from her bag that she got with Jace.

She grabbed the book and handed it to Joel. He flipped through the pages trying to hide his expression. His friend was really making him concerned.

"Anyways, that guy I followed after the club was another hunter, and I've sorta joined their society. Apparently, wolves and hunters are enemies. That's what led to the murder of my family, Joel." Nora said, observing him carefully.

"Nora..I…hmm, Love, are you hearing what you're saying?" Joel asked cautiously.

Nora sighed. She wasn't sure how this would go, but she figured he might not believe her. She needed to prove it to him.

"Joel, I know how it sounds. It sounds like I've made this all up to justify my family dying. To have some type of bad guy that I can blame since the bad guy was never found. And if you even ask if I'm on drugs, I swear." Nora said, looking at him sternly.

Joel made a face looking down at the pizza. Those were the options that he was going with. He didn't realize how badly his friend was coping.

"Woman on the far end of the restaurant is waiting here to see if her husband is cheating. She's in a booth by the bathrooms watching the door. Her husband is just outside the cafe with his girlfriend and should be walking in…..now." Nora said, nodding to the door.

The door opened to the restaurant, and a couple hanging all over each walked in. Joel made a face wondering if it was a coincidence that someone walked in when she said they would.

"Oh, she's pissed. That's her best friend. Please wait for it. 5, 4, 3, 2, and 1." Nora said. As she said one, lots of yelling from the other side of the restaurant happened.

There was another loud female yell and some plates falling. Two seconds later, a different woman emerged and stormed out the door. Following her was the same man that walked into the restaurant several seconds ago. He was damp and looked like someone had dumped a water pitcher on him. Joel watched the scene go on and looked at Nora with his eyebrows raised.

"The waitress is on her way back. She just burned her arm on a hot plate. The burn is right above her wrist." Nora said with a shrug.

Two seconds later, the waitress came back. Joel spotted her wrist, and as the waitress was about to ask them if they needed anything else, Joel cut her off.

"Hey, are you ok, what happened to your wrist?" He blurted out.

"Oh, it's ok. I just burnt on a pizza plate I was taking out of the oven." She smiled at Joel.

Joel looked at Nora but smiled politely at the waitress. Nora gave him a look as I told you so. The waitress excused herself, and Joel proceeded to stare at Nora.

"So, are you like a superhero now?" Joel asked her.

"Um I don't think so, but I am going to find who killed my family and make sure they can never do it again," Nora said, her voice getting dark towards the end of her sentence.

"So I need you not to worry about me. I'm going to be gone a lot. I need to start training to be stronger and understand all of this. But I will call and text you and see you as often as possible." Nora said with a frown.

"Why does this feel like you're breaking up with me?" Joel said, making a face at her.

"Joel, I just don't want you to worry about where I am," Nora said, making a face at him.

"Here's the check, guys. Take your time." The waitress said something back and slipped the bill on the table.

Joel went to grab it before Nora, but she quickly snatched smirking as she did it faster than he did. Joel chuckled lightly. Nora slipped money onto the table and stood. She motions for Joel to come on. Joel followed her quietly outside. She leaned up against her car, watching him process.

"Ok, so I believe the whole superpowers but werewolves," Joel said, handing her the book back.

"Yeah, I know it's weird," Nora said, shrugging.

They had parked on the side of the building, an alley with a dumpster to the left. Joel went on about how it didn't seem possible and how she expected him to believe all that. She was about to tell him then don't but she suddenly got a weird feeling. It was a sickening feeling in the pit of her stomach. She glanced at the alleyway. A man was standing in it. He was a very tall and very huge man. He seemed to be confused, as if trying to figure something out. He locked eyes with her, not sure.

"Your necklace is very pretty." Joel said, reaching out and touching it.

As he did, the necklace fell. Nora must not have fastened it right after her shower. She watched the necklace fall off in slow motion. As the necklace fell, she heard a growl from the alleyway. She glanced at the man. He was vibrating, his eyes starting to glow. The growls echoed off the alleyway. Joel bent over, picked up the necklace, handed it back to Nora, and then glanced to the alleyway from where all the noise was coming from.

"What's wrong with-

"Joel, we need to go now!" Nora yelled, grabbing his arm and shoving him towards the car.

"What I-

Joel glanced back at the alleyway as more loud grunts and noises echoed from it. The grunts then turned to growls. Joel couldn't believe his eyes. Where the man was standing a second ago was now a large brown wolf.

"Joel, car now!" Nora yelled at him as she slid into the driver's seat.

Chapter Twenty One
Close call

Joel flung the car door open and jumped into the passenger seat. You could hear the wolf's nails scrape across the pavement as it came barreling after them. Joel shut the car door just in time. The wolf smashed into the car. It began clawing and scratching at the glass. It's nail pressing into the car screeching as they slid against the glass making small cracks.

"Go fucking go!" Joel screamed as he leaned away from the door.

Nora slammed the car into reserve and backed the car up. The wolf was biting at the car, trying to stay with it. Nora threw the car into drive and peeled out. The wolf was fast, staying with the car the whole length of the parking lot. It kept slamming itself into the side of the car. The car rocked each time the wolf did. Nora punched the gas, trying to get a head of the wolf as they neared the end of the parking lot. She knew by the way the wolf was acting; it would not let them go. Getting ahead of the wolf, she glanced at Joel.

"Hold on." She said as she changed her gears to go backwards.

"What the hell are you doing, Nora?" Joel yelled, putting his hands over his head and ducking down.

The wolf was running straight at the car's back end as Nora reserved. She pressed the pedal down to the car's floor as they went backwards. A loud crashing noise happened as the car backed into the wolf. The wolf was tossed backwards, a loud thud shook the ground as the wolf hit the pavement. Nora quickly put the car into drive and sped out of the parking lot, not letting the wolf have any time to follow them. Joel peeked up from his lap, looking at Nora, shocked and terrified.

"What the hell was that?" Joel whispered.

"A werewolf." Nora couldn't help but smirk.

"A -

"A werewolf. What I was trying to tell you." Nora sighed.

"Oh…ok. A werewolf…ok," Joel said, straightening up and looking around.

"Is he gonna find us?" He asked, his voice shaky.

"From what I know, which is little, is that they like to be hidden from humans, so hopefully not," Nora said with a shrug.

"Hidden, what the hell do you call that? He just wolfed out in the alleyway when he saw you. Did you see its eyes? They were red." Joel yelled.

"Red? They were red! " Nora shouted back at him, anger and excitement in her voice.

The wolf that killed her family had glowing red eyes. She noted it too herself as she continued to drive, ignoring Joel for a second. She didn't think it was the wolf. She remembered dark brown, almost red fur. The one just now was just plain brown. She wondered if there was a connection.

"Yes, he had red devil eyes, and he freaked out when he saw you." Joel said, nudging her.

"Me..when he saw me. Oh, the necklace! Where's the necklace?" Nora said, looking around the car.

"The necklace?" Joel asked, confused.

"Yes," Nora grumbled.

"Of all things, you're worried about a piece of jewelry right now. I will get you another prettier one if you can find a way for that thing not to come to eat us!" Joel yelled at her.

"No, the necklace hides me from them or something. I told you I'm a hunter." Nora said, still looking.

"Ok. so because you're a hunter wolfman wolfed out?" Joel asked, starting to look for the necklace.

"I think so. Jace said to wear the necklace so it would hide my scent or something. Apparently, there's an ongoing kill-or-be-killed thing between hunters and wolves." Nora said, now getting worried she couldn't find the necklace.

"Foot! Near your right foot, near the gas pedal." Joel said, pointing downward.

"Move over. I'll get it." Joel said, squeezing between her and the space between the steering wheel and the floor.

He grabbed the necklace and handed it to her. Nora glanced at it before latching it and placing it over her head.

"I think he might not be able to track us with this on, but I'm not sure." Nora said quietly.

"You're not sure?" Joel asked worriedly.

"Um, not really, but wait, ok, so we need to go to a flower shop or something." Nora said, nudging Joel.

"Flower shop?" Joel said, looking at her like she was crazy.

"Yes, look up one. We can get some plants that our poisons and ward off wolves." Nora said, nudging him harder.

"Ok, ok," Joel said, pulling out his phone and began looking through it.

"2 blocks east on the south side," Joel said, pointing his finger.

"Ok, got it." Nora said, heading that way.

Jace pushed the pizza away as he looked out at the dark sky. He had gone to watch the men train; they were well prepared, which made him feel a little better. The borders were heavily guarded, and he was pretty sure the alliance with the Moonlight pack would happen, but still, something was gnawing at him. Something was making him on edge.

Run. Cole's voice came through.

Jace sighed; he knew exactly where Cole would head if he shifted right now. He tossed a fallen piece of pepperoni into the trash and sighed. He shouldn't, but he really didn't care.

"Going for a run." Jace mindlink Dante and Wyatt.

"Want company, handsome?" Dante linked back.

"No, you stay here; hold down the fort," Jace responded, rolling his eyes.

"Well, how about Matt or Adam? They haven't been out in a while." Dante responded back.

Jace knew what he was doing. Dante was too concerned about him and his weird moods. He could outrun Matt. Matt's wolf was fast, but he wasn't as fast as the other, and no one was faster than Cole.

"Have Adam stay on board patrol. If Matt wants to join me, he can, but if he can't keep up, he's back on patrol with Adam." Jace ordered.

"So you're just going to out run Matt then." Dante responded.

Jace could hear the smirk in his voice.

"Done talking with you. Go do something useful." Jace linked him back, cutting the link.

Jace was out of his bedroom and down by the door in seconds. Cole was freaking out inside of him, wanting out and wanting to get to Nora. Jace groaned at his lack of control.

Shut up. Jace grumbled inward at Cole.

Cole growled back at him in response. Jace walked into the woods, stripping and tying his clothing to his leg. He was about to shift when he heard someone coming up behind him. Jace turned, ready for anything, and made a face seeing Matt. He was half naked, running across the driveway.

"Hey, wait up, Alpha." Matt called, waving his arms about.

Jace smirked and shifted. The more you shifted, the easier it was. The first shift a wolf does is long and painful. There is pain each time, but you get used to the way your bones feel, shifting into places. Cole looked at Matt as he began undoing his pants. Cole huffed at him.

"Hold on." Matt said, falling as he tried to get his leg out of his pants.

Cole sneered at Matt and took off.

They spent the afternoon buying all the plants that Nora kept telling Joel about. They cleaned one entire flower shop out of mistletoe and wolfsbane. Nora only found two plants of mountain ash. She was getting strange looks from the shopkeepers but didn't care. She was now driving Joel home. He was overwhelmed by the day and exhausted. Nora pulled her very beat-up car to a stop in front of his house.

"Take the mistletoe and put it around your house; it keeps them away. Take mountain ash and wolves, bane its poisons. The mountain ash just needs to touch their skin." Nora said, handing him plants.

Joel graciously took them, confused about why Nora was not turning the car off and getting out.

"Aren't you staying?" Joel asked her, confused.

"No, I'm going back to that society. I need to train and learn everything I can about this whole mess. I'll message you when I get there and call you tomorrow. Call me if you need anything." Nora said to him.

"Ok, please be safe, Doll. I love ya." Joel said as he began walking to his house, arms full of plans.

Nora watched him stop at his front door and place one of the mistletoes there before opening the door. He waved to her and ducked inside. Nora waited to see him flick the lights on before taking off and heading to the society. It took her no time to get back there. She parked her car out front and walked to the door. She went to knock but decided just to go in. She held her plants in her arms, her backpack over her shoulder, and fumbled for the door handle. She turned it slightly and pushed the door open. Stepping in, it was complete darkness again. She used her foot to close the door; when she did, she got hit with powder.

"What the hell!" Nora yelled as she felt dust wash over her.

She heard laughter as the lights flickered on. Logan was standing on the entryway's far side, trying not to laugh.

"What the hell?" Nora repeatedly looked at them.

"Mountain ash. It's a trap in case someone just decides to walk in. We really need to show you the back way and how to avoid that trap." Logan smirked.

"That would be great." Nora said, trying to shake off the dust.

"Plants?" Logan asked her.

"Yeah, so this is mistletoe and wolfsbane. You clearly know about mountain ash." Nora said, rolling her eyes.

"Ok…" Logan said, confused.

"Ugh, the mistletoe and wolfsbane are repellents as well. " Nora said, setting them down on a counter.

"So do we hang the mistletoe like we do on Christmas?" Logan smirked.

He grabbed the mistletoe plant and dangled it above his head, making a kissy face at Nora. Nora shoved him lightly with a chuckle. He placed the plant back down as a bell began ringing from where the kitchen was.

"Um…Dinner?" Nora asked.

"Yes, dinner. Come on." Logan said, offering her his arm; she laughed, looping hers through it as he led her to the kitchen.

Chapter Twenty Two
Wounded

The kitchen was huge, with two stoves. She always thought her parents' kitchen was enormous, but this was bigger. A large table was set off to the side. Lilly stopped ringing the bell as people piled in. They all quickly found their seats waiting for dinner. Logan walked over to the table, pulled out a seat next to him and motioned for Nora to come to sit. Kat made a stupid noise from the other end of the table, but Nora ignored it. She was sitting between Lilly and Logan as well as across from Mina. Lilly was running around the kitchen, getting the plates together. She then quickly began passing them out. The plate was sat down in front of Nora, shepherd's pie. She smiled at it. She hadn't had it in so long.

"What the hell happened to your car?" Mina asked her, looking at her strangely.

"Oh, I was attacked by a wolf." She said awkwardly.

"What do you mean?" Logan asked, concerned, turning in his seat to look at her.

"I went out to lunch with my friend Joel, and there was a guy standing in the alleyway next to the pizza place. He was watching me. Then he just turned and came charging at us out of nowhere." Nora explained.

"It's strange." Phil said from the other side of the table, locking eyes with Logan.

"Why is it strange? Isn't that what they do? They attack us and our families." Nora said with bitterness in her voice as she mentioned family.

"Well yeah, but it's not that reckless. They usually plan it out and stage an attack; they just don't go rogue in the middle of the day where anyone could see them." Logan said his voice was puzzled as he was processing what he was saying.

"Yeah, they don't like to reveal themselves to the outside world. It would put their pack in danger and all other wolf kinds." Lily said.

"Unless he was a rogue himself. You know, pack less." Kat said, trying to make sense of everything.

"No, I don't think so. If it was without a pack, he would be in more danger of attacking a hunter. He would have no one to fall back on to help protect him." Logan said, his fingers drumming on the table as he thought.

"What color was his eyes when it was in wolf form?" Drake said, speaking up.

He had been quiet up until this point, but now he was really starting to wonder about his theory. Kat made a huffing noise at the sound of Drake's question. You can tell that she knew what he was going to ask or why and didn't agree with it.

"They were red." Nora said, her face asking him why without saying it.

Drake didn't respond and was quickly up from the table and out of the kitchen. Nora looked around the table, and when no one said anything about him just getting up and leaving, she decided she was going to. She stood up quickly and began walking out the door.

"Wait up, I'll take you to where he went." Logan said, rolling his eyes as he followed after her.

Nora stepped aside and let Logan pass her as she began to follow him. Logan led her to a small room and pushed open the door. The room was set up as a study, with a large desk in the middle of the room, and behind the desk were bookshelves. Drake stood over the desk muttering to himself, looking at something. Nora approached the desk and realized he was looking down at a map. There were markers and all colors, it looked like he had set the map up into territories and had a color for each territory. Drake looked up and looked at her and saw the questions across their faces.

"So I have a theory. I believe we can tell which wolf belongs to which alpha by their eye color when they are in wolf form. I think the Red Wood pack has red eyes while in wolf form. The Red Wood pack is one of the larger ones that take up most of this territory here, and the other larger one, I believe, is called the Cross River pack, and their eyes are blue. There's another pack called The Moonlight pack, and I believe their eye color is yellow, and lastly, The Black Sand pack their eyes are green. " Drake explained.

Nora's mind went to Jace and how blue his eyes were when he was in human form, but Cole's was also the same ice blue. She didn't know if it was a coincidence or if the wolf just had his eye color, but red wasn't an eye color, so maybe Drake was right. Nora thought to herself, listening to him.

"From what I can tell, the wolves mostly keep their pack. They hardly ever mingle, but there is always tension between the Red Wood and Cross River packs. I'm not sure why, but I think if we could narrow down which wolf belongs to which Alpha, it would be easier to understand how they moved and attacked." Drake continued.

"It makes sense if you know what kind of Alpha they have; then you can anticipate how they are as a whole." Nora said, shrugging.

"What else do you know about the Cross River pack's Alpha?" Nora asked curiously.

"Not too much, but from what I've heard, the other pack's don't cross him. They almost fear him, and I'm sure it's because of how he became Alpha. He killed the previous Alpha. Rumors say it was pretty brutal. Although I do not know why. I get information in pieces. " Drake said, still looking at the map.

"How did he kill the previous Alpha?" Nora asked.

"They found him in pieces. Apparently, his wolf went crazy and ripped him to literal pieces." Drake said quietly. Nora listened to him.

She couldn't see Cole ripping apart someone. Something had to have happened. She sighed, trying to remind herself that Jace was a werewolf and her enemy. Logan was studying her. He wondered why she was so interested in the Cross River pack. Just

as he was about to ask her, Mina entered the study
room, looking like something was wrong.

"There's a wolf outside. " Mina said, her voice
twitching.

"What?" Logan said, not processing what she
said.

Mina motioned for Logan to come with her,
and she disappeared. Logan glanced at Drake and
Nora before following her. Drake and Nora quickly
followed them out to the main entrance. The six of
them were assembled in the middle of the room. Mina
looked out the window.

"It's huge and jet black." Mina whispered.

Nora cringed; she slowly walked over to the
window and looked out next to Mina. Cole. What was
he doing? They'll kill him. Nora's stomach twisted in
on herself, and she instantly wanted to vomit.

"Maybe it's just a wild wolf." Nora said, trying to
get them to stop staring at Cole.

"No, that's a werewolf." Kat said, walking up
behind them and looking out the window.

Nora watched Cole sniff the air; he was
searching for her. Nora felt the acid rise up in her
throat. She glanced at everyone; seven hunters to
one wolf. She needed to make Cole leave. Cole sat
down and stared at the window as if he knew where
Nora was.

"Gear." Logan announced.

Kat, Phill, Drake, and Lilly all left the front
entranceway. Nora looked back to Logan, who was
studying him.

"Why is he just sitting outside? Look at him pacing like he is struggling with himself." Logan said mostly to himself.

"Maybe he'll go away." Nora said, hopeful.

"What the heck is wrong with you? We need to take him out before he takes us out. He's probably a scout." Kat said, coming back into the room with a crossbow.

"I don't think he's a scout; look at his size. If he's a scout, then his pack is monsters." Logan said, still wondering what the wolf was up to.

"He looks like he's alone." Drake said, returning to the room.

"I've checked the camera; Drake's right. He's alone." Lilly said, confirming.

"Look at him sitting there. Easy target." Kat said, starting to take aim.

Nora couldn't do it. She couldn't sit by and let Jace get hurt. She watched as Kat looked like she was about to take her shot. Nora threw her shoulder into Kat, knocking her over. She then bolted to the front door. Pulling the door open, mountain ash rained down here, but she kept running.

"What the fuck is wrong with her!" Kat yelled, getting back up

"Nora!" Logan called, going after her.

Nora stepped outside, and as soon as Cole saw her, he started towards her.

"Go!" She yelled at him, but he wasn't listening.

He kept coming closer. She heard Kat setting up again. Logan's footsteps were quicker behind her. She pushed herself to get to Cole. He crossed the road.

"Kat! Take the shot before he can get her!" Logan yelled.

"No!" Nora yelled. She heard Kat release the arrow.

It was spinning towards Cole. Cole didn't seem even to notice. He was so intent on getting to Nora. His ears perked up hearing the arrow fly, and everything began to register, but too late.

"Cole!" Nora yelled as she heard the arrow behind her.

Everything began to slow down. She glanced over her shoulder, seeing the arrow move in slow motion. It was aiming right for Cole. She shut her eyes and moved slightly to her left. Everything sped up in an instant. A sharp pain pierced through her. It brought her to her knees, a yell leaving her lips as the arrow lodged itself into her body.

"Nora!" Logan yelled as he watched it go down.

Cole was by her side in no time, and the world was foggy. She was fading in and out of black. She felt Cole nuzzle into her. His growls echoing around her. She clung to his fur as the world started fading.

"Cole, go." She whispered before slumping over on him.

The mountain ash she was covered in burned his skin. Cole whimpered, trying to help her. As the others circled around them, Cole began to show his teeth. He was standing protectively over Nora. Every now and then, nudging her, a whimper escaping between growls.

"What is wrong with this wolf?" Kat said, reloading the crossbow.

"Kat, stand down." Logan ordered, trying to take a step closer to Nora.

"No, I'm going to kill it." Kat said through her teeth.

"I said stand down now!" Logan yelled at her angrily.

Lilly took the crossbow from Kat as she turned shades of red but listened to Logan. Logan took a step towards Nora and the wolf. The wolf curled its lip up at him. Logan put his hands up defensively.

"Cole..right. Cole, I need to get Nora to help her." Logan said, taking another step.

Cole seemed to be listening as Logan spoke. He didn't growl as he stepped towards them again. Logan went to touch Nora, and Cole snapped at his hand as a warning. He could have bit Logan's hand clean off if Cole wanted to.

"Cole, could you let your human take over for a minute." Logan said, trying to get through to them.

Cole turned his head, listening. He looked down at the small blood pool starting to form beneath Nora. He seemed to nod. Several bone-crunching noises were heard as they watched in horror as the wolf shifted back to a human. Logan took the opportunity to get his hands on Nora to try to see how bad the injury was.

"Get your fucking hands off, my mate." Jace growled, shoving Logan away from Nora.

Jace bent down, trying to study the wound. He ripped her shirt around the arrow site. It had pierced through her upper chest right below her collarbone. He ignored the burns that mountain ash powder left on his skin.

"Listen, we need to get her to the hospital." Logan said, stepping towards him.

"You need to put your friend inside before I let Cole kill her while you watch." Jace threatened.

"I need a car now and bring Wyatt. Northwest Street old mill building. Now!" Jace mind link Dante.

"Listen-

"No, you listen. If anything happens to her, you will all suffer." Jace growled at him

He inhaled, looking at the arrow. He needed to break it in order to apply pressure to get her to stop bleeding. Logan was becoming frustrated and stepped towards him.

"Let me help." Logan said, kneeling.

Jace studied his face and realized he was going to need someone to hold her steady while he broke the tail end of the arrow off. Jace nodded, letting Logan near

"Hold her steady; she might scream even though she is out. I need to break the tail end off the arrow so I can get some pressure to slow the bleeding." Jace explained.

Logan nodded and grabbed ahold of her shoulders. The rest of the hunters watched on, confused. There was a very large, muscular, naked werewolf helping a hunter save another. Lilly stepped closer. There was something different about this wolf, she thought. Jace gritted his teeth and snapped the end of the arrow tail off in one swift motion. Nora screamed in her unconsciousness. Jace immediately pulled her towards him holding her against him as he applied pressure on her wound.

"How do you know her?" Logan asked, confused at how caring a wolf was being to a hunter.

Jace didn't say anything. He heard Dantes' tires screeching in the distance. He looked at Logan, narrowing his eyes.

"I'm taking her." Jace said, his voice daring him to say otherwise.

"The hell you are!" Logan said, ready to fight this fight.

"I am, and not a single one of you will stop me," Jace said, his voice chilling as he looked from Logan to each member of the society.

"She needs medical-

"I have that covered." Jace said, looking towards the headlight coming down the street.

"You are not taking her, Wolf." Logan said, squaring up with him.

Dante's car came to a screeching halt behind Jace. Within seconds He and Wyatt were out of the car and rushing towards Jace.

"Alpha?" Dante said, looking confused.

The smell of hunter overwhelmed both Wyatt and Dante, their eyes narrowing as they looked at the group standing in front of Jace. Their fangs came down, watching them. Dante vibrated with anger; he wanted to kill them all. His wolf crawled under his skin.

"Stand down." Jace ordered them.

"Alpha they are-

"I said stand down." Jace growled; Wyatt and Dante nodded in obeisance.

"Wyatt, the girl, she's hurt. Jace said, and Wyatt came towards him.

"Alpha, she's covered in mountain ash. Look at your-

"I don't fucking care. I need you to fucking fix her." Jace yelled at him.

Wyatt nodded vigorously; he had never seen his Alpha act like this over a random girl.

"I need to take her back to the pack house. All my supplies are there. Can I look Alpha?" Wyatt asked cautiously, stepping forward.

"You are not fucking taking her wolves!" Logan yelled in Jace's face.

Jace snarled, cradling Nora to him.

"Logan. Let her go." Drake said, stepping forward and placing a hand on his shoulder.

"Are you crazy? No." Logan said, looking at Drake.

"She will be fine with him, Logan. Let her go.." Drake said again.

"She will not be fine with him. What the hell is wrong with you? She's a hunter, and he's a wolf. She-

"She's his mate. Let her go; he won't hurt her." Drake said, pulling Logan by his shoulder.

"Mate?" Logan asked, confused.

"Mate?" Dante repeated, his voice just as confused.

Wyatt approached Jace very carefully, holding his hands up as if to say he wasn't going to do anything.

"Alpha, we need to get her back home," Wyatt said, eyeballing the wound.

Jace nodded and began walking to the car, he heard Logan try to follow him, but Drake pulled him back. Jace heard him whisper to Logan that he would explain later. Jace got into the passenger seat with Nora in his lap as he applied pressure to the wound. Dante scanned the hunters, remembering their faces before getting in the driver seat and peeling out.

Chapter Twenty Three
Mate?

Jace didn't let anyone touch her. He nearly kicked in the door of his house as he rushed in. He, with one arm, knocked everything off the dining room table as he gently laid her on it. Wyatt had gone to get medical supplies while Dante was trying to find a way to stop Jace from panicking. The anger rolling off of him was making Dante's wolf nervous. Dante stepped forward and gently nudged Jace. Jace snapped around like he was ready to fight. Seeing Dante holding out his pants to him, he calmed down. He snatched the pants from Dante and pulled them. Dante wanted to ask what happened, but he didn't want to send his Alpha over the edge.

"I don't know why she did that. What was she thinking?" Jace said, holding pressure on her wound with one hand and with the other brushing her hair out of her face.

"What happened, Alpha?" Dante asked cautiously.

"She stepped into the arrow that was coming for me. She didn't even hesitate." Jace said through gritted teeth.

Dante was confused, she was with a group of hunters. Why would she try to save him? The mate pull does not affect humans. It didn't affect anyone but other wolves. He looked at Jace, why would the moon goddess curse him this way? He was an amazing Alpha. His father was a monster. Dante looked at the girl in Jace's arms. She was weak, and she was fragile. She would never make a strong Luna. She would put the pack in jeopardy. She would put Jace in danger constantly.

"Is she really your mate?" Dante asked, watching Jace cradle her.

"Yes." Jace growled at the stupid question.

Wyatt came running back in. The front door was still wide open as he rushed towards the table. Jace watched him carefully. Cole was being overprotective and didn't want anyone near Nora. Jace was having trouble controlling Cole's urges. Wyatt laid out his medical supplies and looked at Jace like he was about to say something horrible.

"Alpha, I need her shirt off." Wyatt said carefully.

Jace growled, but it was Cole flashing in his eyes. Jace tried to push Cole back. He was being unreasonable, but he understood. He didn't want anyone seeing or touching what was his for that matter.

"Alpha, I can't fix her wounds with the shirt in the way." Wyatt said, explaining.

Jace's body tensed up, hearing that he was going to see her topless. The possessiveness Cole was exhibiting was making it hard to think. Dante reached behind him, grabbing a blanket off the couch. He held it out to Jace.

"Jace, the shirt needs to come off. Do you want her to bleed out on the table? Use this to cover her." Dante said bluntly, waving the blanket at his Alpha.

Jace narrowed his eyes at Dante but grabbed the blanket. Wyatt handed Jace scissors and motioned to him to cut the shirt off. Jace grabbed them, and Wyatt turned around, showing respect. Jace eyeballed Dante, who huffed and turned around. Jace cut through the shirt, exposing her midsection. He peeled the shirt away from her. His eyes wandered over her body. She was absolutely perfect; everything on her was …perfect, her breast, her hourglass waistline. His eyes narrowed in on a bruise on her side. He wondered what that could have been from. Wyatt cleared his throat, trying to get Jace to focus. Jace shook his head and covered her with the blanket.

Wyatt turned quickly around and went to Nora. He began studying her wound. Jace pushed Cole out of his mind the best he could. He needed to be less emotional to help Nora through this.

"I need to push the arrow the rest of the way through. She might wake up, and it will be painful." Wyatt explained to Jace.

"Ok, how can I help?" Jace asked, looking down at Nora.

"I'm going to need both of you if she wakes up. Jace, you'll need to hold her down. Dante, if she wakes up, I'll need you to pass me things and keep her arm still." Wyatt explained.

They both nodded; Jace sat her up and held her against his bare chest. The blanket fell away, and he felt Cole stir. Jace pushed him back as he held Nora tightly. Dante was on standby in case he needed help. Wyatt looked at Jace and nodded. Wyatt slipped one hand between Jace and Nora's shoulders, pushing the remainder of the arrow through her chest. On the back side of her shoulder, he grabbed hold of the arrow and pulled hard. Nora jolted her eyes fling open as a curdling blood scream let out of her. Sweat beaded across her forehead as Dante came to help hold her still. Blood began to flow down her back.

"Jace?" She whispered, her voice full of pain.

"I got you." He said back to her as her head slumped forward.

She passed back out. Wyatt was shoving gauze into the hole, trying to see where the bleeder was. The blood was mostly coming out the back.

"I need her on her back." Wyatt said sharply, becoming frustrated that he couldn't see where she was bleeding from.

Jace carefully flipped her over. As he did, he grew tense, seeing a long wide bruise across her back. Cole vibrated; he shut his eyes, stepping back. It wasn't the time to find out what happened. Wyatt glanced at Jace, and when he saw he was getting control began working on her. Jace paced back and forth like a caged animal as he watched Wyatt poke and prod the wound. He heard Wyatt let out a sigh of relief.

"Give me those hemostats." He said to Dante.

"Hema what." Dante said, looking at all the tools Wyatt had.

"The long, pinchy-looking thing." Wyatt said, pointing at it.

Dante nodded, picking them up and handing them to him. Wyatt clamped the blood vessel, and the blood slowed. Wyatt grabbed some more gauze wiping the blood away. He pointed to the needle holders and a pack of sutures. Dante nodded and handed them to him.

"Give me the thumb…tweezers, the tweezers." Wyatt said, changing how he was asking for the tool.

Jace watched as Wyatt tied off the blood vessel and then began sewing up the wound. When he was done, he nodded for Jace to come over and flip her over. Jace carefully flipped her over, and Wyatt began working on the front wound.

"Scissor." Wyatt said, holding out his hand to Dante.

Dante handed them to him, and Wyatt pulled tissue that had curved inwards from the arrow piercing the skin out. He trimmed it up. Dante made a gagging sound before looking away. After he trimmed up the skin, he began suturing the wound closed. When he was done, he stepped away and nodded to Jace, telling him he could have her.

"It's gonna hurt like hell when she wakes up. I have some pain meds and an injection I can give her, but I want her to wake up first. Get her upstairs and get her comfortable." Wyatt said.

"Let us know if you need anything," Dante said to him.

Jace nodded, scooping her up into his arms and quickly moved with her up the stairs, heading for his room. He was up the stairs in no time. Nora was groaning against his chest and moving slightly. He kicked open the door to his room and walked over to the bed. He set her down, studying her, wondering if he should get Wyatt for the medicine. She began to twitch slightly, and the groaning increased.

Wyatt meds. Jace mind link him.

Jace rubbed her face gently, sitting down next to her in the bed. She began to cry slightly, and he laid down beside her pulling her into him. As soon as his arms wrapped around her, she seemed to settle down slightly. He heard Wyatt rushing up the stairs. Within minutes he was in the room.

"Is she awake?" Wyatt asked, walking in.

"Not really, she's crying off and on. She's in pain. Fix it." Jace order.

Wyatt nodded and grabbed the injection. Nora began to twitch more, and the pain looked like it was coming in waves. Wyatt rubbed an alcohol pad over a spot on her arm; he figured with the way Jace was acting, he better not suggest giving her a shot in her butt. He then injected the medicine into her upper arm.

"It will take ten to fifteen minutes to kick in. She will be very loopy when she does come to. I'm going to leave the pills on the dresser. Make sure she eats before taking them. Get me if you need anything else." Wyatt said as he placed the pill bottle on the dress.

        Jace nodded, adjusting his arms around Nora. She nuzzled into his chest, the medicine starting to work. Wyatt left the room shutting the door. Jace watched Nora relax, he was afraid any minute, something bad would happen. She let out a soft sigh, and he couldn't help but fall in love with the sound. He inhaled her scent, and it instantly relaxed him. She was fine, she was in his arms, and he wouldn't let anything hurt her again.

Chapter Twenty Four
Bubbles

Nora winced as she sleepily attempted to turn. She hurt, she recognized the throbbing pain in her shoulder, but her mind didn't care. She opened her eyes as she tried to pull away. She found herself looking up at Jace. He was sitting upright against the headboard of his bed, arms wrapped around her, cradling her. She was trying to figure out what had happened, but her brain was too foggy. She looked at his face while studying it. Her eyes travel from his deep-set eyes to the perfect bridge of his nose. He had the most kissable lips. She reached up, staring at his perfect jawline. His eyes were shut; she listened to his soft breathing and smiled. She reached up and ran her finger under his chin. She could feel the stubble starting to grow there. She chuckled as it tickled her finger. A smile formed on his lips. Nora realized he was awake and froze. She then noticed all of the blood on his bare chest. She reached out, touching it, searching for a wound.

"It's not mine, Little Hunter," Jace said, feeling her touch on his chest.

"Oh good, I thought they hurt you," Nora said, sleepy.

"No, you made sure they didn't," Jace said, his voice sounding angry.

"Why are you mad?" Nora said, trying to sit up and look at him.

"Because you could have gotten yourself killed," Jace said, his anger not leaving his voice.

"No, I can slow things down." Nora said, giving up and settling back into him.

"What?" Jace said, opening his eyes and looking down at her.

"Yeah, it must be a superpower. Only happens when something or someone is attacking me. Everything goes well oooowwww." She explained and then started laughing.

Jace couldn't help but crack a smile. He watched her settle back against him. He loved how she felt against him. She sighed happily.

"Where are we?:" She asked, yawning.

"My house." Jace said, closing his eyes.

"What about the others? Did you hurt them?" Nora said, sitting up quickly.

She winced and let out a small yelp when her shoulder hit his arm when she sat up. She glanced to her shoulder, seeing the sutures. She reached over and touched them carefully.

"Did we go to the doctor?" She asked, wincing as she touched them.

Jace sighed, taking hold of her hand and moving it away from her wound. He shook his head slightly at her.

"No, Wyatt sutured you up, and no, the hunters are fine. Even the one who shot you. She was lucky I had control of Cole." Jace said quietly.

She glanced down at herself and realized she was topless and also covered in blood. She went to grab the bed cover but then didn't want to get blood on it. She scooted away from him, covering her breast with her arms even though moving her shoulder area hurt like hell.

"What the hell are you doing?" Jace asked, annoyed.

"I'm naked." She said, looking around.

"You're shirtless, not naked." Jace said, rolling her eyes.

"Yeah, well. Do you have a shower here?" Nora said, turning herself away from him.

"How are you feeling? Do you think you can stand to shower?" Jace asked, concerned.

"Yeah, I can't sit here in my bra covered in blood anymore." Nora shrugged.

"Ok.." Jace said, sitting up and looking at her carefully He crossed the room and opened a door. She heard him flip on a light, and then seconds later, the shower was running. Nora scooted off the bed and placed her feet on the hardwood floor. She felt the world around her woosh. She grabbed the bedpost, steadying herself as she stood. She shut her eyes and walked across the floor. She felt drunk. She got to the bathroom door and grabbed onto it. She looked down at the gray tile floor. She had been drunk enough that she knew she could do this. She walked into the bathroom, the shower had its own stall, and there was a tub on the opposite wall. Jace was standing just outside the shower, reaching into it. She smiled, watching him test the water temperature on his wrist. Nora leaned against the counter, watching him. He looked up, his eyes locked with hers.

"What?" He asked, withdrawing his hand from the shower.

"Nothing." She said, the same goofy smile on her lips.

He smirked at her as he crossed the distance between them. He stopped just inches from her as he lowered his head towards hers. Nora froze, her stomach doing summer salts as he leaned down towards her. She felt her lower back press into the counter as she realized she was trapped between him and it. He angled his head toward his mouth, inches from her ear.

"What's so funny little hunter?" He whispered into her ear.

His warm breath on her ear gave her an instant shiver. She fought to find words to respond back to him. Her mind was foggy, and the intensity of him was overwhelming. She took a breath, trying to calm herself. She felt his hand on the outside of her bare stomach, pulling her against him. The small little jolts she got from his touch made her want more.

"Are you sure you can shower alone?" He asked, his voice was low and just above a whisper.

Nora cleared her throat before looking up into his eyes. She pulled back from him, pushing herself into the counter.

"Yes, I am perfectly capable." Nora said firmly, nodding to the door, telling him to leave.

Jace smiled slightly, stepping away from her; he pointed at the towels he had laid out for her. Nora nodded her thanks as she watched him walk out.

"Perfect is right." He said to himself, Nora caught a glimpse of a smile coming across his face as he shut the door.

She turned to look in the mirror. She looked like something out of a horror movie. She had a large wound just below her collarbone, and the black suture reminded her of little bugs. She had blood stained down the front of her. She needed to shower. She undid her pants and she slowly slipped them down, almost falling as she kicked her feet out. What the heck did they give her? She thought.

"You ok in there?" Jace called, hearing her almost fall.

"Fine, go away!" She shouted back to him; she heard him grunt in response.

"Using super hearing is just like being in here." Nora yelled to the door.

"So, come back in?" Jace asked; she could hear the smile in his voice.

"No!" Nora snapped, chucking her underwear to the side.

Looking in the mirror, she wondered if the necklace would tarnish in the water. She didn't want to ruin it. She took the onyx necklace off and placed it down on the counter top before slowly walking to the shower. She stepped into the shower; the hot water felt good against her skin. She watched the blood wash down her body, the bottom of the shower turning red. She looked around to find the bottle labeled shampoo and opened it. She smiled a little, smelling it. It smelt like him. She squirted some into her hand and began washing her hair. She let the warm water rush over her, and the bubbles went everywhere. A dizzy spell crashed into her, and the shampoo bottle fell to the floor, soap pouring out. She moved her feet, trying to steady herself until the moment passed, but the soap caught her. She knew she was falling.

It happened so quickly, but she made sure to land on her butt. She tried to stand, but as she tried, the shampoo spilling out onto the floor of the shower made her slip again. She grabbed onto the shelf, trying to keep herself upright, but the shelf toppled over, and she landed on the shower floor again.

The bathroom door flung open, and before Nora could protest, Jace was in the shower with her. He stood in front of the shower head, blocking the water from hitting her. He looked like he was breathing hard, and fear was on his face for a brief second. He realized quickly she was ok. He squatted down, scooping her up into his arms. He went to carry her out of the shower.

"Wait, the soap." Nora pleaded.

He stepped into the water stream, letting the water run over her and soaking him more. Nora couldn't help but notice how the water seemed to make every muscle on him stand out. Once she was bubble free, he carried her out of the shower setting her down gently on the bench next to the tub. He grabbed a large fluffy towel and wrapped it around her.

"Stay here." He said as he began walking out dripping wet.

Nora was too embarrassed to argue; she began drying herself up and scooped another towel for her hair. Flipping her hair forward, she captured her hair. Another dizzy spell hit her as she tried putting her hair up in the towel. She held onto the bench till it passed. Jace walked in; he was wearing shorts and was carrying clothing in his hands. He looked at her face asking what was wrong.

"I don't know what you guys gave me, but I don't want any more of it," Nora explained.

"It was to help so you wouldn't be in pain. It should wear off soon." Jace said, sitting down next to her.

"I would rather be in pain." She sighed, feeling helpless.

Jace smiled at the comment. She was brave, strong, and fearless. He at first thought he was being cursed when Cole uttered mate, but he was starting to see the Moon Goddess chose right for him.

"What?" Nora asked, confused at his expression.

He shook his head slightly and plopped a shirt over her head. It smelt like him, and she was beginning to love the way he smelt. She stuck one arm through it and was struggling with the other. Jace noted she was stubborn, too, he helped her slide her arm through the t-shirt, and it fell down around her.

She was swimming in it, but she had a soft smile on her lips. He didn't respond to it but held up the shorts with a raised eyebrow at her, his eyes sparkled with mischief.

"Oh no, I'm doing those." Nora said to him firmly.

"Yeah, and just how are you going to?" Jace said, holding the shorts out to her.

She snatched the shorts from him and grinned triumphantly. She winced slightly, trying to hide the pain that coursed through her as she moved too quickly. She tried leaning forward but couldn't. She sighed and then dropped the shorts on the floor and tried wiggling her foot into them.

"Seriously, let me help; this is painful and pathetic to watch." Jace said, sighing.

"Fine, but close your eyes." Nora said, folding her arms across her chest.

Jace rolled his eyes as he slipped her feet through the shorts and slowly brought them up. Nora bit her lip to stop from reacting to his fingertips, softly brushing her legs as he pulled the shorts to her knees.

"Stand." Jace ordered.

Nora placed a hand on his shoulder and stood. The T-shirt fell to her knees, so it covered her and she was grateful for it. His fingers grazed her thigh and sent cold chills through her. She was relieved when the shorts were finally up. His hand stayed at her waist after he pulled them up.

"There." He said, looking at her.

"You didn't close your eyes." Nora said, making a face.

"Hungry?" Jace asked, ignoring the comment and offering her his hand as he stepped away.

"Yeah, actually I'm starving." Nora said, feeling her stomach rumble.

Jace helped her out of the bathroom and to the bed. She sat down on the edge of the bed. Jace didn't like where she was sitting. He scooped her up and placed her at the head of the bed, scooting her inward. He then placed the blanket around her. Nora was confused by the whole action, and she just watched him. He hovered over her and then leaned forward, placing a kiss on her forehead. Nora leaned into it, her hand touching the side of his face. His eyes fixated on her lips as he pulled back. He couldn't stop himself from seeing them. He moved into the kiss, his lips meeting hers. Nora was shocked at the kiss, but his warm lips against hers sent shivers through her that she couldn't deny. She kissed him back, her lips moving with his. She felt his tongue graze her lips, and she opened her mouth to allow his tongue access to hers. Nora's hand captured the back of his neck as she kissed him back. Jace pulled away abruptly and left Nora in a little daze. Jace seemed a little breathless, and Nora noticed his eyes were slightly different. He cleared his throat, stepping back.

"I'll be right back. Wyatt might be by soon to check on you." Jace said as he opened the door leaving.

Nora watched him leave, slightly confused. She figured the eyes were a wolf thing. She was left alone in the room by herself with her thoughts. She really needed to check in with Joel, and she wanted to let Logan and them know she was ok. She didn't see her phone anywhere.

Chapter Twenty Five
Caught

" Hunter." Dante mind linked Jace.

"What?" Jace, who was in the kitchen, responded.

" There's a hunter on the premises." Dante said you could feel the rage through the mindlink.

"No. Stand down." Jace said his first thought was going to Nora, his stomach twisting.

"It's in the pack house." Dante said before cutting the mind link.

Nora sighed, waiting. She wanted to get up and move, but she still felt woozy.

She stared at the room; it was plain. No pictures or warmth in it. He seemed like he was all business all the time. Even his room seemed like it. She debated what she was doing here when the door was pushed slowly open. Nora looked at the door, confused. Dante was standing at the door, vibrating. His eyes were glowing blue, and Nora could tell he was on the verge of shift.

"Hunter." He growled, looking at her, his fang already merged.

Nora felt her neck, the necklace. She forgot to put it back on.

"It's ok. I am not going -

"Hunter!" Dante growled.

Nora heard his bone snapping. She needed to get out of here. Her eyes locked on the bathroom, and she raced towards it. Dante was in full wolf mode as he raced across the bedroom floor, trying to beat Nora to the door. The dark gray wolf threw his head at her slamming her into the dresser. Nora hit the dresser with a thud and sank to the floor. Dante's wolf slowly stalked her.

"Stop. I'm not here to cause any problems." Nora said, holding her hand out, trying to reason with the wolf.

Dante's wolf snarled, showing its teeth as it got close to her. Nora was looking around for a weapon.

"Stand the fuck down now!" Jace said, running into the room; the power in his voice echoed like thunder, radiating off the walls.

Dante's wolf whimpered at his presence but was still growling and advancing towards Nora. Jace's eyes glowed Cole's color as he stepped between Nora and Dante. Jace was on the verge of shifting to fight.

"Noah, give control back to Dante now." Jace growled, using his Alpha status.

Noah whimpered and put his head down, shaking lightly. The bone-snapping sound echoed in the room once more. A very naked Dante was in a place where the large gray wolf once was. Dante was breathing heavily, glaring at Jace.

"I told you to stand down." Jace yelled, the power rippling off of him, even Nora could feel.

"She's a hunter." Dante growled; his head hung in respect, but he was fighting the pull to obey.

"Yes, and my Mate. Your Luna." Jace growled back, stepping towards Dante.

"Luna. She can't be Luna. She's a hunter." Dante was trying hard not to cower to Jace, but he was losing.

Jace had his hand around Dante's throat and was pinning him against the wall in one quick movement, squeezing the air from his throat. Dante tried not to show any expression, but with him losing air slowly, he could only hide it for so long.

"I say she can. I am Alpha! Do you forget? Do you want to try to be? Do I need a new beta?" Jace growled as Dante's eyes began to roll back.

"Jace!" Nora shouted at him, standing up.

"Others would kill you right now." Jace growled, not hearing Nora.

He felt a hand on his arm as Nora stepped into his view.

"Stop." Nora said, putting her hand on his arm.

Jace clenched his jaw, fighting with himself not to give in to her calming touch. He let go of Dante, and he crashed into the fall. Dante was on the floor trying to breathe, his body shaking from almost losing consciousness. Dante cowered as he came to. Jace was still running hot. Nora stepped in front of Jace blocking his way from Dante.

"Go! Don't you dare say anything!" Jace's chest vibrated as he spoke.

Dante, stumbling, got up. He looked at Nora, confused, before quickly walking towards the door. He hung his head as he got to the door.

"Lucy." He said quietly at the door.

Nora saw Jace sigh, trying to calm himself down. She rubbed his arm, wanting him to feel better.

"I know….You owe Nora your life. Cole wanted to end you." Jace said his voice was sympathetic at first but then ice cold.

Dante nodded, walking out the door and shutting it behind him. Jace captures her chin with his hand looking down at her. His eyes were full of concern.

"Did he hurt you? Are you ok?" Jace asked, searching her face for pain.

"I'm fine." She answered, a wave of everything that just happened to hit her.

She had so many questions. What was Luna? Why was she it? What was a mate…like animals, mate. Then she felt anger. Why was every wolf hell-bent on killing?

"Are you all just one flip of a switch away from slaughtering people?" She asked angrily; the words just fell out of her mouth.

Jace looked at her, confused. She pulled her face out of his hands and stepped back. Another wave of anger hit her. Was this what happened to her family? Some dumb wolf smelt a hunter and went all kill zone on them. She glared at Jace when he didn't answer.

"Have you killed?" Nora asked, her hand in a fist at her side as she spoke hate in her words.

"Nora…Your necklace." Jace said, realizing why Dante knew she was here.

She needed to put that back on. He looked around the room and then walked into the bathroom. He felt relief as he saw it on the counter. He grabbed it and brought it out to her.

"Put this back on," Jace said, holding the necklace out to her.

"No. Let the next one come." Nora said, fire burning in her eyes as she squared off with him.

"Nora. Necklace." Jace ordered.

"Why do you care? What the hell is a mate or a Lune because it seems so important." Nora said, nearly yelling at him.

"Necklace." Jace growled, holding it up to her and stepping forward.

Nora yanked it out of his hand; her first thought was to throw it, but the image of the wolf from the alley popped into her head. If she left here, she would need it. She wasn't actually keen on spotting wolves yet. She gritted her teeth as she slipped it over her head. Glaring at him, she waited.

"Answers!" She screamed at him when he didn't answer.

"Nora!" Jace growled back, stepping towards her and trying to intimidate her.

She was done. No answers, no need to stay. She took off past him, heading to the door. Jace growled as she got closer to the door and began to follow her. She pulled open the door and saw Wyatt standing there.

"Hey, Nora. Good to see you up. I was coming to see how you were feeling." Wyatt said, confused, looking over her shoulder at a very pissed-off Jace.

"Great. Wonderful. I'm leaving." Nora announced.

"The hell you are." Jace growled from behind her.

"Nora, you're bleeding. Can I see?" Wyatt asked cautiously and not moving from the doorway.

"She's bleeding?" Jace said, the anger falling back.

Wyatt pointed at the blood spot on the t-shirt. Nora glanced to her shoulder, letting out a long sigh.

"I'm fine, thank you. I will go to a walk-in or something if I need to. Thank you for your help." Nora said, waiting for Wyatt to move.

"Please let me look at it." Wyatt said softly, pleading.

"Nora-" Jace started to say, but Nora whipped around to look at him, her eyes narrowed.

"I will let you look at it if someone answers my questions." She demanded.

"Fine, just come sit down." Jace said, his voice almost pleading.

Wyatt glanced at his Alpha. He had never seen someone glare at him and had never once seen him compromise with someone. He almost wanted to smile that this small, fragile-looking girl was not even afraid of the big bad wolf. Nora stomped back into the room and sat on the edge of the bed, annoyed. Wyatt followed her. He walked over and pulled her shirt to the side, looking at the wound. The shirt was so big on her that he simply moved it all to one side and could see the wound.

"Start talking. You know my questions." She said sharply to Jace.

Wyatt's eyes flickered to Jace. He watched him take a deep breath in and hold it. It looked like he was counting in his head to try not to snap back at Nora.

"A mate is something like soulmates but more powerful. We don't decide them. There is a powerful-

"Soulmate.' Nora repeated.

"Yes, that's the closest thing I can think of for humans to compare it to." Jace said.

"I don't even know you. You think I am your ....mate." Nora said, looking at him baffled.

"I don't think. I know. As I said, we don't control it. There is a force between us....I need you." Jace said, trying to explain it.

"An a Luna?" Nora asked, still processing.

"An Alpha's other half. They run the pack together as equals. The Luna is just as important to the pack as the Alpha." Jace explained.

"Have you killed-

"Yes." Jace answered by cutting her off.

"Have you killed a hunter's family?" Nora asked, finishing her sentence; her body began to tremble as she waited for the answer.

"Yes," Jace whispered.

"Why?" Nora's voice cracked as she asked it.

"Nora, it's a kill-or-be-killed thing between wolves and hunters. Do or die. They do the same once they discover a pack. I've never gone out of my way to kill a hunter and their family, but yes, I have." Jace said he didn't want to answer because he was afraid of what she would say or do, but he couldn't lie to her.

Nora was quiet after hearing that. She was trying to process everything he said, but the images of her family kept popping into her head. Then she imagined what Jace had done to other people's innocent families. She couldn't; she began to breathe faster. Wyatt pressed a little hard on her wound, causing her to flinch. She looked at him, and he drew her from her thoughts.

"Did you bump this?" Wyatt asked, trying to stir the conversation.

"Yes." She answered quietly.

"So the bleeding is just from you bumping it. It doesn't look like there's any further damage, but you need to take it easy. Don't use this arm a whole lot." Wyatt said.

"Ok," Nora said, nodding.

"There's some pain med-

"No, thank you," Nora responded to Wyatt cutting him off.

"Ok, they are there if you need them." Wyatt said softly.

"Is there anything else I can help with?" Wyatt asked, looking at Nora and then Jace.

"No." Jace said to him.

"I need some time alone." Nora said aloud, looking at Jace, letting him know she meant from him.

She watched him tense up and look like he wanted to argue with her. Wyatt broke the awkwardness.

"Well, I'm sure you haven't eaten. Alpha, why don't we go get her some food?" Watt suggested.

Jace grunted but nodded, walking to the doorway; he glanced at Nora before leaving. Wyatt nodded to her.

"Please take it easy." Wyatt said one last time before ducking out the door and leaving Nora alone with her thoughts.

Chapter Twenty Six
Past

      Kip sat outside the Black Sand territory, waiting for his cue; it wouldn't be long now. His pack had surrounded the territory. They didn't have enough warriors or men to really fight. The Alpha would either surrender or be taken by force. He would slaughter his pack members until one or the other happened. He waited until nightfall, and Kip sent the signal just as the stars peeked out. Screams erupted as his pack moved in, targeting homes and pulling people from their homes. The ones that fought back were instantly killed. Some of his wolves were setting houses on fire. It was pure chaos and war fair. Kip sat back, watching it all like he was watching a movie with pure joy on his face. The screams, the smell of smoke and blood, all of it sent him into bliss. Twenty minutes. That's all it took. Twenty minutes of attempting to defend themself, and it was all over.

      " Alpha, he will surrender on one condition."

      "Which is?" Kip responded back.

      "That you won't harm any more of his pack members."

      "Oh, all right, tell him to give up."

      "I have him, Alpha."

      "Good, burn the rest of it down."

      "Alpha?"

"I didn't say burn his pack members, just their homes." Kip chuckled.

"Understood."

"Threaten the beta. Let him know if he tries to contact the council, his Alpha will die, and then we will come back and finish this here. Also, if any of this gets to Jace, the same thing will happen. Tell them just to move on or join us either way." Kip ordered.

"Yes Alpha."

Kip cut the mindlink off and waited. He was excited that everything was going according to plan. Kip felt like a kid on Christmas morning as he saw Chadwick the Alpha of Black Sands being dragged to him. Chadwick was a tall, slender man with long blond hair that was braided down his back.

"Chadwick! It's been too long." Kip said, walking over to him.

"Not long enough, Kip. What is the meaning of this? We have never had any problems. My pack is peaceful." Chadwick responded, confused.

"Exactly, your pack is weak and mindless. A poor excuse for our species. You're lucky I don't go wipe them out: " Kip growled.

"Kip-" Chadwick began.

"Don't worry; I have use for you." Kip laughed, motioning for his men to take him away.

"Bring him straight to the lab. I want to get the next batch of them going." Kip said happily as he walked to his car.

Jace made his way into the kitchen; his mind stuck on the conversation he just had with Nora. His chest was tight as he kept replaying the look on her face when she asked if he had killed before. Dante standing in the corner of the kitchen, caught his attention. He gritted his jaw. He didn't want to interact with him right now. He saw Dante debate with himself.

"Not now," Jace said to him as Dante flinched closer to him.

"Do you not understand why?" Dante blurted out.

"Yes, I do. I know what you went through." Jace said, grabbing the leftover pizza from the fridge.

"Then why?' Dante said, coming to the counter, as Jace popped the pizza into the microwave.

"You know why." Jace growled.

"The Moonlight pack will be here tonight." Dante reminded him before he hung his head and walked out of the kitchen as the microwave began to beep.

Jace sighed, grabbing the pizza and heading up to the room. He hesitated in front of the door. He wasn't sure what to expect from her when he went back in. He opened the door and stepped into the room. Nora was pacing the floor. He made a face that said that is not resting. She stopped seeing him. She still looked angry. He set the pizza down. He caught her eyeing it but then turned her back to him.

"I need you to explain." Nora said, looking out the window.

"Explain …." Jace asked her quietly.

"Explain why. Why do you have to kill hunters?" Nora asked, turning around.

"It's been going on since before I existed. I only know the wolf side. From what I was told, when the first person was cursed or blessed, whichever way you want to look at it, their first shift was terrible. You have to imagine the transformation and not have anyone to help you through it. Unfortunately, there were many casualties. The casualties continued. They didn't know how to control their wolf or their urges. Humans then hunted them, finding packs and wiping them completely out. Then it turned into the kill or be killed seranio. Dante. The rage and anger you saw. He watched his family slaughter. His younger sister cut down in front of him. He was left for dead. " Jace explained.

Nora winced at Dante's past. She knew it and felt it. Although she didn't see her family killed, walking into the scene was just as horrific. She looked at Jace, studying him.

"How many families have you killed?" Nora asked him, not knowing if she really wanted to answer.

"When I was younger, my father would cause these wars. I never knew if they were hunting us or if we were hunting them. A lot of them blur together; he would drive the pack forcing us to train constantly and fight constantly. We were always waging war against them. I have no clue how many hunters' dens we attacked or attacked us. I couldn't tell you how many people died. A hunter killed my mother, and my father turned into this warlord." Jace said there was pain in his voice when he spoke about his mother.

"When you became Alpha, how many?" Nora asked.

"Two." Jace said quietly.

"Why?" Nora asked if she could feel her stomach knotting up.

"The hunter that killed Dante's whole family and another hunter that kept attacking us." Jace explained.

"You killed the whole family." Nora asked, her voice cracking as she spoke.

Jace sighed, sitting down and rubbing his face with his hand before looking at Nora.

"Yes, but it wasn't like we killed women and children. It was three grown men brothers trying to eliminate wolves." Jace explained, trying to make it sound better.

"My family was murdered by a wolf…because of me. It's not like my family, or I knew. You literally watched me turn into a hunter in that alley. My family knew nothing about this word, yet their throats were ripped out. Even my brother. He wasn't even out of elementary school yet." Nora said her breathing became fast, and her voice cracked.

Jace was up and across the room in seconds. He pulled her into his chest, cradling her. She didn't fight him; his warmth made her feel calm as she tried to slow her breathing. Warm tears spilled down her face as she felt sick. Jace didn't know what to do. He rubbed her back as she pulled herself together.

"Is that pizza?" She asked.

Jace laughed upon hearing her comment; his laugh was deep and warm. Nora chuckled too at her comment, his own laughter contagious.

"Yeah, why don't you sit down, and I'll bring it over here." Jace chuckled, stepping away from her.

Nora nodded and climbed into the bed, pulling the blanket up around her. She scooted over so Jace could sit next to her as he brought the pizza. He handed her a slice and watched her eyes light up. Her stomach growled as she took the pizza. She didn't realize how hungry she was. Jace laughed, grabbing the remote and turning on the tv. He began flipping through the channels. Nora perked up, seeing something she liked.

"Oh, that." She said, putting her hand on his arm as she scooted closer.

He wrapped his arm around her. This was the first time in the longest that he felt peaceful and normal. He grabbed a piece of pizza and enjoyed the moment.

"Tonight, I am having another Alpha come here. I need to build stronger alliances. Just make sure this necklace stays around your neck." Jace said to the top of her head.

"Why do you need stronger alliances?" She asked, eyeballing him suspiciously.

"There's an Alpha who is crossing lines, and it's becoming too much. I need to ensure that if anything happens, I will have the support from other Alpha's incase we need to put anyone back in their place." Jace said, his voice getting stern talking about it.

She nodded, not realizing she agreed to stay, and she really had not thought past eating pizza yet. She had more questions, but she didn't want to ruin the moment. She was enjoying the simplicity of this all.

Chapter Twenty Seven
Trapped

Kip made his way down to the lab. He was in such a good mood that he was humming as he walked down the stairwell. He met Taylor at the control station. He scanned the monitors looking for the room holding Chadwick. He grinned, spotting it. Although he was a weaker Alpha, it had taken several people to keep him contained. Two nurses had come limping out of the room, and one male nurse was dead. They sedated him slightly and now had him hooked up to the blood pumps. They would slowly be taken blood out to ensure he would be able to stay alive and produce more blood for Kip's experiments.

"How much blood did you want to use this time?"Taylor asked him cautiously.

"Let's do 100 milliliters for the first three and then 50 for the rest." Kip said to increase the amounts drastically.

"Did you want to do all of them or just one right now?" Taylor asked; he was worried they didn't have enough people for when things went bad.

"All of them….ahh well, let's start with the 100 milliliters and see what that does first." Kip said excitedly.

Taylor nodded, and a rush of relief went over him. He was positive they would destroy the lab or get out if they did more than two at a time. The last time they attempted to turn several they did that, many nurses, guards, and other wolves were killed. Kip didn't even bat an eye. They were casualties of war.

"Bring the college student into exam two. 100 milliliters of blood for him." Taylor said, pressing the button in the center and speaking into the speaker.

He saw two guards look up at the monitor and nod as they began moving to get the college student. They dragged him kicking and screaming into exam two, strapping him down to the table. The poor guy was yelling and asking what was going on. A nurse stepped in with nothing spoken. He begged the nurse to talk to him as she injected him with the blood. She looked at the monitor.

"Ready, Alpha." She said before leaving the room.

Kip was excited as she stepped away from the control station and unto room two. He walked into the room, studying the boy. The blood was starting to make him sick; he kept gagging. Kip noted the reaction; that was a first. They normally didn't even notice or react when the blood was injected. Kip walked over with a cruel smile; maybe this one would be different. He leaned over and bit the boy on his arm.

"What the hell is wrong with you? What is going on? You can't be doing this!" He yelled after Kip bit him.

Kip laughed hysterically as he stepped back from the boy. The boy stared at him, confused, and then he let out another yell, and his body convulsed. Kip smiled proudly as to how quickly it was working.

He stepped outside the door, sealing it, watching from the window in the door. He needed this to work.

Logan stared at the gate of the wolf community. If that wolf thought he was going just to let him take Nora and not hear from him, he had another thing coming. He sat in his car not far from the entrance trying to figure out a way in. He took note of two guards. They would know right away he was a hunter; they always did. He was setting himself up for a fight if he went and just asked to be let in. He was too busy focused on the gate and coming up with a plan and didn't see Drake coming up the side of his car. Drake opened the passenger side door causing Logan to jump a mile.

"Dude, what the fuck!" Logan yelled, slamming his fist into Logan's upper arms.

"Hey, nice to see you too." Drake said, rubbing his arm and giving Logan a dirty look.

"Yeah, well, you scared me." Logan said, rolling his eyes.

"No shit, and you should be this kind of death wish sitting outside the wolf's compound, inches away from two wolves that could call for backup and rip you to pieces." Drake rattled out, looking at the gate.

"Yeah, I know." Logan said softly.

"Well, what's the plan, Romeo." Drake laughed.

"That's the problem; this is how far my plan got me." Logan said to Drake.

"Well, you wanna just go ask to be let in?" Drake smirked.

"Sure, what the hell." Logan thought about throwing his car into drive and heading towards the gate.

" Alpha. Alpha. Alpha!" The mind link finally reached Jace; he had fallen asleep wrapped up with Nora.

She was resting quietly next to him. Her arms wrapped around his stomach; he smiled softly. Then frowned, remembering the mindlink.

" Go ahead." He replied back.

"Um, we got a weird situation here at the front gate. Two hunters are demanding to talk to the Alpha, and someone named Nora?" The mind link sounds confused.

Damn it. He knew that dumb ass wouldn't stay away. He glanced down at Nora, trying to find a way to detangle himself from her without waking her. He tried moving her arm off of him. She grumbled and held on tighter. He tried scooting away, but that wasn't helping. He quickly pulled her arm off of him and moved away. That worked.

"Coming." He responded back to the mindlink.

Jace began walking to the door when he heard Nora sigh and sit up. She stretched and then looked around her eyes, asking him where he was going. He made a face.

"Your hunter friends are here. Stay here." He said, annoyed.

"Which one? And why can't I come?" Nora said, not really asking, as she got off the bed and began walking to the door.

"You're hurt and need to stay put. I don't need anything else happening to you." He said firmly.

"They won't hurt me." Nora said, confused, and went to walk around him.

Jace put his arm up, blocking the doorway. Nora narrowed her eyes at his anger flashing in them.

"Look, you don't tell me where I can and can't go." She said, squaring up to him.

'You're not going.' He said, putting himself between her in the door.

"You're funny." She said with a smile and went to move around him.

Jace bent over and picked her up. Before she knew it, she was over his shoulder. She let out a surprised yell but then became angry. She hit him hard in the middle of his back. It didn't phase him. He flopped her down on the bed and moved to the door. She yelled furiously as she was back up on her feet quickly. She didn't make it, though. He was out the door, and the door closed in her face.

"Jace, open this fucking door!" She screamed, banging her fist on it as she tried to pull it open.

She heard Jace start talking to someone who was out in the hall.

"Who is that, and why is she here?" The female voice snarled.

"Rosie, you need to chill out and be on your way." Jace said threateningly.

She heard something snap on the other side of the door. Something metal dropped on the other side of the door, and she heard his footsteps walking away.

"Jace! Jace!" She yelled, slamming her fist once more. She heard a giggle on the other side of the door.

"Hello?" Nora said, confused.

"Looks like you're stuck. He broke the door handle off." A girl's voice came through the door.

"Can you help me out? " Nora asked.

"Why would I go against my Alpha? Who are you, and why are you in his room?" The voice asked for a hint of jealousy in it.

"I'm Nora, and I don't want to be. Are you gonna help me out or not, whoever you are." Nora said, getting annoyed.

"Rose, what will you do if I help you?" Rose asked slyly.

"I'm freaking leaving. Screw that asshole." Nora said, looking around the room, trying to find another way out.

"Perfect. You have two options. The window is on the third floor, so take your chances with that. Or use your brain, dear, and take the door off the hinges." Rose said her voice was coy.

"Thank you." Nora said, walking over to his closet.

The window was too high, and her wound was still killing her. The door was coming down. She needs something to shove in the hinges to knock the screw out and something to whack it with. She began searching his closet. She found a pair of steel toe boots. She was really hoping for tools, but she might be able to use the heel like a hammer. It had metal in it. She then looked around the room. She saw his desk and began searching through that. She found a metal envelope opener. It was slender, and she could definitely use it like a Phillips head screwdriver.

"Try to lock me in." She grumbled, walking over to the door.

She kneeled and jammed the envelope opener into the bottom hinge. She then proceeded to hit the bottom of the envelope opener with the heel of the boot. After several wacks, the screw popped out from the hinge. She did the same to the top and felt so proud of herself when the top screw fell and hit the floor. She smirked at the door.

"Bye-bye, door." Nora grinned and kicked the door.

The door fell forward with a slam as it hit the ground. She stepped over it and began walking out.

Chapter Twenty Eight
Mine

Jace pulled in his car in front of the gate, his headlights illuminating the iron. He saw Logan standing outside the car with another man leaning against the car. He watched Logan stand up straight as Jace approached the gate. He nodded to the men at the gate to open it. The gate creaked open as Jace waited for Logan to approach them.

"Where is she?" Logan demanded.

"She's safe." Jace said through his teeth.

"Kinda hard to see or trust that Wolf." Logan glared at him.

"I wouldn't hurt her. She is safe. What do you want?" Jace growled.

"To see Nora." Logan said angrily.

"I said she's fine." Jace said, stepping towards him.

The guards from his pack left the stand and came to stand behind Jace. Their eyes glowing, just waiting to be told they could shift. Drake came away from the car, standing directly behind Logan in case anything happened. Logan took a deep breath and stepped forward.

"And I said I want to see her." Logan said, squaring off with Jace.

Jace stepped towards Logn miminicking, his move trying to be intimidating. They both were staring each other down. Logan flexed his shoulders; all the muscles down his arms tensioned and showed how cut his arms were. Jace smirked at the act and straightened up; his chest and shoulders flexed as he also showed off his muscles. The anger rolling off both of them made the air around them thick with tension. Just when it looked like they were going to start fighting, a car pulled up at the gate. They both stopped and looked at the car. Logan was worried it might be more back up but judging by Jace's confused look, he assumed he didn't call them.

The door swung open of the red car, and Nora stepped out. Logan relaxed, and Jace looked angry. A big smile came across Logan's face seeing her. Nora walked up to the gate with a smirk on her face that she purposely put there to piss Jace off more. She walked over to them and paused.

"Hi, boys; having a pissing contest, are we?" Nora announced, reaching them.

"How did you get out of the room? I thought I told you to rest." Jace asked her through his teeth.

"Yeah, I have a problem with being told what to do." Nora smirked.

"Out of the room. Did he lock you up?" Logan said, angry.

"Don't worry about it, Logan." Nora said calmly.

"Nora, are you ok?" Logan asked, concerned.

"I'm good." Nora nodded.

"Your chest?" Logan said, stepping forward as if he was going to look at it.

Jace growled and stepped in the way of Logan, blocking his way from Nora. Nora groaned at the two of them, but they completely ignored her, just becoming angry with each other.

"Nora, let's go. You can come back to the society. It's safer there." Logan said, looking at Jace as he spoke.

"She's not going anywhere. That's my mate." Jace said, tensing up; Cole flashed in his eyes at the sound of someone trying to take his mate.

The two guards shifted slightly forward, preparing for a fight. Drake was ready as well. Logan and Jace were locked in a staring contest, and then it happened. Logan shoved Jace.

"She's not a freaking wolf. She's coming with me." Logan said as she shoved Jace.

"I said she's not." Jace said, cranking his fist back.

Nora stepped in between them; as she did, she saw Jace's face turn worried as he released his fist. His fist was heading straight for her face. The world went silent, and everything began to go slow. Nora grabbed Jace's arm and turned it so it would miss Logan. She then ducked and elbowed Logan in the stomach. She watched him in slow motion, wince, and start to bring his hands to his gut. Nora brought her fist forward, hitting Jace in his chest. She stood up straight as the world snapped back into motion.

Logan fell over, holding his stomach, and Jace fell backwards, letting out a groan. They both looked up at Nora, confused about how everything went down. They didn't understand how she just did all that.

"No one decides where I go or what I do. I don't belong to either of you." Nora said, kicking them both in the shins before walking away.

"Nora!" Jace yelled, trying to get up.

"Nora!" Logan yelled as he watched Nora walk over to his car.

She had planned on stealing it as she approached Drake. Drake threw his hands up as if to say don't hurt me. He backed away from the car, leaving room for her to get in. She was about to enter when a bright blue car pulled up beside her. The window rolled down. Her bright pink highlights were the first thing Nora saw.

"Hey girl, need a lift?" Lilly smiled at her. Nora smiled back.

" Yes, please!" Lilly unlocked her door, and Nora hopped in.

Lilly threw her car in reserve and sped off. Nora looked back at Logan and Jace getting off the ground. The confused and angry look on both their faces made her smile. She rolled down the window and flipped both of them off. Lilly saw the gesture and began laughing.

"I really like you." Lilly stated.

"I'm not going back to the hunter club just yet." Nora said, eyeing Lilly wondering what her intentions were.

"No worries. I won't take you anywhere you don't want to go." Lilly said with a smile.

"Thanks for grabbing me." Nora said.

"No worries, I decided we were friends, so friends save friends. I followed Logan to make sure his dumbass didn't get himself killed. Everything looks like it will be fine. They're just fighting over you." Lilly laughed.

"Yeah, I got that. I don't know how to feel about that, really." Nora said, slightly annoyed.

"No judgment here. I have a place we can go until you decide what you wanna do." Lily smiled.

"That sounds great. Do you mind if I use your phone to check in with my friend Joel?" Nora asked, realizing she still hadn't found her phone.

"Yeah, no problem," Lilly said, handing her the phone.

"Thanks." Nora said, taking it and dialing Joel.

Logan hit his car with his fist as he ignored Jace, who seemed unsure of what to do. Logan was happy Lilly scooped her but upset that Nora didn't choose to go with him. Logan glared at Jace before nodding to Drake and getting in his car. Maybe they could catch up if they were quick enough. Logan hopped in the driver's seat and sped off.

"Alpha." Jace heard the mind link and wanted to snap.

Cole was flipping out and wanted to chase down his mate.

"What." Jace snapped back.

"We have a problem." Adam's voice was soft as he said the words through mind link.

*"There's always a fucking problem!"*Jace groweled back.

"What is it?" Jace demanded in the next breath.

" Someone attacked the Black Sands Pack, and their Alpha is missing. Also, the Moonlight Pack and their Alpha are about forty-five minutes out." Adam blurted out as quickly as he could.

"Great. A blue car just left this parking lot. Do your thing and track it. I want its location as soon as you know. I need to prepare for the meeting. Tell Ryan to go to the Black Sands Pack and discover everything that happened. I want as much information as possible and quickly. I want it for my meeting with Alpha Zeke. I feel like it was Kip." Jace demanded.

"Yes, Alpha." Adam said as the mind link ended.

Jace sighed, walking back to his car and peeling out from the gate.

Rose had been watching the whole scene go down, laughing as she watched. Then the word Mate fell out of Jace's mouth, and she felt her insides crush. Mate! He called her his mate. Why was that human his mate? I should be his mate! She screams internally.

From that moment, she knew what she had to do. She needed to get rid of her. She would find a way to end her, and in Jace's sorrow, she would comfort him and be his second chance. Rose had a plan. She took off to her home, forming a plan in her head as she walked.

Chapter Twenty Nine
Gone

Jace walked into his office, slamming the door. He shut his eyes and took a deep breath in. He was fighting hard to gain control of himself. Everything in him was telling him to get in his car and hunt her down.

"Jace?" Dante's voice came from the other side of the room.

"She left." Jace said, gritting his teeth as if it was painful to say.

"What? Where did she go?" Dante asked, getting up.

"I'm not sure." Jace said, pinching his nose, trying to calm the headache.

"Well, let's go bring her back." Dante said, looking at him with determination.

"I fucking want to, but I can't right now," Jace said, frustrated.

"Fuck that! Let's go." Dante said, grabbing his keys.

"Why do you care? You should be happy she's gone; she's a hunter." Jace growled at him.

"Hunter or not, she's your mate. You're my best friend and Alpha. I might be able to get past the hunter thing. She's going to be my Luna. Her place is by your side." Dante said fiercely.

"There's so much going on right now. The Black Sands pack was attacked, and Chadwick is missing. Zeke will be here any minute to discuss Kip, and hopefully, we will get his backing. Nora doesn't know anything about being a hunter or us wolves. Cole is obsessed with keeping her with him. I have to keep fighting for control." Jace said, sitting down, you could see the glimpse of exhaustion, Jace was struggling.

"She didn't know she was a hunter? Didn't her family prepare her?" Dante asked, confused.

"Her family is dead, she came home, and they were slaughtered. She has a scar on her throat I haven't asked her about. I'm assuming the wolf who killed her family did it and left her for dead." Jace said with anger in his voice.

Dante felt his chest tighten. He knew exactly what she felt. The roles were reserved but he watched his family die and was also left for dead. Right then and there, the girl had won his allegiance.

"I will go find her." Dante said, getting up.

"Dante sit; you were wolfing out the last time she saw you. Adam is supposed to be tracking her. We need to prepare for Zeke." Jace said, trying to get his thoughts together.

"Honestly, I think we just need to show them the bodies." Dante said, shrugging.

"A real Alpha will want all the proof before making his pack choose a side to stand. We most likely will be taking on the council as well. There is much more at stake." Jace explained.

He went over to his desk and opened the bottom drawer. A safe was inside. He pressed the code into the keypad, and the door popped open.

Jace pulled out a file; he sighed, sitting back in his chair. This was everything he had.

"Ryan?" Jace mind linked him, frustrated.

"Yes, Alpha?" Ryan sent back.

"What's going on?" Jace asked impatiently.

"I'm bringing back the Beta. Try to stall Zeke until I get there. He's all the proof we need to show Kip is behind this." Ryan said a hint of excitement in his voice.

" We will be waiting on you." Jace sent back.

"Thank you, Alpha." Ryan said proudly.

" Adam?" Jace said switching gear, he needed to know where she was.

"Alpha, she's at a little cafe with a hunter girl. They're having dessert. All is good here."Adam said keeping it short.

" Name of the place?" Jace asked impatiently.

" Mama's" Adam answered quickly, trying not to upset his Alpha.

" Keep me updated." Jace sent, cutting mind link off.

"Jace?" Dante asked, seeing his eyes gloss over.

"Ryan is bringing the Beta of the Black Sand pack; he said he is all the proof we need to prove Kip is behind the attacks. Adam found Nora; she's at a little cafe." Jace said, relaxing slightly.

"Awesome." Dante smiled.

"Maybe we move this to the dining room and have food. We might need to stall this out until Ryan can get him here." Jace said thinking out loud.

"Got it. I will start getting the kitchen ready." Dante nodded, walking out of the office.

Jace leaned further back in his chair, shutting his eyes, trying to calm Cole.

Soon. one thing at a time. He told his wolf.

"So wanna tell me how you knocked Logan. and that hunk of a man on their asses." Lilly chuckled

"Hunk of a man? Jace?" Nora asked, slicing her spoon through her cheesecake.

"Yes, do you not have eyeballs? His muscles have muscles. Girl, he is stunning." Lilly said, taking a long sip from her coffee.

"Yeah, well, his attitude isn't." Nora said, rolling her eyes.

"Yeah, well, wolves tend to be emotional. Doesn't change his hotness." Lilly said with a shrug.

"He locked me in his room but snapped off his door handle. Hotness isn't everything." Nora said, giving Lilly a weird look.

"He could lock me in his room." Lilly said, raising her eyebrows at Nora.

"Perv." Nora laughed.

"But for real, how did you knock them both on their butts? Then I need to know how you escaped." Lilly said, adding more sugar to her coffee.

"I took the door off the hinges." Nora smirked wickedly.

"That is amazing. Imagine him going up to his room, and the door's gone! Oh my god, I want to see it." Lilly laughed.

"Yeah, I bet it will be pretty funny." Nora chuckled.

"So about me knocking them down. Is it a hunter thing that everything goes like in slow motion? It only happens during fights." Nora said, studying Lilly's face as she asked it.

"No. We're stronger, hear and see better. Have better reflexes, but no, we can't slow down time or anything. What do you mean?" Lilly asked.

"Ok, so when I was sparring with Kat, she went to punch me, and literally, as the punch was coming at me, everything went in slow motion. I could move at normal speed, but everything around me slowed. Then again, when I stepped in between Jace and Logan. So I used it to my advantage; I stirred Jace's punch away from Logan and hit them both in their guts. Everything snapped back into real-time as soon as I was out of danger. It's weird." Nora told Lilly, who looked like she was concentrating the more Nora spoke.

"What's your last name?" Lilly asked quietly.

"Chastel." Nora answered, confused.

"I need to call Drake to find out more information, but I remember an old story or legend about the original hunter's having abilities." Lilly said, pulling out her phone and began dialing.

Nora reached across the table and stopped her.

"Lilly, wait, I don't want any more drama. My world is way too overwhelmed." Nora said, panicking.

"Ok, ok. Let me just ask him about the legend. I won't say anything about you. Promise." Lilly said.

Nora looked at her for two more long seconds, and she nodded, taking her hand off Lilly's phone. Lilly picked her phone back up and began dialing. Nora watched her and listened as she got a hold of Drake.

"Hey, Drake, remember that legend about the original hunters?" Lilly said.

"Yeah, that's their last name." Lilly asked.

"Thank you….Yeah, she's ok. Where at Mama's." Lilly said.

"Ok, see you later ... .Am Gasit-O." Lilly said as she clicked off the phone.

Nora looked at her, confused, hearing her speak another language at the end of the conversation. Nora waited for Lilly to explain, but she didn't.

"What did he say?" Nora asked.

"That he's gonna look it up and get back to me," Lilly said with a shrug taking a sip of her coffee.

"What was the end piece? you spoke in another language." Nora asked suspiciously.

"Oh, it's how we say goodbye. I'm going to go get the check." Lilly smiled at her getting up.

"Am Gasit-O." Nora repeated out loud, watching Lilly walk away.

She shut her eyes and repeated the saying, trying to see if she knew it. She shut her eyes and sat it tiring to see if she knew it. All of a sudden, she got a sudden jolt. It meant, I found her. Nora's eyes grew wide as she watched Lilly talk to the waitress. Why did she lie? Nora didn't know why, but she got a feeling that she needed to get out of there. She looked across the table, and Lilly's keys were sitting there. Nora snatched them. She slid out of her seat and began making her way to the back exit. Lilly saw her leaving.

"Nora? Hey Nora, wait!" Lilly called, starting to come after her.

Nora bolted. Racing towards the back door, Lilly quickly caught up. Nora reached for the door handle just as Lily was reaching to grab her shoulder. Then it happened; Nora grinned. The world began to slow down as Lilly reached for her. Nora turned slightly, now facing Lilly. She pushed Lilly back away from her and then slid the booth next to her in front of Lilly and the door. Nora smiled as she pushed the door open, and everything snapped back into real-time. Lilly was flung backwards, hitting the floor. Lilly looked up from the ground, confused, as Nora was nowhere in sight. She heard her car's engine flip on and the car peel out. Lilly groaned, getting up. She flipped open her phone, dialing Drake.

"She got away; she's in my car!" Lilly said into the phone.

Logan snatched the phone away from Drake, hearing what she said.

"What did you do? What did you say to her?" Logan growled.

"Nothing." Lilly said angrily.

"You probably scared her." Logan said, matching her anger.

"Well, now she's not just someone you like. She's actually someone we need to go find her!" Lilly yelled.

"Don't fucking talk to me like that; You've gone and fucked this up. Call Mina to come get your ass." Logan ordered.

He and Drake were not too far from the diner. They knew Lilly's car and could easily track it. Logan hoped she didn't lose her trust in him because of Lilly's stupidity.

Chapter Thirty
Taken

"Ok, ready!" Dante said excitedly, on the verge of pulling Jace into the dining room.

Jace raised an eyebrow walking into the dining room. On the table was a spread of appetizers. There was shrimp, asparagus wrapped in bacon, charcuterie board, and fresh fruit. Dante watched Jace look at the table. He smiled brightly, doing a tada stance.

"Then the main course will be Lamb chops with scalloped potatoes and glazed carrots. Dessert will be trimusie." Dante said proudly.

"I forgot you love to cook." Jace laughed, grabbing a handful of grapes and popping them in his mouth.

"Yup, I'm the whole package. Dashingly handsome, a badass werewolf, and an amazing chef. I have no clue why I'm still single." Dante grinned.

"You forgot Playboy, and that's why you're single." Jace laughed, shoving him as he went to try some of the shrimp.

"Pssh, judgemental much." Dante laughed and then whacked his hand away from the shrimp.

"Hey, don't forget who the Alpha is." Jace said, going to snatch the plate of shrimp.

"You can wait, Mr. Alpha. I didn't cook all this, so you can eat it all before company comes." Dante said, placing his hands on his hips.

"Do you hear yourself?" Jace laughed, rolling his eyes at him.

A knock on the front door stopped. They were joking around. It was time. Jace took a deep breath and quickly changed his composure to serious. He nodded to Dante to stay put, and he heard the door. Pulling open the door, Matt accompanied the Moonlight Pack Alpha Zeke.

"Zeke, it's good to see you. Thank you for coming to meet me." Jace said, extending his hand.

"Jace. I'm intrigued to see what you have to say." Zeke said, taking his hand and shaking it.

"Come this way; we have some food in the dining room. We can eat and go over business." Jace said, leading the way.

"Hi, I need to get a message to Alpha Kip immediately." Rosie said in a quiet voice.

She had walked to the outer part of the woods near her house so no one could hear her. She placed a call into the Red Woods pack. She knew Kip would hunt down and kill Jace's mate in no time just to inflict pain. It would work out perfectly. Jace would be crushed, and she could help him pick up the pieces. She would be a much more fitting Luna.

"No one speaks to the Alpha." The voice came across the phone.

"It's regarding Alpha Jace. It's information he's going to want." Rosie said like she was holding on to the best-kept secret.

There was silence on the other end of the phone. She waited several seconds and when she thought the person had hung up another voice came across the phone.

"This is Alpha Kip; who the hell are you, and what information do you have on Jace?" Kip said his voice sounded angry and irritated.

"Alpha Jace has a mate." Rosie said, throwing out her hook.

"Does he now? And why would you be so willing to let this information out?" Kip's voice changed into a very interesting one.

"Her name is Nora; she is a human. My Alpha doesn't need a weakling. The pack doesn't need a weak Luna." Rosie said bitterly.

"A human. Oh, how perfect. What's your name, girl?" Kip asked as if he was already coming up with a plan.

"It's Rose or Rosie, whichever." Rosie said, annoyed.

"I might be of use to you if you ever wanna change sides. Someone who is willing to go behind their alpha's back I could use in certain situations." Kip chuckled.

"I'm trying to protect my pack," Rosie said defensively.

"It sounds like you're jealous, but I'll take what I can get. What's this human girl's name?" Kip laughed at her comment.

"Nora. That's all I know. She's got dark hair, young. Maybe in her twenties. She took off from Jace this morning." Rosie said, trying to ignore the comment he made about her being jealous.

"Well, Rose or Rosie, thank you for the information. I will take care of your problem. Maybe at some point in the future, you can help me out." Kip said to her, and the line went dead.

Rose felt her stomach knot; what did she just do? She was happy that Nora, the human girl, would be gone, but how did she just make herself in debt to Kip? She looked around cautiously, making sure no one was around before making her way home.

Kip clicked off the phone, a sinister smile on his face as he looked across at Taylor. He chuckled. He couldn't help it; he had just got the best information he could receive. The one person who would stand in his way. The one person who didn't have any weakness now had the biggest one of all. A human mate. A fragile human mate. He was going to crush Jace in no time and then take over his pack as well.

"Taylor, get the boys searching for a girl named Nora. She's in her twenties. That's all I know; get on it and fast. I want her here now." Kip smiled, glancing down at the monitors and the timer on the screen.

The first human has not shifted yet. It had been fifteen minutes since he had bitten him; they were waiting to see how the shift would go. If he could get this calculated right and crush Jace. He could conquer all the packs.

Nora peeled out of the parking lot, looking back in the rearview mirror, hoping no one was following her. She didn't know what was going on, but it didn't feel right. She didn't know what their intentions were. She apparently needed to know more about herself and her family. She raced down the road, eagerly checking over her shoulder and the rearview as she drove along. A paranoid thought entered her mind. What if they could track her with the car? She needed to ditch the car somewhere. She kept driving till she found a dark side road. She pulled the car into the alley. She turned the car off, double-checking her surroundings before getting out of the car. She tossed the keys on the seat. She walked out of the alley and onto the street, trying to blend in. She didn't know what to do right now. She didn't trust the hunters, and Jace was a little controlling. She worried about going to Joel's, not wanting to drag him into this any further. She sighed to herself, walking. She was giving herself a headache trying to figure out her next move.

The air was cold as the sun was just starting to set. She kept looking over her shoulders as if expecting someone to come up behind her and grab her or something. She rounded a corner, still trying to decide what to do. The hunters didn't know where she lived so she could go home but finding out where someone lived was easy. She pulled her hoody around her as she walked. A yellow car pulled up beside her. Nora froze, ready to fight the world if she had to. The window rolled down, and Nora, for some reason, looked down into the car.

"Hey, do you know where Knight Street is? I've been circling the block for like what feels like an hour now. My GPS is all screwed up." A man with light brown hair and green eyes said, flashing her a perfect smile.

"Yeah, if you go back two streets and take a right, it should be the second left." Nora said, relaxing a little bit.

"Sorry, I couldn't hear you. Could you say it again?" The man asked, pulling out a pen like he was going to write it down.

Nora smiled and stepped to the car, leaning on the window a little bit so he could hear her.

"Yeah, if you go back two streets back and take a right-

"Wait, hold on, you're going too fast." He said, leaning closer to her.

Nora leaned into the car more, talking louder this time; the man held up his finger, trying to get her to stop. Nora stopped and then thought of something easier.

"Hey, why don't I just write it." Nora began to say.

She felt a sharp pain in her arm and looked down. The man had reached over and stabbed her with the pen. The world started getting dark as Nora tried backing away from the car. She fell on her butt sitting on the curb. She heard the man's car door open. He walked around to her, scooping her up in his arms. She tried to fight but couldn't move any of her limbs. He popped the door open and set her in the passenger seat.

"Safety first." He laughed as he buckled her in.

She heard him get into the driver's seat. She tried seeing what he was doing, but her lids were getting heavy. As they were closing, she heard him say.

"I got her." and the world went dark.

Chapter Thirty One
Alliance

Alpha Zeke walked into the dining room, eyeing the food. He looked a little surprised, and a smirk came across his face.

"Was I supposed to bring a date?" Zeke asked, looking at his beta.

"No dates needed; we just figured to make it more casual instead of right to business. It's been a while since our packs have sat down, and food improves everything." Dante said, coming out of the kitchen.

"He's right, Alpha. We should do things more this way." Zeke's Beta said.

"Zeke and Levi, make yourself comfortable." Jace motioned for them to sit down.

Levi sat down and began filling his plate with appetizers. Dante chuckled, sitting down opposite him. While Jace and Zeke sat at the heads of the table. Lori brought out drinks from the kitchen. Zeke took a long sip of his while Levi and Dante ate. It was quiet as if they were all waiting for Jace to start the conversation as to why they were here. Jace cleared his throat as the main course was brought out.

"As you know, Kip has always lived on the edge of breaking the laws. Recently He has been letting his wolves run wild. He's letting them attack in the open. Last week he slaughtered a whole theater.

I've been playing damage control for months now and speaking with the council, which has done nothing." Jace said, pausing.

" *Matt brings in my documents from the office, and they are on my desk." Jace mind linked Matt.*

Zeke and Levi waited, seeing Jace's eyes gloss over. Within A few seconds, Matt walked in holding a folder. Jace nodded to Matt to give the folder to Zeke.

"If you want to review the documentation, I've been keeping it all in there. It's getting harder and harder to cover up his attacks as he becomes more and more reckless." Jace continued.

Zeke opened the folder and began reading. Levi watched his Alpha intently, trying to get a read on what he was feeling. Zeke looked up after skimming through the documents.

"What did the council say when you reported it to them?" Zeke asked cautiously as he slid the folder over to Levi, who picked it up and began studying it.

"They said in their findings they didn't find Kip breaking any laws or endangering wolf kind." Jace said, annoyed.

Zeke waited for Levi to finish looking through the documents. Jace could tell they were speaking through mindlink because of their eyes. After a long pause, Zeke looked back at Jace.

"Jace, I'm sure you have more than just this to show me if you called me here." Zeke said, trying to read Jace as he spoke.

Jace nodded, standing; Dante followed his leading standing as well.

"Follow me." Jace said to Zeke and Levi as they stood, following Jace and Dante cautiously.

They began down a stairwell, with Levi growing on edge the further they went down the stairs. Jace could feel the tension coming off of Levi and Zeke. They weren't sure what was about to happen. Jace stepped down into the holding cell. They had the bodies brought there as they were eating upstairs. The smell of blood hit Zeke and Levi as they enter the room. Jace heard Zeke's wolf growl through him, and he could feel the vibration coming from Levi, letting him know he was ready to shift.

"These bodies were left on my land a few days ago. I believe Kip is experimenting on humans." Jace said, stepping aside so Zeke could see the horror.

"What the hell is this?" Levi asked, coming over to the cell.

"Why are some of them half-wolf or have wolf parts?" Levi asked, crouching down and studying them.

"Why do you think it's Kip?" Zeke asked, his face trying to cover up the fact he found this sicking.

"The night Kip's pack was supposed to meet mine to talk about all the destruction he caused. We were supposed to meet at a movie theater. He slaughtered a handful of humans but left one alive."

He pointed to the far left at a body. Zeke looked down at the half-human, half-wolf body; it was twisted and distorted. Blood was stained on the mouth and nose.

"You can only change a human if you give them the blood of an Alpha," Jace said as Zeke continued to look at the bodies.

" Alpha, we are here." Ryan's voice came through mindlink.

"Perfect timing, meet us in the dining room." Jace responded.

"I don't know what to say. Did you show the council these bodies?" Zeke said, standing.

"That bastard." Levi uttered, looking at the bodies.

"Levi, we don't place blame before we know for sure." Zeke said to him.

"The council doesn't care what Kip does. I have one more thing I need to show you." Jace said, heading to the stairs.

"God, it better not be worse than this." Levi muttered, following behind his Alpha.

They returned upstairs to the dining room, where a very bloody and beaten beta from the Black Sands pack was waiting for them.

"Alpha, this is Alpha's Chadwick's beta, Grayson. He is currently acting Alpha for the Black Sands pack." Ryan said, introducing him.

"Acting Alpha? Where is your Alpha?" Zeke asked, eyeballing him.

"My pack was attacked; they took my Alpha and began burning down our homes. Many of my pack members were slaughtered." Grayson said his voice was emotional.

"Grayson, sit. Lori, get him some water, please." Jace said, motioning him to sit.

"Tell us what happened," Zeke said, sitting as well.

"Kip happened, and his lunatic pack. At first, we thought it was just a raid. Maybe he wanted supplies, money, something. We never thought he would take our Alpha. We were outnumbered greatly. We tried to hold our own, but we couldn't." Grayson said, stopping to take a gulp of water that Lori had brought him.

"Why would Kip want your Alpha?" Zeke asked.

Jace knew the answer; the minute he heard Chadwick was missing, his stomach had knotted and twisted in itself.

"Kip said he needed his blood." Grayson stated.

Zeke's eyes flickered to Jace, and he knew at that moment that Zeke's stomach was turning in on itself. His eyes glossed over, and he knew he was talking to Levi. Levi stiffened up on the other side of the room. He clearly had not connected the dots yet.

"I believe Kip is trying to create wolves from humans. I don't know why or what the purpose is. We all know they are not sustainable. Their bodies cannot handle being a wolf." Jace said out loud, knowing that's exactly what they were mindlinking each other.

"You have to be born a wolf. You can't create wolves. That's an abomination. They have no wolf soul. They would be mindless killing machines." Levi said, angry.

"Exactly why they would be the perfect army. If Kip could pull it off." Jace said, locking eyes with Zeke.

"Have you contacted the council, Grayson?" Zeke asked.

"Yes." Jace slammed his fist down on the table, becoming angry that the council kept being brought up.

Levi growled behind Zeke, and Dante flexed, waiting for a fight.

"They do not fucking care. They are sitting in their ivory palace, not giving a fuck what would happen to the rest of us if Kip attempts this." Jace said through gritted teeth.

"He's right. All they did was appoint me as acting Alpha and wish me luck. They said they don't get involved in pack wars." Grayson said.

Zeke rubbed his face thinking. Jace could almost hear him mauling over his options in his head. He gripped the table. He knew without Jace, if Kip turned his sights on the Moonlight pack, it would be a bloody battle; they could possibly lose if he was willing to go after the Black Sand pack for their Alpha's blood. What's stopping him from doing it to others?

"You have my alliance, Jace. If war comes, the Moonlight pack will back you." Zeke said firmly.

"And you have mine; call on me if you need anything as well." Jace said, just as serious as Zeke was.

"We are not much, but the ones that are left will fight. We stand against Kip as well." Grayson said, showing his strength.

Chapter Thirty Two
Directions

They had a tracker on Lilly's car and were able to follow it and find it pretty quickly. They pulled into the abandoned-looking alley. Seeing the car, Logan and Drake frowned. They got out of the car to check it out. Logan let out a frustrated sigh seeing Nora had dumped the car. She must have left on foot, or maybe her friend came and got her.

"It's just like Lilly to go and fuck things up." Logan said angrily to Drake.

"I don't think she intentionally did it, Logan." Drake said, trying to calm him down.

"She freaked Nora out, and now we may have lost one of the biggest assets to our cause. You said she's that Alpha's mate. What if she joins the wolf side? Then what." Logan said, getting more flustered as he spoke.

"Logan, just chill, one thing at a time. The Alpha freaked her out too. I doubt she will go back to him. If it makes any difference, I don't think Lilly meant to." Drake said, trying to ensure Logan wasn't upset with Lilly.

"Drake, you always defend her. Her and her power trips. Just because we're twins doesn't mean she's running the show." Logan said; the anger raiding off of him made Drake nod and look away.

Logan flipped open his phone and called Phillip.

"Nora's gone; I need you to find her friend, check, and see if she's with him. I think his name is Joel." Logan order.

"Wow, that's really easy. I'll get right on that. I'll just go to every Joel's house in the city.' Phillip said sarcastically.

"Watch your mouth and fucking figure it out," Logan yelled.

Drake watched as he furiously opened his phone and dialed another number.

"Hey, find out where Nora lives and go by the house." Logan ordered them.

"Mina dropped Lilly off first. I don't need her fucking things up again. We need Nora to trust us." Logan said firmly.

He could hear Lilly complaining in the background about not wanting to go back and wanting to find Nora. She was telling Mina she was going; there was nothing Logan or she could do about it.

"You tell her I said she's done enough and to get her ass back, or I will have someone take her back and place her in the holding cell." Logan said angrily.

"Don't worry, Logan; she'll be fine." Mina said before ending the phone call.

"Ok, boss, so what do we do now?" Drake asked.

"She couldn't have gotten far; let's keep looking." Logan said, annoyed.

Nora woke up with what felt like the worst hangover of her life. Her head felt like someone had smashed her with a rock. Every time she went to move it, a sharp pain shot through her skull. She felt nauseous and dizzy. She groaned, rolling over, and opening her eyes. She was lying on the bed; she went to move her head but realized she was locked to the headboard with handcuffs clasped around her wrist. The cold metal pressed into skin. She tugged on it, trying to break it off. She heard someone clear their throat from the other side of the room. Nora looked at where the sound came from and saw the same man from the car.

"Where am I?" She said, trying to make her voice sound angry, but her head hurt so bad.

"Don't worry about it. You'll find out shortly. Take a nap." The man shrugged, going back to the book he was reading.

"Seriously. Fucking let me go." Nora said, but the man was back to ignoring her.

She pulled on the handcuffs some more, trying to get them to give or break. Her wrist was beginning to swell from how hard she was pulling. She let out a frustrated sigh. She looked around the room, and it looked familiar.

"So what are we waiting for?" Nora said, annoyed with him.

"Orders." He said, talking to her like she was the most boring thing in the world.

"So we're just going to sit here till then." Nora said, going back to pulling on her handcuff.

"Yup. Oh, and keep trying; those cuffs are designed to withstand a werewolf, so yeah. You're not getting out of them." He said, turning a page.

Nora groaned; she felt horrible, and now she wasn't sure who had her and where she was. She looked at the headboard. The cuff might be unbreakable, but the headboard isn't.

"Hey, could you get me some water? I don't know what you guys gave me, but I feel horrible and really need something to drink." Nora said to the man, making herself look pitiful.

"Fine." He said, annoyed by getting up and closing his book.

"I would say wait here, but that's inevitable." He chuckled, closing the door behind him as he stepped out.

"Confident much." Nora muttered as she turned so she could look at the headboard.

It was a black metal frame, but it wasn't good metal. If she could detach the small metal rod that ran up and down, she could get free. The rod was clearly there for design, but the smart ass lopped the handcuffs through it. She gripped the metal of the handcuffs and moved it up to the top of the rod. She began to pull towards her. She could feel the metal digging into her wrist, cutting the outer part of her wrist. It burned and stung against her skin, but she wasn't going to be anyone's prisoner. She yanked back and forth on the rod until she finally felt it snap. She fell backwards on the bed. Free! Her mind yelled as she got up quickly. Her wrists were still handcuffed together, but now she could run.

She rushed to the door, not really having a plan. She just needed to get out of there. She pulled open the door and went to bolt. She ran into something solid. She went to step back, but an arm reached around her waist, pulling her into a very solid chest. His scent hit her, and she knew that if she looked up, she would see a pair of ice-blue eyes staring down at her. She gritted her teeth; first, he locked her in a room, then he poisoned her and handcuffed her to a bed! She was angry. She was the angriest she had ever been. She went to step back, but he kept her in place. She brought both her hands back and slammed them into his chest with all her might.

"Oh hell no, we're not doing this." She heard him grumble.

Before she knew it, she was up in the air, over his shoulder and staring at the ground. She began to kick and thrasher trying to get away from him. He kicked the door shut behind him and walked to the bed; he flopped her down onto it. She bounced onto her back. She let out a frustrated yell before rolling onto her side, trying to get up. She rolled off the bed by accident, landing with a thud. She didn't care. She got to her feet and started going for the door. Jace caught her by the back of her pants and tugged her back. She landed on her but on the floor.

"How dare you!" She yelled at him furiously.

"How dare I what?" He yelled back, yanking her to her feet.

"How dare you try trapping me here again! Who do you think you are?" She yelled in his face.

"Why do you keep putting yourself at risk!" He yelled, stepping into her.

Nora didn't realize how big he was until he was inches away from her. She stepped back into the wall, narrowing her eyes at him. She wasn't going to let him intimidate her.

"It's not your place to make sure I stay out of danger. Like I am any safer here." She said, standing taller as she spoke.

"You're safest here. And it is my place. You're staying here where I can keep you safe." Jace said, Cole, flashing in his eyes.

Cole was beyond excited to see her. He was overwhelming Jace with the need to be close to her. He wanted to inhale her scent to curl up with her. Jace pushed his emotions back.

"You are nothing to me. You're not my boyfriend or father. A hunter is safest in a house full of wolves. That makes so much sense." Nora said, her voice getting bolder as she spoke.

"You are my mate. I will never let anything harm you." He said with anger in his voice.

"You think making me feel safe is poisoning me and locking me in a room? You think just because of this whole mate thing, you're entitled to me like I'm some piece of property. Look, I am leaving." She said, poking her finger into his chest.

"It isn't safe out there. You need to listen to me." Jace growled, ignoring her poking him.

"Right now, you don't seem safe. I can hold my own. Thank you." She said, going to step away from him.

Jace was taken aback by her actions. He had never had someone step to him and challenge him the way she was just now. Anger courses through him. He shoved her up against the wall, his knuckles hitting it as he did. The wall cracked beneath his first.

"I said you're going to listen to what I say!" He growled, tightening his grip slightly on her arm.

A smirk appeared on her perfect lips. Jace saw the smirk, and it drove him insane. He was confused; most people would shrink away and obey him. Here she is, taunting him with a smirk.

"And I will do what I want." Nora said, her eyes daring him.

Chapter Thirty Three
Stay

Jace had a surge of anger he was trying to push down. Her closeness to him was making Cole wild beneath his skin. Her skin felt soft beneath his fingertips. Her scent was intoxicating to him. He couldn't help but notice that even though she was angry, the way her lips formed the perfect pout made him want them. He didn't want to hurt her. Cole pushed through trying to be close to Nora. Jace's eyes glowed bright as Cole did. Jace let Cole push through just enough to calm himself but not enough to shift. Jace allowed it hoping it would calm him. He leaned forward and nuzzled her neck, inhaling as he did.

Cole. It's fine, look; she's just confused. You need this and you need to calm down before you make us hurt our mate. Jace told him as he pressed his face into the crock of her neck.

Nora was taken back by the sudden action. His light stubble brushed her skin, giving her chills. The chills turned into shivers, and she tilted her head to the side, letting him have better access. His mouth brushed over her collarbone, and he felt her move against him slightly. Cole smirked as she liked this. He nips at the spot where he would eventually mark her, letting the world know she is his.

Cole, don't. Jace's voice came through, worried that he may do it now.

His tongue flickered over the spot as Jace tried to push forward. He could feel Cole's possessiveness coming out, wanting to mark what was his. Cole was fighting hard to keep control. His fangs elongated and lightly scraped her collarbone. A small noise escaped Nora's mouth, a mixture of surprise and excitement. Cole moved his mouth into position. The word mine went through his mind.

Cole! Jace yelled, demanding control back.

Jace took back control just as Cole was going to sink his teeth into her. Jace pulled his head away from her neck, his breathing hard. He leaned his head against her forehead, trying to calm himself. Nora didn't realize, but her finger had slipped into his belt loop, holding him close to her. He opened his eyes, and they were no longer glowing. His hand went to the side of her face, his thumb rubbing it slightly. Every time he touched her, little shivers went through her.

"I'm sorry." He whispered, his lips inches from hers.

She wasn't sure how to respond; him being close to her was overwhelming her senses. The way he just spoke, he felt valuable. She nodded slightly against his forehead, not being able to find words. His thumb traveled across her cheek, settling under her chin. Her body craved his touch. She wanted him to kiss her as his thumb touched her lip. Her whole body was begging for his lips to touch hers. She was done anticipating it. She pulled him closer to her by his belt loop and pushed her lips against his. Jace let out a groan as her lips pressed into his. He took control of the kiss, pushing her further into the wall as he kissed her. His tongue slipped into her mouth, rubbing against her. She wanted more of him, she went to move her hands, but the handcuffs prevented her. She kissed him back, her tongue tangling with his as she implied she wanted more through the kiss.

Jace grabbed her hands, pinning them behind her against the wall as he kissed her harder. His other hand traveled the length of her torso. His fingertips touching her bare skin sent sparks through her. He broke the kiss, his mouth traveling down the side of her neck. A small moan escaped her mouth; he moved down over her collarbone. As he got to the spot, he felt Cole try to push forward.

Mark her! He growled.

Jace gritted his teeth and stepped back suddenly from Nora. His chest was rising and falling hard as he shut his eyes, gaining control. Nora watched him, confused breathlessly. She wondered why he jumped away from her. She stepped towards him. He held his hand up to her as he opened his eyes; they were still glowing. She stopped starting to feel hurt.

"It's Cole. Let me just get control for a second." He said, shutting his eyes.

Nora nodded, stepping back, not sure what his wolf was trying to do. She watched him breathe for another second, and when he opened his eyes, the glow was gone. He desperately wanted to touch her, but he couldn't risk Cole trying to mark her.

"Cole?" Nora asked her question.

"Will you stay?" Jace asked her, ignoring her question about Cole.

Nora looked around; she didn't have a better option. The hunters were looking for her. She wasn't a match for all of them. She could bump into a wolf out in the open. At Least she somewhat knows this wolf.

"I have conditions," Nora said, leaning against the wall.

"They are?" Jace asked.

"One, no handcuffs." Nora said, holding up her wrist to him.

Jace nodded, walking over to her; he pulled a key out of his pocket. He took her wrist in his hand and unlocked the cuffs. He looked at her swollen, slightly cut wrist. He brought his mouth to her wrist, kissing it softly. She bit her bottom lip watching him, the urge to kiss him stirring up in her.

"Conditions?" Jace whispered against her skin.

"Uh?" She asked, his mouth had wiped any thoughts from her mind, other than wanting him.

"You said conditions meaning more than one." Jace chuckled, letting go of her wrist.

"No knocking me out or whatever that asshole did." Nora said, getting upset again.

"Ok, anything else?" Jace asked.

"If I want to leave, I can leave, and you need to tell me everything about wolves and hunters. I need to understand all this." Nora said, feeling defeated that she only knew so much.

"Ok deal." Jace said, holding his hand out to her.

She grabbed hold of it, shaking it. He pulled her into his chest; she chuckled at him. He wrapped his arms around her, kissing her forehead before letting her go.

"Ok first question, explain this mate thing," Nora said, sitting down on the bed.

"I thought I had." Jace said, something flashing in his eyes as he watched her sit on the bed.

"Explain again." Nora said, annoyed.

Jace smirked, walking towards the bed almost like he was stalking an animal. Nora got a grin on her face as she scooted back to the headboard. Jace was on top of her in seconds. His eyes were flickering to the headboard.

"Did you break my bed?" He asked, trying to sound serious, but there was a hint of laughter in it.

"Did you really handcuff me to it?" Nora countered, a smirk appearing on her lips.

Jace growled slightly, pinning her to the bed, a smirk on his face as he towered over her. His mouth was inches from hers, and she found herself trying to inch closer to them. He leaned down to meet her.

"Are you going to explain or not?" She laughed, pulling her head to the side so he couldn't kiss her.

He placed the kiss on her neck, sending shivers through her. She tried to fight it, wanting to know the answers. He saw her skin respond with goosebumps, and he smiled.

"A mate is like what humans call soulmates but much more intense." Jace whispered into her ear; another wave of shivers passed through her as his warm breath tickled her ear.

"Intense?" Nora whispered.

"Mhmm, everything about you calls to me. The way you smell is intoxicating. I have this overwhelming need to have you by me. Cole needs you; you instantly calm us. It's hard to describe; the world makes sense with you near." Jace said, trying to find words sitting back now, just straddling her.

"What happened back there with Cole when we kissed?" Nora said, trying to understand.

"He wanted to mark you." Jace said quietly.

"And that means what?" Nora said, sitting up now and facing Jace.

"It's what wolves do to show they are mated. He wanted basically to let the world know you're his." Jace said, his eyes glowed slightly when he said it.

"Ok.." Nora said, still not understanding.

"It's stronger than marriage; it's a life commitment. You bond with each other to the point you can feel each other's feelings." Jace said, shifting off of her.

Nora nodded, understanding now why he was acting the way he did. She scooted back to the headboard.

"When your eyes glow like that, it's Cole?" Nora asked curiously.

"Yes. sometimes he pushes for control; most of the time, I win." Jace smirked.

"Is it weird? It's like you're sharing your body with someone else." Nora asked, thinking out loud.

"No, I'm so used to him being there, I can't remember what it was like when he wasn't. I know there was a time when he wasn't there, but I think if I were to lose him, it would be like losing a part of me." Jace said, laying down on his back on the bed.

"How am I supposed to stay here when you all hate hunters?" Nora said, sprawling out on the bed too.

"The necklace for now until I figure something else out." Jace said, shrugging.

"But one of your guys already knows. He went all big bad wolf on me, remember." Nora said, stretching.

"He's ok. He's my beta, my second in command. I explained everything to him, and he's ok now." Jace said, watching her stretch, her shirt riding up a little bit as she did.

His eyes wander over her bare skin; the need to reach out and caress her crosses his mind. She smirked, seeing his eyes wander over her, a small flash of Cole peeking through.

"Um, your wolf is showing," Nora said with a sly smile on her lips.

Jace smirked at her comment before pinning her back down on the bed, his eyes glowing brighter.

"What are you going to do about it, little hunter?" He growled into her ear. It sent shivers through her, her body immediately turning into him, wanting to be touched and kissed by him.

She heard a deep chuckle from his chest at her response. She smirked, looking at him. She wrapped her legs around his waist, squeezing. She heard him inhale sharply as she squeezed. He loosened up on her shoulders as she continued to squeeze him. He had to let her sit up straighter to breathe. His hand went to her legs, trying to pry them off of his torso. She smirked, and as he sat up, she pushed her pelvis into him, pushing him over onto his back, and now she was straddling him. She pinned his shoulders to the bed. A grin on her face.

"You're not the only one that can throw their weight around." She grinned.

"You're stronger than I expected." He said, looking up at her.

"Mhmm, so now what are you going to do about it, wolf." She chuckled.

He arched his pelvis upward, sending her closer to his face. She braced herself with her forearms on either side of his head. His arms reached up around her capturing her to his chest. Her hair falling down around them, he nuzzled into her neck before placing kisses there. She wiggled against him, trying to get upwards.

"Alpha!" A knock came from the bedroom door. Jace growled, hearing the knock.

"Uh oh, duty calls." Nora whispered into his ear, and then, being bold, she bit his ear lobe.

Jace growled again, and in one swift motion, he rolled over, capturing her beneath him. A small shriek escaped her mouth as she almost fell off the bed during the roll.

"Alpha! I'm sorry to disturb you, but it's important." The voice came again.

"For your sake, it better be." He growled, looking down at Nora.

"I swear, Alpha, it is." The voice said again. Jace leaned forward and planted a kiss on Nora's full lips.

He scooted away from her before getting up and walking to the door.

Chapter Thirty Four
Secrets

Jace pulled the door open with a frown, expressing how unhappy he was that one of his pack members was outside his door interrupting him.

"What is it, Isaac?" Jace growled.

Nora peeked around Jace, trying to see who it was in the doorway. She recognized him as the guy sitting in the room with her earlier. He looked at Nora. She smiled and flipped him off. Isaac made a face, causing Jace to look over his shoulder at Nora, who was standing there, flipping him off. She smiled at Jace sweetly before he rolled his eyes at her, shaking his head and turning back to Isaac.

"Well…" Jace said, becoming annoyed.

"Our men chased some of Kip's pack off our borders. We are not sure if they saw the other Alphas leave." Isaac said anxiously.

"Ok did they attack? Were they just passing through? What did it seem like they were doing?" Jace said, pinching the bridge of his nose.

"I…I I'm not sure it was almost like they were looking for something." Isaac stuttered out.

"Ok, we're still running double patrol. Send Dante up." Jace said quietly.

"There's another thing, Alpha." Isaac said, uneasy.

"Oh, for the love of god, Isaac, stop drawing shit out. Tell me everything right now all at once." Jace growled.

"There have been some hunters too in the area, also looking like they are searching for something." Isaac said.

Jace glanced over her shoulder, looking at Nora.

Or someone. Cole's angry voice popped up into his head.

Jace nodded to Isaac, letting him know he could go. Isaac bowed and nearly ran down the stairs.

"What the heck was that?" Nora asked as Jace came back into the room.

"Pack stuff." Jace said vaguely.

"Well, duh. I meant why captain asshole was not an asshole anymore and all timid." Nora said, making faces as she talked about Isaac.

Jace shrugged his mind elsewhere. He was getting anxious with Kip's pack acting like circling sharks. Why would he be coming this close? It usually was just to taunt him with minor things but search his territory. He felt his stomach knot up.

"Alpha, Nora." Dante walked in, bowing his head as he acknowledged both of them.

Nora gave him a strange look, moving to the other side of the room. She was ready if he was going to wolf out again.

"Dante, Do you know more than Isaac about Kip's pack searching our land?" Jace asked him.

Nora could sense that this was upsetting Jace. She could practically feel him tensing over it. Dante looked over at Nora, giving her a strange look before answering Jace.

"No, we almost captured one of his pack members, but Isaac wasn't fast enough. We couldn't tell what they were looking for. At first, we thought they were here to dump more bodies, but they had nothing with them. I called Taylor, but he didn't answer. I think we won't hear from them anymore. I believe the news got out, and we contacted the council. Not like that did anything." Dante said, bitterness in his voice as he spoke.

Jace nodded, running a hand through his hair before looking back at Dante.

"Stay here. I need to go speak to Zeke. As well as tie up another loose end." Jace said to Dante.

"Are you freaking crazy? You mean he's staying here, and I'm coming with you, right?" Nora said, narrowing her eyes at Dante.

"Nora, I need you to stay here too. It isn't safe right now. Dante will not hurt you." Jace said, looking from Nora to Dante.

"Nora, I promise I won't. Earlier was a misunderstanding, and I apologize deeply." Dante said to her it was heartfelt and sounded real.

Nora made a face and looked at Jace, determination in her eyes.

"Fine, but if you lock that door or break the handle off, I'm out." Nora said, her eyes threatening him.

"I'm not going to." Jace sighed.

"And if he wolfs out and I kill or hurt him, I am punching you." Nora said, folding her arms across her chest.

Jace blew air out his nose as a smirk came across his face. He glanced over to Dante, who also had a smile on his face.

"I like her." Dante mindlinked Jace.

'Good, keep her safe." Jace responded.

Nora grabbed a pillow from the bed and chucked it at Jace. The pillow hit him, and because he was mindlinking Dante, he didn't see it coming. He blinked, stunned. Dante coughed to cover up his laughter.

"I think I figured that out too. Both of your eyes glossed over. It's some wolf communication thing. Right?" Nora said, looking at both of them.

"Yes, we can speak telepathically." Jace sighed.

"Great wolf secret conversations." Nora rolled her eyes.

"I will be back." Jace said softly, walking out the door.

Nora's eyes flickered to Dante; she studied him briefly before sitting on the bed. The room was so silent you could hear a pin drop.

"So do you like movies?" Dante said awkwardly as he grabbed the remote and went to sit on the couch.

Jace clicked his phone off after calling Zeke. He gave him a heads up that Kip's pack had been circling his lands, and he might have seen them leaving. He sent the same message to Grayson. Grayson was more stressed than Zeke. Zeke was ready for whenever Kip decided he wanted to come at him. They all agree to keep checking in on each other.

"How are you two up there?" Jace mind linked Dante.

"Getting lectured on movie choices and now assaulted because we're having secret conversations." Dante replied.

" Good." Jace chuckled.

"Alpha, hunters at the gate. Same ones from before demanding to speak to you." The guards at the gate mind linked him.

"Coming." Jace responded annoyed.

" Dante, hunters at the gate, make sure you keep Nora there." He ordered.

"Got it." Dante responded.

"Matt and Wyatt meet me at the gate hunters." Jace mind linked them.

" On our way." They both responded.

Jace pulled his car up to the gate. He saw his guards at the gate, ready for a fight. He stepped out of the car and began walking to the gate. A very pissed-off and angry Logan was pacing in front of it. Behind him were two other men and two females. Jace eyed the larger male with a bald head. He was already setting up his attack in his head if this was all to go down. As Jace got to the gate, two wolves flanked his side; he glanced down at them. Right away, he knew it was Matt and Wyatt. They snarled at his side, looking at the hunters.

"I thought I told you not to come back to my territory." Jace said, his voice booming over the sound of the car engines as if they weren't even there.

"She's here, isn't she." Logan said, bowing up at the gate.

"It doesn't matter if she is or if she's not. You're on my land, hunter." Jace said; the two wolves at his side snapped at his words.

"You need to let us have her. You don't understand." Logan said his tone changed from angry to angry and desperate.

"I don't need to do anything." Jace said, anger coursing through him as he grabbed the gate bar and crushed it in his hand.

The metal folded in on itself. The two female hunters in the back shifted, seeing the strength he had in human form.

"You don't know what she is. You don't know what you have, damn it." Logan said, walking up to the gate and yelling at him through.

Jace went emotionless as Logan screamed at him. Jace looked deadly, and the calmer he got, the more the wolves at his side locked in on the hunters. Jace's eyes glowed slightly and caught Logan off guard as Cole appeared. In one swift motion, Jace stuck his arm through the gate, capturing Logan. He pulled him quickly forward, smashing Logan's head against the iron bars. He then shoved him backwards, letting Logan fall to the ground, his forehead bleeding and cracked. It happened so quickly that it took the other hunters a minute to register what had just happened. They hadn't seen a wolf move that quickly, never mind in human form.

"Get off my land now before I gut your hunter friends and let you watch them bleed out. Then I will gut you." Jace said his voice was flat and emotionless.

Logan got up off the ground as all the hunters shifted forward, waiting for orders to fight or leave. He pressed his hand to his forehead and laughed slightly.

"I've heard about you. I heard how ruthless you are and what you have done. You're going to need our help. Others will find her. Others won't care about your reputation or your pack once they know. Let me talk to her; let her come back with us. She's not safe here with you wolves." Logan said, blood dripping down his face.

"She is my mate! She is safest with me! Leave; if she wanted to join you, she would have gone to you, not me." Jace growled, his claws creeping out of his skin as Cole was on the verge of shifting at Logan, mentioning he couldn't keep her safe.

"She will need us, too." Logan said, a smirk on his lips.

"We will see about that. You have about ten seconds to get your asses out of here before I stop being generous." Jace said, his eyes started to glow again.

"Logan, come on. It's not the time or the place." Kat called from behind; she was watching the perimeter, there were two wolves out in front, but she knew with a single summons, his whole pack could be here any second.

Wyatt's wolf smashed into the gate showing its teeth, spit flying out of his mouth as he did. Matt stood behind, baring his teeth, and hackled up. They both were itching to attack.

"You should listen to her and go." Jace said, stepping towards the gate as if he was going to open it.

Logan let out a frustrated yell and began walking back to the car. He knew they wouldn't win this fight, not here and not now, but he wasn't giving up. He needed Nora. He got into the car and slammed the door. The other followed suit. Jace watches Drake shuffle his feet and then slowly approach the gate.

"Alpha Jace, give this to Nora. She is going to want to read." Drake said, holding out a book to him he had kept under his coat.

Jace raised an eyebrow at him before reaching through the bars and taking the book.

"Why?" Jace asked, trying to understand Drake.

"If she is really what we think she is. Then we're going to need to become allies. This is my olive branch to you, so to say. Plus, I like her." Drake said with a shrug.

Jace watched Drake walk back to the car and get into it. He watched Logan start bitching at him for giving the book to Jace. The other cars' headlights turned on as Logan turned his engine on.

"Watch them leave. Make sure they do." Jace said to Matt and Wyatt at his side.

They both growled and nodded; eyes focused on the cars. Jace walked back to his car and got it. He turned it on, waiting a few seconds to make sure the hunters left before turning it around and heading back to his home.

Chapter Thirty Five
Abilities

Logan slammed his fist into the steering wheel, pulling over just a short way from Jace's territory. He punched it again.

"Dude, calm down before you activate the airbag," Drake yelled at him.

"Calm down, calm down. Sure, the bad guys have our girl." Logan yelled at him.

Drake raised an eyebrow at how he said our girl, like Nora, was something more to him than just another hunter.

"Look, I know that she might be of the original bloodline, but this is not how we will get her back. We need to wait it out. If her abilities continue to grow, as the book says, then she's going to need us. I don't doubt the wolf will protect her from the other hunters." Drake said, trying to figure out why Logan was losing his cool so badly.

Logan pressed his head into the steering wheel, listening to Drake talk, knowing he was right. He bumped his head against it before sighing and giving in.

"I know you're right; it's just frustrating. I knew there was something different the moment I saw her. She had no real signs she was a hunter, but I locked in on her." Logan said softly.

Drake didn't say anything. He wasn't sure what to say to that, so he sat there quietly, waiting for Logan to take them back home or continue talking.

"There's something about her. I genuinely care for her, Drake. And now she's some blood thirst wolf's mate. How does that even work? She's human. She went back to him and not us." Logan said before putting the car back into drive.

"She's human, Logan. She doesn't have the mate pull like Jace does to her. So she can choose who she wants in the end." Drake said, now understanding Logan has feelings for her.

Logan sighed and began to head back to their home, his thoughts wondering what Nora was doing, and jealousy pinged in his heart as he pictured her with Jace.

Jace walked up the stairs to his room; he could hear the bickering from the hall. He raised his eyebrow as he heard Dante arguing about a movie with Nora. She was chuckling and laughing at his comments as he tried to defend his selection. He pushed the door open to see Dante standing in front of the tv, hands on his hip, looking irritated.

"Problems?" Jace asked, leaning against the door frame.

"Oh, thank god." Dante turned around, seeing him.

"Hmm?" Jace asked again what was going on again.

Nora had a big grin on her face as she sat criss crossed on the bed, looking at Dante. She had mischief in her eyes, waiting for him to explain what was happening to Jace.

"Tell her, Tell her that this is right here. This movie is the best movie ever." Dante said, pointing at the Tv screen.

Jace's eyes flickered to the screen and then back to Dante, a confused look on his face.

"Well, go on and tell her!" Dante said with a huff.

"Umm..what movie is it?' Jace asked, looking at him.

"Ha!' Nora yelled and then started laughing.

"Seriously! I can't deal with you two." Dante announced before walking past Jace and out the bedroom door.

"Ok then." Jace said, watching Dante stomp down to his room dramatically.

Jace shook his head and stepped further into the room, closing his door. Nora had fallen backwards on the bed laughing harder as Dante stomped off. Jace sat down on the edge of the bed with a small smile on his lips as he watched her wipe a tear away from her face. Jace raised a brow, asking her what had happened.

"It is actually a good movie. It was just hilarious to see him get so worked up that I said it wasn't.' She smirked.

"I've never seen him flustered before; that was actually funny." Jace said, letting out a chuckle.

"Well, I tend to bring out the best in people."
Nora laughed with a shrug.

"Speaking of people, your hunter friends came
by." Jace said, his tone annoyed when he said
hunters.

"I wouldn't say friends, but what did they
want?" Nora said sharply.

"You." Jace said, looking at her.

"I'm not going with them." She said her tone
was firm.

"Good because I told them you weren't. Is
there something happening?" Jace asked, not
wanting to play games.

"Something happening? What do you mean?"
Nora asked.

Jace couldn't tell if she was playing dumb or
just really didn't know. Looking at her, he sighed and
shook his head before handing her the book. She
took the book and looked at it. It was old and bound in
leather. She ran her fingers over the book; it was too
worn out to show its title.

'What is this?' She asked, looking at him.

"The big blad one gave to me said you might
need it ... .which is why I asked if there's anything
going on," Jace said calmly, repeating himself.

"Other than that fact that when something tries
to hurt me, the world goes into slow mode, nope."
Nora said very non-chantilly while opening the book.

"Wait, so drunk you was telling the truth?
Explain." Jace said, his brows turned downward as he
spoke.

"I just did. I don't get it or understand, but that's how I was able to knock both you and Logan on your butts. I stepped in the way of your punch, and then the world went into slow motion, but I could still move normally." Nora shrugged as she scanned the book.

"Adam." Jace mind linked him quickly.

"Yes, Alpha." Adam answered, a sense of worry in his voice.

"I want all information on anything about hunters having special abilities. As soon as you know anything, report back." Jace ordered, without further explanation.

A pillow hit Jace in the side of his head. He shook his head as the mindlink ended. Jace saw Nora looking over at him frowning. He looked at the pillow and then at her as if registering that she had whacked him with it. A low growl rumbled through his chest as he looked at her.

"You asked for it, you and the secret wolf conversations. It's rude." Nora said, ignoring the growl.

He watches her try to ignore him, a smile stretching across his lips. He noticed a spark in her eye, and before she could go back to pretending, he pinned her against the bed. A small shriek escaped her lips as she was pinned down.

"You should really find out who I am." He whispered, taunting in her ear.

His breath teasing her ear and caressing her neck sent chills through her. She moved her head slightly away from his.

"You might be the big bad wolf, but I am not a little red riding hood." She said, locking eyes with him.

The way her eyes flashed made him want her more. It made him want to push her buttons to see exactly what she was capable of. He growled slightly, daring her. His hand pushed up under her shirt, traveling over her stomach. He saw a smirk on her face, and it drove him crazy. He growled as he placed his mouth near her neck. His fangs elongated as he nuzzled into her. She felt his fangs brush over her skin. She was excited but nervous. Suddenly a flash of anger went through her, and a voice somewhere in her mind yelled no. A jolt courses through; she places her hands on his chest and shoves him off of her with no effort. Jace landed on his back on the floor, staring up at the ceiling. A gasp escaped him as he tried to suck air back into his lungs.

"Woah." Nora whispered staring at her hands.

Jace coughed, sitting up. He had never been thrown before. He looked up at Nora, who was now peeking over the edge of the bed. A mixture of worry and excitement in her eyes. He was confused. He had never felt that much strength before, not even from other alphas, and she showed no effort when she did it.

"What just happened?" He asked her, getting up.

"I'm not sure, but it was pretty cool." She laughed.

"Give me that book." He said, holding out his hand.

"Ok?" Nora said, reaching over for the book.

She grabbed the book off the side of the bed and handed it to Jace. She watched him flip through it, his face becoming more and more annoyed as he flipped through the pages. He let out a long sigh before handing the book back. Nora raised an eyebrow at him, asking what he was doing.

"We're going to need a translator; it's nothing I recognize." He groaned, looking at her as if he was studying her.

"Drake gave this to you?" Nora asked him.

"If he's the big bald one, then yes," Jace said, his tone annoyed.

"Well, I think he did it on purpose. He obviously had to have looked at it. So he either knows how to read it or does not and is sure that you will find someone who does." Nora said, thinking out loud.

"Have that much faith in me already?" Jace said with a coy smile on his face.

"I've just noticed that you tend to get what you want." Nora said, making a face at him.

She saw the look again in his eye. The same one he does before his bad habit of pinning her to his bed. She backed away from the bed, but he slowly began walking to her. The coy smile on his face turned into a seductive one. Her body tingled, she wanted to run from him, but at the same time, part of her wanted to be caught. She glanced over her shoulder, looking at the door.

"Don't run." Jace said, but his grin told her he wanted her too.

"Let's see how fast you are, wolf." Nora said, bolting to the door.

Chapter Thirty Six
Catch me

She let out a small shriek as she threw the door open and quickly slammed it behind her. She heard a growl come from behind the door, and she bolted down the hall. She was not sure where she was. She had been here only two times, and both times she woke up in a bedroom. She raced down the hall towards the stairs. She heard his bedroom door open, and it was like he had waited, giving her a head start. She started down the stairs realizing she was on the third floor. She raced down the stairs, nearly falling; her feet hit the second-floor landing. She could hear him just walking down the third-floor hall. It reminded her of a horror movie. She expected him to think she would continue running down stairs. She raced down the end of the second-floor hall, seeing another stairwell. She began climbing it, trying to be as quiet as possible. She got to the third floor. She remembered that Jace said he was the only one who really stayed here. She began trying door knobs. Maybe she could hide in one of the empty rooms. She got closer to his room, and luckily, the room next store was open. She turned the handle and went into the room. She closed the door quietly. The click of the lock echoed in the silent room. It was too loud for her; the noise made her cringe. Her heart pounded in her chest. She froze, waiting, thinking the noise from the lock gave her away.

After several minutes she looked around the room; she needed to hide. She looked at the closet, which was a typical spot, and then her eyes glanced under the bed. The first two places she would check if she was looking were the closet and under the bed. Her eyes glanced at the bathroom. He might not expect her to hide in the bathroom. She walked to the bathroom and got into the tub shutting the shower curtain. She sank down in the tub waiting for what seemed ever, and then it happened she heard the door click open to the room. She held her breath as she heard footsteps. She knew it was him. How did he figure it out? Her heart raced in her chest. She put her hand over her mouth as if it was going to help anything. She was counting his footsteps as she heard him walk around the room. She heard more footsteps, and then the door shut. She let out a breath she was holding, her nerves settling a little. How did he not check the bathroom? She wondered. She slowly stood up and was about to peek out from behind the shower curtain. Suddenly the hiss of the shower head turning on made her jump. She landed right in the line of the water coming out of it. It quickly soaked her as she tried jumping out of the tub. She slipped, trying to get out, taking the shower curtain with her. She landed right into his arms.

Nora glanced up at Jace; He caught her with the biggest smile on his face. Realizing he had her. She struggled in his arms; his arms gripped her tighter. She was wet and slippery, but there was no way he was letting her go. A chuckle rumbled through his chest as he watched her slipping and sliding on the title floor. She was trying everything to get away. Lastly, he heard her let out a long sigh, giving into him.

"Ok, you win." She muttered, still wiggling.

"Oh, I win?" His voice was taunting.

"Yeah, yeah. Let me go; it's cold." She said, a little whiny.

He spun her in his arms, pulling her closer to his chest. The heat radiating from him made her want to lean into him as she shivered. He moved a fallen lock of black hair from her face before settling his hand under her chin.

"What do I win?" He whispered, asking, but his eyes were already saying what he wanted.

She felt goosebumps run over her as she watched his eyes look at her. She couldn't find anything to say to him, her mind going blank as she became very aware of how tight her clothing as it stuck to her. His grin became more taunting as he realized she had nothing to say back.

"So, do I get to pick then?" He said, leaning his head down and whispering it into her ear.

She swallowed, shutting her eyes, trying to force her brain to come back and ignore her body's reaction of "Please touch me." He moved closer, and he could feel her body's reaction to him. His nose brushed hers briefly as he decided to claim her lips. Nora couldn't help it. She stepped into him as he kissed her, following the motion of his lips with hers. His hand wrapped around her waist, pulling her closer. His other hand was traveling down to the small of her back. He could feel her breast brush against his chest through the wet fabric; it was like she wasn't wearing anything. He felt himself grow tense. Nora's hand traveled to the back of his neck and wove her fingers into his hair as she kissed him back harder. Jace pulled back from the kiss, placing soft kisses along her jawline down onto her neck. An intense shiver went through her as his lips touched the skin of Nora's neck. Her head immediately moved to the side, allowing him more access to her neck as he placed more kisses down toward her collar bone. A small noise escaped her mouth as she moved against him. He pulled her into him just as they began to slip. The water from the shower spilled onto the floor behind them. They landed on the bathroom floor with the shower curtain under them and Jace bracing himself over Nora. Jace quickly panicked, looking her over to see if she was hurt. A small laugh escaped her as he realized she was ok.

"This is your fault." She smirked at him.

"And this will be too." He smirked as his hands tugged on her shirt.

Her shirt split up in the middle, leaving her exposed. She inhaled sharply as the rush of cold air sent goosebumps over her. She shut her eyes in anticipation. He looked down at her, his eyes tracing every part of her body. He studied her face before moving his mouth down over her chest. Nora let out a small moan as he neared her breast. His hand cupped it, squeezing it firmly as he took her nipple into his mouth. The sensation of his warm mouth over her breast was so intense she arched into him, craving more. Her body was shaking from the feelings rushing through her, her toes curling into the bed as he began kissing down her stomach. Everywhere his mouth touched sent sparks of cold fire through her. She let out a small moan as his mouth ran over her pants line. His fingers found the button and quickly undid it. He lifted his mouth from her skin, hands on either side of her pants, wanting to rip them off. She lifted her hips in anticipation, and that was all he needed. He grabbed a hold of her pants and popped the button off. He ripped her pants out from under her, taking her underwear with them. She was exposed to him completely. The words mine echoed in his head as he looked down at her. He watched her shiver. He stood suddenly and turned off the shower head. She looked up, alarmed, wondering where he was going. He smirked, seeing her face. He reached down, holding out his hand to her. She took it, and as she stood, he threw her over his shoulder. She let out a playful yell as he carried her into the bedroom.

Getting to the bed, he playful plopped her down on it. She giggled, backing away from him. She took off her half-ripped shirt and flung it at him, hitting him in the face. He growled before crouching on the bed, crawling after her. She let out another small yell as he grabbed hold of her ankle and pulled her down towards him. As he straddled her, he ran his fingers down her center. He could see her body responding to his touch. She let out a small groan and moved her hips slightly. The sight drove him insane. He wanted to taste her. He began to place soft kisses on her, his tongue playfully playing over her slit. She inhaled sharply, letting a small pleasure noise out of her mouth as she once again arched into him. She let out a small groan and moved her hips slightly. He pushed his tongue past her lips and began playing with her bud. Her hand immediately found its way into his hair as if to keep him there. He began making small circles with his tongue over it. She grabbed him, tensed up, and released, enjoying the rush she was getting from it. More sexy little moans escaped her as she moved against him. He inserted a finger into her and began moving it as his mouth captured her bud. She groaned, arching against him. He moved away from her for a second, undoing his pants and quickly discarding them. She didn't even notice he had moved from her. She was too lost in everything her body was feeling. She felt something large at the entrance of her core, and her breathing quickened. Jace saw her tensed up; his fingertips found their way to her bud and began rubbing small circles on it. She immediately relaxed and was lost in the sensation of it.

He slowly pressed his way into her. The sharp rush of pain coursed through her but left just as quickly as it came as Jace made sure to tend to her. He allowed her to get used to the feeling of him before he slowly began to move. The movement hurt at first, but it quickly was replaced with intense pleasure. It felt like she had been missing something and now was full. The tingles and waves of pleasure made her start moving with him. She wanted more and needed him. A pressure was building inside of her like she had been climbing a mountain, and her body was about to give out. She wrapped her legs around him, locking him into her. He could feel herself tightening around him, and he throbbed with need. He could feel his release coming. A warm feeling washed over her as all her muscles began to contract. She let out a moan clinging to him as a wave of intensity rushed over her. He felt her orgasm, and it instantly made him realize. Her body twitched in the aftermath of everything. Jace laid to the side of her pulling her close. He buried his face into her neck, inhaling her scent. She relaxed, running her hand mindlessly up and down his back, enjoying the euphoria of it. Jace placed a small kissing on her shoulder, watching her happily.

"We should probably go back to my room." He whispered into her ear.

"Mhmm." She said, curling into him and resting her head on his chest.

"Dante's going to be really pissed you destroyed his bathroom." Jace chuckled.

"What! This is Dante's room." She said, sitting up.

"Yup." Jace laughed, sitting up with her.

"Oh no." Nora said, looking at the flooded bathroom, the shower curtain on the ground, and now his messed up, wet bed.

"Come, he'll be fine." Jace laughed.

"How I have no clothes." Nora said, needing to leave right now.

She like felt Dante was going to walk in any minute. Jace walked over to his clothing on the floor; he grabbed his shirt and walked over to her. He placed it over her head, and as her face poked through, he kissed her once more. The shirt fell to her thighs.

"Come on, if we go quick, he won't know it was us." Jace laughed, walking to the door.

Chapter Thirty Seven
Threats

They rushed back to the room. Nora kept checking down the hall to see if Dante was coming up. Jace swung open his door and stepped aside, letting Nora go first. Nora scooted into the room quickly. It was not the room she woke up in. This was his actual bedroom. She leaned back against the door, looking around the room. It was pretty plain, a desk in the corner with an open laptop. A Tv facing the bed, there was a small picture frame on his nightstand, and clothes were scattered about. Jace flicked on the night before heading to his walk-in closet. She heard him rummaging around in there before coming back out.

"I don't know if they'll fit, but at least they'll cover you." Jace smiled, holding up a t-shirt and a pair of boxers.

"Yours?" Nora smiled while taking them.

"No, they're Dante's." Jace said sarcastically, rolling his eyes.

"Ok, then I'll go get a pair of his then." She grinned, acting like she was going to leave.

He caught her arm and spun her into him.

"Don't you dare wear someone else's underwear." Jace growled as Cole pushed forward.

"Easy wolfie." Nora said, making a face at him and motioning for him to turn around.

Jace rolled his eyes.

"I've pretty much seen everything now." He smirked, and his voice playful.

"Yeah, well still. It was a one-time thing…. so." Nora said, folding her arms across her chest.

"A one-time thing?" Jace asked, his voice daring her to repeat it.

"Yup." She said, her eyes flashing mischief. He moved towards her and she backed up, a small laugh escaping her.

"Go ahead and run. I like the chase." He growled as Cole flashed in his eyes.

She smirked, squaring up to him, daring him to try to get her. He took a step towards her, standing tall, trying to intimidate her. Her eyes sparkled, waiting for him to make his move. He backed her up against the wall pinning her against the wall and himself. He wasn't sure how he expected her to react, but her reaction wasn't it. She slipped her hands over his neck and pulled him into her. She wrapped her legs around his waist. He groaned, feeling her against him. She was still naked underneath his t-shirt. She laughed at his reaction. He smirked, his hand traveling down her side, sneaking around the front of her, going to touch her.

A loud bang came from the bedroom door. Jace's head shot to the door, his brows frowning.

"Damn it, Jace, you better come clean my room!" Dante's voice came through the door.

Nora heard it and laughed, hearing him being flustered.

"Go away." Jace growled.

"Even my bed is wet! What the hell did you all do?" Dante groaned.

"Go to a different room." Jace said, burying his face into Nora's neck.

Nora shoved him slightly, mouthing the word go. Jace shook his head, grabbing hold of her ear lobe with his mouth. She shivered against him as his hand began to wander.

"Wait till your room's empty." Dante said, nudging the door before leaving.

"See, he's gone." He whispered into her ear.

"Alpha." Adams' voice came through mindlink.

Nora laughed, seeing his eyes gloss over.

"What?" Jace answered.

"So I can't find much other than the original bloodline of hunters who were said to be cursed and had special abilities." Adam said unsure.

"That's it, that's all you got." Jace growled.

"Sorry Alpha…were you busy." Adam chuckled.

Jace ended the mindlink and looked to Nora.

"Come on," Jace said, walking to his closet.

"Where are we going?" Nora said, undressing and placing the oversized T-shirt and boxers on.

"Well, as much as I freaking love how my clothes look on you. You need your own before I have to fight someone. Two, we need to go somewhere to have the book translated." Jace said, his eyes wandering over her as he talked about the way she looked.

"Ok, let's go." Nora shrugged, walking to his door.

Jace stepped in front of her, looking down the hall before nodding for her to follow him. She rolled her eyes at his action but somehow found it cute. She walked down the stairs following him and then watched him halt.

"Nora, we forgot the book. Go back and grab it." The way he said it made her wonder if something else was going on.

"Ok." She said quietly, walking back up the stairs but stalling.

"Go now." Jace said, his voice sounding deadly.

"Mood swings much?" She muttered as she continued.

Reaching the top of the stairs, Nora sighed, unsure what was happening, but headed to the room. Jace waited, listening to her footsteps as she walked away before continuing down the stairs. His foot hit the landing, and he could already smell the blood. He wasn't sure what was going on. No one had alerted him that there was something taking place, and he was angry about it. He cautiously followed the smell of blood.

"Dante downstairs now." Jace commanded *through mindlink*

"Alpha?" Dante asked back, his tone confused and concerned.

"Now." Jace's mind linked him as he wandered into the kitchen; he saw a trail of blood leading to the back door.

He heard Dante running down the stairs. It sounded like he jumped down the last several steps, and he came barreling into the kitchen. Jace glanced over his shoulder at him, telling him to be quiet. He wasn't sure what was going on still. The blood led outside to the back door. Jace swung the back door open, looking down at the cement patio. He gritted his teeth, seeing a message written in blood.

You can't protect her.

Jace shoved passed Dante running up the stairs to his room. He needed to make sure she was ok. He knew he had just left her but. A mind link came through as Dante was giving out orders.

"There's been a breach! Patrol the borders now. We're looking for someone, rouge, or most likely from Kip's pack. Find them and bring them to me. There's also a body somewhere. Perform roll call, make sure all pack members are accounted for and check on everyone." The message went out to his soldiers.

Jace's lungs burned as he raced up the three flights of stairs. He ran down the hall Cole vibrating under his skin, wanting him to shift to be faster. He slammed into his bedroom door, almost knocking it off the hinges as he rushed into his room.

"Holy crap, you scared me! Are you ok?" Nora yelled, looking at him like he was crazy.

He cleared the distance between them and captured her in his arms. He rested his forehead against hers, his breathing fast. He had to touch her, and he had to make sure she was there. He ran his finger over the side of her face. The thought of losing her was very real for a second.

"Hey, want to tell me what the heck just happened?" Nora asked, cupping his face in her hands.

"You're worrying me?" She said, studying his eyes.

"It's fine." Jace said, kissing her forehead.

"Um, if this is fine, I don't want to know what not fine looks like." Nora said softly.

"There was a breach someone got in that wasn't supposed to." Jace explained, still holding her to him.

"Ok...I'm ok. Why are you acting like something would be wrong with me?" She asked him, confused.

"Can you just let me enjoy knowing your ok? God, you talk so much." He whispered to her.

"I-

His mouth captured hers, silencing her. She moved into him as he kissed her like he might never kiss her again. Her knees got a little weak, and she was breathless when he finally let her go. He stepped back from her, still holding onto her hand. He started to open the door, bringing her with him.

"Where are we going?" She asked, still in a daze.

"I need to make sure everyone is ok, and I'm not letting you out of my sight," Jace said, walking through the door.

Nora shook her head, following him, not really sure what was going on. The iron smell flooded her nose as she got to the bottom floor landing.

"Blood." She whispered out loud.

Jace looked at her, wondering how she knew. She began to panic as images of James flashed in front of her eyes, as the world began to spin.

"Hey, hey, what's going on?" Jace said, steadying her in his arms.

She was panicking; she needed to get away from the smell. The longer she smelt it, the more she could see them and their vacant eyes. She began to shake.

"She's having flashbacks." Dante said, walking into the room, recognizing the look.

It took him forever to fight against them, the shakiness, the pale, clammy skin, the way her breathing caught in her throat. It was like a panic attack. Jace looked to Dante for help, not sure what to do.

"Nora, you're fine. You're not there." Dante said, his voice was calm and soothing.

"Focus on your breathing, in through your nose and blow it out through your mouth. Nice and slow." Dante continued coaching her through it. She followed his instructions, her breathing slowing and her panic slowly fading.

The tightness in her chest started to ease, but every time she took a breath, she could smell the iron lingering in the air. She controlled her breathing, her own blood didn't bother her. When she thought Jace was hurt, the worry for him pushed her through the panic. She felt weak but couldn't stop the attack from coming.

"Tell me what you need?" Jace said to her.

"The blood, I need away from it." She said in a choppy sentence.

He nodded and led her to the front door. He opened the door and stepped out. He looked back to Dante, and he already knew what Jace was going to ask. He gave him a thumbs up before Jace shut the door walking outside with Nora. She inhaled the cool crisp air and counted back numbers in her head, calming herself down. She hated when she did that. She felt silly and weak. She looked up at the bright stars. She felt Jace come up behind her and circle his hands around her waist, pulling her back against him.

"Better?" He asked.

She leaned back into him with a small nod. It was crazy that she barely knew him, and he was supposed to be her enemy, but everything about him calmed her. Everything about him felt right. She took a deep breath and sighed happily as he rubbed her forearm. The heat from his hand felt good on her skin. "Want to tell me what happened?" Jace asked carefully.

"Blood, it's all I smelt when I walked into the house that night. Every time I smell it, I see their faces. Their empty, fearful faces, and now I know it was because of me." Nora whispered, shutting her eyes as she said it, the pain radiating in her voice.

Cole whimpered at her pain; he hated his mate hurting. Jace felt the same. He pulled her closer as if he could take the pain away.

"You know the scar on my throat. I sometimes wonder if it would have been better to have died with them." She whispered as if the confession was something she had been hanging on to for so long.

Jace felt a spark of sadness and anger shoot through him as she said that.

"Don't think like that; none of this is your fault." He said firmly.

"It's hard not to." She whispered.

His eyes looked at the scar on her neck. The long slash mark from the canine tooth. If you look closely enough, you can almost see the notches of where the teeth were when they bit into her. Jace became angry again. Nora felt the shift in his emotions. She turned in his arms, touching the side of his face.

"Don't worry; I'm not saying I want to die or will try to." Nora said, stepping into him and resting her head on his chest.

"The wolf that sank his teeth into your throat is dead." Jace vowed.

Nora didn't understand the statement, but she wanted to get away from the topic. She didn't know if he meant the wolf was already dead or if Jace was going to kill him. She felt Jace shrug.

"Cole or I will see to it." Jace said, being able to read the expression on her face.

She smiled slightly and nodded. Dante stepped out onto the front porch. They both turned and looked at him.

"All set, everything reeks like bleach, but it's better than anything else." Dante called to them.

Chapter Thirty Eight
Sorrow

Kip grabbed a hold of the control board yelling, the noise coming out of him was pure anger. He looked down at the video surveillance, and every one of his test subjects was dead. They were twisted in odd shapes, the room was destroyed. Blood splattered across it. He didn't understand what he was doing wrong. More blood was all he could think of. They lasted longer, but not enough to have them win a battle. He felt the control panel begin to buckle under his grip.

"Alpha?" Taylor came to the control station.

"Did you get my message to Jace?" Kip asked, his eyes still scanning the screens as if he hoped one would still be alive.

"Yes, Alpha." Taylor nodded, glancing over his shoulder at the screens.

Kip slammed his fist into one of the camera screens. It shattered beneath his fist, he let out a sigh as blood flowed down his hand. As he growled, his wolf Tovar pushed under the skin he wanted out. He wanted to run, and he wanted to hunt. Taylor watches Kip fight for control over Tovar. He was hard to contain sometimes.

"Did we find the girl?" Kip asked, still looking down at the blood on his hand.

"He has her." Taylor said, afraid of how Kip would react.

"Perfect. He will be more devastated that we took her from him. Knowing he could have protected her and didn't will be so much more worth it." Kip chuckled maniacally.

He saw something move in one of the monitors. He glanced down, and one of the deformed wolves was still moving.

"Look, there's one still alive." Taylor said to Kip.

"Taylor, what if we turn this girl in front of him." Kip said, his grin becoming sinister.

"Can you imagine watching her kill his pack and then dying in front of him, all twisted and deformed," Kip smirked.

Taylor kept quiet; he wasn't sure if he should say anything. He was also worried. Kip was becoming more and more unstable as his project progressed. Taylor watched the one still alive twitch on the floor.

"How much blood did we give that one?" Kip asked.

"I think he got 100 milliliters," Taylor said, grabbing a notebook at the desk and flipping through it.

"Yeah, he got 100. Rooms four and seven did as well." Taylor confirmed and then glanced at the camera to rooms four and seven.

"Well, four and seven are dead. What's different about this one?" Kip asked out loud, leaning over the control board and staring into the camera.

"He was a college student like the rest, he was in his early twenties and played football. The other two were the same in age but not into sports." Taylor said, reading over his notes.

"Ok, so we need to steal a football team." Kip said.

Taylor laughed, but when he saw the look on Kip's face, he realized he wasn't joking. Taylor retracted his laugh as quickly as he could and nodded.

Nora was curled on the couch in the living room, watching Jace pace the floor. His eyes were glossed over the whole time, so she knew he was communicating with his pack. Dante walked into the room, and Jace stopped sensing him. His eyes came back to focus.

"Everyone is accounted for. We didn't find anyone….we also did not find a source for the blood." Dante said his anger came through.

"Everyone is accounted for? " Jace asked, even though Dante had just said that.

"Yes. Everyone." Dante said again.

Jace was relieved, but it didn't make sense. Where would the blood come from? He sighed, running his hand through his hair. He glanced at Nora, who was watching them both.

"How did they or whoever get in?" Nora asked them.

Jace looked at her, slightly surprised, and then his eyes flickered to Dante.

"We have no clue all gates were locked, they didn't trip any of the security features," Dante said, annoyed.

Jace growled, becoming annoyed, and began pacing again. Dante was gripping the back of the couch behind Nora. She could feel the boards to the backrest cracking. She sighed, getting up.

"Jace, you're going to make me sick if you keep pacing. Dante, you're going to break the couch. And the answer to your question is someone let them in." Nora said with a shrug.

A growl erupted through Jace's chest, Nora stepped back, Nora raised an eyebrow at him as his chest began to move rapidly. Nora glanced at Dante, who bowed his head in submission, and a whimper escaped. Nora took a deep breath, Jace was trying to control himself, but the idea of one of his pack betraying him. His hands clenched in fists at his side as Cole pushed forward, trying to make him shift. Cole wanted to go home to home to find the trader. Nora took a deep breath and crossed the distance to him. She reached out slowly and cupped the side of his face with her hand. A growl erupted through his chest again as his hand came and caught her wrist, squeezing it hard. Cole was taking over and was blind to what he was doing.

"Cole, stop." Nora said, and his eyes flickered to her, coming slightly out of a haze.

"You're hurting me, stop. Get control of yourself." Nora said firmly, trying to ignore the shooting pain going through her wrist.

"Jace! Cole is hurting her; stop him!" Dante yelled, trying to muster the strength to move forward.

Jace aura was making him submit. Nora stepped into him. She placed her hand on top of his as he squeezed her wrist tightly. As soon as her hand touched his, his expression shifted. He glanced down, realizing instantly what he was doing. He dropped her hand. His eyes stopped glowing, and he looked down at her wrist. He took it in both his hands, looking it over, trying to see if he injured her.

"Nora, I'm sorry-" Jace said, but she shook her head, cutting him off.

She felt anger coursing through her, a voice in her head telling her that's what wolves do. They hurt people even when they care about them. She gritted her teeth, sweating beading across her forward head.

"Nora?" Jace said, holding her hand.

She ripped her hand away from him, closing her eyes, trying to get control of the rage coursing through her. The voice told her to take him out and that wolves needed to be exterminated. Jace went to touch her again, and she backed away without opening her eyes.

"Get away from me." Nora said, her voice full of venom.

"Nora." Jace said, confused, trying to figure out what was going on with her.

Nora took several deep breaths in her body, feeling like she was shaking. She opened her eyes and looked at him.

"I need air." She said desperately before rushing to the door and going out of it.

Jace looked at Dante, and he shrugged, not sure what that was. Jace went to go after her.

"Give her a minute. I don't know what that is, but she clearly needs a minute …Alpha." Dante tried not to tell him what to do.

Jace groaned, walking halfway to the door but stopping. He could hear her breathing and feel the emotions rolling off her. She was so angry. He heard her heart rate starting to go down, and he decided he waited long enough. He opened the door and walked outside slowly. He saw her standing in the moonlight, looking up at the stars. She looked like she was counting and breathing slowly. He came up behind her and slowly wrapped his arms around her. She sighed and leaned into him.

"Are you ok?" Jace asked her.

"I think so." Nora said quietly.

"Did I hurt you?" Jace asked, hurt in his own voice.

"A little, but that wasn't what that was. Sometimes I get so angry it's like there is this voice in my head telling me to hurt you. To eliminate all wolves. It comes with this surge of rage. I don't understand it." Nora explained, frustrated.

"It's ok, we will figure it out. Jace said to her, leaning down and kissing on the top of her head.

"I hope so." Nora muttered, glancing down at the book.

She sighed, looking up at the sky and the stars. She knew it was too late to go get the book translated. She needed to check in on Joel too.

"Jace, do you have my phone?" Nora asked, she had completely forgotten about it.

"Yeah, it's up in our room." Jace said, looking back at the house.

"Our room?" Nora asked, teasing.

"You're not sleeping anywhere but next to me." Jace said firmly but with a smile on his face.

"Is it a wolf thing to be possessive?" Nora teased him, turning around in his arms to look at him.

"Only about you and you're mine." He smirked and then bent down, picking her up and throwing her over his shoulder.

Nora laughed, not fighting him as he carried her into the house. Dante was sitting on the couch, waiting for them to return. Seeing them, he rolled his eyes.

"Well, I guess everything is all better?" Dante smirked.

"For now." Jace said with a shrug, plopping down on the couch next to Dante.

As he sat down, he pulled Nora from his shoulder to his lap, his arms wrapping around her as she fidgeted in his lap.

"If I'm ever like this, please throw up on me." Dante smirked.

"Jealous. Don't worry, you'll find your mate soon, and then I'll make fun of you." Jace said, nuzzling his face into Nora's neck.

"Jace." She laughed, swatting him, he growled slightly at the swat but ignored her.

"Hey, I really need my phone. I have to check in with Joel." Nora explained.

"Ok, wait here, I'll go get it." Jace said, scooting Nora off of him and almost into Dante's lap.

Dante grumbled and moved over to the couch, grabbing the remote as he did. He flipped the Tv on and began channel surfing.

"Hey, thanks for earlier." Nora said quietly.

"No problem, it took me a while to be able to handle the smell of blood again. You'll get there, but the onset of panic never goes away. You kind of have to work with each time." Dante said with a small smile.

"So your Jace's second in command?" Nora asked, making small talk.

"Yeah, I'm his beta, then it's a toss-up between Wyatt and Adam. then Matt." Dante said, squinting at the Tv, trying to read what the show was about.

"So, are you the better one at fighting?" Nora stepped around the question she wanted to ask.

"What are you getting at?" Dante asked, pausing the TV and looking at her.

"I need to know how to fight. I know the idea of it, and I kind of have the whole super strength going for me, but I still need to know. Can I go to training with you guys? Can someone teach me?" Nora asked hopefully.

"I could throw you a few pointers, have you come to a training-

"No." Jace's voice came from the stairwell as he walked down them.

"Excuse me?" Nora asked, a hint of anger in her voice, she had heard him but was daring him to say it again.

Dante shut up really quickly and tried to focus on the Tv.

"No. You're not going to train. We don't even know what you're capable of or aren't, and I don't need my wolves hurting you or getting hurt." Jace said, holding the phone out to her.

"So just No. Just sit here and be useless." Nora gritted her teeth.

Dante went to stand up, he was done being around the awkward argument. Nora grabbed him by the shoulder and pulled him back down. Dante's eyes shot to Jace as if asking for help.

"I didn't say to be useless. We will figure out a way to teach you to fight, but one step at a time right now, Nora." Jace said, trying not to fight with her right now.

Dante let out a small breath hearing Jace take the high road and not the my way or the highway tone. Dante went to unpause the Tv once more. Nora grumbled, grabbing her phone from Jace. She flipped it open and scrolled to Joel's name, clicking the phone to begin to dial. The phone kept ringing, no answer. Nora got up from the couch and walked to the door. She clicked the end call and redialed his number. It rang and rang still no answer. She was getting annoyed. She checked the time and decided to call one last time. Again the ringing kept going.

"Do you hear that?" Dante said to Jace.

"Hear?" Jace asked Dante, his eyes focused on Nora.

"Buzzing." Dante said, getting up and walking to the kitchen.

The buzzing stopped, and Nora groaned, ending the call. Dante's eyes flickered to Jace as his stomach twisted. Jace approached Nora and held out his hand, asking for the phone. Nora looked at him confused but handed him the phone. Jace clicked the send call button, and the phone redialed Joel's number. Jace shut his eyes, hearing the buzzing start up again. The flash of dread over his face Nora caught as Dante disappeared out of the room.

"What's going on?" Nora asked Jace, starting to be concerned.

The phone stopped ringing, and Jace quickly hit the redial button again. He was focused on Dante, and when his heartbeat sped up, he knew he found something.

"Jace the blood…it was her friend…he's I don't know how we missed it…he's dead." Dante's voice was full of regret and hurt for Nora.

Jace clicked off the phone, hearing Dante's mind link. He looked at Nora; how was he going to tell her?

"Jace, what the hell is going on? Why are you looking at me like that?" Nora said, beginning to panic.

"A message was left in blood on the patio. We didn't know where the blood had come from till now. Till you tried calling your friend." Jace started Nora gasping and bolted through the kitchen.

She was too quick for Jace to stop her. She ran to the back door pushing it open. She ran across the patio, seeing Dante just on the border of the woods. He turned around, hearing her, and his eyes became wide seeing her.

"Nora stay there." Dante yelled to her, but she didn't listen.

Dante didn't know what to do; there was nothing he could do right now to hide it. He looked back at Nora running to him, Jace was just behind, but she was somehow quicker than him. Dante gritted his teeth as she got to the spot.

"Nora…" Dante said his voice was sad for her.

Nora reached Dante's side and looked down into the small wooded area.

Joel's bruised and beaten body was laying there. A few feet away was his phone. Nora inched closer, and Dante caught her. She had seen enough death. He didn't want her to see the rest. She collapsed to her knees next to him. Her stomach turned in on herself as the urge to vomit hit her in waves. She stared at Joel's lifeless body begging silently for him to move, for him not to be dead. Tears streamed down her face. This couldn't be real; this was not happening. She inched closer, wanting to touch him. Wanting to shake him, wanting to scream, get up. As she was about to, she realized his head was severed from his body. She opened her mouth to say something, but a loud scream came out instead. She curled into her knees as another intense wave of pain and the need to vomit hit her.

Jace felt crippled and helpless as he watched her break down. There was nothing he could do to fix this. He went over and kneeled next to her. He placed his arm around her, not sure what to expect. Another sob escaped her as she curled into Jace's chest.

"He was my best friend." She said to his chest through the tears.

"He was all I had." She said, clinging to Jace.

Jace scooped Nora up into his arms and began carrying her back to the house. She shook her head, not trying to get down.

"We can't leave him there like that." Nora said, struggling.

"Nora we won't. I will have my guys get him cleaned up and everything." Jace reassured her.

Nora nodded, giving up on fighting him, her eyes locked on Dante's back, who was now bending over, attending to Joel's body.

Nora felt her heart break more as Jace carried her into the house.

Chapter Thirty Nine
Emotions

"Hey, easy killer." Drake said, walking into the training room.

Logan had been down here for hours, the punching bag he was assaulting looked like it was seconds away from breaking apart. Logan's knuckles were bloody, the punching bag smeared with it. He heard Drake enter but ignored his comment. He reared back and slammed his fist into it again. The bag dropped from the ceiling, and a cloud of dust blew up around it as it did.

"And this is why we can't have nice things." Drake smirked, leaning against the wall.

"Any smartass leads?" Logan asked, catching his breath as he turned around.

"No, no contact has been made. Although there is a situation at her friend's house." Drake said with a shrug.

"Situation?" Logan asked, taking a sip from his water bottle.

"Yeah, her friend Joel's house was destroyed. There was a good amount of blood…pretty sure it was a wolf." Drake said quietly.

"Who knows about her other than Jace?" Logan asked, thinking out loud, whipping the sweat from his head.

"Not sure, but it's gotta be another pack. The way they searched and ransacked the house. They were looking for something." Drake explained.

"More someone. If the news about her is out there, then we need to move quicker. We need to make sure she's safe." Logan said frustrated.

"Logan, why do you care so much? We don't even know anything about the stupid legend. That dumb book Drake has, we can't even read. All we know is they have abilities. Who says they're going to stop this war between wolves and hunters? Who says she's going to win it for us? What if she wins it for the wolves? She's a problem, not a solution." Lilly said, leaning against the doorway.

"You don't know anything, and if you keep going against me, Lilly, I swear." Logan said, stepping towards her.

"Really, Logan." Lilly said, rolling her eyes.

Logan crossed the distance between them, his hand clasped around her throat, throwing her back into the wall behind her. His hand was squeezing deadly around her throat, making her gasp for air.

"Sister or not, I will end you if you keep jeopardizing this for us." Logan said, squeezing more.

"Logan," Drake said cautiously behind him. Logan sighed and released Lilly, She fell to the ground gasping for air.

Logan stepped by her, walking out of the training room, not looking at her again. Drake held his hand out to help Lilly up. She begrudgingly took it.

"Fucking psycho." she muttered, standing.

"Shh." Drake said to her quietly.

"You know it, I know. He is obsessed with this whole hunter thing. I get that we live the lifestyle, but he's in too deep sometimes." Lilly said, going over to the standing mirror and looking at her very red throat.

"Or he could say you're not committed enough." Drake shrugged.

"Oh, ok Mom and Dad, thanks for the reminder." Lilly said, rolling her eyes at him.

"Lilly, that's not what I'm saying." Drake said with a frown.

"Not saying it or saying it is the same thing. You know her friend is dead right." Lilly said, turning away from the mirror.

Drake sighed, he figured but didn't know what Lily was getting at.

"And a wolf did it. maybe that's all we need; Maybe she will just come back to us because of it." Lilly told Drake.

"Even though it seems everywhere she goes, death follows." Lilly grumbled, walking past Drake. She had a point, Drake thought.

Whether the girl stayed with the wolves or came back to them, he didn't care. He just wanted her on their side, and the book translated. He knew giving it to Jace, he would find a way to translate it to help his mate. Drake walked out of the training room in search of Logan. Maybe if Logan reached out to her and offered support, she might build their friendship. He found Logan in the kitchen downing more water.

"Don't." Logan said, looking at him.

"I wasn't going too." Drake said, holding up his hand defensively.

"Then what do you want?" Logan said, setting his glass down.

"Well, Lilly had a good point." Drake said, leaning across the counter.

Logan frowned, his eyebrows turning down as anger flickered across his face. Drake once again put his hands up defensively.

"Hear me out... Her best friend is most likely dead because of wolves. She's probably going to be crushed when she finds out. She might run from the wolves. You need to be there for her." Drake said cunningly.

Logan nodded, replaying all everything Drake said in his head. It made sense, and it could work if he could get close to her.

"Guess I'm going to go swing by the wolf's den again," Logan said, taking a swig of water.

"Or maybe just get your number to her. Jace seemed pretty pissed the last time you showed up." Drake said quietly.

"Right. Well, here you get it to her and check in on them to see if they need help with the book. He didn't seem angry with you. Especially since you gave them that book." Logan said, grabbing a piece of paper and jotting down his number.

"Me...I uh, really?" Drake asked, unsure if he would get a better welcome than Logan.

"Yup. Go." Logan said, walking out of the kitchen.

"Great. I'm going in the morning, then." Drake called back to Logan.

Jace felt helpless as she sobbed into his chest. He cradled her, trying to make her somehow stop hurting.

"This is all my fault." She said in between choppy breaths.

"Shh, no. It's not." Jace said, brushing her hair from her face.

"My mom, my dad, and brother, now Joel. Everyone who mattered is gone." She said, sitting up and looking at Jace.

"You have no control over what others do. Just breathe." Jace said, just wanting her to calm down.

"No, maybe you should run before you end up dead, too." Nora said, scooting away from him.

He frowned deeply as she moved away from him, more tears streaming down her face as she backed off the bed.

"I'm not going anywhere, and neither are you. Come back here." Jace said, getting up.

Nora shook her head, backing away from him. Jace sighed, going to reach for her, but she shoved him back.

"Stop." He growled.

She shook her head, backing herself in the corner. Jace sighed again. He was trying to be understanding, but her not letting him comfort her was getting him annoyed. She sunk down in the corner of the room. Jace came over and bent down, sitting next to her.

"I bring death wherever I go." Nora whispered into her knees.

"I have seen death in person. You are not."
Jace said, pulling her into his lap.

"Then why do I feel like it?" Nora whispered.
Jace ignored her comment, scooped her up, and
brought her to bed.

He pulled her shoes off and laid down beside
her holding her. He let her cry softly in his arms till she
eventually fell asleep.

*"Dante." Jace mind linked him as Nora got
settled.*

"Yes, Alpha." Dante responded.

*"How did everything go?" Jace asked, trying
not to move too much.*

*"They're, um, fixing him up in the morgue."
Dante linked back.*

"How is she?" Dante asked in silence.

*"Ahh, honestly, I don't know. And I have no clue
what I'm doing or how to help her." Jace said back.*

*" Just be there for her. You're doing fine."
Dante said back.*

*"There's gonna be a war. There's something
more to all of this, and not just Kip causing chaos."
Jace said in an angry voice.*

" I know, and I'll be with you." Dante said back.

*"How does he know about her?" Jace's mind
linked back staring at the ceiling.*

" We will find out." Dante said back.

*"I want whoever it is." Jace replied to the
anger courses through the mindlink.*

He had so much running through his mind. He needed more insight from Kip. He knew there was something more.

"Dante, we need a spy. Contact Zeke and let him know where to start making moves. If he's with us, he will need to be ready." Jace said, reopening the link.

"Like sending some behind enemy borders? Who do you wanna send? He knows all your uppers. You'll need someone he doesn't know. Someone he wouldn't notice." Dante said back, thinking out loud.

"Someone who also won't get caught or hurt." Jace said, adding to the thoughts.

"Ok, I'll think about it. Get rest." Dante chimed back.

Jace shifted, pulling Nora into him. Her scent invades his senses, calming him instantly. No one was taking her from him.

Chapter Forty
Sweet Dreams

Nora's dreams were nothing but blood-filled. She kept seeing everyones face, and now Joel's face was added to her nightmare. She jolted up right in her sleep, throwing something very heavy off of her. She heard him grunt as she looked over at him. The moonlight flooding in from the bedroom window shone perfectly on him, highlighting him. His face was frowning as if he was in pain. Nora looked at him, her hand reaching out and brushing over his face. At her touch, his brows moved back into a relaxed position. She smiled, seeing his reaction to her. He was shirtless; her eyes wandered down his defined chest and abs.

Her fingertips brushed down over his neck and then slowly down his chest. She watched his skin shiver under her touch. He rolled over on to his back, groaning softly in his sleep. She smiled, watching him unknowingly search for her. She scooted closer to him and watched him relax. She smiled when he was sleeping, he seemed fragile. She couldn't help but touch him. She ran her finger tips down over his abs and watched goosebumps form. She should run, she should leave, but she wanted him. She wanted to be with him. Her fingertips stopped at his waist line, she ran them softly along it, and he sleepy moaned. She smirked. She wanted to make him make more noises. She brought her hands to the side of his shorts that he had been sleeping in. Gripping them, she pulled them down, taking his boxers with them. Jace, confused and still half asleep, went to sit up. Nora's hand caught his chest, pushing him back down on the bed.

"Nora?" Jace asked, groggy.

"Shh." Nora said as her hand made its way down to his member.

As she enclosed her hand around his shaft, he let out a small groan. She smirked and positioned herself over him as she began to move her hand up and down it. He grew in her hand. She grazed the tip of him across her lips and watched him shutter. She smiled, flickering her tongue over it. He let out a small growl at her teasing him. She ran her tongue down the side of him, watching another wave of chills pass through him.

"Nora." He warned; he couldn't take much more of her teasing.

She smiled before capturing him with her mouth. He arched into her as her warm mouth encased his member. She began to move up and down, her tongue running over him as she moved. His hand found the back of her head, and his fingers wove into her hair as she began to move quicker. She swirled her tongue around the tip of it as she moved upwards.

"Fuck." He whispered as the surge of tingles went through him, his body involuntary twitching as her tongue flickered over the sensitive spot.

She liked it, the way he groaned, the way he cursed because it felt so good. She moved against him and, after several passes, did it again. Swirling her tongue around the very tip. She felt him shutter. She smiled with him still in her mouth. He was all done being toyed with. His hand let go of her hair, finding her shoulders and lifting her up. He sat up just as quickly. His hands went to her shirt, grabbing it at the collar line and tearing it into two. The material fell away at the sides, exposing her perky breast. She let out a small yell, but her smile told him otherwise. His mouth captured her lips, his tongue plunging into hers, demanding more from the kiss. His hands explored further down her. Reaching her underwear, he smirked against her mouth.

"No." She whispered against his lips.

He smirked and pulled on the sides, her underwear shredded in his hands. His mouth moved to her neck, sucking and kissing it as he moved down her. He laid back on the bed, his hands finding her hips and thrusting her forward. She grabbed onto the headboard as her thighs cradled the sides of head, his face buried between them. She felt his mouth capture her bud. He pulled it into his mouth with sucking on it. A moan escaped her as her head dropped, her hand gripping the headboard. His tongue swirling around the bundle of nerves made her mind beg for more. Her hips involuntarily begged to move as he teased her with his mouth. He slid his tongue away from her bud, pushing in her. The sensation of ecstasy made her whimper, her body shaking slightly. His hands captured her hips once more, tossing her gently to the side of him before quickly straddling her. He ran his cock over her slit, rubbing it against her bud. She moaned, twitching slightly as she raised her hips. She wanted him, and he needed to have her now. He smiled, seeing her wanting him. He pressed his way into her entrance; she let out a deep moan as he filled her. He stopped himself from making the same noise. He felt her clamp down around him as he began to move. Her legs wrapped around him, trying to keep him inside her. She moved with him, her fingernails grazing his back as she let the feeling overwhelm her. He thrusted harder and faster as he felt his release coming.

She began to shake beneath him, knowing that hers was not too far away. A warm feeling washed over her as all her muscles began to contract. She let out a moan clinging to him as a wave of intensity rushed over her. He felt her orgasm and leaned down into her as he felt his release happening. His teeth grazed the spot on her neck where he would mark. His fangs pressed into the soft skin. She moaned, arching into him as if she wanted him to. He pulled his head back before it was too late; if she moved like that again, he would sink his fangs into her and mark her.

He moved off of her as he watched her body relax and shake in the aftermath of it all. He smiled, pulling her into him. His hand wrapped around her. She sighed happily against him, and within a matter of minutes, she was back to sleep. He covered them with a blanket before glancing at the clock. 3 am. He shut his eyes, and the relaxing morning was not too far.

The sunlight streamed from the window onto the bed. Nora groaned, pulling the blankets over her head, but the warmth was gone. She looked about curiously. Jace was gone; a small sadness pulled at her as she sat up, looking around the room. Why didn't he wake her? She thought about getting up and holding the blanket to her. She made her way to the bathroom, figuring she might as well shower before venturing out into the house. Getting into the bathroom, she paused in the mirror, her eyes going to her neck. She saw the two small puncture holes his fangs had left from just touching her skin. The last time that happened she had so much angry but last night she wanted him too. She wasn't sure what that meant or what the whole purpose of marking your mate did, but she wanted it.

She sighed, turning on the water in the shower. She stepped into the shower, trying to be as quick as possible. She washed all the important stuff and her hair. She was out as soon as she could. Grabbing a towel, she walked out into the bedroom, wrapping it around her. She sighed loudly in the room. She didn't have any clothes yet, and Jace not being there when she woke up annoyed her.

"Something wrong, sunshine." Jace's playful voice said to her.

"No." She smiled big seeing him.

"Good, here, put these on, and let's go. Don't forget the book." Jace said, handing her a black bag.

Nora raised an eyebrow at him before opening the bag. Inside the bag was a beautiful black sunflower dress and some underwear. She smiled, looking at him. She smirked, dropping the towel in front of him. Cole flashed in his eyes as they ran over her body. She grinned, reaching into the bag and pulling out the black pair of underwear, putting them slowly on in front of him.

"Don't tempt me. We won't leave this room if you don't stop." Jace said, daringly stepping forward.

Part of her didn't care if they did, but a big part of her wanted to know what the book said. The nagging part of her brain was telling her to quit teasing him and get going. Nora made a face at him as she slipped the dress on. It fit her like a glove. Jace's eyes were still wandering over every seductive curve of hers. He took three quiet steps and pulled her into him.

"Hey, now I'm not doing anything this time." Nora chuckled.

"You don't have to. I will always want you." he said as a growl rumbled through his chest as he kissed her lips.

"The book." Nora said, moving her face to the side as if that would stop Jace.

"Mhmm, the book." Jace said, placing kisses along her neck.

"Ok, ok get it together.' Nora laughed, trying to step away from him.

"We need to know what's going on with me." Nora said firmly to him.

He growled softly into her neck but stepped away. His hand captured hers as he made his way to the bedroom door, bringing her with him.

Chapter Forty One
Olive Branch

Nora follows him out the front door stopping and looking towards the woods where Joel's body was found. Her chest tightened as she looked, her eyes searching for the body. Was her chest ever going to stop feeling so heavy?

"What happened to his body?" Nora asked, her voice cracking.

"I had him brought to the morgue. Does he have a family?" Jace said, trying to gauge her feelings.

"His mom lives on the outskirts of town in their family home. His dad passed away a few years ago. I don't even know how to tell her I didn't even know what to do …he had…he…his head ..I.." She stopped talking, not being able to finish her sentence.

"It's ok. I will go with you. I've had to do this once or twice. We might need to borrow and wreck his car. Better a car accident than someone murdering him," Jace said, then regretted being so political.

He looked at Nora, who simply nodded. He could tell she was keeping herself together the best she could. He pulled her against him and kissed the top of her head. They made their way to the car. Nora didn't ask where they were going, images from last night and kept playing in her head. She was so zoned out that she didn't even notice Jace had stopped the car. She glanced over when. She heard the stir wheel squeak from Jace's vice grip on it. A small rumble went through his chest. Nora looked to where he was looking. She was confused as to what had him so angry. She sighed, seeing Drake outside the gate. Nora reached over and placed her hand on top of his. His grip softened.

"You're going to break your car." She smirked.

"Might not be the only thing I break." He said, gritting his teeth.

"Hey, it's ok. I kinda wanna hear what they have to say." Nora said to him.

Jace looked at her, and she saw a flicker of something in his eyes, worried, maybe panic.

"I'm not leaving." Nora said softly, unbuckling her set belt.

"Come on." Nora said, her hand going to the door handle.

He sighed deeply. A few months ago, he would have killed that hunter from coming back, but now we're going to go chit-chat. Jace frowned after getting out of the car.

"Morning." Drake waved.

Jace shot a looked at the guards; they shrugged. Nora felt anger roll off of him as he narrowed his eyes at them. They dropped their heads down and bared their necks to him as if his anger hurt them. Nora watched the scene before reaching over and touching his arm. She felt his anger fade away.

"What do you want?" Nora asked Drake through the gate.

Jace was scanning the background with his eyes. He wasn't picking up on anything. This was weird, a hunter coming alone.

"Adam, Matt, there is a hunter at the front gate, has a patrol report if there's anyone else." Jace sent out his body on alert.

"No, Alpha. No reports of anyone else." They both linked back in unison.

Drake studied Jace.

"I came alone. Logan can be kind of a hothead sometimes, and I'm trying to help build a relationship. He wants one as well, but like I said, he is hot-headed. I came on behalf of him." Drake smiled weakly at Jace.

"Why would hunters ever want to build a relationship with wolves," Jace said, through his teeth.

"Things need to change, there's few of us left, and the hate needs to stop. Nora could be that branch for us." Drake said, glancing at Nora.

"Who says I want to be?" Nora said, her brow frowning at him.

She was still on edge about how Lilly acted towards her. Jace smirked and the look that flashed across his face was proud as if to say "that's my girl". He grinned widely at Drake, acting like he had just won some argument that had not taken place yet.

"I know we damaged your trust; that wasn't supposed to happen. Lilly tends to be a bit impulsive." Drake explained.

"So Logan is a hot head, Lilly is impulsive. You guys sound like you're the package deal." Jace said with a threatening smile.

Drake sighed, trying to talk his way into letting Jace and Nora trust him.

"You might need back up. We don't know too much about it, but there is an Alpha running around causing havoc. We've been tracking him but haven't gotten too close. From what I can tell, you are about rules and order." Drake said with a sigh.

"We know about him, and we have him under control," Jace said, ignoring the offer to help.

"You have him under control? Psssh, I would hate to see what out of control looks like." Drake said, rolling his eyes.

Jace growled, stepping towards him. Nora grabbed his arm, pulling him back to her. Her eyes look to Drake, asking him to stop poking the wolf.

"Look, I just came here to offer our help and give Nora another book that might help her." Drake said, holding out the book to Nora.

Nora looked at him before slowly taking the book from him. He grinned and nodded to her before heading back to his car.

"You know where to find us." Drake said, looking past Jace to Nora; before getting to his car and leaving.

Jace grumbled to himself before walking back to his car. Nora watched Drake leave questions running through her mind. What did he mean she could be the link to build the bond? She heard Jace's car turn on, which snapped her from her thoughts. She sighed, walking to the car. Getting in the car with the book in her lap, she glanced down at it as Jace took off. She ran her fingers down the spine of the book. It was another leather-bound book that had no title. She made a face opening it, expecting it not to be in English. Opening it, she realized it was a journal. She skimmed through it, and as she brushed by the pages, a piece of notepaper came into view. She opened the folded piece of paper. Logan's number was written on it with a note for her to call him. Jace glanced over at her. She wanted to shut the book and pretend she didn't see it, but she could tell he knew something was up.

"Logan left me a note with his number." Nora said to him. Jace suppressed a growl and looked at her trying to read her feelings about it.

"Do I need to worry about the hunter boy?" Jace said quietly.

"Worry like we're a thing?" Nora asked, her voice playful.

"You are my mate." Jace said, not finding it funny.

"Sounds like a wolf problem." Nora said, trying not to laugh.

Jace growled at her response. She couldn't help but laugh.

"Remember, it was a one-time thing." Nora chuckled.

"A one-time thing that happened twice with you making the second time happen." Jace smirked at her.

"Yeah yeah. I was feeling generous." She made a face at him.

"Sure, that's what you wanna call it." Jace said, making a disbelieving face at her.

"It is." Nora said, sticking her tongue out.

"You're hurting Cole's feelings." Jace said.

Nora reached over and patted Jace like she would a dog.

"There, there." She said, laughing.

"You better stop, or I'll let him out, and he'll show you how much of a lap dog he is." Jace said, throwing a wink at her.

Nora giggled and leaned back in her chair, her attention going to the window. She glanced down at the book, debating reading it. She opened the page to the first passage.

November 5th Today is the day before my twenty-first birthday, and I am terrified. We have been safe up until this point. Once I turn, they will know. They will try to end us. It becomes a battle between who can hunt the other and kill them first. I never wanted to ascend. I didn't want the transformation. I am not one of those people who want to be different or unique. I wanted just to live life peacefully, but now it is all about to change. We've moved several times, trying to find a wolf-free zone, and my family is preparing for this day. My mother died being a hunter. My father treated me like the son he never had.

Telling me how proud she would have been, and all I wanted to do was shrink away. I will never have children; I will not pass this down. Hopefully, the bloodline ends with me. Let the wolves just take over.

November 7th It happened. It was painful, but now I am stronger and faster, and my senses are sharper. I can see things across the room and tune into conversations that I shouldn't hear. I am excited. The feeling it gives me is a rush. However, most days, I am just waiting for a wolf to spot me. At night I barely sleep, thinking one is going to come kick in my door. My father said there's a community of hunters. He wants to find them for me. Says we will be safer there. That they will be able to train me, I am worried about traveling that far. My father says it's the only way. There have been rumors of attacks.

The car pulling into a parking lot caught Nora's attention; she looked up from the book to Jace, who was putting the car in park.

Chapter Forty Two
Biting Your Tongue

Jace walked around to her side of the car, opening her car door and holding his hand out for her. A small smile flashed across her face as she took his hand and got out of the car. She realized where they were. This was the same place Jace had taken her where she got the other wolf book. Nora looked at him as she got out of the car, wondering how the book keeper was going to help them.

"Come on." Jace said, ignoring the look.

He grabbed a hold of her hand, and they walked into the book store. Walking in, the bell rang and the man behind the counter came out. His face at first was very pleasant, but seeing Jace, it changed to nervousness.

"Mr. Knight, have you come to return the books you borrowed?" He asked, trying to be brave.

"No, we are not down with them. However, I need a favor." Jace said firmly.

"What kind of favor?" He asked, looking confused.

"I need you to translate something." Jace said, holding his hand out to Nora for the book. Nora handed it to Jace, who handed it over to the bookstore owner.

He looked confused, looking down at the book, and he began to shake his head.

"Tim, your whole family has dedicated their lives to this. If anyone can crack this, it's you." Jace said to him.

"Jace, I don't even know what language this is." Tim said.

Jace shut his eyes and sighed, becoming annoyed that Thomas wouldn't even try.

"Mr. Tim, I'm sure you have resources here that could help you. It's really important I find out what's in this book." Nora said to him, hoping she could sway him.

"What are you?" Tim asked her, looking at her suspiciously.

Jace growled defensively, pulling Nora to him. Nora chuckled, tapping Jace's arm. Tim's eyes almost fell out of his head, seeing the action.

"I'm a hunter, but I need to know more about this book." Nora glanced at Jace, he seemed to be mad that she had told him.

"Hunter, huh…and Mr. Knight is a wolf. Hmmm." Tim said, looking back and forth between them.

"I'm assuming you're his mate by the way he is acting towards you. I don't think I've ever known a wolf to be mated to a hunter. You guys are in for a long struggle." Tim said, looking at them, his face intrigued.

Nora stayed silent while Jace began to get angrier. Jace stepped towards the counter and grabbed hold of it with both hands, his strength making the wood buckle. Tim stepped back, looking at him concerned.

"Are you going to help or not?" Jace growled.

"I'll help, but it's gonna take a while." Tim nervously held his hand out for the book.

Nora smiled, watching Jace make Tim squirm a little bit. She felt bad but liked how Jace took control of things. Nora sighed, seeing Thomas begin to sweat as Jace's eyes glowed. She stepped forward, putting her hand on his forearm.

"Now, now we need him to help us." She laughed, tapping Jace.

Jace sighed, letting go of the counter and stepping back. Thomas looked shocked at how easily Nora tamed the wolf in him.

"We're waiting till you're done." Jace growled at him before walking away down an alley of books.

"How are you not scared of him?" Tim whispered to her.

"He won't hurt me, and besides, I think I can take him." She smirked.

"Sure you can, little hunter." Jace chuckled, hearing her response as he continued down the aisle.

"That is just insane. Do you know about him? Do you know what he's capable of and has done?" Tim leaned forward, whispering to Nora.

Nora looked at him confused, the surge of anger starting in her core.

"He's killed and slaughtered, even his own family." Tim whispered.

"Tim, don't you have something to do, or should I show her what I am capable of?" Jace said, stepping out of the book aisle.

Tim nodded and took off into his back office. Nora looked at him, concerned, as she watched him leave. What did he mean? He killed his own family. Her eyes glanced at Jace. He shook his head and walked away. Shutting her eyes, she could feel the bile bubble in her stomach. A wave of anger hit her as she fought herself to control her feelings. She couldn't stop herself; she followed after Jace. She found him sitting on a brown leather couch by a window with a book in his lap. If she wasn't so angry, she would have wanted to curl up next to him.

"What did he mean?" Nora asked with her hands in a fist by her side.

"Nora, we've talked about my past." Jace said, not looking up from his book.

"He said you killed your family. You never mentioned that." Nora said, anger surfacing.

Jace's eyes glowed slightly as he looked up at her anger circling them. He didn't want to talk about this.

"I've told you about my father; there can't be two Alphas. How do you think I became Alpha?" Jace said to her he was feeding off her anger now.

"Did you have siblings?" Nora asked, ignoring the vibrations of anger.

"I'm not talking about this anymore." Jace growled, the book he was holding snapped at the binding.

"Whatever." Nora yelled at him, walking away.

She didn't even hear him move. Within seconds she was pinned up against a bookshelf. Jace face to face with her. Anger flashed in his glowing eyes. She laughed in his face.

"You don't scare me; you have two seconds to step away from me." She growled at him.

"I don't scare you because you have never seen what I can do. I have done awful things, and just because you feel entitled to know everything doesn't mean you get to throw a tantrum and get your way." Jace growled at her.

She scanned his face fighting with the fact he was right. She should have asked differently, but she felt like he had lied. She gritted her teeth, the anger backing away slightly.

"Let me go." She said annoyed.

Jace growled, pushing off the bookshelf, fighting himself and Cole. He shook his head, sighing angrily before walking back to his spot on the couch. He tossed the book that he had broken aside before laying back on the couch, closing his eyes. Nora blew a large amount of air out her mouth clenching her jaw. She looked at him wanting to fight more but couldn't because she knew she had been wrong. She grabbed the journal in her hand and went to sit opposite him. She sat done on a small lounge chair, sitting down kind of loudly while peeking at him. Jace didn't move. She loudly readjusted herself in the chair, still peeking at him, and he was completely ignoring her. She sighed, opening the book to where she left off.

November 11th We have been on the run for four days now. They found me. It happened all at once in the middle of the night. The front door literally kicked in. Luckily we had been preparing for that moment since I shifted. We managed to get to the car in time. It seems like an endless chase. We keep moving north, trying to find the hunters. Not stopping only for gas. My dad is getting sleep deprived. I don't know how long he can hold out. He's been talking to someone on the phone who keeps giving him directions but only spot to spot. They are worried. If we are caught, we will give away their location. The next checkpoint is on another day. I don't know if my dad can hang on that long. He refuses to switch off driving.

November 16th It's all my fault. If I never shifted, if I didn't have her bloodline running through my veins. He wouldn't be dying. They tracked us to a rest stop. My father nodded out, and I couldn't bear to watch him not sleep. I thought I could keep a lookout. I thought I could tell one if I saw one. They look like normal people till they shift. Their eyes glow right before their bones bend and break. Then the bloodthirsty creature appears. I tried to wake him. He wouldn't wake up. The wolf smashed through the drive-side window biting and snapping. There are so many bite wounds. So much blood. I managed to somehow fight the wolf off the car with a baseball bat. I don't know where the surge of strength came from. In a blink of an eye, he was whimpering on the ground, and I quickly managed to pull my dad to the passenger seat and take off. Two more days.

Nora felt tears swell up in her eye as she read the scene, images of her own horror flashing in her mind. She looked up from the book and needed a moment. She didn't want to read the next passage fearing the girl's father died.

"I had a sister, and yes, she's dead because of me." Jace's voice caught her attention.

Nora looked at him quietly, not saying anything, waiting for him to continue. He was still lying on the couch, looking up at the ceiling.

"My father had gone off the deep end. He had attacked several smaller packs and now wanted to rule them all." Jace said, snorting at the thought of it.

"There was a weak pack, mostly elderly, women and children. He was planning on attacking them. I was older enough and knew better. The pack and I were done with his ways. I asked him to step down, more told him to. After a heated argument, we were in the living room of the pack house. Tables were torsed, the couch flipped over, both of us raging. I went to leave, telling him he was going to step down and we were not going to war with the pack. I heard his bones popping and snapping as he shifted. I was prepared for the fight. I braced for the impact when a piercing scream shattered my ears. I turned just in time to catch my younger sister Emily in my arms. My father's wolf ripped her throat out. She bled out in seconds, as I held her in my arms. I snapped; Cole took over, and when I came to. I was sitting in a pool of blood. My father's body in pieces about the room, Emily's cold, lifeless one in my lap." Jace said, gritting his teeth, he had to stop and paused to get himself under control.

"Dante didn't recognize me as he came running to the pack house. They all sensed the bond break. I didn't bury him, I tossed his body pieces in the woods and let the animals eat him. He didn't deserve a burial. My mother died because of him, and then my sister." Jace said coldly.

"Jace I'm so sor-

"Don't. You know now. I don't intend to keep secrets from you but ask instead of being hotheaded." Jace said, still cold and distant as he shut his eyes again.

Nora swallowed hard. She felt awful. Did everyone have a horror story in this new world she was sucked into? She looked down at the journal and then at Jace. She could feel his sadness underneath all that anger he was projecting right now. She wanted to go to him and wrap her arms around him. She couldn't tell if she had pushed him away or not.

Chapter Forty Three
Dreams

Just when she had decided to go to him, Tim returned a puzzled look on his face. Jace stretched, sitting up and looking at him, waiting for him to explain. Tim took a deep breath looking nervously about. He sensed the tension between Nora and Jace and didn't want to make any more ripples.

"I need more time, but I will tell you what I have found out so far." Tim started and quickly added good news.

Jace motioned for him to get on with it, and Nora gave him her undivided attention. Tim came and sat by Jace but as far over as he could.

"Ok, I haven't figured out the whole story, but so far, I've got that the original hunters were cursed with abilities. They were given powers to fight the original bloodline of the first wolves. The strange thing is you would think they would use the word blessed or gifted regarding the hunters' abilities, but it says cursed. It also refers to the original bloodline of the first wolves being cursed as well, but I haven't translated how or with what they are cursed. It does say a descendant will come from the original bloodline of the first hunters and break or command the curse. The powers will also grow." Tim explained everything he knew.

Nora took it all in, a bunch of questions running through her head. She watched Jace just silently nod and then glanced down at his watch. He let out a sigh and then looked at Tim.

"Do you have a copier?" Jace asked.

"I do." Tim answered, his brows turning down.

"Copy the pages that you haven't finished translating or the ones you're working on. It's getting late, and I can't stay here much longer." Jace said, letting it be known he was becoming bored and almost annoyed sitting around.

Tim nodded and disappeared back to his office. Jace glanced at Nora, who had been looking at him the whole time. She saw something flicker in his eyes before he stood. He didn't say anything to her but motioned for her to follow him.

"Great, the silent treatment." She muttered, getting up.

She knew Jace heard her but continued walking ahead of her. His phone buzzed in his pocket. He flipped it open, looking confused.

"Hello." Jace answered shortly.

"Alpha, I figured a phone call would be less of an emergency." Adam said with a smile in his voice.

"You could have just mind link me." Jace grumbled.

"Well, you've been busy, so I figured if you answer the phone, you're ok." Adam chuckled.

"Ok, so I found the perfect person for the undercover thing." Adam continued.

"Ok." Jace answered.

"You won't like it…but Rosie." Adam said.

Jace could tell he was making an awkward face as he said it.

"Freaking Rosie, really." Jace said, sounding annoyed as he said Rose's name.

"She is a female. He won't suspect her. Her family has been in this pack for years, so she's loyal." Adam said, arguing his stance.

"Talk to her and see what her stance is." Jace sighed, not liking the idea but couldn't think of a better one right now.

Jace continued walking to the front of the store, Nora following behind him. She studied him, half listening to the conversation, half wondering what to do about the awkwardness. Tim came out, handing the book to him as he hung up his phone. Jace nodded and continued towards the exit. Tim smiled weakly at Nora.

"I'll have it done as soon as I can." he said as Nora smiled back.

They walked silently back to the car. Jace opened the car door for her, she got in, and he closed the door behind her. He didn't say anything as he got in and started the car. It was making Nora feel worse but, at the same time, was becoming annoying.

"Where are we going now?" Nora asked, breaking the silence.

"Home." He replied shortly.

Nora gave up looking out the window. If he wanted space, then he could have it.

Kip paced the floor of the control room watching the monitors. He had two Jock college kids brought in. He didn't need them to live long, just long enough to cause havoc and damage. Long enough to wipe out most of Jace's pack. They were taking longer than the others. He didn't know if this was a good thing or a bad thing. He grumbled to himself, waiting.

"Alpha, there's a phone call for you from Rose or Rosie." Taylor said, coming out of the office.

"Rose…Ah yes, let me talk to her." Kip smiled evilly.

"Hello, dear." Kip purred into the phone, a wicked grin on his face.

"The girl is here and still alive. What are you waiting for?" Rosie growled into the phone.

"First off, you are no one to question me. Secondly, we can't exactly waltz into Jace's pack and take his mate. It's more complicated than that." Kip hissed through the phone.

"It might be that easy. Jace has asked me to spy on you. I will be able to know the inner workings of things now. I could report false information. Have them go, and you come to get the girl." Rosie said, her voice chilling.

Kip smiled big. Jace really thought he could breach his pack. He weighed the idea of it all, and his smile grew. This could work.

"I might have to actually meet you. You are about as manipulative as I am." Kip eagerly said into the phone.

"I have no interest in dates. I want Jace, and that girl is standing in my way. So deal?" Rose said, annoyed.

Kip heard bones snapping and popping out of place and back in. Taylor nodded, saying the shifting had begun. He glanced at the phone; this shift had taken the longest. Maybe this time would be different.

"Deal. In two days' time, I might have enough distractions for them. I'll call you, and we will set it up. Good night night she-wolf." Kip said, hanging up and going to study the monitors.

"What was that about?" Taylor asked quietly.

"We have a friend in Jace's pack." Kip chuckled, watching the newly changed wolf.

The car ride had been silent since they left the bookstore. Jace had not even glanced her way. She sighed loudly.

"Can we go check on Joel's mom?" Nora asked, her eyes looking out the window.

"Now?" Jace asked, glancing at the clock on the car dashboard.

"She wouldn't mind. How did you tell her about it?" Nora asked, trying not to see Joel's dead body in her mind.

"Adam staged a car accident. Matt went to her home in uniform and informed her. She had asked if you were ok. She assumed you were with him. Afterwards, Matt let her know the body was taken to the morgue and was waiting for her instructions." Jace said like he was recapping a football game or something.

Nora tried to ignore the tone. He said everything, but it bothered her. She wondered if he was going to take her. She waited a few minutes of odd silence before looking at him.

"So, can we go? Or let me get my car, and I will go by myself." Nora said, letting him know she was going either way.

She watched Jace grind his teeth before glancing over at her. He made the car take a left-hand turn as they started away from his home. Nora raised an eyebrow at him. He let out a deep sigh but didn't say anything. In a few moments, Nora recognized the route and knew he was taking her to Joel's mom. The car ride was silent; she hated the silence. She looked down at the journal in her lap and flipped open to the next page.

November 18 We have been running through the woods for what feels like a week. The sun has only set twice. It was supposed to be two days. I don't know where we're headed. My dad has lost so much blood. The blood is what is helping the wolves track us. We're staying ahead just by chance, but I don't know how much further we can go. The cell service is gone. We are completely lost.

Nora's heart tugged for them as she read, her eyes growing heavy. She fell asleep quickly. She was running blindly through the woods, it was dark. The smell of blood wrapping around her. She tripped over something large, her heart pounding in her chest as she was launched forward, her hands going out in front of her, waiting to brace her fall. She hit the ground with the smell of earth wrapping around her. She tried to get up quickly but couldn't get off the thing she tripped over. The sounds of branches snapping and the leaves crunching enveloped her as she tugged on her foot, trying to get it loose. She pulled with all her might, getting her foot finally free. She got up just in time to miss being lunged at. She turned to see the large red wolf. Blood dripped down from its mouth. Nora froze as it went to lunge at her again. Squeezing her eyes shut, she waited for impact.

A loud yelp was heard as the wolf was flung away from her. A large black wolf planted itself protectively in front of Nora, growling fiercely. Nora could see the ice-blue glow coming from his eyes. The red wolf lunged, and they locked in battle. The red wolf was biting and clawing at the black wolf. The black wolf is trying to fight strategically and push them further away from Nora. The red wolf lunged at the black wolf's throat, snapping and snarling as he did. The black wolf threw the red one off of him. The red wolf slid into a tree, hitting it and letting out a loud yelp. The yelp echoed through the woods. The large black wolf made its way back to Nora. The large black wolf nudged Nora as if checking to see if she was ok. She recognized him and knew it was Cole. Nora ran her hand through his fur, feeling countless wounds. He didn't even wince. He was too focused on making sure she was ok. Loud noises off in the distance sounded like a war was going on. Cole's attention went behind them. He was distracted; he didn't see the red wolf get up and begin to make its way over. It lunged for his throat, Cole still unaware. Nora watched the red wolf sink its teeth into Cole's throat and rip a hunk of it out. Cole slumped to the ground. He struggled, trying to get up as if he wasn't processing what was happening. His ice-blue eyes faded quickly as he collapsed further into the soil.

Chapter Forty Four
Home Away from Home

"Hey, hey, Nora." Jace said, concerned, shaking her; he had pulled the car over when he saw her having a nightmare.

"Cole! Jace!" Nora yelled, jumping up, warm tears slipping from her eyes.

Jace caught her as she sat up quickly by her shoulders. Her eyes looked shocked to see him, and then he watched a rush of relief wash over her. Was she dreaming about him?

"Nora, it's ok. I'm right here." Jace told her calmly as he wiped the tears off her cheek.

She exhaled the breath that she was holding in as she looked at his face. Her hand came up to touch him gently as if confirming he was, in fact, right in front of her. She shut her eyes and leaned her forehead against his.

"It felt so real." She murmured.

"You're ok. I promise nothing ever is going to happen to you." Jace whispered to her.

Nora pulled away from his statement, her eyes looking hurt as if he had just told her something horrible. She's always ok, and everyone around her dies.

"It's not me. I'm always fine. It's you. It was you; the same red wolf that has been ruining my life took you." She said her voice was shaking.

"Red wolf.." Jace repeated her statement, his thoughts thinking of everyone's wolves.

"The night my family died, the night I almost died. All I remember is red fur, red eyes, and teeth. I dreamed he killed Cole and you. Cole was defending me." Nora said, her breath hitching in her throat as she explained.

Red eyes….Kip. Jace thought. He didn't say anything. He got out of the car and walked over to the passenger side. Nora looked confused. He pulled open the car door and, within one shift motion, scooped her out of the car, wrapping his arms around her. She was surprised at first but melted into his arms. He was there, he was ok. Jace kissed the top of her head as he felt her relax.

"I'm not going anywhere; the devil himself couldn't take me from you," Jace said as he pushed down the worry into the pit of his stomach, her dream had somehow created.

He felt Nora wrap her arms around him tighter as she pressed her face into his chest. She relaxed more, the longer he held on to her. Jace smiled; maybe hanging around with wolves was rubbing off on her. The fact that he could calm her just by holding her made him smile.

"Joel's mom's house is the next driveway over." He whispered down to her.

He saw her sigh deeply, still not moving away from him. She needed him a little longer. Jace rubbed her back as she hugged him longer. She watched her inhale before going to step back.

"Ok, I'm ready." Nora said, stepping back from him.

He kissed her forehead waiting for her to step back into the car. She got back into the car and watched him walk around the front of it. She realized in that small moment that she needed him. The pull she had to him was something more than lust or like or even love. She didn't understand it. Maybe it was another hunter thing that they loved, like wolves.

"I'm sorry about earlier. I had no right to get angry with you and push you to tell me about your past." Nora said softly as Jace got back in the car, closing the door.

Jace looked at her before his hand captured her face, pulling her in for a kiss. His mouth crashed into hers fiercely. The amount of chills and shivers she got from this one kiss exploded in her brain. Goosebumps scattered across her skin, her hands weaving into Jace's hair, pulling him closer to her and deepening the kiss. Jace pulled back suddenly; his teeth elongated as the kisses and emotions overwhelmed him. Nora pulled back, looking at his fangs. They didn't scare her like they once did.

"What is it like? Does it hurt?" Nora asked, looking at him.

"No, they just come out." Jace said with a half smile on his face, confused about the question.

"No, I meant when you mark your mate." Nora whispered.

"Nora, don't ask things that you're not ready for or want." Jace said; he could feel Cole becoming excited and trying to press forward.

"I'm not." Nora said firmly, leaning forward to bravely kiss him again.

She could see Cole pushing forward by the way Jace's eyes began to glow. Jace pulled back, slamming down the emotions that were overtaking him. Cole just needed her to say it and he would sink his fangs into her. He wanted nothing more than to mark her. She was playing with fire.

"Jace, I want-

"Nora don't. You need to think about this and not now. You need to weigh the options of what you're even thinking about. You say the words, and I don't know if I can hold Cole back." Jace said, gripping the stir wheel in his fist.

She went to touch him, and he seemed to flinch. She looked hurt as she moved back away from him.

"It's not you, Nora. Cole is just below the surface, and I can't risk this right now. I want you to know that if this is something you want; It will link you to me forever." Jace said quietly.

"Jace-

"Just think about it. We need to go check on Joel's mom. Let's just put it off for now." Jace said, starting the car, trying to end the conversation.

Nora felt hurt; she felt rejected. She didn't know why it bothered her so. She should be happy that he was thinking about her and putting her first, but this small annoying part of her wondered if Jace wanted Cole to mark her. What if he didn't? What if he didn't want to be linked to her because of what she was? Jace looked over at her and could feel the rush of sadness coming off of her. He wanted to console her but he couldn't. He was fighting Cole.

They pulled into Joel's mother's driveway. The drive was a beautiful pebble driveway lined with lights that led to a small country-looking house. In the setting sun, the house seems to sparkle with the various lawn decorations and wind chimes. Joel's mother came out onto the front porch seeing the car pull in. Nora could see she looked worn down and tired from the car. Her shoulders hung downward, and her facial expression was heartbreaking. Nora opened the passenger door before the car even came to a full stop. Jace watched her jet across the front of the car and ran up the steps of the front porch. He watched Nora crash into the older woman. The older woman recognizing Nora, instantly wrapped her arms around her and folded in on Nora. He could hear the sobs from the car.

"Nora, thank god you weren't with him. My poor boy." Joel's mother cried into Nora.

"They said he went instantly. Oh, Nora Bell, if you would have been there, you might not be here. I keep telling myself his father has him now in heaven." She said, squeezing Nora tighter.

Nora squeezed her back tighter, trying hard not to let herself break down. Tears still slipped out of her eyes and down her cheeks. She wanted to tell her he was dead because of her.

"I'm so sorry. I'm so sorry." Nora cried, losing it slightly as she clung to Joel's mom.

"Nora Bell. It's not your fault, baby. Come on now. We've got to pull each other together. I see a young man hanging back there," Joel's mom whispered to her.

"That's Jace." Nora nodded, wiping her face as Joel's mom straightened herself up.

"He's quite handsome," She chuckled, wiping her eyes, one arm still around Nora's shoulders.

"Shh, he'll hear you." Nora chuckled as Jace approached the front porch.

"Evening, ma'am," Jace smiled.

"Evening Mr..?" Joel's mother asked with a smile.

"Jace Knight, ma'am." Jace said, nodding his head to her.

"Well Jace, I am Loretta Wilson. You can call Ms. Loretta or Mama L. Either way, I'll answer. Now let's get you kids in the house before it gets cold." Loretta said, letting go of Nora and walking to the screen door.

Nora smiled, watching her reaction to Jace as she followed her into the house. Jace walked behind them, a small smile also on his lips. The house was warm and inviting. The walls were littered with pictures of the family. Tons and tons of photos of Joel and Nora. Nora's eyes swelled up with tears as she walked down the hall, watching a little Nora and Joel grow up through the pictures. Loretta stopped midway and pointed to one of them by the lake, a smile forming on her face as she touched it.

"Remember that summer and the tadpoles." Loretta chuckled.

"You mean killer snake." Nora laughed. Jace raised an eyebrow asking about the story behind the picture.

"We were swimming, and there was this rocky part. Joel was terrified of snakes. So we were swimming along, and this massive tadpole popped its head just outside the rocks. Joel starts panicking, thinking it's a snake. He tried so hard to get out of the lake. He almost drowned me and busted up both knees and elbows. Took us a second to calm him down enough to tell him it was just a tadpole. Still wouldn't go back in the water. He lost his swim trunks and everything trying to flap his way out of the pound." Nora laughed, reaching over and squeezing Loretta's hand.

"We were still hearing about his scrapes, bruises, and heart attack months after." Loretta laughed.

"Nora, no matter what, you were always there for him. All those hard times in school when he wasn't comfortable in his own skin. You made him believe in himself and let him blossom into that sassy-ass wild cat he was." Loretta laughed.

"In the beginning, I prayed you would marry his silly butt. But once I quickly figured out that wasn't in the cards for him. I knew you were his other half in other ways. I was so thankful you were his best friend and family." Loretta said, squeezing her hand once more before letting go and walking to the kitchen.

Jace saw Nora's shoulder fold forward, and he pulled her back against him. Wrapping his arm around her waist. He leaned down, kissing her shoulder lightly as he tried to comfort her.

"Ok, love birds, get in here and help me cook." Loretta chuckled, her laugh filtering down the hall to them.

Nora smiled, taking Jace by the hand and leading him towards the kitchen.

Chapter Forty Five
Attack

Dinner was nice, the sadness faded away, and they talked about life. Nora was helping Loretta out in cleaning up when she noticed Jace's eyes seemed to be glossed over. She knew he was talking to the pack. Loretta also picked up on it.

"He works a lot? He looks like a man whose life is his job." Loretta said, motioning to the glossed-over look.

"Yeah, he doesn't get a break. He's responsible for a lot of people," Nora said softly.

"Well, that's good because he has initiative and integrity. But in the long run, does that leave any time for you." Loretta said with a wink.

"He makes time for me." Nora smiled, glancing over at him.

"So are you two serious, serious?" Loretta asked with a goofy smile on her face.

"Mama L, we are compl-

"Yes." Jace answered from the table, coming back to the real world.

Nora made a face at him, seeing him snap back, and Loretta began to laugh. She squeezed Nora's shoulder, shaking her head.

"Always said this one was going to be hard to lock down." Loretta said, giving Jace a look.

"Love a challenge." Jace smirked, throwing a wink at Nora.

"Are you going to dress him in the purple tux?" Nora asked quietly.

"You know it, doll." Loretta smiled big.

"He loved that ugly flashy thing." Nora chuckled.

"It's going to be Wednesday at the small white church, and he'll be buried with his daddy." Loretta said, fidgeting with the necklace that hung around her neck.

"I will be right there with you, Mama L." Nora said, squeezing her other hand.

Jace's eyes glossed over, and he snapped out of it pretty quickly. Glancing at Nora, panic flashed in his eyes before he hid it. He cleared his throat.

"Nora, we need to head back." He said quietly.

Nora nodded quickly, recognizing there was something going on. She grabbed Loretta into a big hug.

"I love you. I will see you soon." Nora said to her as she squeezed her.

"Love you too, Nora Bell. You call Mama L if you need anything." Loretta said, squeezing her back.

Nora followed Jace quickly to the car. She was holding in, asking what was wrong until they were inside the car with the door shut.

"What's wrong?" Nora blurted out as Jace got into the driver's side.

"There's been an attack. I'm not sure what's going on. I can't get in touch with anyone, I can feel them, but there's so much chaos they are having trouble responding." Jace said, throwing the car into reserve and taking off.

He knew someone was hurt as he sped in the direction of the pack house. He could feel it through the bond. He kept trying to reach Dante, but he wasn't responding. He was either the one hurt or unconscious. He was using his Alpha aura to reach out to him, and he would have to answer. The car screeched into the driveway of the pack community. He looked at Nora. He didn't have time to stop to open the gate. The guards were gone, helping with the situation.

"Brace yourself." Jace said before pushing the pedal to the floor.

Nora made sure the seatbelt was snapped in tightly before nodding the Jace. Jace took a deep breath and slammed the pedal down to the floor. The car lurched forward, speeding towards the gate. Nora tried her best not to tense up as she shut her eyes waiting for the impact. She was thrown forward with the seat belt snapping her back to the seat as they crashed through the gate. The front of the hood of the car crunched forward, blocking the windshield. Jace glanced at Nora, making sure she was ok as he pushed the car on. As the car sped off into the community, the hood finally broke away from the car. As it did, Jace could see a cloud of black smoke. He immediately knew there was a fire. He shifted the car towards it. He knew it was on the outer part of the community but didn't know how far the attackers had come in.

"Alpha." Wyatt's voice came through mind link.

" Where are you? What's going on?" Jace responded, relieved to hear him.

"We were attacked by those monster things Kip was making. They didn't make it far into the community; they hit several houses in the outer part of town. They set them on fire. We're working on putting it out. Almost everyone is ok." Wyatt said.

"Almost everyone?" Jace asked, clenching his jaw.

"Dante is unconscious. He was fighting three of them when the rest of us showed up. One knocked him out; he's bleeding but not critical. Ryan. I couldn't reach Ryan; he took off after them, chasing them." Wyatt responded, his voice worried.

Jace's stomach knotted up. "I'm on my way."

Nora looked at Jace, seeing his expression that something was very wrong. She didn't know what to say or how to help him. In a matter of seconds, they pulled up to three houses, one still on fire. The families who owned the house stood outside of them, embracing each other. Jace hopped out of the car, spotting Wyatt and immediately going to him. Nora followed quickly behind, trying to find something to help with. A water truck was pulled up and spraying water on the flames, and the fire was almost completely put out.

"Nora stayed with Wyatt. I am going to look for Ryan." He ordered her.

"He headed that way, chasing them through there." Wyatt said, pointing to the wooded area to the left of the houses.

"Matt and Adam?" Jace asked.

"Near the school and hospital. They started trying to make their way there. Matt and Adam cut them off, pushing them back this way. Ryan then chased them off into the woods." Wyatt said, briefly recapping.

"I'll go. If Matt or Adam can be freed up, have them follow after me just in case." Jace instructed.

He started to walk away, but Nora caught his wrist. He looked confused, looking back at her, her face full of worry.

"You should take someone with you. What if it's a trap." Nora said, her gut feeling bad about this.

"The longer I take, the longer Ryan is alone. I need to go now." Jace growled, pulling away from Nora.

She took a step back, her face angry but hurt from his actions. She watched his back as he ran off into the woods.

"He's probably blaming himself that he wasn't here. He will be ok." Wyatt told her as he went back to check on the others.

Nora sighed and then spotted Dante on the ground. She walked over to him. Something had hit him hard on the side of his head. She could see the blood seeping through his dark brown hair. She kneeled down, going to check and see if he was ok. She brushed the hair out of the way so she could see the wound. There was a long crack in his skull running down towards his ear. Blood seeped slowly out of the crack and Dante's left ear. This was bad. She pushed back the quesy feeling the blood was trying to make her hard. She had to fight through it. Dante was hurt.

"Wyatt!" Nora yelled as she looked for something to hold to the wound to stop the bleeding.

He didn't hear her over all the noise. She looked around, and there was nothing. Why wasn't an ambulance or fire truck here? She grabbed the bottom of her t-shirt and ripped it. Her shirt tore and left her stomach exposed. She wrapped the pieces of the shirt in her hand and pressed it to Dante's head.

"Wyatt!!" She screamed at him.

Wyatt's head snapped in the direction of Nora, a worried look on his face as he came walking over. Kneeling down next to her.

"It's not just a bump on the head; his skull is fractured." Nora said to him, removing her now red piece of shirt.

'We need to get him to the hospital now. If his body starts trying to heal that without setting it, it's going to be bad." Wyatt mumbled, looking around for a car.

"Jace's car, come, I'll help you." Nora said, moving to grab Dante's legs.

"Nora, he is heavy." Wyatt said, going to wrap his arms around his torso.

"I got it. Let's just go now." Nora yelled at him as she grabbed his legs.

"Ok, ok. Ready 1, 2, and 3." Wyatt said, hoisting Dante up against him.

Nora picked up his legs and carried him with Wyatt to the car. They placed him gently on the ground next to the car. Nora climbed into the driver's side as Wyatt leaned the passenger seat flat. Nora leaned over, motioning for Wyatt to hand her Dante, he made a face but lifted him to her, and they pulled and pushed Dante into the car. Wyatt shut the passenger door. A loud painful howl erupted from the woods. It was a crushing sound; Wyatt braced himself against the car as it wrapped around them. Nora's eyes shot to Wyatt; she saw hurt flashing through them.

"Go get Dante to the hospital. Go now. I'll follow. The hospital is straight back." Wyatt said, hitting the car.

Nora wasn't sure what happened, but if she didn't get Dante's help, then there would be something else bad happening. She nodded, turning the car on and leaving.

Chapter Forty Six
Damage

Nora pulled the car up to the hospital. She didn't even turn off the engine as she rounded the car to the passenger side door. Opening it, she was prepared to carry Dante into the hospital on her own if she had to. Reaching in and pulling him into her chest. She felt a hand on her shoulder.

"Miss, let us help; Wyatt told us you were on the way." A young man said to another standing behind him.

Nora nodded, stepping out of the way. They pulled the stretcher up to the car and carefully loaded Dante onto it. Nora's stomach was in knots as she watched them wheel Dante in.

"You can follow us, miss. Don't worry about your car; it's fine there." The young man explained as he entered the hospital.

Nora nodded, following behind them. Entering the hospital, they escorted Dante to a room where they began assessing him. A doctor came nodding quickly to Nora before going about the exam.

"We're going to have to take him back for surgery. If we don't get this going quickly, then he will heal wrong." The doctor said to Nora while nodding to the nurses to get going.

They started wheeling Dante out of the room. Then it happened that the world began to slow down. Nora looked around, confused; nothing and no one was attacking her. A small cracking noise coming from behind her, made her turn and looked out the window. The window was riddled with small cracks, and a large deformed wolf was breaking through it. Nora looked back to Dante; they almost had him out of the room. She moved quickly, pushing the hospital bed out of the room. As she got further away from the wolf, the world snapped back into normal time.

"What the- "

"Go get Dante out of here. I will hold off the wolf." Nora told the doctor before slamming the hospital room door.

The doctor and nurse looked at her, their eyes glowing wanting to shift to help. Nora slammed her palm on the door.

"Go, he needs you. He's your Beta. Fix him!" Nora yelled angrily at them.

"We will send help." They said, rushing off with Dante.

Nora nodded, feeling anxious as she heard the heavy breath and snarling coming from behind her. The deformed wolf stood up. It had the legs of a human but was covered in hair, with long talon claws coming out of the feet. The arms were the same. Its face was half wolf and half human. His eyes were human and head shape but the nose and mouth were of a wolf. Its long fangs chomped at her as it breathed heavily. Nora inhaled.

"Hunter instincts, please kick in." She whispered, preparing herself.

"You come. You're different." It growled.

Nora stepped back, hearing it talk. It growled, seeing her move away from him. The wolf charged her. In her mind, the words please work, please work were screaming over and over as she watched it approach. The world faded into slow motion as it came closer to her. She was scared; she didn't know what to do. She was trying not to panic. These were the things you see in horror movies. She looked to her right seeing a chair. She picked up the chair, a surge of energy coursing through her. She cranked back, swinging as hard as she could. Everything in her vibrated as she slammed the chair into the wolf's abdomen. Time went back to normal as the chair hit the wolf. The chair shattered into pieces as The wolf was thrown back into the wall.

"Shit." Nora whispered, seeing the wall crack.

The wolf whimpered and shook its head as if it was surprised too. It slowly stood up, roaring loudly at her. Nora braced herself with what was left of the chair, ready for it to come at her again. The wolf shook its shoulders like it was shaking off the pain. He ran at her again. She felt the surge building up in her again.

The wolf came charging at her, snapping its teeth at her and slashing its claws. The world slowed down as it approached. Nora had the leg of the chair in her hand. She stood back like she was playing baseball and swung as the wolf got close enough. Time snapped back into normal time as the leg of the chair connected to the wolf's chest. This time though, his arm came down, clawing her across her exposed stomach. The wolf was thrown back across the room as Nora doubled over, grabbing her stomach. Three long scratches were across her belly, blood oozing out of them.

The wolf sunk back into the wall. Its nose started to bleed. Nora looked at it, confused. Blood began to leak out of its mouth as it seemed to start twitching. She looked confused, trying to come up with a better plan. She heard a commotion behind her. An earth-shattering growl came from just outside the door; the door to the hospital room flew open. An angry and deadly-looking Jace stood in the doorway, his breathing heavy like he had run the whole way here.

"Nora out," Jace growled, seeing her wounded, and became even moved furiously.

"Jace, I can help, I -

"Out!" Jace yelled, and the walls felt like they shook from his anger.

Nora bit her lip, wanting to argue more with him. She could help. She gritted her teeth, looking angry at him, about to argue, when the world started to slow. She knew the deformed wolf was approaching behind her. She turned as it came towards her. Jace shifted into Cole in slow motion jumping in front of Nora. Nora panicked, seeing the wolf going to injure Jace. Nora yelled, taking the end of the chair's leg, moving around Jace, and plunging it into its chest. The world started back up again, and the wolf was pinned to the ground by its chest in front of her.

She was standing over it, holding on to the leg still. Cole was confused and didn't seem to understand what happened. The wolf groaned, and the life in its eyes started to fade. It reached up, grabbing onto Nora's necklace. Nora held onto it, trying not to let the dying wolf break it off her neck. Cole lunged at the wolf's throat, sinking his teeth into it and finishing the wolf. The wolf's hand fell away, the necklace snapping off from her neck. Nora tried to catch it as it fell. She watched the necklace hit the ground, and she scrambled after it.

"Hunter!" A shout was heard down the hall, and she could hear several people running.

Cole placed himself in front of her, growling at the door, protecting her from his pack. A male nurse came barreling, his eyes glowing, ready to fight as he glanced about the room. His eyes landed on Nora, confused. Cole stepped forward, snarling at him. Nora bent down and grabbed the necklace off the floor, trying to find a way to put it back on. A handful more people came and looked confused. Cole was snapping his teeth, threatening them as he stood there between her and them.

"Hunter?" The male nurse asked, looking at Nora.

She wasn't sure how to answer, so she placed the necklace around her neck, rigging the clasp together so she could wear it. The pack members looked confused as the hunter's scent disappeared. Cole was still not letting one near Nora. Wyatt came pushing through the crowd ordering them to move as he made his way through. Cole was growling at him.

"Cole, I need to check Nora. She is bleeding. I am not going to hurt her. I don't care what she is. She just saved Dante and this hospital from that monster. She has my loyalty. I promise. "Wyatt said to Cole, approaching him slowly.

Cole's ears went down as he listened to Wyatt. He shifted slightly, wanting to trust him. Nora bent down and touched Cole's head. He leaned into her touch.

"Cole, let Jace come back. Wyatt isn't going to let anything happen to me." She said softly to him.

Cole whimpered but allowed Jace to take back control. A loud bone-snapping noise was heard, and within seconds a very naked and angry Jace was standing in front of them.

"Get lost before I let Cole back out." Jace said, sending out his alpha aura to the pack members in the doorway.

They whimpered and backed away. Jace then turned, looking angry at Nora, his chest moving up and down as he tried to control his breathing.

"What the hell were you thinking?" Jace screamed at her.

She wanted to answer him but knew he wasn't looking for an actual answer. She sighed, waiting for him to continue or finish.

"You could have gotten killed. Putting yourself in here with that, that thing." Jace said the anger in him wanted to shake her.

"I'm not dead, and hopefully, Dante isn't either. Oh, if it wasn't for me, that thing would have hurt you, so let's stop overreacting." Nora said to him firmly.

"Nora! Are you fucking crazy!" Jace yelled at her again.

"What would you have done? The same thing. It was to delay the wolf and save Dante or let it kill everyone and Dante." Nora said, holding her hand up to him as if to say the conversation was over.

Jace growled; he was so angry he was vibrating. He went to step towards her to try to intimidate her. She locked eyes with him, daring him to try. He looked at her for several seconds before letting out a long breath.

"Wyatt, fix her." He said angrily, moving out of the way.

Chapter Forty Seven
Stay

"Bandages and something to clean the wounds with now," Wyatt ordered the nurse standing in the doorway; as he motioned for Nora to sit on the bed.

The deformed wolf was still twitching on the floor. Jace's anger was vibrating the room as he went over to it, looking at it. He was literally shaking as it confirmed more and more that Kip was behind everything even more. He was angry at himself for not being there to protect his pack. He gritted his teeth, looking at Nora. Part of him was angry that he let himself get so wrapped up in her and her problems that he left his pack open. Ryan was dead because of his negligence. Dante was in surgery, and who knows what would happen to him? His hands were clenched as he stood over the deformity. He felt a wet substance flowing down over his fingers.

"Alpha, go check on Dante. I have her." Wyatt said, glancing over at Jace.

Jace was squeezing his hands so tightly that his nails were digging into his palms. His nails slowly turned into claws. The more he thought about everything, the more the guilty stabbed him.

"Jace." Nora said, her voice almost a whisper as she watched blood drip from his hands onto the floor.

Jace shot her an angry look before walking to the door and leaving. The intense emotions were walking out with him. Nora frowned, feeling hurt from the look he shot her. It was more than anger, and it bothered her. The nurse brought the supplies that Wyatt had requested, and he began working on her stomach.

"He blames himself." Wyatt said, pressing some wet gauze to her wound.

"What do you mean?" Nora asked, wincing as he touched the wounds.

"He's the Alpha, all the responsibility is on him. Every time something goes wrong. If someone gets hurt, he blames himself because he is supposed to be the one who doesn't let anything bad happen. He's built himself up that way. That's how he thinks. It is like excepts himself to be Superman or something." Wyatt explained.

Nora frowned; this was all out of Jace's control. How was he supposed to know this monster thing was going to attack them? She sighed, trying not to take any of his emotions personally.

"I can't stitch any of these, but we will wrap them. They'll need to heal on their own." Wyatt said as he began bandaging her stomach.

"Ok." She said quietly, her eyes looking out the door to all the random stares she was getting.

"They're confused." Wyatt whispered.

"About what?" Nora asked back.

"We've been raised to hate and fear hunters. They are death, and that's all they caused. You just almost sacrificed yourself to save one of them. They don't know how to feel. They also don't know if you are one. By the way, that was dangerous, reckless, and freaking badass." Wyatt said with a smirk.

"Thanks. Your Alpha is pissed about it, though." Nora shrugged.

"If anything were to happen to you, a part of him would be lost. He would be devastated and would never be able to move past it." Wyatt explained to her.

Nora raised an eyebrow at him; she knew Jace had said they were something like soulmates but didn't realize the impact she would have on him.

"That's why he is angry." Wyatt said, watching her process.

"Do you know how Dante is?" Nora asked as he finished wrapping her sides.

His eyes glossed over for a minute; a painful look flashed across his face. Nora's stomach dropped, seeing the change in his expression. She reached over and grabbed his hand. Wyatt's eyes turned back to normal.

"He's ok. He's in recovery." Wyatt said, patting his hand.

"What's wrong then?" Nora asked quietly.

"It's nothing. It's ok." Wyatt said, but his voice had a sadness to it.

"Liar." Nora said, frowning at him, not moving her hand from his.

"Ryan…he didn't make it. He chased that thing off, and it got him. He was young and was working the way up the ranks. His parents were proud. Jace added him to our close group wanting him to train to become another higher-ranking wolf." Wyatt said, trying to hide how sad and hurt it made him.

Nora reached over and pulled him into a hug. She heard a gasp from the nurses at the nursing station, which was being overly noisy. Wyatt tensed up as she hugged him but returned the hug. A loud growl came from the doorway of the room. Wyatt jumped back from Nora, putting his hands up defensively.

"Alpha I -

"Nora, we're going home; let's go." Jace said shortly, glaring at Wyatt.

"Thank you." She smiled at Wyatt before getting up off the hospital bed.

She looked at Jace, telling him to quit being an ass, but he ignored her. She began walking to the doorway and was about to head out of it when He stopped. He frowned deeply, seeing her exposed stomach. Nora looked at him, confused. Jace groaned, pulling his shirt off and handing it to Nora. She looked at him, making a face.

"Put it on," Jace said shortly and then turned to glare at the people in the hall just staring.

They immediately returned to work shuffling around, and two of them bumped into each other. Nora chuckled at them and slipped the shirt over her head. Jace moved out of her way and waited for her to walk by him. She wiped her smile off her face seeing Jace look at her the same. As she walked by him, she could feel his eyes on her. She ignored it, trying to remember what Wyatt had said. The walk back to the car felt like some walk of shame as she walked ahead of Jace. Getting to the car, she looked at it. It was a complete mess. Jace sighed deeply behind her and then walked over to another car in the parking lot. He talked to a guard at the parking lot. It seemed he parked all the cars for the hospital. He nodded to whatever Jace said and handed him a set of keys. Jace got into a jeep and drove towards Nora out of the parking lot.

Pulling up beside her, he nodded for her to get in. She didn't say anything, she was starting to become angry with him, but she kept trying to be understanding. The car ride was quiet. He didn't say anything as they pulled into the driveway of the house. He got out of the car, turning off the engine. He sighed deeply, wanting to say something to her but chose not to. He opened the driver-side door, got out, and walked over to Nora's opening. He held his hand out for her to take to help her get down. She gritted her teeth because part of her wanted to be petty and not take it. A little nagging voice reminded her that he just lost a member of his pack. She took his hand, and she got out of the car.

Jace dropped her hand as soon as she was out and began walking to the house. Nora's stomach turned nervously in on itself. She didn't know why, but him being angry with her, hurt. She followed after him like she was some lost bad child. She pushed down the surge of anger she felt again. He held the door of the house open for her; She walked past him and kept going. She walked up the stairs to the top floor, purposely trying to be faster than him. She reached the bedroom and yanked open the door angrily. She walked into the room, not really sure what to do next. Jace followed her in closing the door. He glanced at her, not really saying anything. Nora sighed. She couldn't do this not talking thing anymore.

"Jace, it's not your fault." Nora whispered, coming up behind him and putting her hand on his shoulder.

Jace shook off her hand, and Nora stepped back, hurt and upset by the action. She went to say something, but Jace turned around, and the pain on his face was overwhelming.

"It is my fault entirely. I wasn't here, and my pack was attacked." He said angrily.

"So you weren't here. What exactly were you going to do? Your pack still would have been attacked." She said fiercely at him.

"Yeah, but I would have been able to-

"To what? Jace controls everything. You can't control everything. " Nora said harshly at him.

"I'm the Alpha. I should have been here." Jace growled at her.

"Just because your Alpha doesn't mean you can stop bad things from happening." Nora said softly.

"If I was here and not wrapped up in your business. Ryan might still be alive. Dante might not be in intensive care. I should have been here." Jace growled more.

"Oh, so it's because of me. Fine then, I don't need to be here. I don't have to stay. I'm the reason your pack is suffering fine." Nora yelled.

Nora walked to the door, shoving past Jace as she did. She ignored the sharp pain she got in her abdomen as she reached for the door. Jace was quick and pressed his palm against the door, not letting her open it.

"Move." Nora said, her eyes burning into him.

"No." Jace said, standing straight up, showing her his size.

Nora smirked, her eyes daring him to try something. She was so angry inside that she could feel tremors of it throughout her body.

"Get out of my way. I'm leaving." Nora said through her teeth at him.

"No." Jace growled, matching her tone and shifting in front of the door, completely blocking it.

"I'll make you move if you don't," Nora said; she could feel something surging in her.

Like some weird force she could draw upon, she could feel its power, which vibrated in her bones, begging her to use it.

"Do it." Jace whispered, his voice sounding deadly.

Nora was so angry she didn't even think about what happened next. Nora stepped to the side of him. The surge creeping up her arm. She shoved Jace and as she connected her palm to his side the world slowed down and then snapped forward, adding force to her shove. Jace crashed into the wall next to the door. He hit it letting out a groan,a large crack running up the wall from his impact. Nora blinked looking at her hand and then to Jace. Worried flashed across her face as she looked to see if he was ok. He got himself together and then turned to her looking more angry. The worry went away and she grabbed the handle of the door. Jace moved quickly, placing himself between the door and her.

"Move!" Nora yelled at him, getting frustrated.

"No." Jace said firmly.

"You just said everything's my fault. You know I know that. Everything from the minute I started to turn twenty-one has been my fault. Everything! My family was murdered, Joel was murdered, and Rylan. Now your pack is being attacked. I know all of this already, so you didn't have to tell me. I'm leaving before I bring anything else down with me. Move!" Nora yelled, tears welding up in her eyes as she started to shake.

Jace stood there solid, blocking the door from her. The pain in her voice tore into his stomach. He felt horrible for saying what he said, but he didn't mean it was her fault.

"Jace, move or I'll make you." Nora said, her voice cracking slightly as she tried to contain her emotions.

Jace pulled her against him in one swift movement, his hands going to the side of her face, pulling her in for a passionate kiss. Nora was shocked at first, not expecting that to be his response; she was more ready to fight. She gave into the kiss, kissing him back. Ignoring the pain shooting through her stomach as it brushed against Jace's stomach. Jace pulled back the kiss leaning his forehead against hers.

"That's not what I meant." He whispered.

"I don't blame you. I meant I shouldn't have allowed myself to be distracted. Don't go." Jace said, pressing his lips to her forehead.

Nora wanted to stop fighting; she wanted to stay with him. She craved his touch, his presence; everything about him made her feel safe, calm and wanted. She found herself nodding, but a piece of her deep down told her she should go. That what she said was right. Chaos follows her.

"Come to bed with me. I need you." Jace whispered.

It tugged at her heart; she understood it. She needed him, too, and she couldn't help but say yes.

Chapter Forty Eight
Deceit

"Only one casualty?" Kip groaned, listening to Taylor go over what happened.

"All that and just one!" He yelled again, letting his fist come down on the desk, his red hair scattering loose from his pulled-back ponytail.

"Yes, Alpha." Tayler said, flinching as he watched him become angry.

These days Kip was wound up so tight Taylor was becoming actually afraid of him. Taylor was worried something would flip in Kip's mind, and he would be the next one in a hospital bed being experimented on. He wouldn't put it past Kip. Taylor was walking on eggshells for weeks.

"Explain. Explanation now!" Kip yelled, his eyes not looking at Taylor, but it felt like he was looking through him.

"One casualty, and Dante was hurt pretty badly. The girl got away. She is there at the pack house with Jace. One of the wolf....things got to the hospital. I am not exactly sure what went down there, but the wolf thing was killed. I'm assuming Jace and his pack ended it." Taylor said, recapping.

"And the houses that were set on fire?" Kip asked, annoyed.

"No one was in them." Taylor said with a shrug.

"Not one person was home.....not even a house pet, nothing with the fires?" Kip ranted on, asking angrily.

"No, I'm sorry, Alpha. The houses were destroyed if that's any positive." Taylor smiled at him. Kip sighed, waving Taylor off with his comment.

He stretched, looking out over his lab. He needs more of them. If he had more, they could do so much more damage....but how could he get more?

"I want a whole football team like the entire team. We're going to give them double what we gave the ones we sent out today. That should cause enough damage, and then we will kidnap more than that and create an entire army." Kip said, thinking out loud.

Taylor's gut twisted as he began talking more and more crazy. Did they even have enough blood for all that? How were they going to even? Do they have enough pull to draw enough people to a spot to take them? Kip saw his worried wheels spinning and slapped him in the shoulder. His lips curled into a skin-crawling smile as he brushed one of his stray red hairs out of his face.

"College kids love parties. Free booze, we will drug the booze. You think way too hard about things. We can also steal another Alpha. We need to research to see if there's a pack out there or a rogue Alpha, but get the victims first." Kip laughed maniacally.

"And we have holding cells, so don't even start thinking about where to keep them all." Kip said, shaking him.

"Ok, so…I just-

"Have you not been to a party? Get booze, lots of booze, and make flyers and pass them around at the dorm. Jeez. Send someone to scout out the territory to the left of us. I feel like we're missing a pack; maybe there's an Alpha we can take." Kip said, rolling his eyes.

"Where and when are we holding this party?" Taylor asked Kip, still trying hard to see how this was all going to work.

"Make it easy, the pack house." Kip smiled.

"And when people go missing, and the last place they were was on our property." Taylor said, thinking of human police showing up.

"I got it, so we only let the strong ones in. We turned all the other ones away at the door, telling them it was a mean prank played on us." Kip said, making a surprised face.

"You really think this is going to work?" Taylor asked out loud by accident.

"It will! Go now and do what I asked before you piss me off more." Kip growled, sending out his alpha aura.

Taylor whimpered, lowering his head and leaving to go complete his task. Kip turned to the monitor; he glanced down at the holding room Chardwick was in; he was sedated and hooked up to IVs. One was making sure he stayed alive, and the other was stealing his blood. Kip sat down in his chair, staring aimlessly at the monitors. He took out his cell phone and dialed the number Rosie had called from.

"What?" Rosie whispered into the phone.

"Figure I give you some information that you could pass on to your Alpha. Make you look credible." Kip snickered.

"Ok, and that is…?" Rosie asked, trying to rush him.

"I want something first." Kip said, ignoring her impatience.

"What?" Rosie asked him, annoyed.

"Do you think you could get some of Jace's blood?" Kip smirked, it would be wonderful if he created a monster using his blood to kill Jace's own mate; it would be like he was killing her himself.

"No, are you crazy? How would I do that?" Rosie blurted out.

"I don't know. You're smart. Tell me something about his mate if you can't do that. Something that will be helpful." Kip said, keeping her on the phone longer on purpose.

There was a long pause on the phone as if Rosie was thinking, but there was something awkward about the pause like she was debating telling him something.

"Out with it, Rosie, or this partnership could end any time I feel like it." Kip said sing-songy into the phone.

"So something happened at the hospital, and for a minute, a few pack members thought they smelt a hunter." Rosie said carefully.

"Ok, and was there a hunter?" Kip asked, confused at why she was telling him this.

"Several pack members swore they smelt one," Rosies explained.

"Can we cut to the chase? Who did they think was the hunter?" Kip asked, annoyed.

"They swore it was coming from her. They all thought she was a hunter." Rosies said her voice was very serious.

"So why are you not sure if she is a hunter or not?' Kip asked.

"Because as quickly as they smelt it. They said it went away, and Nora didn't even move. But She took down that monstrosity you created." Rosie said quietly.

"Uh….Are you sure?" Kip asked, sitting up; everything just got a whole lot more interesting.

"That's what the rumors are." Rosie responded.

"Hmm, Jace's mate is a hunter? How do you not know for sure? You've been around her, can you tell?" Kip asked, needing more information.

"I've been around her once and had no clue that she was one." Rosie said, stressing that she didn't know for sure.

"Hmm, a hunter that has found a way to mask their scent. She is either really smart, or there's something else going on." Kip said more to himself than Rosie.

"If there is a way to mask the scent, I don't think she's smart enough to know." Rosie answered with jealousy clearly slipping through.

"But if she is ... .Hunters are already super strong. This will be perfect." Kip chuckled, forming a whole new plan in his head.

"What will?" Rosie asked, confused.

"Don't worry about it. Tell Jace I am building an army of those things, and then I am coming for him and every pack that stands in my way." Kip said, his voice chilling when he said it out loud.

"You want war?" Rosies asked, confirming that's what he was saying.

"Yes, and the next time we speak, it will be so you can lead Jace's mate to me." Kip said, laughing as he ran through his entire plan in his head.

"What do you mean?" Rose asked.

"I mean, I am going to stage a distraction, and you take her for a walk or maybe to safety in the woods between our packs, and I take your problem off your hands." Kip smiled into the phone.

"Fine, call me beforehand so I can come up with something. Now I gotta be friends with her." Rosies said, her voice full of disgust.

"Make sure you tell him the information." Kip said with his smile coming through the phone.

"Ok, I will tell him." Rosies said as she heard the phone line click off. Kip laughed to himself.

This was going to be perfect, he will kidnap the girl. Force feed her his blood, and it will be his blood. He wanted every part of this glorious plan to be his alone. He then will bite her, turn her into one of these creatures and turn her loose on Jace. He will die by her, and she will die shortly after her body starts to try to break down. He wondered if being a hunter would make it special somehow. It was so perfect and utterly tragic. He laughed, sitting back down in his chair. Everything was falling into place so perfectly for him. His phone began to ring, and his smile grew as the council called him.

Chapter Forty Nine
Friends?

Nora rolled over, a sharp pain coursing through her stomach as she did. The bed was cold and empty. She didn't open her eyes yet but reached out, searching for him. She knew before she opened her eyes, he was gone. She sat up, a feeling of sadness rushing over her. He didn't wake her. She sat up and slowly, her side burning. She stood, pulling the shirt up over her head. The bandages were dried, but they stung so badly. She decided she was going to take a shower and then go to the hospital to see Dante. She sighed, realizing she really didn't have anything here. She would have to come up with something. She wandered into Jace's closet, it was massive, and she giggled a little that a man would have this much clothing. Walking in, she stopped short, seeing a whole side of the woman's clothing. She felt jealousy surge through her. Whose clothing were these? She went over to a slender black dress, ran her hand over the material, and a tag flapped out as she touched it. Was it new? She then moved on to a dark blue shirt to have a tag. The more she looked, she realized the clothing had tags on them. She pulled down a dark brown shirt with gold glitter flakes on it and looked at the size. Medium. She made a face, finding a pair of jeans; she read the size, realizing they matched her size as well. She chuckled, seeing a draw of underwear, and thought, well, this will be the icing on the cake. She picked up a pair of black lace undies and looked at the size. As she did, a brand new tag fell off of them. Either Jace was a man whore and had a section of women's clothing in his closet so his flings could replace clothing that matched her perfectly, or he had done all this for her.

She smiled brightly, knowing in her heart that he had this done for her. She looked at her options. She wanted to be simple today. She grabbed the dark navy blue t-shirt and a pair of dark wash jeans. She kept the lacey undies and made her way out of the closet. A buzzing was heard as she walked out of the closet. She placed the clothes on the bed and wandered to the buzzing noise. It was coming from inside the nightstand. Nora bit her lip, debating with herself if she wanted to find out what it was. Curiosity got the best of her, and she pulled the drawer open. As the drawer opened, her cell phone slid forward. She smiled, grabbing it. Plopping down on the bed, she saw a text message from Jace. she laughed. He must have put his number in her phone.

Nora, I had to go help Ryan's family make arrangements to make yourself at home. There's a whole kitchen full of food; help yourself. The closest I had stocked with clothing in your size. I will see you soon.

Nora smiled brightly at the message and was about to respond when she saw another text message in her inbox from an unknown number. She clicked on it, opening it.

Nora, we need to talk. I am sorry how things went with Lilly and sorry I managed to find a way to get your number. But we really need to talk. We are not the bad guys - Logan.

Nora sighed. She went back and forth about responding to him. She didn't want to; she was still really creeped out by the way Lilly acted towards her and how persistent they were about communicating with her. It was like they wanted to own her. Like she was an object. On the other hand, she felt she should warn them about those things. They are hunters, and maybe they could help take them down if there were more of them out there. Shower first, she thought to herself.

She showered quickly. The worst part was the bandage being stuck to her. She had to let it get wet first before she could tear it from her skin. The wound was healing, but it looked like it may have become infected. She would see if Wyatt could look at it for her when she got there. She threw her hair up in a towel and wrapped another around her body as she stepped out of the bathroom. She nearly jumped, seeing a woman sitting at the end of her bed.

"Who the hell are you?" Nora yelled at her.

"Easy doll face, it's me. The girl who talked you into taking the door off the hinges." Rose smiled.

"Ok, but what are you doing here? How did you get in?" Nora asked her, pulling the towel closer to herself.

"I have a key." Rosie smiled with a shrug.

Nora felt something inside her become angry; it wasn't your normal angry, jealous feeling. It was possessive and almost dark. Nora shut her eyes, trying to push it back.

"What do you want? Nora said, trying to control her anger.

"Calm down. I just wanted to come to check on you. See if you are ok. Maybe have some girl time." Rose smiled sweetly at her.

"I'm actually on my way out." Nora said quietly.

"Oh, does Jace know?" Rose asked.

Nora's eyes narrowed at her saying his name. She had noticed all the pack members called him Alpha out of respect. Why was she saying his name like that? The tinge of anger started creeping up again. Nora gritted her teeth, trying to figure out how to stop the urge to hurt her.

"I am going to meet him, so don't worry." Nora lied, not knowing why she was.

"Ok, well, you guys enjoy the day. Maybe we hang out at a different time. I hope we can be friends, Nora." Rose said, getting up and walking to the door.

Nora couldn't respond; she just nodded as Rosie walked out the door, closing it behind her. She was going to have to ask Jace about why she had a key to his room. She quickly got dressed, slipping the navy blue t-shirt over her head and pulling up the jeans. She decided to let her hair air dry. She went over to her phone, picking it up in her hand; she decided to text both Jace and Logan.

Hey, I am going to head over to the hospital and check on Dante. She messaged Jace.

Hey, I am not sure how open I am to communicating right now while I am trying to figure everything out. But you need to know about these things. I am not sure what they are, but they are half-human, half-wolf creatures. They are deformed and are destroyers on steroids. If I can get a picture of one, I will send it to you. Have your guys be on the lookout. Nora messaged Logan.

She started walking to the door when there was a knock at it. Nora sighed, not knowing who it was. She opened it slowly, and she saw a redhead man standing there. He smiled brightly at Nora and her confused look.

"Hello, I'm Matt, and Jace asked if I could give you a ride to the hospital." He said his smile was still warm.

She looked at him suspiciously, and her phone buzzed in her hand. It was a text from Jace saying Matt would take her to the hospital. She sighed softly before nodding to Matt.

"Did you eat anything yet?" Matt asked, walking down the hall next to her.

"Not yet, but I don't mind. I want to get to the hospital and check on Dante." Nora said quietly.

"We can stop by the kitchen. There are some muffins, granola bars, and fruit. There's bound to be something quick you can grab so you don't go hungry." Matt said, walking down the first flight of stairs.

Nora was going to say no, that they should just leave, but her stomach growled and reminded her that she needed to eat. She smiled as Matt raised an eyebrow, hearing her stomach, and she nodded to the kitchen idea. Matt chuckled, leading the way to the kitchen.

Walking into the kitchen, she was overwhelmed with the smell of breakfast. There was everything you could have asked for. Waffles, pancakes, muffins, toast, cereal, fruit. You name it was laid out like a buffet.

"Is this always like this?" Nora asked, grabbing a cinnamon bun and apple.

"Yeah, Jace, make sure there's food here for every meal laid out like this. If someone is having trouble at home, they know they can stop by and grab a meal. Also, if they're training or too busy, they know there's food here." Matt explained, grabbing a chocolate chip muffin.

"That is really awesome." Nora said, impressed, her heartwarming at how Jace looks out for everyone.

"He's a very good Alpha. We haven't had one like him." Matt said a hint of sadness in his voice when he said it.

Nora noted the tone but didn't say anything to it. She grabbed her cinnamon bun and apple walking to the door. Matt followed behind her. A black jeep was pulled up front, waiting for them. Nora looked at him, and he nodded. She hopped up into it and, while waiting for him to do the same, ate half of her cinnamon bun.

"Hungry?" Matt chuckled.

"Starving." Nora said, biting into the apple.

Matt turned the car on, laughing some more as Nora took another big bite of the cinnamon roll as they headed towards the hospital; the car ride was mostly silent. Matt kept glancing at her. Nora's first thought it was because of how she was eating, but she wasn't eating anymore, so now it was becoming annoying. She pressed her lips together before turning to him and staring at him. She smirked as she noticed him feeling awkward.

"Exactly. Awkward when someone keeps looking at you. So what is it you want to ask me?" Nora said with a smirk.

Matt laughed out loud at her actions and shook his head, realizing she was right.

"I'm sorry. You're funny; you know that." Matt laughed.

Nora looked at him like he was crazy and motioned for him to tell her what was on his mind.

"Are you really a hunter?" Matt asked.

"Yup. The necklace here makes me incarnito to you guys. I'm only telling you because I gather you're like Dante and close with Jace; otherwise, he wouldn't let you take me anywhere." Nora said, rambling a little bit.

"Uh…and your Jace's mate?" Matt asked, his eyebrows coming together.

"Yeah, he's been very adamant that I am." Nora chuckled with a small smile saying she kind of liked it.

"Did you know you were a hunter?" Matt asked curiously.

"Nope, that wonderful day came out of nowhere, the same day I met Jace." Nora shrugged.

"Your family didn't tell you?" Matt asked, surprised.

"I don't think they knew. They were killed because I was turning soon. It was like they had no idea." Nora said, trying to keep her voice still and not think about them as she said it.

Matt made a hmm noise as he looked forward on the road. He looked like he was thinking everything over. He nodded a few times and then looked back at her before looking forward again. Nora made a silly face at him, not knowing what he was doing.

"Ok, you're cool…not to mention what you did at the hospital was badass." Matt announced.

Nora shook her head, laughing at his announcement, and looked out the window.

Chapter Fifty
Mine

Jace left Ryan feeling completely drained. It was brutal. Ryan had not been in training long with Matt. Matt would have shown him how to be a great warrior and leader. He was young, and it killed him to see his father and mother like that. Jace told them that he died doing his duty and defending the pack. That if it wasn't for Ryan, more deaths would have happened. It was the complete truth, and Jace felt it in his chest. He wished he would have been there; maybe he could have saved Ryan. Jace flipped open his phone and dialed Zeke's number.

"Alpha Jace, I didn't expect a call so soon." Zeke's voice came across the phone.

"Kip arranged an attack on my pack with more of those things." Jace said, his anger could be felt across the phone.

"He has more?" Zeke asked, his voice shocked.

"I don't know, but I think he's planning to." Jace said, and then it reminded him that he needed to speak to Rosie to see what she found out.

"What are you planning?" Zeke asked.

"I'm done waiting around. I'm declaring war." Jace said, his voice deadly.

"We will fight with you. When are you planning to move?" Zeke asked.

"Dante has been in the hospital after the attack, I am going there shortly to touch base with him and my warriors, then I will let you know when. It will be soon. The quicker you can get here, the better." Jace said as he got into his car.

"I'm sorry to hear about Dante. We will have what warriors we can spare sent to you without compromising our pack here. Chadwicks pack is here as well. We still haven't found him or heard back from Kip about returning him. They know he is alive because the bond is still there. I will send you warriors there as well." Zeke said, coming up with the game plan as he went.

"Thank you. I will speak to you before night falls." Jace said gratefully.

Nora walked into Dante's hospital room nervously, but all of that went away when she saw him sitting up on the end of the bed looking bored. His face lit up seeing her. He was out for all of it, but they told him what she did for him.

"Nora!" He smiled excitedly. Nora crossed the room and wrapped her arms around him in a tight hug.

"Oh, thank god you're alive." Nora said as she squeezed him.

"Thank you." Dante said as he squeezed her back.

"I keep forgetting you wolves heal so quickly." Nora said as she stepped back from the hug.

She grabbed his head and began looking through his hair. She was shocked to find a thin pink line where the large skull fracture used to be. She shook her head in disbelief.

"You guys are amazing." Nora said out loud.

"She's crazy." Dante laughed, looking back at Matt, who nodded to his statement.

"Well, this crazy saved your life, so there." Nora said, folding her hands across his chest and stepping back.

Dante laughed, squeezing her into a hug again.

"So, are you guys breaking me out of here?" He asked Nora.

"Can you leave?" Nora asked.

"I don't know. I feel great, but who knows? They have all these stupid rules, and Jace ordered me to listen to them." Dante grumbled.

"Is Wyatt here?" Nora asked him.

"I'm sure he's here somewhere. Why are you ok?" Dante asked, getting nervous.

"I'm fine. Just wanted him to look at the scratches. Oh, next question I need to learn to fight. I got this neat trick thing I can do, but I don't know if it's going to save me. I mean, clearly, the thing wounded me." Nora motioned to her stomach.

"Neat trick?" Dante asked, looking to Matt to see if he knew what she was talking about.

Matt just shook his head.

"Yeah, so can someone teach me to fight?" Nora asked, making a face at them.

"Yeah, I mean, why not? You're already fighting things." Dante laughed.

"She can't come to training." Matt said to Dante.

"Well, duh, I wouldn't want to make all your wolfies upset." Nora said, making a face at Matt.

"Wolfies." Matt repeated, giving her a strange look trying not to laugh.

"But, like, when you guys get free time." Nora asked them both.

"No problem." Dante nodded and Matt shrugged.

"Hey miss, can you send Wyatt in here?" Matt said, sticking his head out the door and speaking to a very cute nurse.

He smiled brightly at her, almost too brightly, and talked a whole lot sweeter. The nurse giggled and nodded before hurrying off. Nora chuckled, rolling her eyes at Matt. He let out one of his own chuckles and shrugged. Just then, the atmosphere changed. A low growl was heard in the doorway. Nora turned fist up, ready to fight another one of those things; why isn't her cool trick working, she thought. As she spun around, ready to knock whatever it was lights out, she spun into Jace. The growl was coming from him. He caught Nora mid-swing.

"Alpha." Dante and Matt said in unison, nodding their heads.

"You smell like him." Jace said, still growling.

"Hi to you." Nora said sarcastically to him, he was still holding her arm.

"Why?" Jace asked.

"Why what? You can let go. The threat has been neutralized." Nora said, motioning to her arm.

Jace blinked like he didn't realize he was still squeezing her arm. He let go of her arm and pulled him to her.

"Why do you smell like Dante?" Jace said, still softly growling.

"Because I hugged him. What is wrong with you? Can you stop growling like an angry puppy?" Nora said, putting her hand softly on his cheek.

He growled louder at the word puppy, but she watched the tension slowly leave him a little as if her touch took some away.

"Why did you hug him?" Jace asked less angrily.

"Oh, for the love of- Because I was happy he was alive. I was happy he didn't die. That I actually saved someone for once. I'll probably hug him again when I'm gonna leave." Nora said, now getting mad.

"You know this weird pose-"

Jace pulled her against his chest and pressed his lips into hers. The kiss wiped any anger away she felt and caused her mind to go blank. She curled her fingers into his hair, kissing him back just as fiercely as he was her. Someone clears their throat from the doorway. The sound broke through to Nora, and she pulled back from the kiss.

"Hey, Wyatt." Nora smiled at him.

"Someone needed me?" Wyatt asked with a smile on his face looking at each one of them.

"Yeah, I did." Nora said, patting Jace's shoulder to let her go.

He grumbled softly and let her go. He looked at Dante; his eyes narrowed as if scolding him. Dante chuckled a little, he had been holding it in since Nora called their very scary and deadly Alpha a puppy. Matt cracks a smile at the sound of Dante's chuckle. Nora shook her head at the boys and walked over to Wyatt.

"So those claw marks I need you to look at really quickly. I took the bandage off; they are healing, but I think they might be infected." Nora said, starting to roll up her shirt.

As she exposed her stomach, Jace was by her side, now growling at Wyatt. Nora was thrown off by his weird behavior. She let her shirt go and placed a hand on his chest. He eased up, Cole still dancing in his eyes.

"What is the matter with you? He's a medical professional. He's fine, I just wanna make sure I'm ok." Nora said Jace but more to Cole.

"Cole, these men are your friends." Nora said softly, seeing Cole pushing forward.

Dante, Wyatt, and Matt all stood stunned as Nora talked Cole down with simple touches and words. The fact that she didn't know much about wolves or how it all worked made it even more astonishing.

"Cole, I need to make sure Nora is ok. I won't hurt your mate or ever try to take her from you." Wyatt said softly to Cole.

"My Mate." The words came out in a harsh growl from Jace's mouth, but everyone knew it was Cole.

"Yes. I'm your mate. Now let Jace back, Cole." Nora said, standing on her tippy toes and placing a kiss on Jace's forehead.

A small whimper came out of Jace's mouth as Jace's eyes went back to normal. He looked at Nora with almost the same look Dante and Matt had on their faces. Nora shook her head at him before turning around and facing Wyatt.

"Dante and Matt, why don't you guys step out for a second." Wyatt said to them, trying to make it easier on Cole.

Dante and Matt nodded, quickly getting out of the room. As they left, Wyatt shut the door. He motioned for Nora to sit on the bed. Jace grumbled but let her go. She went and sat down. She began to roll up her shirt, and the growling started. Nora patted the bed next to her, telling Jace to come sit. He reluctantly did, and Nora entwined her fingers through his. Her touch made him less on edge. Wyatt looked over the claw marks. He pressed on one, and Nora winced. Jace got angry and wanted to throw Wyatt across the room, but Nora squeezed his hand, telling him to stop.

"We're gonna start you on a strong antibiotic. These look like what you thought. They are getting infected. I will go fill those meds right now. I would like to give you an injection of them now to restart everything, and then you can start taking the pills tonight." Wyatt said as Nora nodded in agreement.

"Wait, can you fix him?" Nora said, poking Jace.

"Umm, are you sick, Alpha?" Wyatt asked, confused.

Jace groaned in response, rolling his eyes at Nora's statement.

"No, he's just extra Coley late. He's all flustered because I hugged Dante." Nora said, sighing.

"That's because you're his mate, and he hasn't marked you yet. The urge to become more and more almost possessive over our mates is stronger and gets worse when they are unmarked. Cole is acting out because he wants everyone to know you belong to him." Wyatt explained before heading to the door.

"So if he marked me, then Col-

"Nora, you don't even know what that means. Don't throw ideas out there like that." Jace said quietly but in short.

"I'll let you guys talk while I go get the med." Wyatt said, excusing himself.

"Well, I won't understand unless we talk about it, so spill." Nora said, looking at him annoyed.

Jace sighed deeply and sat down.

"Well, I already told you about the whole soulmate thing. Well, when a wolf marks his mate, he bonds with them. It's bigger than marriage, Nora. Besides, I have to bite you." Jace said quietly.

Nora nodded, feeling sad that he talked her basically out of it. Cole clearly wanted to do it. If she was ok with it, why was Jace trying to talk her out of it? Why was she upset? Nora shook her head at herself, not understanding her emotions. She should be happy that he was looking out for her. What if Jace didn't want to mark her? The thought crept into her head. She looked down at the ground, starting to get more upset.

"Nora?" Jace asked, confused by her response.

"It's nothing. I'm ok." Nora whispered.

"Ok, here we are." Wyatt said, walking into the room, shaking the pill bottle, and holding up the injection.

Nora smiled, grateful for the timing. Nora rolled up the sleeve of her arm, getting ready for the shot. Jace cleaned off a spot on her arm with a wipe and then looked at her.

"Ready?" Wyatt asked.

"Yeah, go for it, shots don't-

As she said the word, Wyatt injected the antibiotic into her arm.

She made a hissing noise at him as she pulled back, rubbing her arm. It burned; she continued rubbing it.

"Sorry, Yeah, it stings pretty bad but don't worry, it should go away pretty quickly," Wyatt said, and the stinging had already lessened.

"Home?" Jace asked Nora, and she nodded quietly.

Chapter Fifty One
Jealousy

Are you ok? A text message from Logan came through the phone, responding to her message. The phone beeping made her jump. She picked it up in her hand as she sat down on the bed. Jace was on the phone speaking with another Alpha. She could tell by the way he was talking that something big was coming. He was talking about war.

I'm ok, but something big is coming. Your hunters need to be ready. From what I can gather, someone is making these things. Or so Jace thinks. Nora replied back.

Thanks for the heads up. You let me know if you need anything. We are your friends, I promise. Logan texted back. Nora sighed, swiping the text away. She wanted to trust him, but she just didn't know.

"Ok, we will hold a meeting once you arrive. Thank you, Zeke," Jace said, clicking the phone.

Nora placed her phone back in the nightstand drawer and looked over at Jace. He was rubbing the back of his neck. He sighed deeply, thinking as he looked at the ground.

"Everything ok?" Nora asked, looking at him.

"It will be. Have you eaten today?" Jace asked, looking from the floor to her.

"Yeah, breakfast." Nora said, shrugging.

"Ok, why don't I meet you in the kitchen? I need to go talk to Rosie, and then I can cook for you." Jace smiled at her.

"Rosie?" Nora asked, hoping she hid the jealousy in her voice.

"Yeah, I asked her to look into something for me." Jace nodded, going to the door.

"Something?" Nora asked, getting annoyed with all the vagueness around here.

"Yeah, she was checking up on someone. I'll meet you in the kitchen." Jace said with a nod before walking out the door.

Nora felt her blood boil. She was done. He doesn't tell her anything that's going on, and now he's having little meetings with Rosie, who has a key to his room. No thanks, this wasn't what she signed up for. She didn't know what she should do. She was angry because part of her wanted to track him down and yell at him. The other part of her told her to go. But where would she go…home? She couldn't go home. She sighed, grabbed her phone, and headed out to the kitchen. She was hungry.

"Hey, look at you. Did you escape, or did they kick you out?" Nora laughed, coming into the kitchen and seeing Dante sitting at the breakfast nook.

"They basically threw him out." Matt laughed while he was looking in the fridge.

"Well, I'm glad you're doing good." Nora said, sliding into the nook across from him.

"I'm starving." Matt groaned from the inside of the fridge.

"Yeah, being in that room drove me nuts. I'm glad to be out. Matt shut it. You're always hungry." Dante said to Nora and then yelled at Matt.

"Doesn't change that I'm hungry. You're not?" Matt asked, peeking over at him.

"Well yeah, but I'm not being a drama queen about it." Dante laughed.

Nora chuckled, getting up from the nook and walking over to the fridge. She checked Matt out of the way, who laughed, moving. She looked in the fridge.

"Want something fast or something that takes a little longer but is good?" Nora asked them.

"Good." They both chimed in at the same time.

"Italian, ok?" Nora asked, seeing the chicken breast.

"Heck yeah." Matt smiled, sitting down at the nook.

Nora laughed, grabbing the chicken breast and placing it on the island. She then turned her attention to the pantry. She walked in, finding her ingredients. She walked out with everything she needed and over to the counter.

"So normally I would make my own marinara but don't have time for that, so this jar sauce is gonna have to do." She told the boys.

They both shrugged, looking at her like she was crazy anyways. She set up a small station for her chicken and turned the oven and stove top on. She grabbed a deep frying pan and coated it with olive oil before getting her chicken ready. She coated the chicken in flour, then dipped it in her egg wash, and then dipped the chicken in parmesan cheese mixed with breadcrumbs. She then placed the chicken in the frying pan to get a nice fry on each side.

"So, who taught you to cook?" Matt asked Nora as she moved about the kitchen.

"My momma." Nora smiled. It had been a really long time since she made food for anyone.

"Well, thank goodness, it's not even fully cooked, and it smells amazing." Matt smiled brightly.

Nora just laughed and continued cooking. She had forgotten all about being angry at Jace as she moved about the kitchen. The oven beeping going off made her realize how long it had been, and Jace still wasn't down here like he said he would be. She inhaled, trying to push back the overwhelming feelings creeping up. She took the pasta off the stove top, drained it, and placed it in a large bowl. She placed it on the countertop, and Matt moved quickly like he was a starving animal. Nora shot him a look, and he stopped in his tracks. She got the chicken out of the oven and placed it on a cutting board on the island. She poured the warm sauce that she added bits and pieces to make tastier into a sauce pourer on the counter as well.

"Ok, now hungry hungry hippo." Nora laughed at Matt.

"Don't have to tell me twice." Matt laughed, grabbing himself a plate and began serving himself.

A giggle caught her ear as she glanced at the doorway. Jace and Rosie came down together. She chuckled at something tapping his arm as they entered the room. Nora was struck by anger and sadness all at once. She placed her hand down on the counter but brushed her wrist against the glass pan she just took out of the oven. She heard her skin sizzle.

"Shhit." She muttered, pulling her hand away and going over to the sink.

"Nora you ok?" Dante asked, hearing both the hissing noise and her curse.

She nodded, not saying anything because she wasn't sure what was going to come out of her mouth if she opened it. She turned on the sink, getting it to a lukewarm temperature before sticking her wrist under it. She could already see the blister. She sighed, letting the water take the sting away. She felt Jace behind her and became angry all over again.

"Hey, let me see." Jace said, concerned.

"No. It's fine." Nora snapped. Jace was taken back by her tone and tried to figure out what was wrong, but at the same time, he was getting mad at the way she snapped at him.

"Nora, let me take a look." Jace stated, this time not asking.

"Running it under lukewarm, not cool water is the best treatment for it right now. You can see it later." Nora said, trying to play it off as medical info and not her about snap on him.

"Hey Nora, can I get some? It smells amazing." Rosie asked with a smile.

Nora shut her eyes, trying hard not to rip her face off. She just nodded, looking back at her wrist. Jace wasn't sure what was going on with her. He stepped closer to her, going to wrap his arm around her waist. She felt it coming. She shut off the sink and sidestepped before he could wrap his arms around her. Nora was quick and moved even quicker when she was mad. She walked to the overside of the kitchen, grabbing a plate. She fixed a plate really quickly and brought it over to Dante, who hadn't gotten up yet.

"Nora, I would have gotten it. Thanks." Dante said, a little surprised at her actions.

"No worries. You're just out of the hospital. Matt should have gotten you yours first." She said, shooting Matt a look whose face was covered in red sauce.

He gave her a look as if to say what and then went on about eating his food. Nora saw Jace coming for her again.

"Jace, do you want me to make you a plate?" Rose asked sweetly.

"Um, Sur -Jace started to answer but then saw a very pissed-off Nora walk straight out the back door.

Where was she going? He shook his head and followed after her. The cool breeze rushed into her. She shut her eyes as the warmth of the sun spread down over her. She was holding the railing to the small porch, trying to calm herself. She heard the door open and closed behind her. She instantly wanted to run.

"Nora, what is going on?" Jace asked, becoming annoyed.

"I don't know, you tell me." Nora snapped, not turning around to look at him.

"How the -" Jace stopped himself before he swore and started again.

"How am I supposed to know? You're the one who's upset." Jace blurted out.

"Why does she have a key to your room? What took so long?" Nora asked, turning around.

"A key to my room? What are you talking about? Rose does not have a key to my room." Jace said, looking at her confused.

"Not what she told me, and it took you an overly long time to make your way down to the kitchen ... .with her" Nora said angrily to him.

"Nora, nothing is going on between me and Rose. She does not have a key to my room, and I was talking about pack business with her. She was giving me information she found out." Jace said, coming to stand in front of her as he spoke.

"Pack business, which means none of mine. How was she giving it to you?" Nora snapped, pushing past him.

Jace caught her arm and pulled her back to him. She was too angry and too upset to let him manhandle her right now. She felt a strange surge come from her core. All of the anger foamed into a ball. She turned to him, shaking her eyes and tearing into him. She placed her hand on his chest with the slightest motion as if she was going to gently push him. Jace was thrown back into the house. Nora barely even moved. Jace hit the side of the house, the air rushing out of him. He gasped, looking confused at Nora. Nora was shaking, looking at her hand. How the hell did she do that? Matt and Dante were at the back door in seconds, both looking for the enemy.

"Woah." Matt whispered.

"You guys ok?" Dante asked.

"Yes. Go back inside." Jace growled, getting up from the house and standing tall.

Dante and Matt nodded quickly before disappearing. Nora's eyes locked with him, she was still angry, and part of her didn't even feel bad. How dare he make her feel like nothing.

"Want to explain what the hell was that?" Jace growled. Cole pushed forward in his eyes in case he needed him.

"Hunter business." Nora said, a cruel smirk on her lips.

"What the fuck, Nora? I'm not playing these games. I'm not fighting you either." Jace growled.

"Your eyes say differently, Wolf." Nora said, being hurtful on purpose.

"That's bullshit." Jace said to her, stepping towards her.

"Cole could never hurt you, and neither would I. The only person trying to hurt anyone here is you....hunter." Jace said, adding a jab to prove a point.

Nora blinked; his statement seemed to get past his anger wall. She gritted her teeth, forcing the strange feeling down. She stepped back away from him, tears building up in her eyes.

"Just leave me alone." She said quietly.

"No." Jace said firmly.

"Jace, I am done with all of this. I am an outsider and you're making sure it stays that way. You're keeping me in the dark about everything. And then Rosie. There's nothing going on." Nora fake laughed.

"You're upset because you think something is going on with Rosie?" Jace asked, walking towards her.

She backed away a little but not like she was going anywhere. She nodded and as she did he took a deep breath in and let it out in a sigh.

"Nora, there is nothing with Rosie." Jace said softly to her, boxing her into the porch railing.

"Why does she have a key? I was showering earlier and then she was just in the room. Said she had a key to it." Nora said, making a face at him.

"If she does, she won't any longer. I never knew she had one made. I will take care of it. I did not ever give it to her." Jace said a little anger in his voice.

"Why do you leave me in the dark?" Nora asked, her eyes flickering up to him.

"What do you want to know?" He asked, leaning his forehead against hers.

"Everything." Nora said, closing her eyes as she felt his hand snake around her waist, pulling her into him.

"I will tell you everything then." Jace said, pressing his lips to her forehead.

At his touch she seemed to melt into him. She wrapped her hands around his neck and moved to kiss him. His mouth met hers as soon as he saw her head tilt upwards. He kissed her deeply. He kissed her like he was trying to show her that she was it. His only, she was his everything.

Chapter Fifty Two
Lobo

"Come on. Whatever you made smells amazing." Jace said, pulling back from the kiss.

"You can't have any." Nora smirked at him.

"Well, that's rude." Jace smirked, pushing her back into the railing, his face nuzzling in her neck.

"No, what's rude is saying that you will cook for someone and then showing up late." Nora chuckled as his facial hair tickled her neck.

"I will make it up to you." He smiled down at her as he pulled back.

"I'm holding you to it." Nora said firmly.

Jace grabbed a hold of her hand and walked back inside. Matt and Dante were arguing over the last piece of chicken. Nora sighed letting go of Jace's hand. He watched her walk over and stop the argument between Matt and Dante. Then cut the chicken in half and give a piece of it to each of them. Jace smiled watching her. She didn't know but she was going to be a great luna once she started trusting herself.

"Jace, I made you a plate and saved you a spot." Rosie called over to Jace.

Nora stiffened, gritting her teeth. An image of slamming Rosie's face into the plate of food flashed in her mind. Jace pulled Nora back against him, wrapping his arms across her stomach as he did. She leaned back into him as he kissed the top of her head. Nora watched Rosie put her head and hide her expression. She seemed like she regrouped and then looked back up.

"There's room for Nora. come on." Rosie said, scooting down a seat on the table.

Jace unwrapped himself from Nora and took her hand leading her over to the table. Dante and Matt were eating their seconds. Jace pulled out Nora's chair for her. She sat down not liking that she was sitting next to Rosie but didn't want Jace sitting next to her either.

"Nora, this is amazing." Dante said as she sat down.

"You should cook more here." Matt said with his mouth food.

"Nora, could you pass this to Jace?" Rosie smiled at her.

Nora nodded and slid the plate over. Jace looked down at it and smiled at her, pushing the plate more to her.

"It looks amazing, but since the heathens have eaten everything, you can have mine." Jace said as he did.

Nora shook her head but Jace narrowed his eyes at her pushing the plate towards her. Nora let out a long sigh before grabbing the knife from the table. She made a face, cutting the chicken in half. She pushed the other half towards him. He chuckled and took it. He cut into his chicken and placed a piece in his mouth. He instantly made a mmm noises and glanced at Nora. She let out a small laugh.

"Good?" She asked, still chuckling.

He nodded and then looked to Matt and Dante who gave him an I told you so look. Nora smiled as it had been a long time since she had cooked and she was glad everyone enjoyed it. She ate happily seeing everyone happy with it.

"So we're going to let Nora know everything that's going on." Jace announced, moving the pasta around and trying to get more sauce on it.

Dante nodded, finishing his food, Matt shrugged, but then a small voice perked up from beside Nora.

"Jace, do you think that is safe?" Rosie said softly.

Nora whipped her head towards Rosie, looking at her with daggers. Everything in her tells her to just let this woman have it. Jace's hand went to Nora's thigh, and he squeezed it softly. Letting her know to relax. She was trying her hardest to buy the way she said his name. The way she was acting towards him. Now saying she was a threat. Her leg was shaking from being angry.

"Nothing against you Nora but your brand new. You're also rumored to be a hunter. I just want to make sure the pack is safe." Rose said softly to her.

"Make sure the pack is safe?" Nora said it as if it tasted bad.

"Rosie, you have no place to say anything. She saved my life. I owe her one. If she was this evil badass hunter, she would have killed me and not taken on a super wolf to make sure the rest of the

pack was safe. What did you do to save the pack?”
Dante growled.

"I-...Jace-" Rose started to say.

"Alpha, do not say my name again without it.
You know your place. Dante is right. Nora risked her
life and I decided what's safe and best for this pack.
Nora is no threat." Jace said shutting her down swiftly.

"Yay, Nora's in the club." Matt chuckled from
his plate.

Nora sent him a silly look and shook her head
when he made a face back. She was growing to love
each of them pretty quickly. She heard Rosie sigh and
shut down next to her. Nora felt bad, she didn't know
what it was like wanting something she couldn't have
and she didn't know what their relationship was
before. She hated that she was trying to see things
from Rosie's side. Nora took a deep breath choking
down her anger and looked at Rosie.

"Rose, I know I am new and I know trusting
outsiders is scary. I get that your whole world changed
when I showed up and I'm sorry for that. But I promise
I am not a threat to your pack. Hopefully in time you'll
see that. " Nora said softly, She looked over to Matt
and Dante.

Jace smiled, listening to Nora. He could tell
Nora had just seconds ago wanted to strangle Rosie,
heck he wanted to but he watched her take control of
her emotions and address the problem fairly. The
moon goddess had chosen right for him. Rose smiled
weakly but nodded.

"Ok, recapping the chaos." Matt announced, looking at Jace, who nodded, giving him the go ahead.

"So There are other wolves out there, and they all have an Apha...wait, should I explain how the hierarchy works too?" Matt asked.

"Oh, for the love of god. There's an Alpha named Kip who we believe is creating those super wolves-" Dante started explaining.

"We need a better name for them." Matt announced, cutting off Dante.

"By forcing humans to change into werewolves. We don't know his exact plans -" Dante said, being cut off again.

"He wants a war." Rosie said next to her.

"He wants to take control of all packs and be king with his army of -

"Abominations," Matt blurted out a word.

"No, that won't work..." Matt said, thinking out loud.

"Werewolves X...no, that makes them sound cooler than us." Matt muttered to himself.

"Whatever. We're going to war." Dante blurted in frustration.

"Wow..."Nora said out loud, looking at them. Jace started laughing next to her.

"Maybe next time you give the breakdown." Nora said to him, laughing.

"Oh, I can tell you how that works. So Alpha is the head wolf, he calls all the shots and they also have this thing that once you pledge your loyalty like if they tell you to do something you have to do. It's hard to explain ummm. You're human it's like magic then -" Matt started rambling on about the command chain.

"That's horrible." Nora said out loud.

"What?" Matt asked.

"Being forced to do things you don't want to do because someone said you should." Nora said, her eyes brow in a frown.

"That's why the person who becomes Alpha has to be a good person, they put their pack before everything. The position is scarred." Dante spoke up.

"The Beta is second in command. He is the Alpha's right hand and helps him through everything." Matt said, shaking Dante's shoulder.

"Then there's Gamma, which is Wyatt," Matt said with a smile.

"What's your title?" Nora asked him.

"Delta. Wyatt and I are on the same level below Dante." Matt said, yawning.

"Can we go back to the going to war comment." Nora said, looking at Jace.

"Yeah, sure, so war-like-

"Matt." Dante groaned.

"What?" Matt blinked, looking at Dante.

"I'm going to bed. Nora, the food was amazing, thank you." Dante said, getting up and nudging Matt to come on.

"Uh..ah yeah, Nora, great food. See ya tomorrow." Matt said, still confused about getting up.

Nora laughed at them as Dante basically dragged a still-chattering Matt out of the room. Rose stood up and nodded to Jace.

"Alpha, Nora, have a good night." She said almost too formally before leaving the room.

"Oh, thank God." Nora said, holding her head and leaning forward.

"Imagine if their voices were actually in your head." Jace whispered.

"What?" Nora asked, looking at him.

"Yup, the whole secret conversation. Anytime they want, chimes right in my head." Jace laughed.

"Oh, I don't envy you." Nora laughed, scotting over and leaning on his shoulder.

"It's a tough job." Jace smirked, wrapping his arm around her waist.

"So, can you explain everything to me?" Nora said with a yawn.

"Kip is in control of the Red Woods pack." Jace said as Nora cut him off.

"As in the Red Woods, you told me to stay away from?" Nora asked, the name jogging the memory.

"His pack is equal in size to mine. However, Kip, in the last few months, has lost it. He lets his wolves do whatever they want. Then we started discovering bodies. I reached out to the council, which is a group of high-ranking Alphas who are supposed to help regulate and control things so stuff like this doesn't happen. They must have a connection with Kip because they're doing nothing. Then whatever

Matt wants to call them starts popping up. We watched a young man try turning." Jace said, trying to explain the madness.

"You can turn a human into a werewolf?" Nora asked.

"No. You need to already have it in your bloodline to be a wolf. However, there is an old legend that if you ingest the blood of an alpha and then are bitten by an alpha, you can turn a human. As you see, it holds some merits, but they aren't right, and they die. I'm sure the ones that attacked us the other day would have if we didn't stop them. Kip, I'm positive, is using his own blood, but that can only get you so far. We thought we had more time until the Black Sand's pack Alpha went missing. Kip is holding him, and I am sure he is using his blood to turn these new ones. So after the attack, I contacted Alpha Zeke from the Moonlight pack about going to war. He is going to back us when we take on Kip." Jace said, explaining everything.

"How big is Zeke's pack?" Nora asked, taking in all the information.

"Almost as big as ours, but he can't spare all his warriors. They need to have some at home to protect his pack. The Black Sand's pack is also offering what they can. They want their Alpha back," Jace said, rubbing his forehead; talking about it all made him start thinking about strategies and how to go about attacking Kip.

"You're going to need more help. Those things are intense and strong." Nora worried, her mind drifting to Logan and his hunters.

"All I have is Zeke and what's left of the Black Sands pack; it will have to be enough." Jace said softly.

"I want to train to fight. I can get by with whatever weird ability I have, but clearly, I am not untouchable." Nora said, pointing to her stomach where just under her shirt lay claw marks.

Jace looked like he was debating with himself, but then he nodded.

"I'll have Dante and Matt switch off training you when they're not with my warriors."

"Thank you," Nora smiled. Jace stood suddenly and held his hand out to her.

She took it without even thinking about it. He walked out of the kitchen and started towards the stairs.

"Hey, what are we doing now?" Nora asked.

"Bed. All that just exhausted me.' Jace said, his voice sounding tired.

Nora nodded, following him; she could see his shoulders sag a little. She didn't notice it before, but there were dark circles under his eyes. He looked absolutely exhausted. His eyes glossed over as they reached their floor. Nora wondered what message was coming through.

"Fucking Matt." Jace said, half annoyed, half laughing.

"What did he say now?" Nora chuckled.

"Lobos. He wants to call them Lobos." Jace said, shaking his head as they reached the door.

"Lobos?" Nora asked.

"It's the Spanish word for wolf. He's a real original." Jace said, opening the door and shaking his head.

Chapter Fifty Three
Power

Nora rolled over again to another cold bed. She sighed, annoyed. She sat up, stretching and reaching for her phone. She groaned. A text message was flashing on her screen from Jace.

Had to go meet with Zeke; you looked so peaceful sleeping didn't wanna wake you. Matt and Dante are waiting for you when you're ready to start training.

Tired of waking up to a cold bed. Nora sent back with a silly face letting him know she wasn't really mad.

I'll make sure you're warm later, promise. Jace sent it back, and she could see his sexy smirk of a smile on his face as she read it. She stretched again before walking over to the closest and getting dressed. She was out of the room and down the stairs in no time. Matt was sprawled out on the couch, flipping through channels on TV.

"Here's sleeping beauty now!" Matt yelled over the couch towards the kitchen.

"Morning sunshine." Dante yelled out from the kitchen.

"Get yourself something, and we need to get out on that field and start training." Dante said, giving her orders like she was one of the pack members.

Matt chuckled as she hurried to the kitchen, grabbing an apple and an orange. Then I went to the door. She looked at both of them impatiently. Matt laughed, shaking his head as he made a grunting noise getting off the couch.

"Come on, Dante, we don't have all day." Matt yelled, a smirk on his face.

A loud sigh was heard before he appeared out of the kitchen, giving them both the death stare. Nora laughed before taking a loud bite out of her apple and walking out the door. They drove out to the smaller training ground. Dante had ordered it to remain empty and for the other warriors to train elsewhere for the day. Dante turned the car off and walked out to the center of it, waiting for Nora and Matt to catch up.

"So we're gonna just start. I'll have Matt start attacking you, and we'll see what you got. Then once we evaluate, we'll build on that. Clearly, you have something since you took down one of those-

"Lobos." Matt blurted out.

Dante rolled his eyes at him and motioned for him to get moving. Nora stood on the other side of Matt, waiting. She was wondering if her body would recognize him as a threat when he went to attack since she knew him. She waited.

"No hard feelings." Matt said before running at her.

As Matt approached her, the world slowed down. She sighed. How was she ever going to learn to actually fight if her body kept cheating? She stepped aside as Matt got to her, getting out of his reach. She stuck her leg out, tripping him. Matt fell forward, and the world snapped into place; he hit the ground and was shocked. He rolled over on his back, looking up. Dante came over and looked down at him.

"What was that?" Dante said to him, confused, and then looked at Nora.

"It was like she didn't even move? Did you see her move?" Matt asked, looking at Dante from the ground.

"Did you even move?" Matt asked again, now looking at Nora.

"Yes, I did. I tripped you." Nora said with a small smile, but she was also frustrated.

"How?" Matt asked to get up.

"I got this thing…it's a hunter thing." Nora said, looking at Dante.

"Oh snap, the rumors are true." Matt whispered.

"Shut up, Matt." Dante said, annoyed.

"Yeah. So when someone or something goes to attack me, everything goes in slow motion, but I can more freely." Nora said, frustrated.

"Badass, you got superpowers." Matt smiled.

"Why are you upset?" Dante asked, confused.

"Because how am I supposed to learn to fight if my body keeps letting me cheat? What if it doesn't work one time, and then what?" Nora said, annoyed.

"Clearly, it's not foolproof." Nora said, lifting her shirt to show the wolf's claws.

"Hey, hey, Jace will kill us; you do that again." Matt said, yanking down her shirt.

"Well, we keep training. Use your power when you can and if it falters, we will go over defensive moves." Dante said, making a plan.

Matt nodded and went back to the other side, ready to start training. Nora stood out in the middle of the field, her breathing rapid as she waited for Matt to make his move. They had been training for over an hour. She was covered in sweat, and she was trying hard not to use her power so she could be prepared for whatever could come her way. Matt charged her Nora stood still, waiting, focusing on telling herself that she wasn't endangered, hoping that the slow motion wouldn't kick in. It tried, but she fought it. Matt slammed into her, causing her to fall back on the ground. She hit the dirt with a loud thud. The wind got knocked out of her. She rolled to her side, gasping for air.

"Oh shit Nora. Why didn't you do anything?" Matt said, going to her side.

He helped her up to her feet, looking at her like she was crazy.

"I was trying to make my power thingy not kick in." Nora said in between gasps of air.

"Ok…well don't. Use everything you got. It's a gift and weapon. We have super strength and speed. Even in human form. Use all you got." Matt said, shaking his head like she was crazy.

"Ok, let's go again, let's go again." Dante yelled from the sidelines as Matt circled around Nora.

Nora was standing ready, breathing rapidly due to the many rounds they had already done. She was fast, and Matt couldn't catch her, but she was getting tired, and he was getting closer and closer with his punches.

"Dante, I want out. Your turn." Matt said, tired, and laid down on the ground.

Dante sighed and walked out into the field. He looked over at Nora, he could tell she was tired, but she was determined to get this down.

"How would you feel about fighting our wolves?" Dante asked quietly.

Matt sat up, looking at him, he was right; she would need to be prepared for everything. Matt glanced over at Nora, who was debating about it. She struggled with seeing wolves with flashbacks, but she needed to be prepared for everything. She nodded.

"Let's do it." Nora said, mentally preparing herself.

Dante nodded and began walking towards the woods. Nora looked at Matt taking a step forward, not sure if she was supposed to follow. Matt shook his head, not seeing her step forward.

"He's going to shift." Matt said with a shrug.

"Ok.."Nora said, confused.

"He'll be naked. Jace will kill him if you see him naked." Matt laughed out loud.

"Oh..right." Nora said quietly. A few seconds later, a wolf emerged out of the woods.

It was massive, not as big as Cole, but still huge. The wolf was dark gray, and his eyes were a bright ice blue like Coles.

"It's a pack thing." Matt noticed Nora looking into Noah's eyes.

"I heard a rumor that the pack's members match the Alpha's eye color when in wolf form." Nora said, remembering Drake going on about one of his theories.

Matt nodded. She noted that she needed to find the Alpha with red eyes to find out who killed her parents. Noah walked out to the center of the field, not too far from Nora. He locked eyes with Matt. Nora was starting to shake slightly, but this overwhelming feeling of anger began to build up against the fear. She shut her eyes, trying to force it back and to remain calm, but it was winning.

"Noah…Noah is Dante's wolf. He wants to know if you're ready?" Matt asked her quietly.

Nora nodded, and Noah snarled at her. She felt herself go numb. All except this force that was in the pit of her stomach. It was swirling and building. It was stronger than what happened the other night with Jace. She locked eyes with the wolf. Something took her over, and she forgot it was Dante. He was her enemy. Noah began to run at her full force chomping his teeth at her. Nora stood, not moving, her breathing slow and steady, waiting for the wolf. It jumped mid-air when it got close enough to her, lunging for her. As its feet became airborne, the world snapped into slow mode. Nora waited for the Wolf to be just in front of her. She slammed her fist into its sternum. A force of energy burst from her stomach to her fist, blasting the wolf back away from her. The world snapped into normal mode. Nora was thrown backwards, sliding the opposite way. Her body hit the ground, digging into the ground, and her head flung back. As her head hit the ground, the world went dark. Matt jumped up, not sure what happened. A very naked Dante lay unconscious, feet away from Nora. His body hit the ground so hard it was imprinted into the ground. Nora was flung in the opposite direction, her body also leaving its mark on the dirt. Matt rushed over to Nora. She was fine, breathing well, just unconscious. He ran over to Dante, he could tell his body was working on healing itself. His chest looked funny as it moved when he was breathing, but they both were alive. Matt gritted his teeth, knowing he had to contact Jace.

" Alpha." He sent the mindlink as his stomach flipped.

Chapter Fifty Four
Trance

"What Matt? I am in a meeting with Zeke." Jace responded to the mind link, letting him know he was annoyed at being bothered.

"It's Nora. We were training, and something happened." Matt responded back.

"Where?" Jace's stomach dropped hearing that something was wrong with Nora; he felt Cole start pushing to be let out. Zeke looked to Jace, knowing something was wrong. He could see his wolf trying to push through.

"Training field C, Dante, I think, might be hurt too." Matt mind linked back.

" Wyatt." Jace's mind linked him as he stood up.

"I have to go. Stay here, and make yourself comfortable. I will be back." Jace said, standing trying to force Cole back again, trying not to let him take control.

"Yes, Alpha." Wyatt sent back immedately.

" Training field C Nora and Dante might be hurt." Jace linked him, walking out the meeting room door, his body shaking his stomach in knots.

" On it." Wyatt responded.

"Adam get to the hall. I need you in the meeting room, keeping Alpha Zeke company." Jace linked Adam as he rushed out the front door.

"Yes, Alpha, everything ok?" Adam responded back.

Jace ignored the question, his mind racing on how to get there as quickly as possible.

Out ! Now! I'm faster! I'll get there quicker! Cole screamed in his head.

Jace gave in and let Cole take control. He was right; they would get there quicker, running as a wolf than trying to navigate the roads with the car. Cole's paws dug into the earth, cutting across the fields and then dodging into the woods. Cole was running as fast as he could. He needed to get to his mate. He needed to know she was ok. He could hear another wolf in the distance behind him. He saw a flash of white, almost golden fur behind him, and he knew it was Wyatt. Cole dug harder into the ground as he saw the woods opening up. He ran towards the opening. Crashing out of the woods, Cole's eyes scanned the field. Matt was kneeling next to Nora, checking on her. He could hear Dante's groans, but no noises were coming from Nora. Cole ran full force towards her, skidding to a stop in front of her. He reached down and nuzzled her head with his. She didn't respond. Cole whimpered and tried to move her head again.

"Cole, she's out cold." Matt whispered.

Cole showed his teeth to Matt, and Matt bowed his head in response. Cole lay down whimpering next to Nora as Wyatt's wolf came up beside them. Matt heard the bone-crunching snapping noise as Everett shifted back into Wyatt. Cole curled his lip as Wyatt kneeled to touch Nora. He began snarling.

"Cole, I need to help her. Let Jace back." Wyatt said softly.

"Matt, I need you to go see if you see any visible wounds on Dante." Wyatt said to Matt ignoring Cole's growls.

Matt rushed over to Dante, looking him over. He heard Cole growl some more as Wyatt picked up Nora's hand to check her pulse. Cole snapped at him.

"Jace, you need to come back." Matt tried mind linking him.

"Trying." Jace responded as Matt glanced over, seeing that Cole was twitching, trying to stay.

"Cole, I promise I will take care of her." Wyatt said to him in a smooth, steady voice.

Matt looked over at Dante; he couldn't see anything. No bruising, no wounds, nothing. His head was solid in place despite it just being fractured a few days ago, but wolves heal quickly.

"Wounds?" Wyatt yelled over.

"No, he's just out cold." Matt yelled back, shaking his head, not understanding why.

Cole whimpered again and then shifted back into Jace. Jace was hunched over, breathing hard. Jace groaned as if he had hurt himself trying to get back control.

"What's wrong with her?" Jace asked, looking at Wyatt.

"I'm not sure, she had no wounds, neither of them do. They're just unconscious." Wyatt said, shaking his head.

"How do we wake them up?" Jace said, touching Nora's head.

"We need to get them back to the hospital and see. They might just wake up in time, but at least if we have them there, if anything else happens, we can be prepared for it." Wyatt explained.

"Matt… car and clothes." Jace ordered as he watched Nora's breathing.

Matt got up and raced to the far parking lot where Dante's car was. Matt rushed over, sliding across the hood; he smiled to himself about it and then got into the driving seat. He turned the keys over and drove across the field towards Jace and Wyatt. Getting out of the car, as he reached them, he popped the trunk.

"Dante keeps extra clothes in his trunk." Matt yelled to Jace and Wyatt as he started over to Dante.

Matt tried picking up Dante, but he was so heavy. He scooped him against his chest and began dragging him towards the car. Wyatt came overdressed, picked up Dante's legs, and helped carry him into the car. Wyatt got in the back seat with Dante. Jace was sitting in the front with Nora cradled in his lap.

"Ok, I'll drive." Matt said to himself as he got into the driver's seat and started driving to the hospital.

It was dark and foggy like she was watching an old movie. A flickering light began just like before a film started, and then there was the countdown. 3...2....1 The world in front of her flickered and then went dark. The world opened up to a black-and-white scene of a young couple meeting in the middle of the woods. They were acting secretive, like they were not supposed to be there. The girl had long dark hair, from what she could tell, she wrapped her arms around the young man as he pulled her into a deep kiss. Nora watched them kiss, trying to figure out what exactly this dream was trying to tell her. The young man pulled back, his eyes glowing, they were glowing ice blue. Nora looked at him. He had similar features to Jace. Could they be related?

The world was soundless around him, but she could tell by their sudden panic expression and the way the girl with the long hair kept shoving the man something was happening. She wanted him to go. Lights in the background, the color of fire appeared. She begged him to go. She didn't want whoever was coming to find him. Nora's eyes were focused on the male, his eyes growing brighter as they would before shifting. Her gut told her that he was a wolf. She looked at the girl, who looked like she was on the verge of crying. The torches were coming closer. He pulled her in for a fierce kiss. She kissed him back fiercely but pulled back, shoving him away from her.

"Go!" She yelled at him, shoving him again.

Her scream of go breaking the silent film. Nora felt her pain pour into her as if it was her own pain.

The girl's eyes were now glowing an ember color. Nora was confused why the two wolves were not able to be with each other. She felt him growl as he looked at the girl touching her cheek one last time before taking off. As he left her, the world around Nora went dark. There was hushed yelling and crying. She knew it was the girl.

"You are never to be with him again." The word echoed in the darkness.

The world flickered, and a new scene unfolded. A small town, an old town. All the homes were built by hand and from stone. The roofs were made from some type of straw. There was destruction around. A family crying as they held on to a dead loved one, a house on fire. Smoke and blood filled the air. It was as if the town had been raided.

"This ends now." A voice echoed, and the world faded; only one person remained clear, an elderly woman dressed in black looking around at the heartbreaking chaos.

The world went black. Seconds later, soft chanting was heard. Nora couldn't make out the language or what was being said. It was softened and mumbled. The world flickered around, and a young woman with long hair appeared in front of her. She let out a horrible shriek as she collapsed forward, her body shaking and trembling. Her eyes glossed over, and the ember glow faded from them, almost like someone had taken them. She hit the ground, shaking. The young man appeared rushing towards her, but he was thrown back when he reached out to touch her. The same force trembled through his body, but the glow from his eyes didn't fade but burned brighter. Both of them collapsed.

Nora watched the scene in horror, trying to decipher what was happening. The young man and woman stood up, confused. The girl's eyes narrowed when she saw him, and as he looked at her, his face turned into disgust.

"Wolf." The girl sneered at him.

"Hunter." The man growled. The world flickered dark.

Chapter Fifty Five
Moon Child

Darkness she had been sitting in darkness for what seemed ever. Part of her began to wonder if she had died. She was a little upset she didn't get the flashback and get to see her life play over. Why did she get to see people's lives she didn't even know? At some point of waiting, she gave up and sat down in nothingness. Maybe this was hell. She didn't think she did anything so wrong she would go to hell.

"Nora, you need to fight." She knew the voice, the warm way it tugged at her heart.

She could hear him; she shut her eyes, trying to remember the smooth sound of it.

"Nora, wake up." He pleaded; he sounded broken.

"Jace." Nora said into the darkness.

"Nora, I need you." It was a faint whisper.

Her heart broke hearing the pain in his voice. She needed him too. She got up, looking around. There had to be a way out. She needed out. He needed her; she wasn't going to sit here and wait any longer. She began walking forward, not knowing where she was going. She could barely see, but she had to try. A light flickered on in the distance, and she began walking to it. She didn't know if it was some type of trap, but she had to find out. She had her guard up as she got closer. The light was cast over a door. She looked at the plain wood door debating on whether or not to go in. She took a deep breath and told herself that it was this or sitting out in the darkness doing nothing.

She grabbed the door handle and yanked the door open. It was a room in a cabin, maybe? It was old and rustic. Nora stood outside the door looking in. It was dark but not as dark as where she was. She took a step in, and the door slammed behind her. As the door slammed, the fireplace flickered on. The whole room took over a vintage look in color. She looked confused. A dark pot was hung over the fire, boiling. Nora stepped forward, looking around. She could tell that she was someplace old. A loud noise made her jump as the girl from the previous images walked through the door Nora just entered from. Nora looked at her, and a silly grin was on the girl's face. She took off her cloak and hung it by the door as she walked over to the fireplace. She poked the lid of the pot peeking in.

"You'll burn yourself." a voice called from the other side of the room.

"I'm ok, Mother." The girl replied.

The woman got out of the rocking chair and walked over to the table, setting down plates and forks.

"Go change before your father gets home. You can smell that boy on you." The mother said her tone was harsh and disapproving.

"Mother, I-

"Nadia, you were forbidden by the Alpha to go to see him. You're going to cause a war." Her mother said sharply.

"He's my mate's mother." Nadia pleaded.

"And you are the daughter of the Alpha; you are betrothed to another, regardless of mate or not. Our pack needs this. You must do your role." The mother said, pointing for her to change.

Nadia hung her head and walked out. They didn't know that her mate was the Alpha's son of another pack. They didn't know that he would fight for her if she didn't go. Nora watched the scene and felt horrible for the young girl. Everything went black again, and Nora was left in the dark.

Nora looked at the door; it was the only way in or out. Maybe if she went out into the darkness and traveled around more, maybe she would find another door and a way out. She pulled open the door and walked out of it. She was back in the forest from the previous vision.

"Nadia go, the villagers are coming. Run!" The girl's mother shoved her away from her.

"No, I can't leave you." Nadia cried, going to go help.

"You are my only child and my everything; go now!" The mother yelled, shoving her.

Nadia fought with herself, but she took off running in the words. The mother stood proud, waiting for the mob. Nora felt the urge to protect her, but she could not do anything. This was just another vision.

"Yetta. I have been waiting for this day." an older woman stepped forward as the mob found her.

"Sorinah." Yetta responds, but not saying anymore.

"Yetta, your kind has finally done enough damage, and we are sick of it. We have lived by each other for years in peace, but now your kind has caused death and destruction to our people." Sorinah said, the crowd behind her agreeing.

"Sorinah, it was not meant to be that way" Yetta said, her voice showing sadness.

"Children and women killed between your battles. Our homes were off-limits. We had an agreement." Sorinah screamed at Yetta.

Yetta did not respond; she knew she was right. She knew her daughter had caused the war, and their poor village was the battleground. The boy that was her daughter's mate chose to go to war to get her.

"We might not be able to fight your kind, but we have something better. We will make something that will." Sorinah said, walking forward and grabbing hold of Yetta's hair.

She motioned for another woman to come forward; she was carrying a knife and a bowl. Sorinah grabbed a hold of Yetta's hair and ripped a handful out of it. Yetta bit down on her lip, refusing to cry out. Sorniah dropped the hair into the bowl; she then grabbed the knife. Yetta's eyes grew wide as she saw the knife. Sorniah nodded, and three men came forward and grabbed ahold of Yetta. Yetta's eyes glowed amber as she tries to shift. Sorniah dumped a powder over her, and Yetta screamed in pain.

"Mountain ash." Sorniah smiled as Yetta was unable to call upon her wolf.

"Yetta, I am sorry, but this is the only way to ensure our safety. You understand. You would do the same." Sorniah said as she pressed the knife across Yetta's throat.

She caught her blood in the bowl and then began chanting. Nora froze her hand over her mouth as she watched the graphic scene. It faded quickly and was replaced by the image she saw before, of Nadia turning into a hunter and hating her mate. The world went dark again.

"Nora."

"Hello?" She called out to the darkness; she didn't know this voice.

"Nora."

"Yes?" Nora asked, her voice uncertain of everything.

A warm light filters down onto another door. Nora started at the door.

"Nora, I have shown you this; so you can understand the path laid out for you. You will have to make a choice. It will not be easy. Only you will be able to stop the chaos ahead. It will take a hunter and a child of the moon. You, my dear, are both. Go now," The voice said to her sternly.

"Child of the moon? I am both what?" Nora yelled back.

"Find your wolf. Make the right choice." The voice said as the door opened.

"Wolf? Jace? I already found him. What do you mean? What choice? Who are you?" Nora said, her voice becoming more annoyed as she wanted more answers.

The door flew open, and a force shoved her through it. Nora fell forward, tumbling into more blackness. Nora jolted up right in the bed; she began fighting as a force was holding her down.

"Nora. Nora. Stop. It's me." Jace said, holding onto her.

Nora froze, hearing his voice. Relief rushed over her as she wrapped her arms around him. He pulled her into him, cradling her against his chest; she could feel the stress leaving him as he squeezed her tighter.

"Jace, I'm ok." Nora laughed as she tried to pull back.

"Don't ever. I mean, ever do that again." Jace growled, his eyes glowing slightly.

"I didn't mean to." Nora laughed.

His mouth smashed into her kissing her deeply like he hadn't seen her in years. He pulled her closer to him, wrapping his arms around her as he kissed her more. She returned the kisses and melted into him. She was glad to be back. She felt at home in his arms. She had so much to tell him and pulled back. She wanted to tell him all about everything she had seen, but when she looked at him. She saw the bags under his eyes, the way his face looked a little paler. He looked sick. She couldn't tell him right now. She needed him to have a moment where he didn't have to worry about everything.

Chapter Fifty Six
Awake

"Hey, we heard you were up. Hungry?" Matt asked from the doorway.

"Starving." Nora said with a smile.

"Dante ate all the tacos, but there were some burgers and Chinese food left and some pizza. I don't know. I shouldn't order food when I'm hungry." Matt smiled.

"Dante, is he-

"Just fine." Dante said, waving at her.

"Oh, thank god. Dante, I am so sorry. I don't know what that was. Did I hurt you?" Nora asked, pulling away from Jace to look at him.

"You knocked me out." Dante laughed.

"Otherwise, I am fine." Dante said, winking at her when her face looked hurt.

Matt shoved a plate of mixed-match food at Nora and plopped down at the end of the bed. Jace growled at him a little bit; Nora subconsciously rubbed his forearm, settling him down. She looked at the plate; there was lo mein, a burger, a slice of pizza, and half of a taco. Nora smiled; Jace shifted behind her and pulled her back against his chest. She leaned back as she swirled her fork around the noodles.

"How long was I out for?" Nora asked the room.

"Almost two days." Jace's voice vibrated through her back.

She finished the lo mein and moved the plate away. Her stomach was overwhelmed by the influx of food.

"You ok?' Jace whispered into her ear.

"Ate too fast." She smiled.

"Dante, when you were out, did you dream anything?" Nora asked quietly.

"No, I don't remember anything." Dante said with a shrug.

"Hello, all. Alpha. I've come to check on the patients. She's awake, which is exciting. I will let Wyatt know. I will take their vitals before I go." The young woman said as she bowed her head, addressing Jace.

The woman went to check on Nora, but seeing her leaning comfortably against Jace, she decided to start with Dante. She took his blood pressure and heart rate. He smiled at her, noting how beautiful she was.

"Jace, can we go home?" Nora whispered to him.

"Let's get you checked out, and then I will take you home." Jace said, smiling, hearing her call his home, home.

"So what's the verdict, nurse? Good to go?" Dante asked her with a flirty smile on his face.

"You're perfect- I mean, your vitals are perfect. I will run it by Wyatt." The nurse stuttered out, bushing deeply.

Dante flashed her another charming smile as she stumbled out the door, completely forgetting to check on Nora. Nora laughed, shaking her head at him.

"What, don't be jealous. I'm perfect." Dante smiled brightly.

"Mhmm.' Nora said, rolling her eyes at him.

"Stop harassing the nurses." Wyatt said to Dante walking in and heading over to Nora.

"I didn't do anything," Dante laughed.

"Go home." Wyatt said, listening to Nora's lungs.

"No problem, I might need help out. Can someone get a nurse?" Dante said, laughing as he stood.

"Matt helps Dante." Jace said, his voice annoyed.

"Why do I always get crappy jobs?" Matt muttered, going to grab Dante by the hand.

"Come on, handsome." Matt chuckled.

"But Wyatt might miss me." Dante smirked.

"Go." Wyatt said as he took Nora's blood pressure.

Nora was laughing at the scene. Dante made faces at Wyatt as he walked past them.

"Nora, great sharing a room with you; we should do it again sometime." Dante said, a mischievous grin on his face.

"Dante." Jace growled from behind Nora.

"I'm kidding." Dante laughed, winking at Nora as he and Matt left.

"I swear, one day." Jace grumbled.

Nora patted his arm that was draped around her.

"Well, everything sounds and looks great. Heart, lungs are all good. How do you feel?" Wyatt asked her, studying her face.

"Fine...sleepy but fine." She smiled.

"How are you sleepy?" Jace asked, looking down at her worried.

"I don't know bad dreams." Nora shrugged.

"Well, get her home, Alpha, and let her rest some more. Nora, don't do anything too strenuous the next few days. We don't really know what happened, and you look great, but just in case, there's something underlining that was missing. Just take it easy." Wyatt instructed her.

"How long is a couple of days? I need to go back and start training. Well, I'll have to see if Dante is ok with training again, but I need to know how to handle myself." Nora said, annoyed.

"No." Jace said behind her. Nora shifted away from him, turning to look at him. Her face scrunched up, confused.

"What?" She asked him.

"No more training." Jace said; his tone was sharp and authoritative, like he was talking to a pack member.

"I need to know how to fight." Nora said, trying to ignore his tone.

"No, not now." Jace said, sharpening his tone.

"I don't know who you think your-

"We will talk about it when we get home," Jace said, cutting her off as he stood up from the bed.

"Nora, take it easy, ok. Have Jace call me if you need anything." Wyatt said, giving her a small smile as he went to head out.

Nora could feel her blood boiling. How dare he try to tell her what to do. She narrowed her eyes at him, trying to control her anger. He sighed deeply as he looked over at her.

"Not now, Nora. I just got you back. Can we just go home?" Jace said quietly.

Nora exhaled and nodded, getting up off the bed. She wobbled a little, and she grabbed a hold of the bed. She shut her eyes to stop the world from spinning. She got up too fast and had a head rush. Before she could even process moving forward, Jace scooped her up and carried her against his chest.

"I just got up too fast. I can walk." Nora said to him with a sigh.

Jace responded with a small noise and didn't say anything else. She leaned back into his, resting her head against his chest. She loved the smell of him; he was starting to feel more and more like home, even when he thought he was the boss of her. The car ride was quiet; he kept looking over at her as if he thought she would disappear or explode. She smiled softly, seeing his concern. She reached over and entwined her fingers into his, letting him relax at the feel of her touch. She was angry but couldn't stay angry at him because of how he was worried about her and how exhausted he looked. She felt bad. They were home before she knew it, and he was at her door, opening it up and going to scoop her again. She frowned at him.

"Jace, I can walk. Stop." Nora said, swatting his hand away.

"What if I just wanted to carry you?" He said with a smile, offering her his hand.

She made a small face and took his hand, and they walked into the house. Dante was sprawled out, asleep on the living room couch. Mouth hanging wide open. Nora laughed at him. As she walked by, she pushed the blanket off the top of the couch so it would fall and cover him. Jace smiled, shaking his head at her actions. Nora was happy to be back home as she walked into Jace's room. She heard him walk in behind her as she went to turn on the tv. He caught her by the wrist, spinning her back into him. She collided with his chest with a small yell. She laughed as he ran his hands down her sides, reached her hip, grabbed ahold of them tightly, and pulled her pelvis closer to his. He rested his head against her forehead.

"Don't ever do that again." He whispered before his mouth claimed hers.

She kissed him fiercely back, her hands traveling to the bottom of his shirt as she pulled it up over his head, breaking the kiss. As soon as his shirt was off, his hands went to hers, quickly discarding it. He pulled her back in for another deep kiss. He kissed her like she hadn't seen her in years. The want and need portraying through the kiss. His mouth moved to her neck, kissing the spot where he would someday mark her. Sharp electric tingles flow through her body as he touches the spot. She moved into it, her body wanting him to mark her. She didn't understand it; all she knew was her whole body needed and wanted it.

"Jace." She whispered, saying his name like she was telling him to do it.

He moved his mouth down her shoulder away from the spot, trying to control himself and Cole. His eyes glowed slightly as Cole pushed forward, trying to make him go back to her neck. Jace focused on the curves of her waist, his tongue and mouth moving over her abdomen. Nora shivered against his touch. He grabbed her by the waist, picked her up, and carried her to the bed, burying his face into her neck as he did. His fangs elongated as he did. His fangs scraping against her skin sent chills through her as she hit the bed. Jace laid her back on the bed and yanked her pants off in one swift motion.

Nora sat up as he tossed her pants behind him. She grabbed ahold of the belt he had held him up and began undoing it. She then unbuttoned and unzipped his pants and pulled them down. His pants fell around his ankles, and Nora did the same and pulled his underwear down. His member was exposed. Nora remembered how he felt in her mouth and wrapped her mouth around his member. Jace inhaled sharply, a small growl escaping his lips as she began sucking and moving her head. Her mouth pleased him. After her mouth made several passes over his member, he caught her chin in his hand, having her let go of himself. He then laid her back on the bed. He pushed her legs apart, positioning himself above her. His manhood pressed against her entrance. She wrapped her legs around his waist and pulled him into her. Tidal waves of ecstasy passed through her as he began to move her, legs wrapped tightly around him as she moved with him. They moved together and felt the heat building up between them. Nora's moans became louder as she reached her climax. Her muscles tensed as her release happened so did his. They laid entwined with each other. Nora drifts off to sleep, her legs still wrapped around him. Jace smiled down at his sleepy mate. He unwrapped himself from her. He laid down next to her, his mind at rest for the first time in a long time. He pulled her against him, cuddling her till he drifted off to sleep.

Chapter Fifty Seven
The Argument

The next morning rolled over, and she sighed, frustrated when she felt an empty bed. She sat up a little angry. At times she wished she could do the whole talk through minds; she would so cuss him out right now for leaving her again. She grabbed her phone and went to text him. Looking down at it, she saw a new message and assumed it was from him explaining where he had run off to. Tomorrow she decided she was going to get up early and leave him in a cold bed. Clicking into her messages, she saw that it wasn't from Jace but from Logan.

Hey, how are things going? She made a small face.

Apparently, I have superpowers and knocked myself out for two days. Also, Jace is going to war with the Red Woods pack. I would make sure your guys are ready for anything that trickles down your way. Nora debated a second before sending it.

So you are what we thought. Nora, you're from the original hunter bloodline; that's why you have abilities. We were trying to tell you that before Lilly got all …Lilly on you. She really didn't mean it. Thank you for the heads up about the war coming. I will make sure my guys are ready. Let me know if you need anything at all. Logan responded.

What does that mean? Original Hunter bloodline? Why do they have powers? Do you know anything more? Nora texted him back.

Did you get the book translated? That's all we know; it was passed down by word of mouth. The only written information we have is in the language no one can translate. Logan messaged read.

Jace was working on it. I'll let you know as soon as I can. Nora said, sighing.

She had forgotten about that with everything that had been going on late. She stretched, yawning as she clicked on Jace's name on her phone.

Where did you run off to? She sent him with an angry face.

As if on cue, Jace walked through the door holding two plates of food. The smell of breakfast hit her nose and her stomach instantly growled. She felt bad for sending the message and seeing him bring her food.

"Morning Sleeping Beauty." He smiled at her, setting the food on the nightstand.

"Hungry?" He motioned to the food.

"Very. Thank you." She smiled, looking over her plate.

He literally made everything. Eggs, bacon, sausage, English muffins, and waffles. Her stomach growled again as she looked at the food. Jace laughed, hearing her stomach. He placed his plate on the other nightstand and glanced down at his phone.

"You sent me an angry face?" Jace smirked, looking at her.

"You keep sneaking away. You're lucky you brought back food." Nora said in between bites.

"So you miss me?" Jace said, his smirk turning into a teasing grin.

"Maybe." She shrugged as if she didn't care. In an instant, she was pulled back across the bed, looking up at Jace.

Who began to place kisses on all the right spots. She struggled not to give into the rush of sensation that spread all over her body.

"Say you miss me." He mumbled into her skin.

"Miss you? I don't know." Nora giggled as he playfully bit her shoulder.

His hand traveled down over her breast, cupping it with his hand as his mouth captured her earlobe.

"Say it." He whispered into her ear, his breath hitting her ear sent shivers through her.

She inhaled sharply as his hand began to travel down from her breast to her stomach, tucking her into the shorts she had slept in. Her body moved upwards to meet his hand as he began searching for her spot.

"Your body misses me." He whispered to her.

Her hand grabbed a hold of his wrist as he explored. A small moan escaped her lips as his fingers found it. She arched against his hand as his fingers continued to please her. She felt her body begin to twitch as she felt her release coming. His mouth kissed hers, muffling the moans coming out of it. He felt her tense up as she reached her climax and then relaxed underneath him. He smiled as he kissed her forehead.

"Miss me?" He teased her once more.

"Shhh." She muttered, kissing him.

He chuckled against her mouth and then sat down on the bed, getting his food. Nora laid there for a second, composing herself. Jace took a bite out of his English muffin and laughed. Nora made a face at him before rolling over to her side. She sat back in the bed, happily eating.

"So I need to go make sure my men are ready for what's coming. Matt and, up until recently, Dante have been training them. But I need to go down there myself and train them." Jace said, eating the rest of his food.

"Ok, that's great. I can come and maybe train a little." Nora said nonchalantly, looking out of the corner of her eyes at him.

"I don't want you going; we need to keep your powers a secret." Jace said, getting frustrated.

"I get that, but I need to know how to handle this. If I don't figure them out, then I am just a ticking time bomb." Nora said, trying to choke down the anger bubbling up in her.

"Now's not the time." Jace said shortly.

"So you rather I be some damsel in distress, some weakling," Nora growled.

"You are not weak." Jace said to her, sighing.

"No, but useless because I don't know how to use what I have." Nora said, turning away from him.

"Nora, I can't risk something happening to you; again." Jace said, becoming annoyed.

"Fine, I'll just ask Dante for a lesson away from everyone again." Nora said, trying to compromise.

"No, I can't risk either of you getting hurt, right Nora. This isn't up for discussion." Jace said, becoming angry.

"Dante wasn't worried about it." Nora said, becoming angry.

"Yeah, and look what happened; you could have died, and your powers went haywire. We still don't understand them." Jace said, trying to get her to see this was for her safety.

Nora was silent, giving him the cold shoulder as she turned her back completely on him. Jace went to go to her but heard the commotion downstairs. War was coming any day, and the pack needed him.

"Nora, I have to make sure they are ready." Jace said, trying to be soft with his words.

"Go. No one is keeping you here." She said coldly.

He gritted his teeth holding back words as he walked out the door. It slammed it behind him, and Nora heard a locking noise.

"Did he really just lock me in?" Nora growled, going to the door.

She turned the handle, and sure enough, it was locked. She was going to strangle him.

"Stay outside the door and make sure she doesn't leave till I come back." She heard Jace say to someone.

"Yes. Alpha." He responded.

She didn't recognize the voice, but there was no way in hell she was staying in this room. She looked down at her phone, she scrolled through it, debating between calling him and yelling at him. She saw Logan's name. If Jace wasn't going to let her train, she knew Logan would. She couldn't be useless, she couldn't just sit by with whatever was going on. She wanted to help. Nora walked to the window, looking down; she watched them leave to go to the training grounds. War was coming, and she was not going to just sit here in this tower like a princess to be protected. She wasn't going to let people die while she could help.

She had already known Jace put someone outside her door and probably down the hall as well. She looked at the ground and took a deep breath, her stomach knotting at her thoughts. She wondered if she jumped if the world would slow down. She would technically be in danger, and that's when it happened. Logan would train her; Logan would not treat her like some fragile thing. If she could get to the hunters, she could be valuable. She could try to understand and use her powers and then come back and help Jace. She tugged on the window wanting it to open, but it refused. She became angry and slammed it open. The glass around it began to crack. She glanced at the door, expecting whoever was guarding it to come running in. When they didn't, She looked out the window, studying how far the ground was. She knew the definition of a fatal fall and looking down from the third floor, this could be that.

"Fuck it." She whispered angrily as she stuck her foot out the window and dangled it over the edge.

"Worse…well, worse case, you die, but second to worse case, we break something." She muttered to herself.

"Please, I need you to work." She whispered, looking at the ground.

She felt herself go numb and let herself fall forward. As she started to free fall, everything turned in slow motion. She smirked excitedly that she wasn't falling to her death. The ground came at her so easily. It was like she was just floating downward. What else could she do? How else could she use this? She thought as the window shattered up above her and the glass pieces began to fall down in slow motion. Nora shifted herself out of the line of falling glass. As her feet touched back down on the safe ground, time snapped back into place. The glass sprinkled around her like glitter from the sky. Nora glanced back up at the window, waiting for someone to catch no noise from above; she looked to the front no one was coming out the door after her. She may have actually pulled this off.

Chapter Fifty Eight
Legend

Jace felt guilt in the pit of his stomach mixed with anger as he walked out the door of his house. He didn't mean to lock her in and shut her down, but he needed to keep her there. Adam met him at the car as the rest of them followed behind. Matt caught up to them; Dante was hanging back.

"Lady problems?" Matt asked, approaching the car.

"You're sparing with me first." Jace growled, getting into the car.

"Shit." Matt muttered, getting in.

"Shouldn't have opened your mouth." Adam laughed from the driver's seat.

"Any news from Rose?" Jace asked Adam.

"She said that he is working on creating an army. He has figured out the more fit and physically conditioned the person is, the longer they last as those monsters," Adam explained what he had heard from Rose.

"Lobos." Matt shouted at them all.

"Lobos." Adam rolled his eyes.

'When is she coming back?" Jace asked as they drove to the training grounds.

"She should be back now. I just didn't check." Adam said with a shrug.

Jace's phone began to buzz; he looked down at it thinking it was going to be Nora. Seeing Tim's antique shop come up on caller id, he hit the accept button and placed the phone to his ear.

"It's about time." Jace said into the phone as he answered it.

"Mr. Knight, I am sorry for the delay. The book was very old and very hard to translate." Tim began.

"What did you find out? I know you're not calling me with nothing." Jace asked, his voice threatening.

"From what I have been able to translate, it's a story." Tim began.

"A story?" Jace asked, his voice annoyed and confused.

"Yes, Mr. Knight. It says in the beginning, there were two powerful werewolf packs. They lived, for the most part, in peace but were rivals. Then a young female fell in love with a young man from the rival pack. They were both the Alpha's pack successors. They were supposed to marry elsewhere, but they were mated and fated to be together. They tried against all odds to unite the two packs, but war happened. The war took place in a by-standing village. Killing the humans that lived in the village. The villager fought back by cursing one of the lovers. This is the part that gets a little hard, but from what I can understand, they curse one of the werewolf lovers to become, for lack of better terms, a hunter, to forget they were a wolf and to hunt and kill werewolves. Have this overpowering hate for them. They also gave them abilities to sense danger, and it says something like slow down time. They also can harness the energy and use it against their enemy. If they don't take the energy from elsewhere, they can use their own but at the risk of draining themselves." Tim explained.

Jace was quiet for several seconds, trying to process everything he had just heard.

"Mr. Knight, did I lose you?" Tim asked over the phone.

"So, if I understand correctly, Nora is a wolf that was cursed to be a hunter, and she can harness energy and slow down time. Why doesn't she have a wolf if she is one? Cole would have found hers." Jace said, confused. Matt and Adam looked at each other and got quiet, trying to listen to the conversation.

"I don't know if Nora has a wolf or is one, but her ancestors were until they were cursed. It's the ultimate Romeo and Juliet scenario, but unlike Romeo and Juliet, Juliet kills Romeo and forgets she loved him. You'll have to do some research on your own about Nora. This is all the book has." Tim said.

"Ok Thank you. I will send for the information and book shortly." Jace said, ending the call.

He sighed, hanging up the phone. There were more and more questions every time he found out a little more about Nora, it became more complicated. Cole was a little excited at the fact she might have a wolf. He felt him stir in him when Tim said it. Cole desperately wanted to find his other half. He looked away from the phone and found Matt and Adam staring at him.

"You're worse than teenage girls" Jace said, shaking his head, spotting the look Matt and Adam had.

"Nora might have a wolf?" Matt whispered a hint of excitement in it as well.

"I don't know; I'm going to have to tackle that at another time. We need to do this now. We need to focus on getting everyone ready." Jace said, trying to push it from his mind.

His mind is still on the fight he had with Nora. The longer he thought about it, the more he felt bad. He could have handled it better. He was not used to people arguing with him or going against anything he said. He needed to remember that she wasn't a member of his pack. He sighed deeply as they got to the training site. His pack is waiting, as well as the members from Zeke and the Black Sands pack. Matt got out of the car and waited for Adam.

"It's gonna be ok, Alpha." Matt whispered to him before heading out towards the group.

"Alpha's here; line up, get ready. Cut the chatter. We aren't here to talk; we're here to work. You wanna live through this; then you're gonna listen and learn," Matt started yelling, taking on the role of a drill sergeant.

Jace smiled briefly at Matt's comment and then watched how Matt's composure changed as he walked out onto the field. For how goofy he was in person, he was deadly on the battlefield. Jace approached the group, and as he did, a loud hush fell over them. The members of the Black Sand's pack eyed him cautiously; they were beaten down and broken. They looked almost terrified of Jace. Zeke's pack tried to not show their nervousness towards him, but they weren't masking it well. He knew his reputation, and he didn't care. He liked it that way. Mess with what was his, and you wouldn't live to see the next day. Now Kip was going to find that out the hard way.

"Pair off in groups of two to three. We will do close-quarter combat. I wanna see what you got, and from there, we will critique and mold you. This isn't going to be a walk in the park. These th- Lobos that Kip is creating are fast, strong, and have no thought process except to kill. We will fight in human form first and then wolf form. We need to make sure your wolves are ready for this as well." Jace yelled out over the group, Matt and Adam standing behind him.

Although Adam had no official title like Dante, Wyatt, and Matt, he still held just as much authority. He had gained Jace's respect and favor as he worked his way up to be one of the best fighters he had.

"Matt, you take the groups on the right, Adam left, and I will keep an eye on the middle till Wyatt is freed up," Jace instructed them.

"Yes, Alpha." They both nodded to him before going out to the groups.

Jace watched the men fight, he was weeding them out as he watched them. He will find the weakest ones and pair them with Matt. He was good at motivating and teaching. The stronger ones he would give to Adam, he was good at fine-tuning kills. He and Wyatt will work with the ones most needed.

"Alpha." Wyatt said, approaching him quietly.

"Wyatt." Jace said quietly, his eyes still fixated on the warriors.

"What's wrong?" Wyatt asked.

"Nothing." Jace said quietly, but Wyatt knew better.

"Nora, ok?" Wyatt asked.

"Probably angry as all hell, but ok. I locked her in the room…again." Jace said quietly. Wyatt laughed.

"You remember she took the door off the hinges last time." Wyatt continued laughing.

"I left someone outside the door just in case. Dante is also laid up on the couch." Jace said shortly.

"I'm sure you can smooth things over with her later." Wyatt smiled.

"Wyatt, are there any tests you run on people who haven't found their wolves yet?" Jace asked.

"No, it's usually more of a psychological issue. Why? " Wyatt asked.

"Psychological." Jace said to himself, thinking out loud.

"Someone having trouble ?" Wyatt asked again.

"No…maybe.. I'll fill you in once I know more. Wyatt, go take the tall one that doesn't know how to block and show him something before he ends up with his face reconstructed." Jace said annoyed.

Wyatt hurried out into the field, stopping the two men sparring, and began to show the one have difficult different ways to block incoming blows.

"That's enough!" Jace yelled out over them.

"Line up if I tap you; go over to Matt. If Wyatt taps, you go over to Adam. The rest will stay in the middle." Jace yelled as they fell in line.

Wyatt, Matt, and Adam looked at him with the same confused look.

" Matt, you're going to get all the weaker ones to work on technique and strengthening. Adam, you'll get the better fighters, fine-tune them, teach them to be lethal, and Wyatt, you and myself will work with the in-between." Jace explained through mind link to them.

They all nodded, and Jace walked out into the crowd and began the selection.

Chapter Fifty Nine
Retaliate

Nora rushed away from the house, quickly heading towards the woods. Ducking into the woods, she debated what she wanted to do. She really wanted to text Logan and tell him to come get her, but at the same time, something was tugging at her, telling her not to leave Jace. She was debating as she walked further out into the woods. When she felt she got far enough away from the house, she flipped open her phone.

Hey, can I come train with you guys for a little bit? Nora typed it out and then erased it. Hey, could I learn some fighting skills? Nora sighed as she typed out another sentence and erased it again. Hey, I have crazy power that knocked me and the person I was sparring without for two days…would you be comfortable trying to teach me how to control it? Nora typed out, feeling like she needed to let him know the danger of it all.

Yeah, I'm sure we can figure out something so that way you don't knock us all out; lol Logan texted back.

Awesome, can you come get me at Jace? Nora replied.

"What are you doing?" A voice asked behind her as she hit the send button.

She gritted her teeth, realizing she was caught; she turned around slowly and smiled brightly at Rosie.

"Taking a walk. What are you doing?" Nora said to her, confused.

"Same. I was actually on my way to come find you." Rose said to her with a small smile.

"Really? Why?" Nora said, putting her phone in her back pocket.

"Well, you know I wanted to…I wanted to say I was sorry." Rose said, coming to her slowly.

"Sorry for-

Just as Nora was about to ask why she was sorry, the world slowed down. Her body was sensing danger, but she wasn't sure where it was coming from. She watched Rose walk towards her slowly, and then her hand reached out to grab her. Nora stepped out of reach. Was Rose the danger? As she stepped out of the way, she noticed that Rose's eyes were glowing red. Red? Jace's pack was blue. Nora felt the energy building up in her as Rose realized she missed her as time snapped back into place. Nora had moved far enough away from Rose that there was a good gap between them.

"Sorry for even tolerating you. Sorry for not killing you soon. But now we have bigger plans for you." Rose grinned, her fangs coming down.

"We?" Nora asked, trying to think about what happened when she was sparring with Dante to make her power come forward.

"They said I couldn't kill you, nothing about not hurting you." Rose laughed at her claws coming out of her fingertips as she let pieces of herself slowly shift.

"Bring it." Nora said, taking a deep breath. Rose growled, running at her.

Nora stood still, and just as Rose was close enough, everything slowed down. Nora stepped out of her way just as the claw swiped at her midsection. Nora threw her fist forward, connecting with Rose's jaw. Time snapped back into place as Nora hit Rose. It sent Rose backwards a few steps, a few drops of blood coming out her mouth. Rose looked frazzled as she touched her lip; seeing the blood, she growled louder. This time running at her faster. Time slowed down, but it was like Rose had moved too quickly, and it caught her as she was too close to Rose. Nora raised her forearm, blocking the slash, Rose's claws raking across her skin, peeling it open. Nora threw a punch into Rose's gut as she blocked the hit. Time snapped back into place as Nora's fist connected with Rose's stomach.

Rose let out a gasp and doubled over. Nora wasn't playing anymore as she went forward; Nora grabbed a handful of hair and brought her knee up to Rose's face. She kneed Rose hard in the face. She placed her foot on the ground and brought her knee up again, slamming Rose's face again. Nora then shoved her back away from her. Rose fell backwards on the ground, blood pouring out of her nose as she let out a yell. Nora stood ready, waiting for her as blood dripped down off her arm from her wound. Rose let out a growl looking up at her as she caught her breath.

"Oh, you think you're so strong; let's see how you can hold up against a real wolf." Rose said as she let herself shift.

Rose's dark brown wolf appeared in front of Nora after several bone-snapping sounds were heard. She then felt it as strong as ever. The surge of power is coming forward. She needed to not do what she did last time but just enough to hurt Rose. Rose's wolf looked at her, growling, showing its long sharp fangs. She seemed to almost smile as she walked at her slowly. Nora waited for her to attack. She could feel the power forming in her stomach. Her hands were trembling but not because she was scared but because her body felt like it was getting overwhelmed with energy. She was trying to focus on not letting the feeling take over her like it did when with Dante.

Rose's wolf lunged at her, and Nora moved out of the way just in time. Rose's wolf snapped at the air. She turned quickly around, catching Nora on her calf with her teeth sinking them in as Nora let out a scream. Nora slammed her fist down on the top of the wolf's head as hard as she could, a jolt of energy coming with her hand as she did. Rose's wolf let out a loud whimper as she dropped to the ground.

Jace stood there watching the men fight. His eyes study each one before moving onto the next.

"Alpha... hunters at the front gate... seem to be frantic about Nora." Jace's stomach knotted as he heard the mind link.

"Dante, go check on Nora now." Jace mind link Dante.

"Ok?" Dante replied, confused.

"Hurry." Jace told him back as he heard the confusion from Dante.

Without a word to anyone Jace started for his car. His anxiety got worse as he waited to hear back from Dante. Jace got in his car and drove to the front gate. Getting out of his car, he slammed the door showing his anger; his eyes glowed as Cole became just as angry seeing them. Logan was slamming his hand into the gate, yelling.

"What the hell is your problem!" Jace yelled, going to the gate.

"Nora! Listen, she's being attacked!" He yelled, holding his phone up to hear as he clicked the speaking phone.

The sound of yelling and fighting came through the phone; he heard Nora let out a small yell, and then animal-like growls were heard. Jace's heart dropped to his stomach.

"Alpha, she's not in her room; the window's broken. I'm going out front to see if I can find her." Dante linked back.

"Dante, something is attacking her! Hurry!" Jace sent back, not hiding the panic in his voice.

Jace shut his eyes and he was hoping If he strained to hear, he could pick up anything from the phone call or around him. His stomach was gliping around inside of him panicking. Cole was pacing fiercely inside of him.

"Alpha, I can smell blood near the pack house. I'm going after it." Dante linked him.

Jace tensed up, letting Cole take over. Logan jumped back away from the gate, seeing Jace shift. Cole took off, running towards the pack house as fast as he could.

Dante raced through the woods; he could hear fighting. The smell of blood was getting strong as he made his way through the trees. Getting to a small clearing, he rushed out into it. His eyes widened, seeing Nora's blood dripping down her calf and forearm. Dante didn't see the wolf coming at her.

"Nora?" Dante said, coming out of the trees.

Nora heard her name and turned to see Dante. She looked relieved seeing him, but then Rose's wolf lunged at her. The world slowed down as Rose's wolf went for Nora's throat. She decided that a dead Nora was better than taking her back. Nora threw her arm up in time, Rose's Wolf teeth clamped down on her forearm. A loud snap was heard as Nora's bones broke underneath the power of the wolf's jaw.

"Nora!" Dante screamed as he watched the wolf latch onto Nora's arm and broke it.

The wolf pulled Nora down to the ground, shaking her with the broken arm. Noah came forward, and Dante shifted as quickly as he could, charging after the wolf. Nora shut her eyes, pushing the pain out of it and taped into the energy she had been holding back. She pressed her palm into the center of the wolf's chest. Nora let out a loud yell as the energy jolted through her and into Rose. The wolf let go of her arm and dropped to the side of her. Noah stopped short just in front of them. Nora braced her arm to her chest, looking at Noah. Noah went over and licked Nora's face.

"I'm ok." She said weakly as she shut her eyes, trying to stop the pain.

Noah went over to the dark brown wolf and nudged it. A growl emerged from Noah as he realized who it was.

"It's Rosie....is she- " Nora started to say when a noise coming from the other side of the clearing caught her attention

Cole came sprinting into the small clearing with panic and anger in his eyes; he was already growling, ready to take on whatever was attacking. Nora smiled weakly at Cole. Cole rushed over to her once he realized the threat was gone. Cole whimpered, laying down next to Nora, trying to be as close as possible to her.

"I'm ok, Cole." Nora said, tapping his head lightly with her other hand, wincing as she did.

The wolf shifted back into Rose's human form. Cole narrowed his eyes at the body, growling fiercely. A loud gasp was heard as air rushed into her lungs. Nora had thought for sure she killed her. Cole began growling even more. He left Nora's side and walked over to Rose.

"Cole." Rose whispered. It was the last thing she said.

Cole grabbed her by the neck. He sank his teeth into her, and with one forceful tug, he ripped the front of her throat out. He dropped the flesh out of his mouth as he walked back over to Nora. Nora didn't know how to feel about it, she knew Rose would have done the same to her, but the way Cole just did it was so effortless.; like it didn't even matter. Cole whimpered again and nudged Nora.

"Cole…I need Jace." Nora whispered to him, resting against him slightly.

Noah came over and braced Nora's other side as she began to feel lightheaded. Cole stepped away from her once Noah had her. Nora shut her eyes, trying to stay with it. She heard Cole switch back into Jace.

"Damn it, Nora." She heard Jace say as he got to her side.

"Noah. Wyatt no.," Jace ordered Dante to send for Wyatt as he carefully pulled Nora into his arms.

"Don't be too mad, ok." Nora said with a small smile.

"I am furious." Jace whispered as he picked her up.

"Well, I'm broken, so even?" Nora smirked and then winced as her arm brushed his.

"You wouldn't be broken if you listened." Jace said, trying not to be angry with her since she was in pain.

"I wouldn't be broken if you were a tyrant." Nora said, angry.

"No more. Let's just get you home. "Jace said, cutting off the conversation.

Nora nodded and leaned her head against his chest as he carried her out of the woods to the pack house. Blood was dripping from her forearm, steadily bleeding all over herself and Jace. Her leg was also dripping blood. With each step Jace took, she felt more tired. She closed her eyes briefly.

"Hey no, you stay with me." Jace said, poking the top of her head with his chin.

"I'm here, just tired. That took a lot out of me, I feel drained. No energy." Nora said quietly.

"I know, just stay awake and stop scaring me." Jace said, and for the first time, Nora heard the vulnerability in his voice.

"You're really afraid of losing me?" She asked him.

"Yes, Damn it!" Jace growled as he started walking up the steps.

Nora was quiet as he held her carefully through the house and up to their room. The guard at the door opened the bedroom door for them. Jace walked in cold air rushing in from the broken window. He made a disapproving noise as he walked over to the bed, setting her gently down.

Chapter Sixty
Repercussions

Jace sat down next to her, looking over her wounds. He got up, walked to the bathroom, grabbed a towel, and returned to bed. He wrapped it tightly around her leg to stop the bleeding; as he tightened the towel, Nora winced but said nothing. He looked at her arm.

"You're crazy if you think you're doing what you did to my leg to my arm." Nora said, moving her arm closer to her.

"No, I'm pretty sure it's broken." Jace said, not touching it but looking at it.

"It feels pretty broken." Nora said with a small smile.

"Bite wound on the calf, broken forearm, and claw marks on the opposite forearm." Jace mind link Wyatt so he knew what he needed.

"Stopping by the hospital to get supplies. Is she alert?" Wyatt sent it back.

"She's alert, just tired, but she said it from fighting, not the wounds. There's a good amount of blood, but I don't think she's hit anything crucial." Jace replied back.

"Be there as soon as I can." Wyatt linked back.

"Calling for backup?" Nora asked with a small smile.

"Wyatt, I think I might just move him in here with us." Jace said sarcastically.

"No, I'm not into that type of relationship." She smirked with a wink.

Jace let out a long sigh shaking his head as he looked at the claw marks on her other arm. He went to the bathroom, got a damp washcloth, and returned to bed. He began to clean her other arm.

"What happened?" Jace asked, confused; he knew Rose was jealous, but to do this?

"I don't know, she was talking about us and them. Whoever it was wanted me, and I was to come with her." Nora said quietly.

Jace looked confused about who Rose was talking about. He hasn't asked anyone to get Nora.

"Jace, when she shifted, her wolf's eyes were red." Nora told him.

She knew what it meant but didn't want to come out and say it.

"Kip. She went over to Kip's pack." Jace said through gritted teeth.

Jace pushed the cloth onto her less wounded arm as he said it. Nora winced slightly, moving her arm back away from him.

"Sorry." he said quietly, asking for her arm back.

"It's ok. I'm sorry too." She said, talking about Rose.

"There's no reason to be sorry about her. I just don't know why she went over to Kip's pack. She was invested here. Her whole family, generations have been part of this pack. I don't know why she would risk it all and leave," Jace said out loud, confused.

"Why does a girl do anything crazy? Could she have been in love or mated with one of Kip's members?" Nora asked out loud.

It was like it clicked as Nora said it.

"I sent her over there, not thinking about her not finding her Mate. She had to have gone over and met her mate. A mate should never ask the other one to put themself in danger like that." Jace said, angry.

"I don't know about the wolf world, but in the human world, men are dicks, and if they can use someone to get ahead or something they want, they do it." Nora said quietly.

"Maybe," Jace said, using another towel to dry off her arm.

"Should I even ask about the window?" Jace said, feeling like Nora had something to do with that.

"Probably not. You're already grumpy." Nora said quietly.

"Did you jump out the fucking window?" Jace growled, his eyes flickering from his to Cole's.

"Maybe." Nora said quietly, taking her arm away from him just in case.

"Are you insane? This is the third floor. How did you not get hurt? I swear, Nora, I am going to lock-

"You're not locking me anywhere! Maybe if you would stop acting like I'm some fragile piece of property that you can shut away. I wouldn't be so extreme. News flash, I get to say where I go, what I do, and how I do it! Not you! Oh, and guess what? I've figured out my powers the hard way! If you even try shutting me away, I will leave. Clearly, I am resourceful, and I will leave, and you will never ever see me again!" Nora said, standing up and looking down at him sitting on the bed as she yelled at him.

Jace looked a little taken back, anger flashing in her eyes. Her chest moved up and down quickly as she tried to calm herself down from being so mad at him. She cradled her arm against her chest, but she didn't even look like it was hurting her right now. She was staring him down, daring him to go against what she had just screamed at him. Cole whimpered inside of him at the thought of never seeing her. Jace was becoming angry the more she stared at him like that. Cole whimpered louder as if he wanted him to stop.

I'm not letting her leave quietly. Jace told Cole.

You're wrong. She can handle herself. You need to trust her more. She is not weak. She is our perfect match. Wolf or no wolf. Cole shot back.

He sighed slightly, rubbing his forehead with his hand. Cole was right. He had sparred with Rosie in both forms; she was deadly. He glanced up at Nora. She was waiting for him to argue.

"Nora-

"I mean it, Jace. I-

"Nora, listen to me." Jace said, raising his voice above hers.

She stopped talking and looked at him. The volume of his voice took her back a little. He sighed again, getting up and motioning for her to sit down. She made a face, but her arm and leg were throbbing, so she sat.

"You can train on conditions." Jace started, and Nora made a face going to cut him off, so he stopped talking and put his hand up, telling her to wait.

"The condition being you train with me." Jace finished.

"Ok, deal. Why was that so hard?" Nora asked quietly.

"Well, you knock me out for a few days, and this whole place might fall apart. So be prepared for that. " Jace smirked.

"I won't. I think I've figured it out." Nora smiled.

A loud knock came from the door, and before anyone could answer, a shirtless Dante entered the room. He didn't care if he was going to be in trouble; he wanted to make sure Nora was still alive.

"Hey, she ok?" Dante said, walking in.

"You ok?" Dante asked, seeing her.

"I'm ok." She smiled at him, masking the pain she was in with the smile.

"What the hell was that? I mean, you were great but Rose. What the fuck?" Dante said, his sentence staggered.

"Rose joined Kip's pack. From what I can tell, Kip's pack knows Nora is my mate and wants to take her. Rose was trying to do that. I don't know how much Kip's pack knows about Nora." Jace explained to Dante.

"Oh, ok. Dude, you scared the crap out of me. What were you doing in the woods? " Dante said, coming over to look at Nora's wounds.

"Running away." Nora said simply, watching Jace tense up.

"The hunters." Jace growled.

"You were leaving us?" Dante asked with a hint of sadness in his voice.

"Yes and no. I was going to go train and learn to defend myself from the hunters, and I would come back afterwards." Nora said to Dante, trying to ignore an ice-blue-eyed Jace.

"Nora-

"I hadn't exactly decided I was more mad that Jace locked me in the room again. That's why I was still in the woods. I was debating. I didn't want to leave." Nora told Dante.

Dante frowned, not saying anything else; he understood. He wouldn't have stayed somewhere against his will, either. He looked at her arm and made another face.

"Oh, that looks gross." Dante said out loud.

"Thanks." Nora laughed.

"So, was that what you did to me? It was the weirdest thing to watch. It was like something threw her away from you. Something unbelievably strong. I don't know how she came back because you had stopped her heart with that." Dante stated.

"Kinda, I don't remember yours. I was locked in on a wolf attacking me. I completely forgot it was you and went overboard." Nora explained.

Another knock came from the door, and in walked Wyatt and Matt. Jace frowned seeing Matt but kinda expected him. He had also grown fond of Nora. Matt was carrying supplies as he walked in.

"Housekeeping." Matt smiled, trying to mask how worried he was. Wyatt frowned, seeing her arm.

"I can tell you right now that it's broken. I need to do an X-ray, but I have a stabilizer with me until we can get you over to the hospital." Wyatt frowned.

"You ok? I know it's a stupid question while you're sitting there with your arm dangling.' Matt said.

"It is a stupid question." Jace grumbled behind them.

"I'm fine." Nora said, making a face at Jace about his rudeness.

"Wyatt, I will meet you at the hospital. I need to finish up with the troops. Dante stay next to Nora. Like next to her until I am back," Jace said, getting up and heading to the door.

Nora felt her stomach knot a little. She knew he was going to be angry, but part of her hated the fact that he was mad at her. She watched him leave, and her stomach twisted more, seeing him not even say anything or look back at her. Wyatt moved towards her, and Nora shut her eyes, getting ready for more pain, knowing Wyatt was gonna have to touch her arm.

Chapter Sixty One
Defense Mechanism

Jace walked down the hallway, his mind repeating Nora saying she was planning on leave. He felt Cole's pain at the thought of her leaving. He pushed it aside, he needed to focus. His pack needed him to be strong and make sure they were ready. Getting to the bottom of the stairs he remembered Rose's body and Logan, He let out a long sigh.

"Hunter still at the gate?" Jace linked the front guards.

"Yes, Alpha. He's demanding to see Nora."

Jace growled his first reaction was to tell the guard to tell Logan to go fuck himself but then he thought about Nora. She was calling him. Jealous tugged at his heart but he tried to control it.

"It's up to Nora. Hang tight." Jace was sent back.

"Dante asked Nora if she wants to see Logan?" Jace mind linked Dante.

"He'll be ok…you eh not so much." Dante joked with her nodding at her arm.

"Thanks, I feel loved." Nora responds sarcastically. Dante's eyes glossed over.

Nora caught the look and knew one of the wolves was talking to him. She looked at him curious, sometimes she really hated being left out.

"Nora Alpha wants to know if you want to see Logan?" Dante said looking at her confused.

"Logan? He's here…um yes," Nora said, confused.

" *Alpha, she said yes." Dante mind linked him back.*

Jace gritted his teeth somewhere inside of him. He wanted Nora to say no, like it was her choosing him over Logan. He shook his head. He needed to stop being so damn emotional.

"Let the hunter in and escort him to the hospital so he can visit Nora there." Jace linked the guards at the front gate.

"Yes, Alpha."

He had made it to his car, he got in and sat down. He gripped the steering wheel in his hands, becoming angry. Stop, you'll break it. Her voice echoed in his head from before when he had done the same thing, in front of her. He let out a long sigh and rested his hand against it.

"Attention all a hunter will be on the premise: do not engage, do not attack. He is welcomed right now. I will advise when he is gone." Jace's mind linked his entire pack.

"Adam." Jace's mind linked him.

"Yes Alpha?" Adam linked him back.

"What's the deal with the hunter?" Adam asked before Jace had a chance to respond back.

" Friend of Nora's. Rose is dead, she attacked Nora. She lined up with Kip. I need you to inform her family and bring her body to them." Jace linked him back.

"Will do." Adam replied shortly.

Jace noted that he didn't react to the Rose piece at all. He didn't have the energy right now to worry about that. Maybe he just didn't care.

"Ok Nora this is gonna hurt. I need to slide your arm into this to stabilize it." Wyatt explained.

"Ok, I think I'm ready." Nora said, looking down at her very painful arm and the air splint that Wyatt was about to put on her.

"Ok, I'm going to try to be as gentle as possible." Wyatt said.

He reached out and touched her wrist and the world went slow. The pain of him touching her arm was even worse. He moved in slow motion bringing the air splint towards her arm. Nora bit down hard on her lip trying to stop her power from working. She didn't need it to be slow right now; she needed it done and over with as he lined up her arm with the splint and went to push her arm in it. It was beyond painful Nora let out a yell and where Wyatt was touching her a jolt shot out of her skin. Wyatt whipped his hand back, the world snapping back into the right time as he looked at Nora confused.

"You just shocked me." Wyatt chuckled like it was static electricity and not Nora's doing.

He looked at Nora confused when he saw how painful her face was. He knew it was going to hurt but not as bad as her face looked.

"Hey I'm sorry it's going to be ok. I'll go quickly and be gentle." Wyatt said going to pick up her wrist again, but her body said no and shocked him once more.

He pulled his hand back and looked at Nora. She made a small face at him.

"Sorry." Nora said quietly.

"Yeah, imagine that, but like a thousand times more." Dante started laughing as he responded.

"You're shocking me?" Wyatt asked.

"Not intentionally, it's like a weird defense mechanism my body is developing. It knows you're going to hurt me so it said not today." Nora smiled.

"I know it's gonna hurt but I gotta do it to fix it. Can you turn it off?" Wyatt asked.

"Not really; I just started understanding it." Nora said with a frown.

"Ok, what if we distract you?" Matt asked, coming over.

"We can try anything." Nora said with a shrug.

"Ok, so I need you to think of a number from five to twenty." Matt said.

"Ok." Nora said with a nod as Wyatt picked up her wrist gently.

"Now think of that number but in objects." Matt glanced over at Wyatt who was now lining up the splint to her forearm.

"Ok, now, what?" Nora asked.

Wyatt pushed her arm into place with the splint. Nora let out a small yell and her body zapped Wyatt. Dante was quick and fastened the straps as Wyatt walked away shaking his hand.

"Good work Matt." Dante smiled.

"You ok Nora?" Matt asked.

"I'm ok...Wyatt?" Nora asked, bringing her arm towards her lap.

"My hand's numb but I am fine. We might need to sedate you once we get you to the hospital if you need a cast." Wyatt said standing up.

The drive to the hospital was quiet. Dante kept looking over at Nora to see if she was ok. She would smile weakly at him every time he looked. She then started making faces. The ride was literally about ten minutes but he had to have checked on her at least fifty times. Wyatt had called ahead and the x-ray room and hospital room was already set up for her. Getting to the hospital they were rushed in like she was some celebrity and taken straight to x-ray. Dante followed closely behind.

"Ok we will do the x-ray with the splint on. If the bones aren't broken or lined up right we won't have to take it off and redo." Wyatt said motioning for her to come over and set her arm on the table.

"Any chance of pregnancy?" A nurse asked me to come over.

"What?" Nora asked her, taken back by the question.

"Could you be pregnant? The x-ray could be harmful to the baby which is why we ask." The nurse smiled explaining.

"Um...I don't know." Nora answered.

She really didn't know. She couldn't remember her last cycle and she was active, everything had been so strange since she turned twenty one. The nurse smiled and went and got a lead apron.

"It's ok. We will just be cautious anyways." The nurse said, placing the apron on her.

"Look I don't know, I don't feel pregnant whatever that feels like. And obviously I am not a virgin so keep your looks to yourself." Nora said, making a face at Dante.

"Woah woah, chill. No harm meant." Dante said through his hands up in defense.

"Ok we will just be in the other room." The nurse motioned to Wyatt and Dante to step behind the wall.

"Nope. I'm staying right here." Dante said quietly.

"Beta Dante, hospital policy says for your own safety-

"Don't care, go," Dante said, waving the nurse off. The nurse bowed her head in defeat and walked behind the wall with Wyatt.

Nora looked at Dante curiously. Did he have the same power over pack members that Jace did? Dante said her look and smiled.

"Alpha said to be right next to you, literally. So yeah, I'm up your butt until he says otherwise." Dante said, throwing a wink at her.

"Wonderful." Nora said as the X-ray clicked, taking a picture of her arm.

"Ok, perfect; Nora will have you wait in the room across the hall with Dante while we look at the X-ray." Wyatt said to her.

Nora nodded and started walking, she smirked
" Coming buttplug?"

"Hey, that's gross." Dante said, laughing,
walking after her.

They walked across the hall to the room. Nora
hopped up on the hospital bed waiting for Wyatt to
come back in. She watched Dante listening to the
conversation in the hall. He frowned deeply.

"What?" Nora asked in a whiney voice.

"Sorry." Was all Dante said as Wyatt walked in.

"Bad news, the splint needs to be readjust and
the bones aren't lined up. It's a pretty bad break."
Wyatt said his face showing that he was sorry.

"Shit." Nora groaned.

She took a few deep breaths and then looked
at Wyatt calmly. Wyatt raised an eyebrow at her.

"Ok, let's do it." Nora said, holding her arm out
to him.

"Ok, let's get the splint off." Wyatt said as he
walked over to Nora, and just as she dreaded, the
world went slow.

She shut her eyes and waited. Maybe taking it
off wouldn't be so bad. Wyatt slowly peeled back the
velcro strip holding a portion of the split in place. Nora
let out a breath she had been holding in as he undid
the middle velcro strip. She sighed seeing that it was
taking so long and undid the last one before Wyatt
could even make it over there. He looked up at her
slowly questioning why she undid it. She wasn't going
to try to explain to him right now that he was moving
in slow motion. She shook her head and he then went

to take the splint off. Pain shot through her arm as she gritted her teeth. Wyatt slowly peeled the splint away from her arm. Once it was off and he was away from her the world snapped back into place.

"Ok, now the hard part. I am going to have to pull your arm out straight and keep it taught while someone slips he splint on and tightens it." Wyatt explained to her.

Her mind screamed, this was going to hurt. Dante came over to her to help steady her shoulders. Wyatt went to grab her wrist but Nora's body reacted sensing her fear. As Wyatt touched her skin, her body zapped him and at the same time Dante jumped. Dante also got zapped.

"This isn't going to work." Wyatt said, shaking his hand from the pain.

"You're telling me." Dante said, rubbing his hands together.

"I'm sorry. I'm really trying to stop it." Nora said with a frown.

"Ok, maybe we can give you a light sedative and see if we can do it then." Wyatt said, looking at the nurse, who nodded and walked out.

"It's kind of cool. To be honest." Dante said with a half smile.

Nora smiled, the pain taking its toll on her. She wished Jace was there. Jace, I need you. She thought in her mind as Wyatt walked in with a cup.

"I was going to try an injection but I figured your body probably would fight that too. So drink this, it will make you sleepy." Wyatt said.

She took the cup and drank the liquid. It was warm going down. Within a few seconds she began to feel a little drunk. She kept thinking about how she really wanted Jace there. Wyatt went to touch her hand again and her body zapped him but not as strong as it had been.

"Well give her a few more seconds and I think we will be good." He said to Dante.

"Ok." Dante said, watching Nora closely.

Chapter Sixty Two
Fracture

" Jace, I need you." Jace blinked hearing Nora's voice come through his head like she had mindlinked him. He stopped in his tracks as he walked towards the training field. He had to have made it up. He desperately wanted her to reach out to him. He shook his head, clearing his thoughts. Part of him felt guilty he had left but he needed to put his pack first right now.

"Jace."

It happened again. What was going on he knew this time he wasn't making it up. Could she mindlink him? Was this part of her weird abilities? She wasn't a pack member and she wasn't a wolf. How else would she be able to? This couldn't be real, he thought.

"Jace. Jace. Jace."

He heard his name in her voice over and over again like she was calling to him to come to her.

"Dante everything ok with Nora?" Jace mind linked him.

Nora began to panic the drunker she got. She kept saying Jace's name over and over in her head wanting him to appear. Her body had gone into over defensive mode. Wyatt and Dante were standing on the other side of the room making sure she didn't think they were coming near her.

"I'm sorry." She whispered to them.

"It's ok, you just need to relax." Wyatt said cautiously.

Nora had zapped them hard a few times when they came near her. She actually sent Wyatt across the room, which is where Dante and Wyatt were now standing, trying to figure something out.

"Where's Jace?" Nora whispered, putting her face in her hands.

"Where's Jace?" It echoed through his mind, another link from her.

"Dante! What is wrong with Nora?" Jace sent through mindlink his tone stern.

"Um, we got into a little bit of a situation. We couldn't get her arm splinted without her body zapping us. So we gave her a sedative and now she's drunk and we can't get near her without her body thinking we're a threat." Dante sent back.

"I'm coming." Jace sent back as he turned and ran back to the car.

"What if I don't look at you guys sneak out of the room." Nora said, her face still in her hands.

"I'm not leaving you." Dante said quietly.

"Well, I can't promise you're safe in here. It's not like I'm going anywhere." Nora growled.

"She might be right. Maybe if we leave, her body will calm down without sensing any threats," Wyatt said quietly.

"Alpha said to stay by her." Dante said, arguing with Wyatt.

"How are you going to look after her if she knocks you out again." Wyatt growled.

"Fine. Nora, we'll be right outside the door." Dante said as he began to walk out the door, they were lucky and the room had two exits; they didn't have to pass by Nora.

"Maybe we can find a way to sedate her fully?" Wyatt said once outside completely.

"Your drink is doing wonders." Dante said sarcastically.

"Well, that's not something I expected to happen. I was thinking she might get happy, drunk or sleepy. Only one of those has happened and made everything worse." Wyatt said, shaking his head at Dante.

"Where is she?" Jace said, walking up to them.

"She is in there, but be careful. She has no control, and she could hurt you." Wyatt said quietly.

He didn't want to say that about Nora, but that was the fact right now. Jace ignored the warning and walked into the hospital room. Nora's head shot up looking worried as she saw him but relieved.

"Be careful." Nora whispered.

"I feel really weird and can't control it," Nora said quietly.

"You know I would never hurt you, so I'm not worried about it." Jace said, walking to her side. Her body didn't react to him.

Jace sat down next to her, Nora relaxed a little seeing that she hadn't hurt Jace yet. Jace pulled her against him carefully wrapping his arm around her. She instantly relaxed against him. His scent took over her senses and she nuzzled into him more. Her body's defenses dropped.

"You're ok. I'm here now. I got you." He whispered to the top of her head.

She felt calm and felt the anxiety in her leave. Even the pain she was having seemed to lessen. She looked up at him and smiled.

"I'm sorry." She whispered.

"You don't need to be sorry; this is not your fault." Jace whispered to her.

"No, you are upset with me. You think I was leaving you for Logan." Nora said, a little drunk against his chest.

She felt him stiffen and she felt sad for him thinking that. How could he think that? She thought looking up at him. She took her good hand and put it to his cheek.

"Jace, I promise I am not ever leaving you." Nora said and then winced when her forearm brushed his stomach. She watched his eyes glow and fade very quickly as she said it.

"Cole happy or mad?" Nora asked quietly.

"He was worried but happy." Jace said with a small smirk.

"We gotta fix your arm." Jace said to her.

"Ok but i don't know how we are going to do this." She said, shutting her eyes.

"How did you guys get it on?" Jace asked.

"Matt kept asking me questions, but I don't think that will work this time." Nora said softly.

" *Wyatt, I'm going to distract her. When I do you need to get this splint on her right. What do I need to do to help?" Jace mind linked Wyatt who was still in the hall.*

"I need someone to pull her wrist out straight and to the left to line the bone to get the splint on correctly." Wyatt responded.

"Fuck. Ok I'll do it." Jace said, hating the thought of hurting Nora even though it meant fixing her arm.

If Rose was still alive he would kill her again for causing all this.

"Nora Wyatt's going to come back in the room, but he's not doing anything." Jace said to the top of her head.

She nodded, her eyes still closed resting as the sedative was taking more effect on her. Jace reached down and touched her hurt arm. A Little spark zapped him but didn't hurt him.

"Sorry." She muttered.

"I just want to look at it; I'm not going to hurt you." Jace said, and he felt her body relax.

He moved his hand down towards her wrist. Nora's body didn't react, trusting him. It made him feel worse, it felt like he was about to betray her trust completely. Wyatt. Wyatt walked into the room and he felt Nora's body going tense sensing Wyatt in the room. Nora kept her eyes shutting hoping that if she didn't see her body would react but she could sense that it knew.

"Nora." Jace said quietly to her.

Nora opened her honey colored eyes and looked at him. Jace felt guilt in the pit of his stomach. Wyatt on three. Jace bent his head towards hers and kissed her softly. He felt her body relax as she began to kiss him back. He deepened the kiss as Nora's body began to respond to him. Jace's hand traveled down towards the bottom of her hand.

One… Two… Three. As Jace said three he pulled her wrist forward and to the left. In an instant Wyatt slipped the splint on and closed the velcro straps. Nora let out a loud yell as her bones relined. A jolt shot through her, shocking both Jace and Wyatt. Wyatt jumped back shaking his hand as the jolt felt like electricity shooting up his arm. He looked over to Jace worried since he had his whole chest to Nora. He couldn't even tell Jace had been shocked.

"You ok?" Jace whispered down to her.

"Oh god that hurt. Are you ok?" Nora whispered to both of them.

"We're fine." Jace whispered to her, kissing the top of her head.

"That was sneaky." Nora smiled up at Jace.

"I know I'm sorry love. We needed to fix your arm." Jace said, pulling her closer to her chest.

"Your eyes? They're still glowing. I hurt you didn't I?" Nora asked, her face showing sadness.

"No, Cole is just concerned." Jace said, trying to calm her down.

It did hurt; it wasn't as bad as he thought, but Cole came forward, helping him take the pain.

"I'm okay, Cole." Nora said, sleepily patting Jace's arm; Jace smiled at her reaction.

"I'm going to go get some pain meds and medicine fixed up for her. If you want Jace, you can take her home." Wyatt said.

"No pain meds. The stuff you gave me last time was awful." Nora said, nuzzling into Jace's chest more.

"Are you sure?" Wyatt asked.

Nora nodded, starting to drift off to sleep against Jace. Jace scooped her up and nodded to Wyatt, letting him know he was heading out.

"Check on Adam and the rest of the men. Take Dante with you. If he's feeling up to it, have him start helping the weaker ones." Jace orders, walking out.

Chapter Sixty Three
Feud

Kip hadn't heard back from Rose. She was supposed to go and trick Jace's mate into leaving with her. He had men waiting near the border of the Jace's territory. Kip paced the floor in front of the control station. A sharp pain ripped through him, sending him forward into the control station. He shook with pain as he felt the bond rip away. He knew that one of his pack members was gone. An overwhelming sadness rippled through him. Kip's wolf howled inside of him feeling lost. Kip felt his wolf's pain. He knew the minute she took her last breath she was gone. Rose was dead. He pulled himself upright trying to control the shaking feeling rushing through him. Then the sudden rage coursed through his veins. He paced the control room angry. He wasn't attached to her yet but his wolf inside was going crazy that his mate was gone.

"Dumb Bitch." He muttered.

He knew the only reason she would be dead was because she messed up and let Jace know their plan or did something stupid. His wolf whimpered as he cursed her.

"Shut up." He muttered to him.

She was clearly weak and not fit to be his Luna. His wolf growled angry inside of him wanting revenge, wanting to rip something apart now that his mate was gone. There was this fire.

"You'll have your turn, don't worry. Good, we can use that rage when the time comes." Kip told his wolf.

He looked over the monitors and his army was almost ready. He had learned that if he kept the bodies of his new creations unconscious and kept the body temperature low that the breakdown didn't happen. He had been making his soldiers and setting them asleep inside of a just above freezing room. He looked over at Chadwicks monitor, he didn't know how much longer Chadwick could hold out. He had become so weak, he didn't look good. Kip started saving his blood in blood bags just in case he didn't make it. He shrugged at the thought of Chadwick dying. If he died and his Beta became Alpha he could just go take him. It might be better that way.

He needed a new plan, Rose had ruined the one plan he had to get close enough to Jace's mate. Jace was too strong on his own. There were rumors now that he had an alliance with Zeke's pack and the remainder of the Black Sand. He wasn't sure if his army of freaks could take on all of them. He had sent his own pack into training overdrive. He had never really trained them. He let them go on their natural instincts. Most of their wolves were savages, and they attacked like such. No organization, just pure emotion. It made them deadly, but in war, when he needed them to listen, he wasn't sure if that would happen. He clenched his jaw, annoyed. Suppose he could have just gotten the girl. He now more than ever wanted to crush Jace by killing his mate; even worse, he would turn her into one of his monsters. He just needed to find a way to her.

"Alpha, we need some supplies from town." Taylor said softly, seeing his anger.

He hated even bringing it up and he wasn't sure what he was so angry about but his job was to also look after the pack, so he had to speak up.

"Supplies?" Kip growled.

"Yes, Alpha, we are low on food." Taylor said, trying not to make sure none of his emotion showed with Kip being as angry as he was.

If he shows anything, Kip could take it as a challenge or threat. He didn't want that. He needed to make sure he was still around to protect his pack as much as he could.

"Send some of the women. We need the men learning how to actually be warriors." Kip said, looking at him, waiting for that flicker of disapproval.

Taylor didn't show any expression but nodded and left as quickly as he came. Walking out he let the breath go he had been holding. Kip was losing it more and more each day. He headed to the woman's pack house. Their pack was very segregated. The woman kept to themselves unless married and were to be seen and not heard. They did all the major errands for the pack and were kept under lock and key. When a girl came of age they would present them to the pack and hopefully she would find her mate. It was a brutal tradition but up until that point they were rarely out and about.

Taylor pulled up to the pack house and walked up to the door, he knocked twice and one of the older girls answered.

"Yes Beta?" She asked, lowering her golden blond head.

"Kayla takes a few girls into town and buy enough food and supplies to last a while. We might not be going out anytime soon." Taylor ordered.

Kayla kept her forest green eyes on the ground as she nodded, ducking back into the house.

"What did he want?" Kayla was asked as she came back into the house. Kayla looked over to see Sarah.

"Go get Abby; we're going into town to get food and supplies for a month or so." Kayla said to her.

"A month or so? What's going on?" Sarah asked curiously.

"I didn't dare ask. Beta's order. Just hurry. You should be excited we get to leave." Kayla hurried her.

"Maybe we can just not come back?" Sarah whispered.

"Shh. don't say such things go, now." Kayla said, glancing at the door, hoping the Beta was already gone and not within listening distance.

Sarah nodded her dark red brown head at Kayla as her sky blue eyes lit up at the thought of getting to leave the pack house. They hadn't been out in months. Sarah rushed up the stairs to find Abby.

"Abby!" Sarah yelled as she almost tripped going up the stairs.

Jace carried Nora out into the hallway of the hospital walking towards the exit when he saw him. He had forgotten about him. Cole growled softly steering Nora.

"What's wrong?" She asked sleepy.

"Nora? Holy crap are you all right?" Logan said, seeing her, and coming to them.

Jace stiffened up and pulled Nora closer to his chest, protecting Nora away from Logan.

"Logan?" Nora asked, lifting her head away from Jace's chest.

Seeing him she cracked a small smile realizing why Jace was acting jealous. She reached up and rubbed Jace's cheek with her good hand. Logan looked confused.

"I'm okay." Nora said with a smile, putting her head back against Jace's chest and nodding back to sleep.

She let out a small, happy sigh. The noise settled Cole slightly as he looked from her to Logan. He grumbled slightly, realizing the way Lohan was standing; he wasn't going anywhere anytime soon.

"She's fine. Her arm is broken but everything has been taken care of." Jace said to Logan who looked at him skeptical.

"Wolf?" Logan asked him, his voice exposing the anger he felt for seeing Nora hurt.

Jace didn't answer but it was obvious by the way his face tensed that what Logan said was true. He wanted to tell him how this was his fault and if she was with him this wouldn't have happened. He clutched his hand in fist, as he stared Jace down.

"I need to get her home." Jace said shortly through gritted teeth.

"She needs to go somewhere safe." Logan said, matching his tone.

"She doesn't need anything from you." Jace said, his eyes glowing.

"You don't know what she needs." Logan said, bowing up to him.

Nora groaned; she just wanted to lay in her bed. She was sick of hearing them bicker.

"Jace and Logan shut up." She mumbled into Jace's chest.

Jace smirked hearing her and Logan raised an eyebrow hearing her tell Jace to shut up. Logan felt bad seeing her in pain and moved aside.

"I'm coming with you." Logan said as he stepped aside.

"The hell you are. You're lucky you're even in my territory." Jace growled.

"Jace." Nora said, her voice soft but pleading.

"Fuck fine." Jace growled, walking past Logan.

Logan followed quickly after him, surprised at how easily he gave in to Nora. He was taught his whole life that wolves were evil. No emotional bond to anything except hurting others. They were pure violence but watching Jace cradle Nora closely to his chest and walk across the parking lot to his car. Made him second guess. He got the car as Jace loaded Nora carefully into the passenger side.

"Get in the back." He muttered going over to the drive side and getting in.

He didn't even look to see if Logan had gotten in the car as he pulled out of the parking lot. He drove towards the pack house glancing in the rearview mirror. Jace didn't trust Logan, maybe he should have blind folded him, he didnt think about how he was giving a hunter a free tour of his home. He clenched his jaw at the thought. His main job was protecting his pack and lately he felt like he was failing.

Chapter Sixty Four
Unlucky

Adam sighed as he walked from his car towards Tim's. Jace had him running around all afternoon. He had what felt like a never ending to do list. He had to train the pack members, then deliver bad news and Rose's body to her family, and lastly he was fetching some book from Tim's. He sighed he hadn't even showered yet. He started towards Tim's when he caught something's scent. He turned on his heels, his wolf stirring inside of him. He began walking fast towards it. His wolf wanted him to run. Before Adam knew it he went from jogging to running down an alleyway and cutting across a street. He stopped short on the sidewalk of a busy street. Across the way was a small local grocery store. He looked across the way confused as the car sped by. His wolf urged him to go. He didn't understand what he was after. Adam stood watching the cars speed by looking at the grocery store.

A few seconds later a woman walked out with golden blond hair. Adam's wolf began howling inside of him. The woman looked across the way her green eyes met his. His heart dropped into his stomach.

"Mate." He whispered out loud.

Without even thinking he stepped out into the road and began crossing it. A yellow car skidded to a stop, stopping just before hitting Adam. The woman let out a small yell as she watched the car almost hit him. Adam ignored and rushed the rest of the way to her. The woman stepped back away from him, casting her eyes down to the ground.

"Don't worry, I won't hurt you." Adam said, confused by the way she was acting so timid.

She didn't say anything but kept her gaze down. Adam's wolf inside was going crazy wanting to find her wolf, wanting her to talk and accept them back. Adam stepped closer to her.

"What's your name?" Adam asked, wanting to know why she wasn't as excited as he was right now.

"Who are you?" Kayla asked very politely, keeping her eyes on the ground.

"I'm Adam. You're my mate." Adam said, stopping himself from reaching out and touching her.

"Yes, Sir." Kayla answered, acknowledging that she felt the mate pull too.

"It's ok, you can look at me." Adam said, not liking the way she avoided him at all.

Kayla was tugging on her ring finger, trying to get herself under control. Between being overwhelmed with feelings, knowing that she shouldnt act on them and being scared of her new fond mate.

"Why are you scared?" Adam asked.

"I- uh." Kayla stopped talking.

Adams wolf was becoming angry, who had hurt her? Why was she so timid? Adam's wolf pushed forward, his eyes glowing a light blue as he did. Kayla looked up and her eyes flashed red.

"Kip." Adam said his name like his mouth tasted gross as it passed through his teeth, Kayla stepped back with the tone of Adam's voice.

She even whimpered. Adam's hand went to the back of his neck, rubbing it as he was trying to come up with a plan. He wasn't letting her go back there.

"What's your name?" Adam asked, softening his tone.

"Kayla, sir." Kayla answered, her eyes still cast downwards.

"You don't need to call me sir. My name is Adam. You are my mate, and I will never hurt you." Adam said, vowing it.

Kayla looked up briefly hearing what he said and Adam saw a flash of hope. He didn't know what situation his mate was in but it ended today.

"You're coming with me to my pack." Adam said, holding his hand out.

"I…I can't," Kaya said, shaking her head.

"Why?" Adam said frustrated.

"He has my sister." Kayla whispered.

Two other girls came out of the store and stopped short, seeing Adam with Kayla. Sarah rushed over to Kayla, stepping almost in between them. She hesitated but looked up at Adam, her eyes glowing red as she did.

"Kayla, are you ok?" Sarah whispered.

"He's my mate." Kayla leaned forward and whispered to her.

"What?" Sarah said, shocked.

Abby stood off to the side, her eyes still on the ground as well but she heard the comment and let out a small noise. Adam couldn't tell if she was excited for Kayla or scared.

"We can't have mates outside the pack." Abby whispered.

"Is your pack a cult? This is crazy. Why are you all acting like this?" Adam said frustrated.

The girls didn't answer. Abby walked over and tugged on Kayla's arm.

"If we take much longer, we're going to get in trouble." Abby said, fear in her voice.

"This could be your way out." Sarah whispered to Kayla.

"I can't leave you and Abby. Also Millie is still back there. I can't leave her." Kayla whispered back.

Sarah gritted her jaw and then looked at Adam.

"Look, our pack is horrible to women. We are to be seen and not heard. If we do anything wrong, they hurt us and sometimes they hurt us even if we don't do anything wrong. We need to get back, but if there's a way you can save Kayla-" Sarah started to say.

"Sarah, I already- " Kayla interrupted

"Then you need to do it. She has a little sister. If I can find a way to get them both out, will you them?" Sarah said, raising her hand to Kayla.

"Of course." Adam was amazed at this girl's selflessness and strength.

"You gotta take Abby too," Sarah said firmly.

"Ok." Adam said, not sure how Jace would react to him recruiting all these new pack members, but once he told him what was happening, he knew Jace would.

"What's your phone number?" Sarah asked.

Adam reached into his back pocket and pulled out a pen. He looked around, looking for paper. Not finding any, he began to look at the store.

"No, they'll search us, um…" Sarah said, trying to think of something.

"Sarah, it's ok." Kayla whispered.

"No hush. Here." Sarah said as she rolled up her shirt, exposing her belly slightly.

Adam looked confused and motioned for him to write on it. He shook his head. It was strange.

"They'll patt search us, it will be fine. Hurry." Sarah said, urging him.

Adam sighed and bent down to write his number on her belly. That's when he saw the scars. They were long, stretching across her abdomen and looking like they wrapped around her back.

"What happened to you?" He said, angry.

"Sarah plays the hero a lot." Abby said, with sadness in her voice.

"It's fine, write your number." Sarah said, stomping her foot slightly.

Adam wrote his number quickly in pen on the girl's stomach. He glanced at Kayla; he wanted just to take her now. He knew what family meant. He couldn't let her abandon hers, especially if this is what happens.

"Do you have any marks on you like that?" Adam asked, his jaw clenched as he waited for the answer.

"Not as bad, thanks to Sarah." Kayla said with a small smile.

"We have to go." Abby said, fear in her voice.

"I can't let you all go back there," Adam said firmly.

"We have to. He will kill my sister." Kayla said, turning away from him. Adam reached out and caught her hand.

"We will find another way. Come with me." Adam said fiercely.

Sarah looked at Kayla, trying to figure something out. Abby whimpered slightly. Sarah couldn't think of anything. They would know if they didn't come back with Kayla, and the first thing they would do is tell Alpha. The first thing he would do was torture Mille; Sarah could do nothing to stop that. Sarah let out a frustrated sigh.

"If you don't let me go, I will reject you." Kayla said, her voice cold and steady.

Adam dropped her hand, hearing the words come out of her mouth. The way she was so calm and focused, he didn't doubt she would. His wolf inside him whimpered.

"I don't want to, but I will. I need to go back. I need to make sure my sister is safe. We will find a way to get all of us out. Until then, I need you to trust us and wait." Kayla said, her voice not pleading but telling him how it was going to be.

"Fine. I will give you two days; if I don't hear from you, I will come for you myself." Adam said his voice was almost like a threat.

"Two days, got it." Sarah said, grabbing Kayla's hand, and they all piled into the car.

Kayla's forest green eyes burned into his mind as he watched the car leave. He gritted his jaw, not knowing if he made the right choice.

We shouldn't have let her go. Landon, his wolf, growled frustrated.

Did you want to be rejected? Adam said, his own voice matching his wolf's anger.

We could have called her bluff. Landon said, still grumbling.

She wasn't bluffing. Adam said, turning on his heels and making his way back to Tim's.

He would get the book and get home as soon as he could. He pulled out his cell phone, turning the volume all the way up. His stomach is in knots. He needed to talk to Jace as soon as possible.

Chapter Sixty Five
Glowing

Nora was asleep. Jace had laid her gently on the bed, making sure she was as comfortable as could be. Logan had followed him in and was standing awkwardly in the middle of the room. Jace sighed heavily.

"If you insist on being here, sit down." Jace growled.

Logan didn't say anything but made a noise, scoffing at Jace before sitting down on the loveseat across from the bed. He plopped his elbows on his knees, resting his chin on his hands, just staring at Nora and Jace.

"Well, this is going to be wonderful." Jace said sarcastically as he pulled his phone out of his pocket.

"Lori, could you bring up some water and those chips Nora likes." Jace said into the phone, turning away from Logan.

Logan let out a breath and took his phone out as well. He had several text messages from Lilly and Drake asking how it was going. If Nora was ok? Did they need to storm the gates? He wrote a quick reply to both of them, letting him know he had it handled and was waiting to see how Nora was.

Adam rushed to the pack house, squeezing the book he fetched for Jace too tightly in his hand. He passed Lori on the stairwell, who was carrying drinks upstairs. He mumbled an excuse to her, but it did not stop him from moving faster. Getting to Jace's door, he knocked once, opened it, and went inside. His mind screamed at him that he needed to see Jace now. Walking in, he was hit with the smell of a hunter and immediately threw his guard up. Landon was already just below the surface, and smelling the hunter, he pushed forward even more, causing his eyes to glow bright icy blue.

"Adam?" Jace said, confused he didn't think he would be back this soon.

"Hunter?' Adam growled; he completely forgot about Jace's mindlink early, letting them know a hunter was on the ground.

"He's with me. It's ok," Jace said to him with an eye roll.

"I need to talk to you." Adam said in a hurry.

"What's wrong?" Jace said, sensing that he was on edge; Adam was always calm and collected.

Adam glanced at Logan, who was sitting up right now, studying him with his eyes. He was waiting for this wolf to lose it and turn.

"Adam, it's ok." Jace said, confused.

"I've found my mate," Adam blurted out.

"That's great. Congratulations!" Jace said, stepping forward and clapping him on the shoulder.

"She's in Kip's pack." Adam said, his mouth sour as he spoke it.

"Ok...If she's not with you, I'm assuming there's something wrong. If you're worried about me accepting her. Adam, all you have to do is vouch for her, and she's in." Jace said like it was nothing, he trusted Adam.

"She's not with me because she went back-

"Did she choose her pack over you?" Jace asked Adam, a little angry for him.

"No. The women there are treated like animals. I met three of them, and they were terrified to even talk to me or look at me. They were gathering supplies. The one girl brave enough to speak to me was covered in scars." Adam said, his voice trembling with anger as he spoke.

"So why did she go back?" Jace asked, confused.

"She has a little sister." Adam states, shifting his stance.

Jace looked at him, wanting him to explain more, wanting him to tell him what he needed. Adam paused, biting the inside of his cheek.

"Adam, just ask or tell me already." Jace said, commanding him.

"I want to go get her and them. There would be four girls in total. My mate, her sister, and her two friends. It's horrible, and my mate won't come without them," Adam blurted out.

Jace took a deep breath and let it out as he ran his hand through his hair. He needed to weigh the options. He was about to head into war with Kip's pack. If he attacked beforehand just to save the four girls, he could risk the advantage in battle. He needed everything to go smoothly. He couldn't risk anything. He knew Kip already knew that he had a mate, and

Nora now became a target. He couldn't risk anything else happening before they attacked.

"Alpha, I can't let her stay there," Adam said softly.

"Adam I-" Jace started to say.

"Jace, we have to help him," Nora spoke up, sleepy, as she shifted herself in the bed.

"Nora." Jace said, going to her.

Logan got up to walk to the opposite side of the bed, then Jace. Jace looked at him, and his eyes glowed as Logan went to see Nora.

"Hey, Logan! I thought I made you up." Nora said with a smile, and then her attention went back to Jace.

He sat down next to her and cupped her cheek gently. She leaned into it, enjoying his touch.

"Nora, are you ok?" Jace asked her, concerned in his voice.

"I'm okay, sore and well broken, but I'm good. You need to help Adam. If there's really a bunch of girls being abused and treated like animals, we can't let that happen." Nora said, her eyes flickering to Adam.

"Nora, I have to do what's best for the pack right now," Jace told her; he felt Adam's emotions rise.

"Adam, I'm not saying we won't help them, but I need to plan it all out. We're about to go to war. I can't have anything to tip Kip off. I need to have the element of surprise and attack first. If we go guns blazing and into his territory, before we are ready, we risk losing people. Let me think about this." Jace said firmly.

Lori walked in carrying a tray holding water and the chips Jace asked for. He motioned for her to set them down by the nightstand next to Nora. Nora frowned deeply, seeing the hurt in Adam's eyes.

"When are you planning on attacking?" Logan asked.

He had been listening and slowly starting to see that Jace might be the better wolf.

"What's it to you hunter?" Jace growled.

"You're going after the guy creating those monster things, right? He's kidnapping people and trying to turn them into werewolves?" Logan asked carefully.

"How do you know about that?" Jace asked as he narrowed his eyes at Logan.

"Wolves aren't the only ones with intel," Logan said simply.

"It's a wolf's business." Jace growled.

"It's not. A wolf is running around hurting people. The people we protect are innocents. Therefore, it is now a hunter business. Before you, wolves would just look away at the havoc that was caused, and we did all the cleaning up and putting an end to the chaos. I don't know what made you step up, but it is not just your business." Logan said, beginning to bow up at Jace.

Adam growled from the other side of the room, Landon so close to becoming unleashed due to all the stress. He wanted out; he wanted to let loose. Jace's eyes glowed as well as he was taking what Logan said as a threat. Logan started Jace down his eyes, daring him to do something.

"Boys!" Nora yelled, and all of their eyes flickered to her.

She was hurt, tired, and sick of the petty nonsense. She felt her body beginning to tingle as a response to her annoyance. She talked the electricity down as she watched them all stare at her. Lori dropped the tray she had been carrying and walked out. She looked at them, confused; she hadn't even yelled that loud at them.

"I don't know what the hell your problems are. Actually, I know what your problem is, who's the bigger man? Well, guess what? Both of you have the same problem, and it's a madman running around making whatever the hell Matt is calling them, Lobos or whatnot. Why not put your pissing contest away and join forces." Nora yelled at them.

Logan was staring at her, very confused, and stepped away from the bed. Adam ducked his head as if ashamed and stepped back away. Nora looked at them all confused, she didn't even threaten them. What damage could she do anyways? Her arm was broken. She thought. Her eyes flickered to Jace. He hadn't moved away from her but reached out and touched her arm. A few zaps went through him, but he didn't even flinch.

"What? Why are you all acting weird." Nora said, annoyed.

"Your eyes…Nora, they're glowing amber." He said quietly.

Nora got up slowly, and with Jace following her closely behind, she walked into the bathroom. She flipped on the light and looked into the mirror. He was right; her eyes were glowing amber. She looked haunting; it was scary but beautiful at the same time. She leaned forward, looking into the mirror harder. Now, why would this be happening? She thought, pulling her cheek down, making the inside of her eyelid show. Everything looked normal; they were just glowing. She shook her head and sighed. She looked at Jace, who was watching her carefully.

"Ok, and we all know I am weird at this point." Nora said, rolling her eyes.

Jace didn't say anything. He wasn't sure what to think about it. It normally was a wolf trait to have eyes that glowed, but it was only when your wolf pushed forward and wanted to take over.

"How do you feel?" Jace asked her.

"Annoyed, tired, and painful. Mostly annoyed," Nora growled as she walked back into the room with Logan and Adam.

Jace could feel the power coming off of her, hence the reason Adam was ducking his head. His wolf didn't like it and was reacting. Adam looked up at Jace, looking for an answer. Jace shrugged.

"Now, can we all play nice? Logan, if you offer assistance, just come out with it. Yes, we could use all the help we can get. Jace, if he offers help, you should accept." Nora said, ordering the two about.

"Adam, stop bowing your head at me; it's weird. Your eyes glow all the time randomly. I don't know what this is, but like I told Jace, we all know I'm a little weird lately, so stop it." Nora yelled at him. In an instant.

Adam's head snapped up like an Alpha had ordered him. Jace watched the reaction and couldn't understand it. He should be the only person that could order Adam like that. He felt Nora growing more annoyed as her emotions pushed out words. Cole whimpered slightly inside of him. Jace walked over to Nora and pulled her back against his chest.

"Hey, calm down. You're right; we should help each other. You're hurt. I need you to relax." Jace whispered sweetly into her ear.

He felt her instantly relax as he touched her. She relaxed even more when he spoke softly to her. She leaned back into him and let out a small breath. He looked down at her as she shut her eyes, allowing herself to let go of her anger and annoyance towards them. She opened her eyes, and they were no longer glowing. Jace felt the room relax.

"We will find a way to join forces with the hunters and help Adam." Jace announced, looking at the room.

Logan and Adam nodded quickly, not wanting to piss Nora off again.

"Good, that's amazing. I'm tired again." She whispered.

Jace nodded and motioned for Logan and Adam to get out as he scooped Nora up. He carried her to the bed.

"We will talk downstairs in my office. Adam, have Wyatt or Matt come to keep an eye on Nora." Jace said to Adam as he was ducking out the door.

"Logan, please follow Adam to my office." Jace said nicely to him as he began tucking Nora back in.

Logan nodded and followed Adam out; they closed the door gently. Jace leaned down and kissed the top of Nora's head. She sighed happily, closing her eyes.

Chapter Sixty Six
Cell phone

"You're late." Kip growled, greeting the girls.

They hung their heads low, not answering. Abby was shaking, and Kayla was nervously playing with her pinky finger as she kept her gaze on the ground. Sarah just stared at the ground, counting numbers in her head, trying to keep her cool.

"Alpha said you're late. What took so long?" Taylor said, his voice just as threatening.

"We had trouble finding some of the items you requested. The owner went looking for them in the back. It took a little bit longer, but we got everything. Beta, Alpha." Sarah said, addressing them both, her head still hung low and her gaze staring at the ground.

Kip made a noise and then began searching through the bags, seeing if they got the things he wanted. Taylor was eyeing the girls. Abby could feel his eyes on her, and she desperately just wanted to disappear. She hated attention, never mind forced attention. She began to fidget, shifting her stance.

"What's your problem?" Taylor asked, looking at her.

She could feel his eyes burning into her; it felt like her skin was on fire. She was trying to come up with a reason for her mind yelling at her not to tell him about Kayla and her mate.

"I..I- " Abby stuttered out trying to find a reason.

"Beta, she was worried we would be in trouble for getting back late, but we were also worried about coming back without the items you wanted." Kayla spoke up, sensing Abby's panic.

"Does she have a problem speaking, too?" Taylor growled.

"No…No Beta. I'm sorry." Abby said quietly.

"It's all here. Good job, girls." Kip said with a smile, standing up.

Kip's announcement took the heat off the girls. Taylor settled down and looked over to Kip. He picked through a few things, taking what he wanted. As Alpha, he got the first pick of everything. He motioned for Taylor to come get his stuff. He shook his head; Kip shrugged and went about his business.

"Take the rest and divide between the pack houses, men first." Taylor growled at them.

They all nodded, and a rush of relief swept through all of them as they were allowed to leave. They loaded the groceries back up into the car and left to go to the men's pack house.

"That was so close." Kayla said quietly, getting into the driver's seat.

Sarah fastened her seatbelt in the passenger seat. She let out a loud sigh and glanced in the back seat as Abby was on the edge of hyperventilating.

"Now all we gotta do is steal a cell phone." Sarah smirked.

"What the hell!" Abby shirked.

"Sarah, you're going to get hurt if you get caught." Kayla started to lecture her.

"Exactly, get caught, which won't happen. So no worries." Sarah smiled.

"How exactly are we going to get a phone?" Abby pouted.

"Ladies, I got this." Sarah smiled brighter.

They pulled up to the men's pack house. Kayla let out a long sigh. She hated coming here. The men would harass them, and they had to just stare at the ground. If they offended anyone and word got back to Taylor or Kip, they would be punished.

"We're going to find a phone?" Abby whispered from the back seat.

Sarah made a motion to the men's pack house, and Abby's face went white.

"Don't worry, you can wait in the car. It actually works as part of the plan." Sarah said as Kayla raised an eyebrow at her.

"What is the plan?" Kayla sighed.

"So Henry kind of has a thing for me. He always has his phone on him. So I'm going to flirt with him and get his phone. But so things don't get too weird, I need you guys to come rush in with something and get me out of there." Sarah said, looking at them.

"Sarah, it sounds a little risky." Abby said, shaking her head.

"The wind blowing wrong is risky for you." Sarah said, rolling her eyes.

"Abby's right, Sarah. It's a little risky," Kayla agreed.

"Well, it's all we got, and we need a phone," Sarah said, not going to talk about it anymore.

Sarah opened the door and got out of the car. As the car shut behind her, the door of the men's pack house opened. Kayla got out and popped the truck, going to retrieve groceries for them. Henry, Kyle, and George spotted them and opened the door. Kayla and Sarah walked to the walkway with the groceries in hand, waiting for them to come get them. Henry walked out to Sarah, his hand going to take the groceries. She didn't release them.

"Sarah, let me have the groceries." Henry said firmly but confused.

"I was thinking I could help you bring them in." Sarah said, her voice low with a hint of flirting in, her eyes on the ground.

"All right." He smiled and then held his hand out to Kayla, asking for her groceries.

Kayla let Henry take them as Kyle stood staring her up and down. Kayla's wolf inside was growling. Now that she found her mate, she hated being ogled even more.

"Where's Abby?" George asked Kayla as she gave the rest of the groceries to Henry.

"She's in the car; she's not feeling well." Kayla said quietly.

She watched George go over to the car and lean against it, trying to talk to Abby. Kayla shifted slightly, being uncomfortable with Kyle just staring at her.

"You know you could show me those pretty green eyes of yours." Kyle said slyly to her.

"Alpha said females are to look at the ground only." Kayla said; her voice was monotone with no feeling in it.

"He wouldn't have to know." Kyle whispered, stepping near her.

"Sarah, what's going on? Kyle is starting to bother me." Kayla mind linked Sarah.

"It's going; hang on." Sarah replied.

Henry followed Sarah in as she set the bags on the counter in the kitchen. She kept her eyes on the ground as Alpha had ordered, but she could sense Henry giving her the once-over. She could see his phone bludging in his back pocket. She was still trying to come up with a plan to get it.

"Is there anything else you need help with?" Sarah asked coyly.

"There might be." Henry said to her, stepping towards her.

Sarah stepped back, acting shy, but she was calculating her moves. Henry's hand brushed Sarah's hip unsteadily like he was uncertain about it. Sarah fluttered her blue eyes up at him and ran her hand around his hip. He looked down at her quickly, his eyes slightly shocked.

"The Alpha might be upset with your bold moves." Henry said, trying to make his statement sound flirty and not shocked.

"He might be, but are you?" Sarah smiled seductively as she slid her hand over his butt, resting it there.

"I-I."

Sarah squeezed his butt, making him push into her; he was still shocked at her actions that he didn't notice that she pulled the cell phone out of his back pocket. Henry growled slightly, his wolf coming forward and becoming possessive.

"Want." Henry's wolf said through him.

Henry slammed her hard into the counter, pushing himself against her. His face buried into her neck as he nips at it.

"Now, emergency now! Come save me!" Sarah mind linked Kayla and Abby.

Abby heard the mindlink, and it sent her into overdrive. George was leaning in the window trying to talk her up when Abby felt it coming up. She leaned forward and vomited everywhere. The nerves of everything get the best of her.

"Shit!" George yelled.

"Kayla, go get your friend and get out of her. Abby's puking and no one wants to catch whatever she has." George yelled, backing away from the car like it was a ticking time bomb.

Kayla nodded and rushed into the men's pack houses, finding her way to the kitchen. She walked in, her stomach turning, not knowing what she was walking into. Henry had pinned Sarah against the counter, his hand starting to travel up the back of her shirt while the other hand was playing with her pants button. A rush of relief flashed over Sarah's panicked face as she saw Kayla.

"Abby's throwing up. We need to get her home." Kayla announced.

Henry pulled back, his eyes glowing red as his wolf was just below the surface.

"What ?" He growled.

"George told me to come get Sarah. Abby is vomiting all over the car, and we don't know if she is contagious," Kayla said, her voice evenly toned.

Henry let out a frustrating sigh as he stepped away from Sarah. He looked her over once more before letting her go completely.

"If my mate never shows up, I may mark you." Henry said to Sarah's back.

A chill went through her knees at the thought of being marked by Henry. She would rather rot in a cell than be marked by him. Forever bonded to him. The girls rushed out of the pack house and got into the car as quickly as they could. Kayla turned the key and pulled out of their driveway.

"We are never doing that again." Kayla announced.

"Dude, quick thinking with the vomiting Abs." Sarah chuckled.

"It wasn't a show; you all made me so sick to my stomach. All I needed was the panicked mindlink, and my stomach couldn't take any more stress." Abby said hopelessly.

"Well, it was perfect." Sarah laughed.

"Did you even get it? We are not going back anytime soon." Kayla grumbled.

"Ta-Da!!" Sarah laughed, pulling her cell phone out and showing them.

"What was that?" Adam asked Jace as he came into the office.

Jace walked over to his desk, letting a deep breath out. He ran his hands over his face as he looked down. A rough map of Kip's territory was rolled out onto his desk. He looked down at still not answering Adam. Logan walked over to the desk, glancing down at the map.

"So, are we doing this or not?" Logan asked quietly.

Jace gritted his teeth. What Nora said was right; he could use all the help he could get. The Black Sand's pack was weak, and Zeke could only let so many men come help. Jace sighed heavily again.

"I need to see how your team fights. Will they come here and train side by side without problems?" Jace said quietly.

"Alpha- " Adam started to protest, but Jace's eyes flickered to him, and the look was all Adam needed to be quiet.

"They will." Logan said, his voice was firm and sure.

"Fine. Have your team here early tomorrow," Jace said firmly.

"Sounds good." Logan said with a nod.

"Has Zeke returned to his pack?" Jace asked Adam.

"Yes, he went this morning." Adam answered, still wanting to talk about what just happened with Nora.

"I will stay here the night." Logan announced.

Jace eyed him slightly but nodded. Adam could tell he didn't like it, but he wasn't going to argue. It made sense. Adam frowned.

"Adam get Logan a room and whatnot." Jace said, his focus still on the map.

"Yes, Alpha." Adam said as he motioned for Logan to start going to the doors.

"Here, Alpha." Adam said, holding out the book he collected for him from Tim's.

"Thank you, Adam." Jace said, taking the book from him.

"Let's go hunter." Adam muttered.

Chapter Sixty Seven
Stolen

*"Alpha, I think Sarah stole my cell phone."
Henry had been debating whether to link Kip for a
while now; it had been almost two hours since the
girls left.*

He at first thought he misplaced it, but then
when he couldn't find it, he started thinking about
Sarah. She had never acted attracted to him. He tried
wondering if she was coming into heat, but he would
have sensed her hormones and wouldn't have been
able to control himself.

*"What." The way Kip shot back with anger
made Henry cower even though they were not
anywhere near each other.*

*"She was acting strange early and came on to
me. Now my cell phone is gone." Henry responded
timidly.*

*"Well, have your boys meet Taylor and me over
at the woman's pack house; things are about to get
ugly if this is true." Kip sneered.*

*"Yes, Alpha." Henry responded, now wishing
he would not have said anything.*

"George and Kyle let go." Henry yelled.

"Where are we going?" George yelled down
the stairs.

"To the girls." Henry yelled back.

"Ooo like -

"No, Sarah stole my phone; we're meeting
Alpha there." Henry said regret in his voice.

"Shit, I don't want to go see that." George said back.

"If he's calling for us, it's because Alpha said so, so get your shoes on." Kyle said, walking down the stairs.

"Fuck." George muttered as he went back up to his room.

The car ride to the girls was too short. Henry drove and was torn between taking his time and not wanting to go see what was going to happen and not wanting to be there after or long after Alpha got there. He didn't want any of the rage or anger that he kept just below the surface. They arrived first, and Henry felt a little relieved. They got out of the car and stood outside of it, leaning against it. Henry left the headlights of his car on and pointed at the house so the girls would have a heads-up.

"Men are here!" A panic shout came from downstairs.

"Men are here!" It echoed through the house as all the young girls shuttered.

They never knew why they came when they showed up but whenever they did, someone was in trouble or worse. The girls piled out into the living room, each one shrinking away. Each one trying to be the one that was overlooked.

"Shit, Sarah, the phone. You know they're here because of the phone." Abby mind linked her from across the room.

Kayla's eyes fell on Sarah's as she pushed Millie behind her. As they locked eyes, Sarah could see the fear in Kayla's eyes. She knew it was for her and Millie. Sarah took a deep breath in. This wasn't her first rodeo at being in trouble. She was used to it by now. It will be fine.

"Don't say anything. I will take care of everything." Sarah said, looking at them both.

Kayla shook her head at her, begging her not to take the blame or fall, to be quiet. Sarah winked at her. Within the next second, the boys came in. Henry locked eyes with Sarah, and she saw a flash of sadness. The girls in the room all lowered their heads, shivering, staring at the ground.

"Sarah, Abby, Kayla, and Millie, outside now," Henry said sharply.

Sarah looked over at Kayla, who looked physically hurt when they called Millie's name. Sarah knew that they would use Millie to get to them. She couldn't let her get hurt.

"Henry, sir, whatever it is. I can assure you Kayla, Millie, and Abby had nothing to do with it." She spoke up, and the girls around her let out a small breath as she spoke without being addressed or permitted.

Kyle went over and grabbed Sarah by the back of the neck, slapping her hard on the back of her head as he did.

"Speak when addressed. Eyes down. No one asked to hear you. Alpha wants Sarah, Millie, Kayla, and Abby outside." Kyle growled, pressing his thumb on her collarbone and making her wince.

Abby was the first one to move towards the door, eyes plastered on the floor as she walked. Kayla squeezed Mille's hand tightly as she walked out the door after Abby. Kyle let go of Sarah and shoved her forward. Sarah began walking out the door, trying to come up with a way to keep her friends safe.

"Ladies." Kip said as they came out, his voice was charming and pleasant.

It was never good when he was happy. It always meant something was going to entertain him, and that was never good for anyone. He paused dramatically for effect before continuing.

"Henry here says after you left the male's pack house, his phone went missing. Have any of you seen it?" Kip asked them, almost sarcastically, and the girls didn't know how to respond.

"Answer me!" He shouted, spit flying out of his mouth as he yelled.

"No, Alpha." Abby responded first.

"No, Alpha." Millie said quietly.

"No, Alpha." Kayla repeated the answer.

This was going to get bad if someone didn't step up and say they had it. Sarah knew what she had to do, and it wasn't like she was lying.

"Yes, Alpha." Sarah responded.

"No." Kayla sent it through mind link to her.

"Ahhh, the little rebel again. Sarah, what are we going to do with you? Why would you want a cell phone?" Kip said as Taylor, and he both locked eyes on her like she was prey.

"I was jealous." Sarah said, making up some reason she didn't have a good one.

"Jealous? Jealous of what? You know what they used to do to thieves back in the old days?" Kip asked, his face curling into a smile.

"Jealous of the boys having everything. And no, Alpha, I do not know." Sarah said, not sure which question she was supposed to answer.

"They would cut off the hand that stole. So they couldn't steal again." Kip snickered.

"Do you know what they did to liars?" Kip asked, moving towards her.

Sarah could feel his aura as he was coming to her. She lowered her head more as she felt the pressure to submit. Her wolf inside her whimpering at her Alpha being upset with her. She then felt his hand entwine into her hair and yank her head up.

"They cut out their tongues." Kip growled as his other hand pressed on either side of her jaw, wanting her mouth to fall open.

Abby whimpered, and Kayla let out a small breath, not wanting to cause Sarah or any of them more trouble. Kip's eyes flickered over to them.

"So, what is it? Why did she want a cell phone? If I have to commend you, I will rip out her tongue and feed it to each of you." He growled.

Sarah shut her eyes, focusing on a memory from her childhood. It was one of her mother and her planting wildflowers. She would run in this large open field afterwards with her mother playful chasing behind her. She could still feel the breeze on her skin and feel the warmth of the sun dancing on her skin. She heard a snap; her eyes jolted open as pain shot up her arm. She watched her pinky finger dangle backwards. Kip looked over at the girls as a sharp, small yell came out of Sarah's mouth.

"I don't think I will make you. I think the fun way will be to break Sarah's bones until you tell me. The longer you take, I might have to start cutting things off." Kip nodded to Taylor, who pulled a boning knife out of his pant leg.

"It's to contact -" Kayla blurted out.

"My mate." Sarah blurted out.

"Your mate?" Kip growled.

"Sarah, please." Kayla begged her through mind link.

"Kayla, don't say it's your mate; you might get hurt. Mille needs you." Sarah mind linked her.

She felt her ring finger arch back and snap.

"What did you just mind link to?" Kip growled.

"I'm sorry, Alpha; I was telling them where the phone was so one of them could return it to Henry," Sarah said through a painful yell.

"Who is your mate? Abby, go get the phone." Kip asked, growling.

"His name is Adam, and he is with the Cross River pack. I was supposed to call him when I could sneak out and get away." Sarah stammered out.

Within a few minutes, Abby came out with the phone in her hand. She walked over to Kip, handed him the phone, and quickly went back to where she had been standing before. Kip took the silver cell phone in his hand and shoved it into Sarah's good hand.

"Call him." Kip grinned. He now had a way to get someone to do something for him. He would have Jace's mate for sure now. He smiled big, thinking of it.

Adam showed Logan the way upstairs. He walked over to the middle room. He was going to put this hunter in between Dante and Jace; that way, if he was up to any funny business, they would literally be right next store. Adam opened the door and let it swing open, revealing the room. Logan looked at him before walking in.

"Sweet dreams." Adam grumbled, throwing the key at him.

"Thanks." Logan said as he caught the key.

Adam began to walk away, and his cell phone started to ring. An unknown number came up on the screen, his stomach in knots as he slid the phone to answer.

"Hello?" He said quietly.

Chapter Sixty Eight
Border

A scream echoed through the phone. Adam pulled the phone away from his ear as he looked down at it briefly. His stomach turned in on himself; he knew who was calling before they even said anything.

"Don't fucking touch her!" Adam yelled, growling.

Another scream rippled through it. Adam's wolf pushed forward and began to growl; he wanted to kill him.

"You shouldn't tell people what to do with their things." Kip's voice came through the phone.

"Leave her alone!" Adam yelled, anger in his voice.

"I will. I'll even let her leave with you, but favors don't happen for nothing." Kip's sick smile could be heard in his voice as he spoke.

"What do you want?" Adam said, his voice shaking from rage.

"Meet me on the border of our packs. Bring Jace's mate." Kip chuckled.

"No. I can't bring Nora." Adam growled. Another loud, painful yell came through the phone.

Adam was starting to sweat, hearing her in pain.

"She's only got so many fingers before I have started breaking bigger bones. If we can't make a trade, I'll just give her to my men after she's all broken. Let them have their way with her, and then we will put her out of her misery. I will send her to you in pieces." Kip threatened as a whimper came over the phone again.

"Stop.!" Adam growled.

"You have twenty minutes to be at the border with Jace's mate, or that's exactly what's going to happen." Kip said, and the phone went dead.

Landon was clawing at the inside of him; he was sweating, and he felt his chest burning from the panic. He was going to kill him. He was going to rip him limb from limb. He needed his mate safe first. Adam didn't know what to do; he knew Jace would not allow him to take Nora to him. He was trying to think of someone he could bring, he didn't think Kip knew what Nora looked like. He found himself staring at Jace's bedroom door. He glanced down at his phone, the time ticking away was eating at him. He knocked softly. Matt opened the door, giving him a confused look.

"Jace sent you to switch out?" Matt asked.

"Yeah." Before he could even stop the lie, it fell out of Adam's mouth.

"Cool beans, buddy, she's been asleep this whole time. I was starting to get bored. Let me know if you need to switch later. I think Jace is off preparing for what's coming." Matt said, slapping him on the shoulder as she walked out the door.

Shit, what did we just do? Adam asked himself. We need to find a way to keep our future Luna safe and our mate. Landon responded.

Even his wolf was loyal to Nora. Adam walked into the room, trying to be quiet, but his emotions were causing him to shake slightly. His mind kept screaming for twenty minutes, the sounds of her screams echoing around inside his brain.

"Adam?" Nora said, sleepy.

"It's me. Matt and I traded out," Adam said quietly; he heard his voice tremble.

Nora's eyes shot to him. Something was wrong; she could see the panic in his eyes, his muscles twitching, and she could sense his wolf just begging to be let out.

"You have five seconds to tell me what is going on? Is Jace OK?" Nora said, standing up and facing him.

Her heart rate increased, fearing that someone she cared about was hurt.

"I..I." He didn't know what to do.

Twenty minutes, just tell her we have fucking less than twenty minutes! Landon growled inside of him.

"I found my mate. Kip has her, and he's torturing her. He says if I don't bring Jace's mate to the border in twenty minutes to trade, he will send her to me in pieces." Adam blurted out.

Nora's stomach twisted hearing that Adam's mate was being tortured. She looked at him, her eyes sad for him.

"I don't know what to do. I thought maybe Jace was here. I don't have much time. "Adam said, pacing now and grabbing his hair as he talked.

"Let's go." Nora said, getting up and heading to the door.

"Nora, I can't. I can't hurt Jace or betray him. He's my Alpha. I can't hurt you or let someone else." Adam said, tugging on his hair more; he was breaking.

"You're not doing anything. Let's go now." Nora said, opening the door, anger coursing through her.

She was done with this Kip guy, and she was going to make sure no one else got hurt. Adam followed her out.

"Nora, we can't." Adam said, reaching for her and grabbing her arm.

As he touched her, a shock went through him. She turned her head quickly back to him, watching him shake the voltage out of his hand.

"We can, and I will. Now, let's go. We don't have time." Nora said, her eyes flickering as she looked at him.

Adam's feet began to move without him even telling them to. The way she said let's go to him was a command, and his body automatically reacted to it. Jace had not marked her yet; she was not officially Luna, but even if she was, Luna's did not command their pack. Adam went to mindlink Jace.

"Don't! We will tell Jace when we are almost there. We don't need him to risk getting himself hurt or stopping us before we can get your mate." Nora said, heading down the stairs.

Adam hung his head and listened; he had no choice. The packed house was completely empty. He knew that Jace had everyone preparing for war. He was hoping Dante would have come home by now and he could get him to stop them. They walked outside; Nora went over to the only car in the driveway and stood by it. She motioned for Adam to hurry up. He got in the driver's seat, shaking his head. Dante! He thought.

"Dante, Kip has my mate at the border, and he wants me to trade Nora for her. I told Nora in a panic. We're heading there now. She's commanded me not to tell Jace and to go." Adam frantically mindlinked Dante.

"Fuck! I am on the other side of our territory. How is she commanding you? Where are you now?" Dante responded.

"We're heading to the upper border between Kip's and our territory. We have ten minutes left before he kills my mate. Tell Jace." Adam said, his voice sad and worried.

"I will!" Dante responded back.

Nora missed the mindlink going on. She was focusing on the overwhelming amount of energy she was feeling in the pit of her stomach. She needed to figure out somehow how to use it. Maybe she could zap them all if she got close enough to Kip and his men. Maybe they would be left unconscious, and they could get back to the territory safely. This was her only plan right now. She glanced over at Adam as they started down a dark tree-covered road. He pulled over and parked the car on a gravel patch.

"We will have to walk from here." Adam told her.

Nora nodded, her stomach turning in on itself as she became worried. She was going to get his mate, and everything was going to be fine. If she pulled this off, maybe there wouldn't even have to be a war after all. There was some hope. She exited the car and waited for Adam to show her the way. Landon begged him to let him shift so he could get to the border quickly.

"Maybe I should shift and get there ahead of you. Throw Kip off a little bit." Adam said quietly, hoping Nora would agree.

"No, we do this together." Nora said, heading down the dark dirt path.

"Alpha, we have trouble on the border. Kip is there with Adam's mate. He wants to trade Adam's mate for Nora." Dante mindlinked him quickly.

"What! Where's Nora." Jace linked back anger in his voice.

"She commanded Adam to take her to the border." Dante said, anger in his own voice as well.

"Get to the border now." Jace growled.

"I'm on my way, but I am not close." Dante said. Jace could hear through his voice that he must be running, he sounded like he was pushing himself.

"How did she command him?" Jace asked, but it was more of a thought.

Cole pushed forward, and Jace let him take over. He took off running towards Kip's territory. He would destroy him if he even so much as breathed on her. Cole's feet kicked up hunks of grass and dirt as he raced across his territory. He knew now why Dante sounded the way he did. He was in wolf form and sprinting.

"All available men to the upper border, where Kip's and our territory meet. We have a situation. Your Luna is endangered; be calm and quiet about it. If she gets hurt because someone fucks up, they will regret it." Jace mind linked the entire pack, except Adam.

He didn't want anyone to know there was a mindlink going on. Their eyes give them away, and Kip would know.

"Alpha, I just left Nora with Adam. What do you mean she's endangered?" Matt's voice came through mindlink.

"Border now, Matt!" Jace growled back, and he felt Matt shift through the link.

Jace felt better knowing that Matt was the closest one and he would get there as quickly as he could. Jace knew Matt wouldn't let anyone hurt Nora. Cole's rage pushed him to run like he'd never run before. The thought of Kip taking Nora was unbearable, and he wasn't going to let that happen.

Chapter Sixty Nine
Trade

They walked into a small clearing. Nora's body was vibrating as it sensed danger. She kept telling herself not to give away what she was. Her newly found glowing eyes made her nervous; she didn't want it to happen. She didn't want Kip to know she was a secret weapon, regardless of what Jace thought. She gritted her teeth, seeing a girl on her knees cradling her very broken hand. Three other girls were off to the side, two of them with tear-stained cheeks. Her eyes landed on the man she knew instantly, Kip. His medium-length hair pulled back in a ponytail, a sickening victory smile on his face.

"So you came!" Kip announced happily.

"We didn't have much of a choice!" Nora said, glaring at him.

"You came willingly?" Kip said shocked; he was expecting Adam to have tricked her.

"Yes. Now hand over….all the girls," Nora said, looking quickly to the left.

Adam was confused; he saw the girl named Sarah on her knees. Her hand mangled, Kayla was unharmed off to the side, and Landon eased up a bit. Why was Sarah hurt? Adam thought as he studied each girl. His eyes landed on Kayla, and they glowed slightly. He was on the verge of losing it and letting Landon go.

"All the girls. Who do you think you are?" Kip chuckled.

"Well, I think I am worth more than one girl, someone's mate or not. I am Jace's mate and a much bigger prize to you. So you either hand over all four girls or Adam and I are leaving." Nora said, her head held high, power raiding off of her.

If Adam didn't know any better, he would have assumed Nora was his Luna already and a wolf. He was hoping Kip would think the same and not sense that she was different.

"You do have a point, but I will slaughter all four of these girls if you don't come," Kip smiled wickedly.

Adam growled and stepped forward. Nora's hand hit his chest as she narrowed her eyes at Kip.

"Go ahead. When Jace finds out you attempted to capture me; he will be enraged. If you attempt to kill them; Adam here will make sure he rips at least one of you limb from limb. You also will have a much bigger problem on your hand when Jace shows up. You will have nothing to bargain with…. No me." Nora said with a shrug.

"Let's go, Adam." Nora looked at him using the same tone she used to get him.

Adam's eyes panicky went to the girls. He dropped his head, not being able to fight the command, and they started walking out of the clearing.

"Trust me." Nora whispered to him.

A loud growl came from behind him as Kip realized he could only get what he wanted if he listened to Nora. He shoved Sarah forward; she landed on her hand, making her cry out in pain.

"Wait!" Kip yelled angrily.

Nora and Adam stopped at the edge of the clearing, pausing a moment but not turning to face Kip.

"I will give you all four of these sorry pieces of shit for you. You come willingly, no fighting." Kip announced.

"Done deal." Nora said, turning around and walking back to the middle of the clearing.

It was like an invisible line was between them as she stepped to the edge of Jace's border. Adam whimpered, hearing Nora say she would go with him.

"It's fine, Adam." Nora said, patting his arm.

"Girls first." Nora said to Kip.

"How is Jace mated to you?" Kip said, becoming frustrated.

"Girls first, let's get this going. I am not coming over till we have at least half. The injured one and the young one first." Nora announced.

"You are a clever girl," Kip sighed. He nodded to Taylor, who shoved Millie away from Kayla.

The little girl looked frantic as she walked slowly over to stand behind Adam and Nora. She looked helpless as she stared at her sister, still over near Taylor. Nora waited to move towards them, waiting for Sarah to be safe. Kip kicked her.

"No, not me first, send Kayla to be with her sister," Sarah said from the ground.

"Shut up and go." Kip said, kicking her in the side.

Nora felt herself vibrating more, her power wanting to let loose and protect them all. She gritted her teeth, still waiting. Sarah got off the ground and began walking slowly over towards Adam. He helped her the rest of the way.

"Ok, I sent the good faith part." Kip announced, waiting for Nora to start moving towards them.

Something was off, and she kept sensing something bigger. There was something more dangerous nearby. Her body was picking up and reacting to it. She looked around, trying to figure out what caused it. Then, two of those creatures emerged from behind Kip and Taylor. This changed things. They had these collar's around their neck. She looked at Taylor, who seemed to smile, and saw he had a remote in his hand. This is what he must be using to control them. Otherwise, they would be uncontrollable.

"Come before I let my beasts just tear everyone apart." Kip smiled.

"As I start walking, they start walking. If they don't make it to the middle at the same time I do, I don't come." Nora said, her voice threatening.

"Fine, let's move on." Kip growled.

Abby and Kayla started to walk towards Jace's territory, their eyes locked on the ground. Nora went to start walking, and Adam caught her wrist. His eyes begged her not to.

"It's fine; let go and stay." Nora said in a commanding voice.

Adam dropped his hand, giving into her. A low growl came from him as he watched her start walking. Landon was howling inside of him, watching Nora start walking away. His eyes glowed fiercely as he began to rock in place, trying not to shift. Landon wanted out. Nora got to the middle at the same time as the girls. They paused; Kayla's eyes flickered form the ground to hers, thankful but filled with sadness.

"When you get to my territory, get as far back as you can. Head to the far side of the clearing quickly." Nora whispered to her before continuing to walk.

Nora was taking several deep breaths as she got to Kip. She needed to focus her energy when the time was right on the two giant monsters. If he released them, he could cause major damage; they would surely lose the girls, and Adam would die defending them. Then, those things would travel onto Jace's territory, doing more damage and hurting more people. She couldn't have that. She needed to get all four of them close enough to each other: Kip, Taylor, and the two lobos. She shifted slightly, trying to inch closer to the Lobos. Kip raised an eyebrow at her. Adam and the girls began moving towards the edge of the clearing. Nora felt a little relieved everything was going to work out. She saw Kip nod to Taylor from the corner of her eyes.

A loud noise erupted from the direction of Taylor, followed by a second loud noise. Nora turned to see Taylor holding a gun. The world slowed down as Nora realized he had fired it twice in the direction of Adam and the girls. She watched the bullet spin towards Adam. She went to run towards them when the world somehow snapped back into place. Kayla ran in front of Adam, blocking the bullet. Adam caught her in his arms as the bullet pierced her back. Adam tried to spin her in time so the bullet didn't hit her. The second bullet hit him in his back.

"No!" Nora screamed as she moved towards them.

Kip pulled her back towards him, and a sharp jolt vibrated through his hand as he touched her. She ripped her arm away.

Jace!! She screamed his name in her head. She felt a sharp pain in the back of her head. She knew someone must have hit her over the head with something hard. She fought hard to stay conscious. She needed to get to the Lobos. She took several steps forward, reaching out to the creatures. She fell forward just in front of them. Her outward hand brushed their feet. She gave all she had and sent the bit of energy she had felt into them, and her world went dark. The electricity went up the Lobo's legs, shocking them as it traveled up them. It settled into the collars they were wearing and fried them, causing them to malfunction. They were shock collars and began continuously shocking the Lobos. They fell to their knees.

"What the hell is going on?" Kip yelled, walking over to Nora.

The Lobos began to yell out in pain with each zap; they began convulsing as the zaps became stronger as the collars continued to malfunction. Kip looked to Taylor, who was holding the remote; Taylor shook his head, saying he had no idea what was going on. Kip growled as one of the Lobos fell over dead. In a few short seconds, the other did the same thing. Kip growled as he picked Nora up and slung her over his shoulder. He glanced back at the girls and Adam.

Adam held Kayla to him, pain radiating through him as he watched the front of his own chest turn red. He ignored his pain, trying to find where the bullet had pierced Kayla. Millie sat down next to them, tears streaming down her face. The front of Kayla's chest had a large hole in it. Adam panics, shaking her lightly as he realizes that she isn't responding. Sarah let out a small cry as she kneeled down next to them. Abby began crying. Adam brushed the hair out of Kayla's face as reality set in. She wasn't breathing. The bullet pierced through her heart, killing her instantly.

Adam pulled her close to him as he let out a blood howling. Cradling Kayla to him. He felt himself going weak as well. Suddenly, it was hard to breathe, and it was getting cold. He watched Kip laugh as he walked out of the clearing. Adam fell back to the ground as he became weaker. The front of his chest became more and more red. With her good hand, Sarah applied pressure to the hole in the front of his chest.

"He's dying." Sarah whispered to Abby.

Abby kneeled down behind Adam, supporting his head.

Tears slip down her face as she watches his skin begin to fade to gray. His arms still wrapped around Kayla as he held on to her. A dark red-brown wolf sprinted into the clearing. His eyes searched the clearing, the wolf's hackles standing up as he was growling, looking around. Spotting Adam on the ground, the wolf skidded over to them. There was a puddle of blood forming underneath him quickly. In one instance, the wolf transformed back into Matt.

"Shit...Shit ..Shit Adam. Adam, what the-?" Matt said, coming to the side of his head.

"He's got Nora, they just left. Go." Adam coughed out, blood coming out the side of his mouth as he spoke.

"Adam -

"Matt …..I'm dead …..go. Jace ….I'm …sorry." Adam said his breathing became short and fast as he struggled.

Matt gritted his teeth; he could tell he was about to pass. He squeezed his hand hard before shifting back into his wolf. He dashed towards the other side of the clearing, heading after Kip. A large black wolf came running into the clearing; his growl was vicious, making everyone cower. Adam couldn't feel the pain anymore. He closed his eyes as he felt the world starting to slip away. The large wolf nudged him frantically. Adam knew it was Cole. He shook his head lightly. He was too weak to talk now.

" Kip has Nora go. Matt is chasing after him, not too far behind and not too far ahead of you. Go, he's going to need help. Jace, I am so sorry." Adam mind linked him.

Cole whimpered, watching his friend take his last breath; the anger he had towards him for letting Nora do this slipped away. He let out a howl before rushing across the clearing, chasing after Matt, hoping they would reach Kip before they could leave.

Chapter Seventy
Gone

Seconds later, a swarm of wolves appeared in the clearing. The girls were huddled around Adam's and Kayla's bodies. A large gray wolf came rushing over. The wolf nudged Adam fiercely with his nose. Adam's body moved, but nothing happened. The large gray wolf let out a howl, and the wolves around them hung their heads. A wolf a little smaller than the gray wolf came hurrying forward; he was white with golden streaks in its fur. Getting to Adam, the wolf shifted back to his human form. Abby covered Mille's eyes at the naked man; Sarah watched the man reach down and check Adam's pulse. She saw his jaw clenched, realizing he didn't have a pulse. He then went to Kayla to do the same. His eyes flashed pain, and he locked eyes with Sarah.

"What happened?" He said, his voice trying to control his anger.

"Kip, he took the girl; I think Adam said her name was Nora. Kip's beta shot Adam and Kayla before leaving. The red-brown wolf and black wolf took off after them that way." Sarah points across the clearing.

Without any words exchanged, the large dark gray wolf took off towards the other side of the clearing, several of the other wolves following him.

"All of you go; I only need four to stay behind. Go make sure the Alpha doesn't need you." The man said, looking at the reminder of the wolves.

The wolves took off following the dark gray wolf. The remaining four dark brown wolves came over and sat just off in the distance, waiting for instructions. Wyatt bit his lip hard, seeing that there was nothing he could do for his friend. He forced back the tears that were swelling in his eyes. He felt like a failure if he could have gotten here quicker. He looked at the hole in Adam's chest, knowing he could have done nothing to save him or the girl. He felt the anger rushing through him. He glanced over to the girl who looked the oldest. She was cradling her hand. He cleared his throat, looking at her.

"Let me see your hand." He said, his voice softening.

Sarah shook her head, not making any contact with him; they all were not actually. He was confused; he looked over at one of the four wolves. He realized he was still very naked. He let out a long sigh.

"Bring me some clothing. The others bring things to take back Adams and his mate's bodies." Wyatt said calmly; he was trying to hide the emotion in his voice as he ordered the other wolves to go.

"Kayla…her name was Kayla." Abby spoke up. Wyatt hadn't even got a chance to look at any of the other girls.

There was something in her voice; his head snapped to her.

"What's your name?" He asked, feeling his heart rate increase as he looked her over.

"Abby." She said softly; the way she said her name and her voice spoke sent shivers through him.

"Look at me." Wyatt said, annoyed that she hadn't yet.

He was then hit by the sweetest smell. His wolf felt like he was running around inside of him, full of excitement. The smell was her; it was her scent.

"Mate." Wyatt said as his eyes locked with hers, and the whole world seemed to snap into place.

"Mate." Abby whispered back, shocked, and her eyes shot to the ground.

Cole raced through the trees, his feet digging into the dirt as he pushed himself to go fast. Thoughts of Kip touching Nora rushed into his mind. Cole's anger ignited more, and he dug deeper. He could smell Matt's scent getting stronger as he traveled through the woods. He was catching up. His paws hit gravel, and he knew that he had crossed into Kip's territory. A smell hit him hard and fast as he crossed over the gravel. Strong like iron, he knew in a second it was blood.

"Matt!" Jace mind linked him.

No response. The blood was getting stronger as he ran. He could see headlights from a car up ahead. It had to be Kip's. He pushed himself more; he could feel his pads cracking from how hard his feet were hitting the ground. He didn't care; he would break, bleed, and die to make sure nothing happened to Nora. He caught up to the cars. His nose searched for the blood. There was a car still there; the driver-side door was wide open. He was searching for

Nora; her scent was strong, and he couldn't tell if she was still there or had just left. He circled the car, his teeth bared, hackles up, and a low growl coming from his throat as he went to attack. As he got to the other side of the car, he found Matt. He had Taylor by the throat, he was still in wolf form. Matt had large wounds all over his sides, blood dripping down him, but he still held on to Taylor. Taylor was in human form, unclothed. Telling Cole that they must have fought and Taylor wasn't strong enough to stay in wolf form. Cole looked around and realized there had been a second car.

"Kip left with Nora; I was able to get Taylor." *Matt answered Cole's reaction, through mind link.*

A loud growl erupted through Jace, it was blood chilling. The kind of an animal in pain, it made Matt's hair stand on end. Cole's lips pulled back, revealing his long, sharp teeth as he moved closer to Taylor. Cole wanted blood, wanted to rip him from limb to limb.

Wait, we could use him. Jace said to Cole.

Kill him. Cole growled back.

We don't know the inner workings of Kip's main house where he will be keeping Nora. We could use him to get her back. Jace growled back.

Cole growled, and before Jace could fight control, he chomped down on Taylor's hand. He would have screamed if Matt's mouth wasn't around his throat. A low gurgle came out instead. Cole's teeth connected through her wrist, and with one swift pull, he ripped Taylor's hand from his arm. Blood gushed out of his handless limb.

Fine, but he doesn't need his hand. Cole growled.

Jace forced the shift and turned back into human, his breathing was rough as he stood looking over Matt and Taylor. He was forcing the anger down so that he didn't lose control and kill Taylor.

"Ryker let Matt shift back." Jace commanded.

Ryker let go of Taylor's throat. Taylor let out a painful scream as he rolled into himself, clutching his hand to his chest. Ryker moved back and shifted back to Matt. Matt reached down, grabbing a hold of Taylor by his neck again. His fingers went into the puncture marks Ryker had left. He left out another yell.

"Alpha?" Matt asked, growling.

Jace shut his eyes, fighting the urge to go over there and kill Taylor. Cole pushed forward, wanting him to do it.

"Where is he taking her?" Jace growled.

Taylor clenched his jaw shut, refusing to talk. Matt looked at Jace, waiting for instructions. Jace walked over to him, grabbed his other hand, and yanked back hard on his wrist. The bone-snapping sound of his wrist breaking echoed in the surroundings. Taylor let out a gut-wrenching sound as his hand dangled. The bone from his arm protrudes out of the wrist joint. Jace was expressionless.

"Where is he taking her? Last time I am asking." Jace growled.

Taylor refused again, and a small chilling smile spread across Jace's lip. He leaned down, grabbing a hold of the bone sticking out of his wrist. As Jace barely touched the bone, Taylor whimpered. Jace grabbed a hold of it, wrapping his hand around it. Taylor screamed as Jace twisted it, rotating the bone. Taylor let out another agonizing cry as his eyes rolled back in his head from the pain. Matt slapped him in the face.

"Oh no, you're not getting out of this that easy." Matt growled again, slapping him.

Taylor blinked, sweat pouring off his forward head from the pain. Blood dripped from his barely attached wrist. Jace waited a few more seconds, letting him take in the pain. He reached for the other bone hanging out of the opening. He grazed it with his fingers.

"Matt, next it's his legs." Jace said, his voice was cold.

Taylor still wasn't talking; Jace wrapped his hand around the bone, pulling forward slightly. Taylor whimpered in pain. Jace began to rotate the bone in the opposite directions; he did this one slowly, so the pain was overbearing. The bone was grinding against the other as he twisted. Taylor screamed furiously, his sounds bouncing off the trees that surrounded them. Jace let go and moved down to his leg.

"Ankle then knee or knee then ankle?" Jace asked Matt.

"Ankle then knee, you sever that artery near the knee, he might die quicker." Matt said indifferently like they were talking about the weather.

Jace grabbed hold of his ankle in his hand, glancing up at Taylor, who was still remaining silent. He twisted quickly and fast; another loud snap echoed off the trees. He didn't even wait. He grabbed his other foot, doing the same, Taylor screaming through the pain as he did.

"Hmm, you think they have a tire iron in the car? Instead of snapping the knees, maybe I'll just crush them." Jace said, getting up and moving to the car.

Taylor was letting out long breaths, trying to control the pain. He was broken. Cole had removed his right hand completely, and blood was dripping out of it. His other hand was being held on by skin, his arm broken beyond repair, and now both of his ankles. He was in pain all over and couldn't take another thing. He didn't even realize Jace had come back and was standing over him with a tire iron. Jace tapped the tire iron to the knee he was planning on smashing into pieces. Taylor was debating giving in and telling them what they wanted to know. His head told him that he couldn't betray his Alpha. Then a small voice told him that he was dead already. If he even managed to get back to his Alpha, he knew Kip would see him as useless being caught. He would kill him for that alone. He was taking too long thinking. Jace raised the tire iron above his head and slammed it down onto his right knee. The bones crumbled beneath the iron. Taylor caterwauled again; the noise was full of pain and defeat.

"Stop!" He managed to choke out.

"Stop?" Matt said coldly.

"I didn't hear stop." Jace said, placing his foot on top of his knee and applying a small amount of pressure.

"He took her to the pack house." Taylor screamed out.

There was a commotion behind them as Noah came bolting into the area. He skidded, almost slamming into the car; he had been running so fast. Noah's eyes searched the area quickly. His eyes landed on Jace.

"Kip has her." Jace said bitterly, the words hurt his mouth to say.

Noah began growling viciously as he walked fur standing on end. He walked up next to Jace, waiting for orders. Noah stared down at Taylor, wanting to rip him limb from limb.

"Noah, I have this." Jace said, applying more pressure to Taylor's knee.

"I told you he went to the pack house." Taylor cried.

"There's more you're forgetting." Jace growled.

Noah wandered up to his face, Matt still had a hold of his throat. Noah settled next to his head, he took one of his claws and ran it down the side of it. His skin slowly peeled as Noah's claw ran over Taylor's face.

"There's a lab underneath the pack house. He will take her down there." Taylor yelled out.

"How do I get in?" Jace growled.

Several more wolves appeared in the clearing, circling around them. They bowed their heads, seeing Jace. Jace ignored them, waiting for Taylor to answer.

"There's two ways through the back room in the pack house. There's a door that leads to it. Then there's a house on the far side of our territory. It's bright yellow. There is a hatch in the living room floor," Taylor coughed as he spoke.

"How far is your pack house from here?" Jace asked, looking over to his wolves.

"Twenty minutes." Taylor said, closing his eyes.

"Wars is now! Get back to the house and gather our supplies. Get all troops out here, Zeke's and the Black Sands. Tell them we're doing this now. If that hunter is still around, tell him as well." Jace said to his pack.

They bowed their heads and took off in the direction of the pack house. They didn't even flinch. They didn't even guess his judgment. It was more than the bond. Nora had made an impact on all of them from the hospital act alone. They would fight for her without question. Jace stepped off of Taylor's knee. He motioned for Matt and Noah to move away from Taylor. They instantly followed his command. He let out a small breath and shifted into Cole. Cole moved over to Taylor. A small smile appeared on Taylor's lip.

"There's the demon wolf." Taylor said, seeing Cole.

Images of ripping his father apart popped into his head. Cole wanted to do it again. Wanted to feel his teeth pierce and tear through his flesh repeatedly before letting him slowly bleed out. Cole clamped down on Taylor's throat. His fangs piercing his jugular blood began to pour into Cole's mouth. He ripped his head to the side and tore the front of Taylor's throat off. He dropped his flesh from his mouth and walked away. The only sound in the woods was the gurgling from Taylor as he drowned.

Chapter Seventy One
Amber

"I need to reset your fingers so they don't heal like that." Wyatt said, taking his eyes off Abby and looking at Sarah.

"I'm fine." Sarah said quietly.

"Do you want to heal and not be able to use your fingers?" Wyatt asked quietly.

Sarah was still busy watching the men come and take Adam's and Kayla's bodies away. They were taking them to prepare them for burial. She was watching their backs as they walked out of the clearing. She didn't mind the pain, she felt she deserved it. Regret and guilt flooded her system. She wouldn't have stolen the cell phone, She would have made Kayla believe there was a way to get out. To escape. Things may have been rough with Kip's pack, but at least Kayla was still alive.

"Just let him fix them, Sarah. It will be no use to have a hand that doesn't work." Abby said to her.

"We will need to go back to the hospital; that way, I can bandage it once I get it in place. We need to do this quickly. I don't know what Jace needs." Wyatt said, knowing that this meant full out war.

The girls nodded and began making their way out of the clearing. Logan came rushing into the clearing, almost bumping into Sarah and Abby. The girls backed up his scent, hitting them. Sarah stepped protectively in front of Abby and Millie, growling fiercely. Logan threw his hands up, taking a step back.

"Hunter." Sarah growled, snarling, her eyes glowing as she blocked his way.

"Easy, he's on our side right now." Wyatt said, looking at Logan.

"Nora." Logan said, looking around.

"Kip took her." Wyatt said, his voice full of anger with a touch of sadness.

"Where's Jace?" Logan said his hands went into fists immediately.

"He went after them; I am not sure what's going on. Matt is with him, and others are not too far behind." Wyatt explained.

Logan rushed towards the other side of the clearing. Wyatt watched him, wanting to stop him, but knew he wouldn't listen. Wyatt and the girls began making their way out of the clearing. A swarm of wolves came rushing out of the other side of the clearing. As Logan approached, he braced himself, waiting for an impact of one of them at the speed they were running. A larger red brown wolf barreled into him. The wolf was angry that something had stopped him. Logan was flung back, and the red wolf rolled into him. The wolf got up, snarling and snapping, clearly pissed off at Logan. Seeing Logan, the wolf gritted its teeth and stopped growling. The wolf sat back and looked like it was muttering to itself. In a quick motion, the wolf hunched down and then began to transform in front of Logan. Logan made a gagging noise as he watched the bones shift, snap, and pop into place. Within a second, Matt was kneeling in front of him.

"That was disgusting." Logan said to him, trying to recover.

"War is happening now. If your hunters want to help take down Kip, we are doing this now. He's got Nora. I wasn't fast enough." Matt said, his voice shaking with rage as he stated he wasn't fast enough.

Logan looked at him and nodded. He stepped back, pulling his phone out of his pocket. He called Lilly.

"Get to the Wolf's Den now. We're going to war. The Red Woods wolves took Nora. Let our members know we are fighting with the Cross River pack and allies. No one is to hurt any wolves but the Red Woods ones. Get here now." Logan ordered.

Sarah overheard Logan and stopped walking. She watched Abby and Millie halt as she did. They didn't have time to go to the hospital. They needed to help. She needed to get Millie to safety, but she and Abby could help. They grew up in the Red woods. Even though Kip kept them basically locked up, she still knew her way around.

"What are you doing?" Abby asked her quietly as Wyatt slowed down to a stop

"We can't waste time fixing my hand. Your Alpha needs you, and that girl did everything to save us. We need to help them. Put my hand back in place here, and we are going with you." Sarah said, looking at Wyatt.

"We as in me and Abby, not you, Millie." Sarah said, looking down to Millie, who was excited to help.

Mille frowned, "Sarah, I want to help…. Kayla. She was my sister."

"You are seven and can help by keeping yourself safe. Your sister would have wanted that." Sarah told Mille, who frowned deeper.

Millie looked exactly like Kayla, except her eyes were hazel. Even the way she was frowning right now was like a younger Kayla was looking at her. Sarah felt her chest tighten.

"It's going to hurt." Wyatt said quietly as he walked over to Sarah; he wasn't arguing he needed to fix her hand but needed to get with Jace.

"It doesn't matter," Sarah said, holding her hand out.

Abby stepped into Sarah, bracing her. Wyatt grabbed a hold of her wrist and looked at her. He could get three of her fingers back in place at once if he did it right. It still left the pinky and thumb needing to be done separately.

"Little one, there is a car on the other side of that tree right there. Inside it is a medical bag. If you want to be helpful, grab it for me and bring it back," Wyatt said to her quietly as he examined Sarah's hand more.

Wyatt had always had his medical bag on him, but recently, he had over stocked it due to Nora being hurt quite often. Millie was on her way, and Wyatt locked eyes with Sarah.

"I am going to count to three and reset your pointer, middle, and ring finger all at once. I will have to do the pinky and thumb completely separately. You need to somehow keep still after until I can get your hand in a splint." Wyatt explained to her.

Sarah nodded as Abby grabbed her shoulders and pulled her against her. Wyatt watched Abby brace her, and Sarah seemed distracted. He took that moment to grab a hold of her three fingers and pulled forward. Sarah fell into Abby, a scream escaping her mouth as her bones relaxed; a loud popping sound was heard.

"You said three!" Sarah growled, her eyes glowing, as her wolf pushed forward to give her strength.

Abby pulled back slightly, trying to get ahold of Sarah. She looked at Sarah, and confusion went across Abby's face. Sarah narrowed her eyebrows at Abby.

"What? Why does your face look like that?" Sarah growled at Abby.

"Your eyes, Sarah." Abby whispered.

"My eyes Abby, no, my fucking fingers." Sarah said, getting angry with her.

"No, your freaking eyes Sarah. They're not glowing red." Abby said, annoyed and shocked.

"They were not red when Lilliana pushed forward." Abby said to her, calling Sarah's wolf by name.

"What?" Sarah asked.

Wyatt had no idea what they were talking about but seized the opportunity of Sarah not paying attention and snapped another finger back into place. He grabbed a hold of her pinky and pulled with a slight twist. It's popping back into place, echoing in the woods. Sarah let out another deep growl. Lillian, under the surface, gives her strength.

"See, they're not red." Abby said again.

"What color are they?" Sarah whispered, taking the wave of pain in stride.

"Amber." Matt said, walking out of the woods with Logan behind him.

Wyatt looked up over Abby's shoulder and was confused.

'Kip's pack is red." He stated.

"Sarah, did you renounce Kip as your Alpha?" Abby whispered, a hint of fear in her voice.

Kip would kill you if you left his pack.

"I guess mentally I did." Sarah said with a shrug; her mind had screamed it as she watched Kayla die.

"Rouge's eyes don't glow." Abby said, confused.

"No Alpha, no glow." Abby said again, not understanding.

"What color is your pack?" Sarah asked Matt, her eyes flickering.

Wyatt yanked on her thumb as she got lost in the conversation, snapping into place just as Millie came in sight with the medical bag.

"Blue." Matt answered.

"So you didn't align with Jace mentally." Abby said quietly.

"I don't think that's how that works. I would need to take an oath to swear into a pack, and the

Alpha would need to accept it." Sarah whispered to Abby.

"She's right." Wyatt said, motioning for Millie to hurry.

"In the bag, there is a splint for the hand. Fetch for me." Wyatt said to her.

"Cross River is blue, Black sands are ironically Green, and the Moonlight pack is white." Matt said, going over all the colors.

"I have only seen amber once." Logan said, piecing stuff together.

Wyatt slipped the hand splint onto Sarah's fingers and hand, securing it into place before looking at Matt confused. There was no pack with amber glowing eyes.

"Who? Abby was right about rogues. They do not get a color." Wyatt said, narrowing his brows as he talked.

"Nora. Her eyes glowed, amber." Logan said; a chill seemed to go through the air.

"She's not a wolf." Wyatt said, trying to think how it was possible.

"She's not, but her eyes glowed amber, and she commanded Adam like an Alpha." Logan whispered.

"Is that even possible?" Sarah asked.

"Who knows what is possible now," Matt said, shaking his head.

"We need to get going to help. I need someone to take Mille somewhere safe. Abby and I can help you get through Kip's land without trouble." Sarah said.

"I am meeting my members at the front gate. I can take Millie to the pack house. I am assuming that's the safest place." Logan said.

"I don't know about you, hunter." Sarah said, her eyes glowing amber again.

"I am going with him." Matt said, reassuring her.

"Fine. You two take Mille to safety, and we will start heading to meet Jace with him." Sarah said, pointing to Wyatt.

Mille squeezed Sarah tightly.

"Listen, you are going to be fine. I will see you soon." Sarah said, kissing the top of Millie's head.

Chapter Seventy Two
Help

Nora groaned; her head was killing her. She went to reach up to touch the back of her head; she felt wetness there. She pulled her hand down, opening her eyes, she saw her fingertips stained with blood. She saw shackles on her wrist. They were silver; she rolled her eyes slightly at the silver shackles. There was a faint, familiar smell in the air as well. The silver chain was coated in something.

"It's Wolfsbane." A voice said from the other side of the room.

She forced her eyes to focus; the room was dark, and her head was still foggy and painful. The only light in the room was a dim light coming through the small window in the door.

"Well, it's dumb." Nora said, holding her head in her hands, trying to make it stop throbbing.

"Well, we mostly have everything set up to hold other wolves. Humans aren't really a threat." The voice explained.

"But here I am." Nora groaned, whoever this was liked the sound of his voice.

"It's because you belong to Jace. No hard feelings." The voice smiled.

"I don't belong to anyone. You wolves are possessive over things you don't have or own." Nora said, annoyed.

"How do you know about wolves? Jace, I'm assuming." The voice said again.

"I'm done talking to you." Nora said, fighting back a wave of nausea.

Her headache was getting increasingly worse, and the chains were starting to bother her. She was getting hot; she could feel the sweat starting to drip off her forehead. She leaned back against the wall she was next to. The cold from the stone felt good.

"Feeling sick?" The voice asked again.

"No, I'm just peachy." Nora replied sarcastically.

"I bet Jace loves your personality." The voice chuckled.

"He's also going to love ripping you to pieces when he gets here." Nora said, trying to coat her mouth with spit; it was becoming so dry.

"Well, see about that." The voice said as the lights flipped on in the room.

The blinding light from the overhead hanging lights causes Nora pain. She shielded her eyes as her head throbbed more, and the urge to throw up crept up her throat. She heard another person move towards her, but she was too busy trying to keep herself from vomiting. She didn't care. She felt something cold press against her cheek. It was a wet cloth and water bottle.

"Drink…slowly." The man said his voice was calm and soothing.

Nora took the bottle of water, looking at it carefully, deciding if she wanted to risk drinking it. She sighed, opening it and taking a sniff into the water.

"You broke the seal. Clearly, it hasn't been opened." The voice muttered.

Nora took a big swig of it, covering her eyes from the light. She could see the man now. His hair was dark brown; he was tall with broad shoulders. He was not who she expected. She thought that it was Kip in there taunting her, but it was someone she had never met. He reminded her of Jace in the way he held himself.

"Who are you?" She asked to take another sip of water.

"Just some peon you don't need to worry about." He said, leaning back against the wall.

She could make out the color of his eyes now. She thought, for some reason, they were going to be ice blue, but they weren't. They were a deep, rich brown. It reminded her of the ground, soil. They were warm, and she found that surprising.

"He hasn't marked you yet." He said to himself out loud.

For some reason, the announcement hurt Nora. She felt sad, and somewhere deep inside of her, this strong wanting. She wanted Jace to mark her. She was upset he hadn't yet, but she didn't understand those feelings. It wasn't like he was giving her his college ring or letterman jacket. Some type of small symbol. He was going to sink his teeth into her and leave a mark. From what she could understand, it would link them together, and it was a forever thing. More scared then marriage. She wasn't ready for something that serious, but deep down, there was this whimpering, nagging, and almost heartbreaking feeling about it. She pushed it down and turned away from the man. Her wrists felt like they were on fire. She pushed the pain from her mind, shutting her eyes and waiting. She needed to get her head together and come up with some type of plan.

They walked quickly through the woods, searching for Jace. Wyatt was leading the way while the others followed quickly behind. They crossed into Kip's territory, and Sarah saw Abby stiffen up. She didn't want to be back here. Sarah went to comfort her and as if he knew. Wyatt reached back and grabbed a hold of Abby's hand. Abby didn't react act like Sarah, except she saw a smile form on her lips as she wrapped her fingers around Wyatt's hand. Relief rushed through Sarah; she was happy for Abby. She had been so shy and scared most of her life; maybe Wyatt would change that for her.

As they crossed the gravel that divided Kip's land, the smell of blood rushed into Sarah's nose. She saw Wyatt become attentive. She could tell he was trying to gauge if there was danger or not. Sarah took a step towards the car they came upon, and a large gray wolf darted out, showing its teeth and growling. Sarah backed up, bumping into Wyatt. Jace stepped out from behind the front of the car.

"Noah, easy." He yelled, anger still in his voice; he was pacing back and forth like a caged animal.

Noah ducked his head at the command, but as if he couldn't control himself, he bolted at Sarah. His large paws landed on her chest, tackling her to the ground. Hitting the ground, Sarah let out a yelp. Noah began licking her face and nuzzling into her neck. Wyatt went to get Noah but realized he wasn't attacking.

"What is he doing?" Abby whispered, concerned.

Sarah's wolf pushed forward, her eyes glowing amber. Sarah's wolf, Lilliana, was excited. She was yelling to come out inside of Sarah's head. Sarah fought back, confused by everything going on. Noah buried his face into her neck, and she could feel him inhale. Jace sighed loudly as he was pacing. He kept looking to the woods over their shoulder. Cole screamed inside of him that they needed to leave now. The longer they waited, the more time she had alone with Kip.

"Noah, that's enough; shift back if you can't control yourself." Jace commanded.

On command, Noah stepped back and began shifting. As Noah shifted into Dante, his scent hit her. She was overwhelmed by it; it was intoxicating. He smelt like the earth after it rained but with a touch of something warm. Sarah moved towards him, her eyes glowing brighter. Lilliana shouted mate inside of her. Dante looked at her, Noah howling inside of him. She was perfect. Dante stepped towards her, not realizing he was fully naked.

"Mate." He said to her, his eyes glowing blue.

Sarah stepped back, her senses trying to overwhelm her. Lilliana pushed forward, wanting to go to him, wanting Sarah to accept him, to say mate back. Sarah fought hard against her urges. Her eyes glowed a bright amber. Dante grunted, seeping closer to Sarah.

"Why are you fighting it?" Dante growled at her.

"Because of what's happening." Sarah said, her eyes looked from Dante to Jace.

Jace stopped short, seeing her eye color, and walked over. He caught her chin in his hand, and Dante let out a small growl, already becoming protective of Sarah. Jace shot him a look, and Dante lowered his head, taking a step back.

"Your eyes." Jace said quietly.

"It happened when Kayla died." Sarah answered honestly.

Jace looked at her like he was looking for an answer, his eyes shooting over to Wyatt, who shrugged in response to the question of how and who came silently to him. Jace let out a sigh.

"Dante is your mate?" Jace asked, his voice remaining even toned.

"Yes." Sarah answered.

"Dante, take your mate and her friends back to the packhouse where it is safe. We Don't know what to expect yet." Jace ordered, his expression softening, realizing that Dante had found his mate and did not want anything to happen like Adam and Kayla.

"No." Sarah spoke up, stepping further away from Dante.

"We came to help. Abby and I have lived in Kip's pack. We can get you to where you need to go the quickest and without alerting people." Sarah said.

Her eyes peered into Jace's, and they glowed. Jace stared at her for a minute, the amber color throwing him off. Was Sarah somehow connected to Nora? Why did they have the same color glow? He thought to himself as he debated on if he should accept the help. Jace let out a short sigh.

"Fine, as long as you agree to follow my orders and stay out of the way." Jace said to her.

"Agreed. Do you have a map?" Sarah asked.

Dante let out a grumble, and Sarah's eyes flickered to his. She knew he didn't want her here. She clenched her jaw together, trying to ignore him. Jace walked over to the car and began searching for a map. To his surprise, there was an old one in the glove box. He motioned for her to come here as he unraveled it and laid it across the trunk. Just as they began looking, they could hear the sound of paws hitting the ground. It sounds like the soft rumble of thunder. Sarah looked at Jace nervously.

"It's ok, they're coming with us." Jace said before nodding back to the map.

Chapter Seventy Three
Move out

She could hear screaming and shouting from the rooms down the hall. Nora sat up, the metal from the cuff causing her pain. She didn't know she was this much of a weakling. The man sitting across the way from her didn't even act like he heard the screaming. She looked at him like he was crazy. She slowly got to her feet and began moving across the room.

"Where are you going?" He asked her, annoyed.

"Obviously not far." She said, rolling her eyes at her and holding up her hands.

She went to the door, and he got up like he accepted her to bolt. He went up behind her incase he needed to grab her. She ignored him, standing on her tippy toes, trying to see out the tiny window in the door.

"What are you doing?" He asked, annoyed.

"Do you not hear all that?" Nora said, still trying to see.

"Yeah, it happens quite often here." He said, his voice filled with no emotions.

"What's going on?" Nora asked again.

"Alpha is making more of his. ... .pets." He said, leaning back against the wall.

"And you're ok with this?" Nora said, turning around to look at him.

"It's not my place." He said with a shrug.

"So you're a mindless person; you have no thoughts of your own." Nora said, angry.

"I have a good thought to knock you in your mouth," He smiled at her.

"Do it." Nora said, her eyes narrowing at him. Maybe this was what she needed, some threat.

Maybe her powers would kick in, and she could get out of there. He stepped up off the wall with a grin on his face. He backed her up against the door. She started to panic a little when her powers did not show.

"I don't hit girls." He whispered into her ear and stepped away.

"What's your name?" Nora asked him.

"Asher." He said, giving in.

"Asher." She repeated it for some reason.

He gave her a weird look before looking back down at the phone he held in his hand. He looked so much like Jace. His nose was slightly longer and narrow. His cheekbones were as pronounced as Jace's beside the eye color. She thought, looking back to the door.

"Do you want to go see one?" He asks, his voice teasing.

"I already have." Nora said quietly, and then a thought entered her head.

If she could get an idea of the layout, maybe she could somehow tell Jace. She knew he was on his way to get her; she worried he might get hurt. She was worried that someone might die. She knew he wasn't coming alone, and she didn't want anyone dying for her.

"I'm not afraid of them." Nora said, baiting him.

"You're not." Asher said, interest flashed in his eyes.

"Nope, but for some reason, you are afraid of some humans." Nora said, motioning to the cuffs.

"I am afraid of nothing." Asher growled.

"Mhmm says the man holding a human girl hostage and cuffed." Nora said with a chuckle to add to it.

She wasn't sure what her next move would be. She knew the cuffs had wolfbain on them. She knew they would be painful to any wolf. She just didn't know how she was going to use them just yet. Asher growled, getting her attention, and then began walking to her. She narrowed her eyes at him, waiting for him to do something. He backed her into the door. She was ready for whatever he was going to do. He reached behind her and unlocked the door. He pushed the door open, and it swung outward.

"I don't have a key." He said to her, motioning for her to walk out the door.

She looked at him, confused like it was a trick. He stepped back away from her, waiting for her to go. She stepped towards the door; she was not sensing any danger, and then she took a deep breath and walked out the door. She waited, and nothing happened. Asher stepped out the door behind her and motioned for her to go left.

"Where are we going?" Nora asked, stepping to the left.

"To scare you." Asher grinned.

The noise of thunder surrounded them as Sarah and Abby drew on the map. Going into details about which roads not to use and the quickest way to both entries to the pack house. The thunder stopped as they were surrounded by wolves. Sarah didn't look up as she was marking the best route to the yellow house. Jace had said that Taylor had told him there was an entrance there.

"Done," said Sarah as she pushed the map towards Jace.

"Dante, Wyatt came here. Grayson shifts back and comes forward." Jace commanded outwards over the crowd of wolves.

Wyatt and Dante moved to the car as a blonde wolf navigated through the crowd. He came out and shifted into his human form. He then made his way to the car.

"Wyatt and Grayson, I want you to take Zeke's and Grayson's pack to the yellow house and begin making your way. I will take our pack and head to the pack house. Kip will be waiting for me. You will be our surprise. Dante, I need you with me. Kip knows I move with my beta. If you're not there, he will know something is up." Jace said, pointing to the map as he spoke.

"When we get inside, we find Nora." His eyes flickered to Grayson.

"You find your Alpha." Jace said, knowing that's where Grayson's head was at.

"Will do," Grayson said with a nod.

"We just need Matt-

"Present." Matt shouted with a smile.

Walking into the clearing, Logan and four people follow behind him.

"Bout time." Dante grumbled to him. Matt walked up to the car and nudged Dante lightly.

"Missed you too handsome." Matt winked at Dante.

"Jace, these are my hunters. Drake, Phill, Mina, and Kate. It's not many, but we are deadly." Logan nodded to them.

"And I am Lilly." Lilly announced herself, walking in from behind the crowd.

"And Lilly." Logan said, rolling his eyes; she had been taking too long, so he was going without her.

Matt tensed up and turned to see Lilly. His eyes began to glow as his world seemed to slow down. He looked to Jace as the feeling began to overwhelm him.

"Oh, for fuck sake, do you all have to find your mates as were going to war." Jace growled, knowing what was happening to Matt.

"Sorry, bossman, fate isn't mine to play with." Matt said, walking to Lilly.

"Watch it, wolf." She sneered a little at him.

"Mates?" Logan said, watching Matt walk by him.

"I'll be your wolf, babe." Matt smirked, throwing a wink at her.

"No." Logan said, looking from Matt to Jace.

"Yup." Jace growled.

"Matt pulled it together. I assume Abby, you're going with Wyatt, and Dante Sarah is coming?" Jace said annoyed.

"Yes, Alpha." Wyatt responded.

"No." Dante growled.

"I am going with you, like it or not." Sarah growled back.

"We don't have time for this. She's going with us." Jace growled at Dante, who went to protest but stopped at the commanding sound in Jace's voice.

"Matt and Logan, you need to work this shit out. You two are sticking together and will hang back until I summon you. I will leave a small number of our pack behind with you and the hunter. You will be our reinforcements." Jace ordered. Logan glared at Matt, who ignored it and looked fondly at Lilly, who was staring back, completely confused.

"Let's move out," Jace said, stepping forward.

"Let's go get our girl." Dante said, stepping forward with Jace.

Dante, Wyatt, Sarah, and Abby all shifted into their wolves, waiting for Jace.

Jace looked at Matt, nodded quickly, and shifted into Cole. The wolves parted into sections. Dante's wolf, Noah, stepped up next to Cole. Wyatt's wolf, Evertt, moved forward. Cole howled, and they all took off their own ways.

"Well, I guess it's just you and me…brother." Matt smirked and winked at Logan.

"Don't call me brother." Logan said, glaring at him.

"Can someone catch me up?" Lilly smiled, playful, as she moved out from behind Logan.

"Well, gorgeous, I'm-

"Nothing and no one," Logan said, angry.

"What is your problem?" Lilly asked, shoving Logan.

"This wolf here thinks he's your mate." Logan said angrily.

"Mate?" Lilly repeated.

"Mate." Matt said, the words rolling off his tongue sounded perfect to Lilly.

There was something in the way he said it like there was some promise to it. Lilly was taken back by it. She swallowed hard as she looked at Logan.

"Where's Nora?" She asked, concerned.

"The Red Wood's Alpha has her. We are back up. Jace is going after her." Logan explained.

"That psycho has her." Lilly said, angry.

"Not for long." Matt said, matching her anger.

Chapter Seventy Four
Can't

Nora stepped out into the hall; it was cold. The walls, ceiling, and floor were all white. She looked to Asher, and he nodded for her to go left. She walked down the hall slowly. Part of it was because it was aerie with the random screaming, and the other part was because she was trying to make sure she remembered everything. Walking past the first room, the sound of soft crying was heard. Asher saw her interested, and he tapped lightly on the glass of the door. The small shade pulled up, the person inside stepped aside, and Asher moved to the right, moving out of the way.

"Go take a look." Asher said, no emotion in the comment.

Nora stepped up to the door. Looking inside was a medical room; there was a girl strapped to a chain in the center, the kind you would see at a dentist. Tears stained her cheeks. She watched someone who looked like a nurse come over to the girl. She grabbed her mouth and took a vial that contained a red solution into her mouth. The girl was too weak to struggle. Nora hit the glass.

"Hey!" Nora yelled, the nurse turned around.

Nora was taken back by the sadness she saw in the nurse's eyes. She bowed her head and stepped away from the girl. Nora looked to Asher.

"What did she do to her?" Nora asked, confused.

"What she was ordered to do." Asher said quietly.

She saw something flash in his eyes: regret, maybe sadness. It was the same look the nurse had when she locked eyes with Nora.

"What did she give her?" Nora asked again.

"Blood." Asher said, walking down the hall.

Nora followed after him; Asher stopped at the next room as Nora caught up. He tapped on the window again. The blinds went up as Asher stepped aside. Nora looked into the window; it was the same hospital room set up, but this time, a man was strapped into the dentist's chair. He was fighting. The nurse injected something into him, and he began to calm down. The same thing happened; she took a vial with blood out of a cabinet, walked over to the man, and forced him to drink it.

"Why?" Nora asked, stepping away from the door.

Asher didn't say anything, but instead of continuing down the hall, he walked to a gray door. He pulled it open and motioned for her to follow him. They entered a stairwell, and Asher walked down a flight of stairs. Getting to the bottom, he waited by the door. As Nora caught up, he opened the door and walked out. This hallway was darker; strange noise was coming from the rooms. The walls were gray down here, and the doors were so dark they were almost black. Nora followed close behind Asher. Getting to the first door, he pressed a button on the wall, and the dark gray wall turned into a glass. As the gray faded to clear, Nora saw what looked to be someone who used to be human. They had half wolf parts, half human. They were laid on the ground, blood pooling from their nose and mouth. Their eyes glossed over, staring lifelessly at her. Their breathing was so shallow that she had to focus to see that they were still breathing. It was a horrifying scene. A loud scream ripped her eyes away from the poor soul in the room. Asher was already heading down to the next room.

He paused outside the wall where the screaming was coming from. He looked at Nora, debating on pressing the button. His hand lingered over it. Nora walked over to him and pushed his hand to it. The wall faded from gray to clear. A Lobo was standing in the middle of the room, a nurse in the corner trying to get away. The room was destroyed, the chair was in pieces, and a surgical tray was flung across the room. Another nurse lay dead in the middle of the chaos while the one still alive tried to hide in the very back corner of the room. Nora quickly bolted to the door, reaching for the handle. She tugged on it, but it was locked. She began pulling fiercely on it, her eyes flickering to the glass wall, trying to see if the Lobo had gotten the girl yet.

"Asher opens the freaking door, it's going to kill her!" She shouted at him.

"I can't." Asher said quietly.

"Open the door!! What is wrong with you!" Nora yelled, going over to him and grabbing him.

She attempted to drag him to the door, her eyes locked with the scared, frantic nurse. Her eyes glowed red as her wolf pushed forward.

"Asher opens the door before it gets her. She's a member of your pack! Don't you feel nothing!" Nora screamed, pulling him closer to the door.

The nurse in the room shifted into her wolf form. A small red wolf cowering away from the savage and giant Lobo. It walked towards her, and if the thing could grin, it was. The small red wolf's hackles went up as it tried to look fierce. It didn't phase the Lobo.

"Let me in! I'll save her if you can't. Just please open the door!" Nora screamed at Asher.

It was no use; he didn't move, didn't budge. Nora began patting him down for a key. The Lobo snatched the small wolf up in its arms and began squeezing it. Nora couldn't find a key. She ran to the glass wall, wondering if it could see. She began pounding on it. Maybe he would put the small wolf down if it got distracted. The Lobo's eyes flickered to the wall. He carried the small Wolf over to the glass wall. Nora was slamming her fist into it. The Lobo smiled, showing all of its teeth to Nora.

"Put her down!' She screamed as she heard the wolf's ribs begin to crack.

The Lobos smiled widened, and then, with one quick motion, it bent forward, reaching down with its massive teeth and crunching the small wolf's throat into its jaws. Blood fell down from its mouth and down its chest, falling onto the white floor. The red wolf went limp in its mouth. Nora turned away, seeing the blood tears stung in her eyes. She was shaking. She turned to Asher, rage rushing into her.

"Why!" She yelled as she stuck him in the chest.

He didn't say anything. She hit him again; this time, she felt a jolt, her powers starting to wake up. The jolt caught Asher off guard. He didn't know if it was the wolfbane-dipped cuffs hurting him or if something actually happened.

"You could have saved her!" Nora screamed.

"You let one of your members die like that! You're pathetic." She yelled, hitting him again; he caught her arms this time.

"I told you I can't." Asher said, a crack of emotion came through his emotionless voice. Nora stepped back.

"What do you mean you can't?" Nora asked, confused.

"I just can't." Asher said again, letting go of her hands.

Footsteps coming down the hall caught Nora's attention. She was angry; she could feel her powers trying to push forward, but something was holding them back. She gritted her teethQ

"Can't isn't a good enough reason to let people die." Nora growled at Asher.

Kip rounded the corner, an ugly smile plastered on his face. He looked amused as he walked up to them smugly. He glanced at the window. The Lobo was still holding the poor dead red wolf in its mouth.

"Well done, Asher. Did the little miss enjoy her tour?" Kip smiled brightly.

"You're sick." Nora whispered to him.

"Maybe." Kip said with a wink before looking at Asher.

"I might make you my beta; you've done a great job so far. I mean, I do have your daughter, but I think you've gone above and beyond." Kip smiled.

Can't…that's why he can't. Nora thought of looking at Asher. He saw her make the connection, and he made a subtle nod so she would know that was the reason.

"Beta Alpha? Is Beta Taylor ok?" Asher asked to keep his eyes low.

"He's dead. I'm assuming Little Miss's mate got a hold of him." Kip shrugged his eyes, still inspecting the Lobo.

"Look at this piece of beauty. This fierce, mindless, killing machine. They're going to help me take out your lovely mate's pack, and then I'm going to rule all packs. From there, we will start enslaving humans. It's going to be a whole new world." Kip grinned.

"You're insane," Nora said quietly.

"How is any of your pack still with you?" She asked.

"Most of them are debited to me. Others, I keep their family safe. More importantly, they are bonded to me by the moon goddess. Just like any other Alpha's pack members are." Kip shrugged.

"Well done, Asher. You can go see your daughter. Hurry back," Kip said, waving him off.

"Little Miss, come with me. I have your suit awaiting you." Kip grinned viciously at her.

Kip started walking, and as Nora moved to follow Kip, Asher bumped his hand into hers. She felt him force something into her closed fist. She glanced at him quickly. He made no eye contact and continued walking. She felt the object in her hand as she walked. It was a key. She was surprised. She hoped it was the key to her cuffs.

Chapter Seventy Five
The One That Got Away

Nora followed Kip down the long hall. She kept her eyes focused on her surroundings but didn't try looking into any of the rooms. She didn't want to see any more horrors. Kip glanced over his shoulder, noticed Nora's discomfort, and began hitting the buttons on the wall as he passed them. The dark gray wall became clear as Nora walked by each one. Each room held the same horror but a different stage. Somewhere, just starting to shift, some didn't make it and lay dead on the floor. The nurse in the room looked relieved. Others were the Lobo standing over the person nurse's dead body.

"Why don't you let the nurses out?" Nora asked as they passed by another room.

"At first, it was because I didn't care; I wanted to see what my creation would do. Now, it's more of a fear-control thing for the rest of my pack. Keeps everyone in line." Kip said it like it meant nothing.

He opened one of the dark gray doors and smiled at her. He was leading her into one of the hospital rooms. She felt dread in the pit of her stomach. She was developing a plan in her head. If she could get the cuffs off, maybe she could get them on him. She held her head high and walked into the room. The room was chilling and terrifying. She thought of all the poor souls who were shoved into here. Kip motioned to the seat.

"So what's your plan?" Nora turned around to face him; the question was said more as a statement.

"Sit down." Kip said, shoving her towards the chair.

Nora sighed, sitting in the chair and giving him a look, saying now what. He went to say something, but then his mouth shut. He looked at her throat; he saw the scars on the left side.

"How did that happen?" Kip asked as if he knew.

"Wolf killed my family and tried to kill me." Nora said through gritted teeth.

"Did you see the wolf?" Kip asked, stepping forward.

"Just his eyes . They were red, and his fur was brown-red as well." Nora said, rage in her voice.

"Do you live in a house with a yellow door?" Kip said, trying to control his grin.

Nora's eyes snapped upwards towards him; his eyes glowed red as she locked eyes with him.

"It was you!" She yelled, The rage boiling in her stomach as she lurched forward. She slammed the wolfbane handcuffs into his chest. They sizzled against his skin. Kip jumped back, a sinister smile coming across his lips.

"So Jace's mate is a hunter! I had suspected this! Oh, that is precious!" Kip laughed; he shoved her forehead backward, and her back hit the chair.

"If I cared about the legal part of everything, I would be able to kill you no problem now. Killing humans is frowned upon in the wolf world." Kip snickered.

"I can't believe I slaughtered your family. Jace's mate's family. I can't believe you're a hunter. This is so…so exciting." Kip laughed, walking about.

"I am going to kill you." Nora said; her voice was deadly and soft.

"No…no, you're going to kill Jace for me. You know hunters are stronger than humans. If I can turn above-average humans. Can you imagine what you will be like as one of my creations? You're going to be stronger, faster, and better in every way!" Kip said, shoving her back against the seat again, this time grabbing a strap from the chair and securing her in.

"The one that got away will be the one that helps me get everything I want!" He chuckled to himself.

Nora shut her eyes, trying to block him out as he continued to ramble on about how he was excited. She could hear him fumbling around with things.

Jace. She thought I don't know how this wolf thing works, but I'm hoping it can work with hunters, too. If you can hear me, I am on the bottom floor of his pack house. He has a sick hospital down here where he is making the Lobos. He wants to turn me into one. Nora then focused on sending images of what she saw.

She focused, using everything she had. She knew it was silly; she wasn't a wolf, she wasn't in Jace's pack, but she was feeling hopeless, and she figured it didn't hurt to try.

Cole was running as quickly as he could. The group he was leading was not too far behind, but he couldn't control how quickly he was going. Everything in him was pushing him into overdrive. He needed his mate; he needed Nora. He needed to make sure Kip did not harm her.

Jace. Her voice fluttered through their heads.
Nora? Jace thought, hearing it.

There was nothing else; it was static as if someone was trying to mindlink him, but it was like a cell phone that had a bad connection.

I don't know if it's going to work. Packhouse Bottom Floor Hospital Lobos Turning me into one.

He knew it was Nora's voice, and he was worried that he was making it up, but when he heard her say that Kip was going to turn her into one of the Lobos, Cole panicked and began running even harder. He could feel Cole's pads cracking from how hard he was pushing off the ground. A jolting pain sent Cole flying forward, his face planting into the ground and smashing forward. Images flashed through their mind. An all-white hospital room and a man he recognized; his stomach turned seeing Asher. Then, a hallway leads down to a dark stairwell. An all gray hall with haunting rooms that showed horrors. He saw an image of a Lobo holding a red wolf in his mouth. Then, he was shoved into a small hospital room. Kip laughed crazily in front of him as he was shoved into a chair. He was overwhelmed with emotions. Fear, panic, rage, anger, disgust. He then realized these were images from Nora. She was sending him.

"Alpha?" Dante's voice came to him as Noah helped Cole up.

Lilliana flanked Noah's side, going to help Jace as well. She was just as fast as Noah, and it surprised him how fast she was and how she was able to maintain that speed. Once Cole was up on his feet. Noah rubbed his face across Lilliana's, waiting for Cole to signal to go again.

" Nora is in trouble. I know where she is." Jace replied back as Cole shook off the dirt.

Nodded to Noah and took off again.

"We were almost there, Nora." Jace replied back like he would a normal mind link, hoping it made its way to her.

"Matt slowly starts moving out; from what I've just seen, we are going to need everyone. Make sure the hunters know this might be life or death for them." Jace mind linked.

Matt's eyes glossed over as Jace's message came through. Logan saw the look and was starting to realize that's how they communicated. He stood up straight, his stomach twisted, waiting for Matt to come back and tell them what was going on. He saw Lilly shift uncomfortably. Even though Matt was being mindlink, he felt Lilly's discomfort, and he reached down and grabbed hold of her hand. Logan waited for Lilly to rip her hand away or to smack him, but she didn't. She just held on to it back. He made a face confused as he looked back, waiting on Matt. Matt came back to them, and he frowned.

"Jace needs us to move out; he says it's worse than what we thought. We need to move now. He also wanted to make sure you hunters understood that this might be a life or death thing for you." Matt said quietly, his eyes flickering to Lilly.

There is a mixture of emotion in them as he waits for their response. He wanted to tell Lilly to go and make sure she was ok. He could already tell from her personality she wasn't going anywhere. Logan looked over at his group.

"It won't be held against you if you do not want to come." Logan announced to them.

"Let's do this." Lilly said as she unknowingly squeezed Matt's hand.

"You stay by me." Matt said, leaning his head down towards her and whispering into her ear.

Lilly made a face and then, as if she realized she was standing a little too close to Matt and holding his hand. She dropped it and stepped out. Matt grumbled at her.

"Listen, wolf, I got this." Lilly said to him.

"You keep up that tough girl act, Love. It suits you." Matt winked at her, stepping closer to her with a smile on his face.

"Ok, if you're coming, we'll move out now." Logan said but then realized that Matt was going to shift and be a wolf running; there was no way they were going to keep up.

"Don't worry, hunter. I got you covered." Matt smirked.

He nodded to the back as three ATV's came through the trees. The young man on them stepped off and nodded to Matt before shifting into their wolves and heading back into the woods. Jace had most of the pack on the move, but he kept a number of them back home just in case Kip had other plans. Jace also had Zeke monitoring Jace's pack from his home. If anything happened Zeke would send men to Jace's pack house.

"Hope on and follow me." Matt nodded to the ATV's.

Logan tapped Lilly, and they moved to one; Mina and Drake got on the other, and Lastly, Kat and Phill on the last ATV. Lilly sat next to her brother, watching Matt. Within seconds, loud bone snapping sounds were heard. Lilly watched in shock as Matt turned into his wolf. She had never seen a wolf shift before, and it looked painful. Ryker nodded to them as if to say this way before bolting into the woods. The ATV'S revved up and followed after Ryker.

Chapter Seventy Six
Hold on

"We're almost there; hold on, Nora." Jace's voice whispered into her mind.

She didn't know if she had made it up, but something in her told her it was real. She needed to stall him from trying to turn her.

"Why kill a whole family?" Nora said, angry.

"Why not?" Kip shrugged.

"So you like killing?" She said, trying to move out of her straps.

"Like isn't the right word. Love isn't even the right word. I crave it. Humans are easy prey. They are worthless, and honestly, they do nothing for this world. They are weak and bottom feeders. Hunters, now hunters. They are fun to kill. They fight, and they fight hard. It's actually a challenge to fight them. It's exhilarating. Do you know how runs get a runner high? It's like that; it's like an addiction," Kip said as he stopped what he was doing to explain.

"How many hunters have you killed?" Nora asked.

She finally got the strap that was lying across her loose; she could easily slip out of it now.

"I thought I had gotten them all. Thanks to you, maybe you're the last." Kip laughed.

Kip didn't know about Logan and his members. Nora noted it. She wondered how long he was tracking and killing them just for the fun of it.

"So you're just an out-of-control maniac." Nora said.

"It was nothing special. Maybe..do you know, your parents didn't even see it coming for hunters. Their faces stuck on the screen in front of them. They didn't even taste like hunters. Hunter's blood is sweeter. Maybe you were adopted." Kip snickered.

"I promise I will see you die." Nora growled at him.

"Oh, such big scary words." Kip laughed.

The door opened, and Asher stepped in. Nora's eyes looked at him, and she saw regret. She could see him flexing his jaw as he stepped into the room.

"All the nurses are occupied, so I need your help. There's no blood in here, so I need you to take some out of me and put it into this vial. It's going to be even more satisfying that it's my blood that turns you." Kip laughed.

Asher tied a tourniquet around Kip's upper arm. He felt his skin, looking for a vein. Finding it, he took the needle off the shelf and inserted it into his arm. He pulled back on the syringe, and Kip's blood began pouring into it. After getting enough blood to fill the vial, Asher released the tourniquet and inserted the needle into the vial, letting Kip's blood into the vial. Asher handed the vial back to Kip, waiting for instructions.

"Now all we need to do is have you be a good girl and drink this. Then I'll bite you, and you'll become a masterpiece." Kip smiled, took the vial, and began walking to Nora.

Reaching Nora, he shoved her head back against the chair, the other hand going to her jaw as he tried to pry it open. Asher resisted the urge to pull Kip off of her.

"Asher, come help me." Kip demanded.

Asher didn't move; he didn't want to. He was done with this all. He didn't realize how hard he was breathing, trying to fight the urge to help his Alpa.

"Asher now! I command you to come hold this girl's head now." Kip said, using his Alpha status on him.

As if he was a robot, Asher begrudgingly walked towards Nora. With one hand, he pressed her forward head back into the chair, holding it in place while she struggled. Asher's eyes said how sorry he was. Alarms went off. Just as Kip was about to force the vial of blood into Nora's mouth, his head whipped upwards towards the sound. Asher was still holding her head in place as he was commanded to, but the other hand went to the strap holding her in place. It was loose, and she could, with some struggling, get through, but Asher wanted her out now. He exposed his claws and sliced through the strap. Kip was too busy focusing on the commotion. "Asher, go see what's going on," Kip ordered him; he smiled relieved as he stepped away from Nora.

As he stepped back away from Nora, she took her chance; she slipped the key down into her hand from her wrist and undid the cuff. Kip was trying to figure out what was going on. Nora quickly got off the chair and stepped towards Kip as the handcuffs slipped off her wrist. She reached forward, clamping them down onto Kip's wrist. The wolfbane burned his skin as the cuff touched his wrist. Kip let out a yell and flung his arm back. His hand whacked Nora in the chest. She was flung back. Kip grabbed a hold of his wrist, letting out a small yell. His eyes narrowed at Nora.

"Give me the key!" Kip growled, his eyes glowing red as he cornered her.

"No." She said, stepping back.

"Give it to me, or I'll finish what I started with you." Kip said, motioning to her neck.

Nora looked at him, daring him with her eyes. He stepped towards her, his eyes glowing. Her body vibrated now, knowing that danger was coming. She felt the energy being built up, and she waited for her moment. Kip reached out to grab her, and she sent out the jolt. As his hand touched her skin, it shocked him, throwing him backwards. As he hit the counter, Nora ran for the door. Kip was up in no time, shaky but moving towards her. She threw the key to the back corner of the room. Kip changed directions, going after the key. Nora rushed out into the hallway, running for the white door. She knew she had to take that one to go upstairs. She raced for it, and a loud growl echoed behind her as she reached the door. Yanking the door back, she ran into the stairwell. The loud growls echoed behind her.

"Asher, she got away, stop her, and hold her for me." Kip mind linked Asher.

Asher had made it to the white floor and was standing at the control center, trying to see why the alarms were going off. He saw it. The large black demon wolf ran towards the pack house. He knew it was Jace. The large, smoke-gray wolf at his side was his beta. Asher smiled; he prayed they made it. The noise down the hall caught his ear. Nora came sliding into the white floor. She saw Asher and ran towards him. He made a face; the girl was running right into her enemy. The command to stop her and hold her echoed through him. He fought hard against it. Nora stopped at the control center, glancing at the camera.

"Cole." She whispered, seeing her wolf.

"Nora, there is a stainless steel door at the end of this hall. The code is 1493. Remember 1493. I have to stop you and hold you. I'm fighting, so do something quickly." Asher said.

She could see him shaking.

"So stop me and hold me, and let me go. He didn't say "keep me." Nora said with a wink.

Asher smirked as he grabbed a hold of her and squeezed her to his chest.

"If you can stop him, this pack will follow you. No one wants him here, but he has too much over us. Stop him." Asher said to her.

Kip barreled through the door to the white room. He chuckled, seeing Asher holding Nora. He hurried towards them.

"You thought you could get away that easily. This is my pack, this is my home." Kip yelled.

"Go." Asher whispered as he squeezed her tightly.

Nora looked confused as she stepped back; Asher looked to Kip and let her go. Nora stepped out of his grasp, confused as to what he was doing.

"Go." Asher repeated to her; this time, his eyes glowed amber as his wolf pushed forward.

Nora was confused by the color but looked to the end of the hall. She squeezed his arm before she started to hurry down the hall.

"Asher, I command you to stop her!" Kip shrieked, seeing him let her go

"No." Asher said, squaring off with him.

"Do you have a death wish?" Kip growled; he then saw the glow in Asher's eyes.

"Did you renounce me as Alpha." Kip growled.

Asher didn't say anything but remained silent and blocked Kip's way to Nora. Kip smirked as he hit something on his wrist. The doors to the white room opened, and out stepped newly turned Lobos. Nora glanced over her shoulder in a panic. Asher couldn't take on all three of them, Kip and the two Lobos. Asher didn't flinch; he stood resilient, waiting. Asher was acting beta; as he stood there waiting for his death, he sent out a mindlink to his pack members. If Kip has not commanded you to fight, stand down and let Jace and his pack pass through. It ends tonight. This is our way out.

"Bring him to me," Kip said to the Lobo, who bowed their heads and followed his command.

Nora turned back around; Asher needed help. She couldn't let him die. She watched him start to fight them; they were slashing at him. Their claws ripped through his skin. She watched him try to fight. He would fight one of them off, but the other would attack, causing him to falter. Asher crashed to his knees. The Lobo raised its deadly claws above his head, waiting for Kip to signal.

"Stop!" Nora screamed, reaching the control center.

Kip held up his hand, and the Lobos just held Asher there. He was covered in blood. Nora didn't know if he had a spot on him that was not bleeding.

"Come here then." Kip smirked. "No." Nora said, fighting herself.

"Kill him." Kip said with a shrug.

"No!" Nora yelled.

"Come here and drink this, and we won't kill him." Kip said like it was the easiest thing to do.

"Let him go, and I will." Nora said, stepping towards them.

"Fine." Kip sighed, rolling his eyes.

Nora walked slowly towards them, her eyes watching the Lobos carefully. She stopped short in front of them. She watched Kip jingle the bottle out in front of him.

"I want these things away from him, and I want him in a safe spot." Nora said, her eyes glancing back at the door to the exit, debating if she needed to run or if she could make it.

Kip let out a long sigh; he glanced at one of the Lobo's.

"Take him somewhere safe. He's probably just gonna bleed out anyways." Kip shrugged as the Lobo picked up Asher and began walking to the stairwell.

"All right, I kept my end of the deal, drinky drinky." Kip smiled, holding out the vial.

Nora walked the rest of the way to Kip, her eyes on the Lobo that had Asher. She took the vial in her hand.

"Drink it, or I'll order it to kill him." Kip whispered.

Nora shut her eyes, letting a small breath out as she brought the vial to her lips. She watched Kip motion for the Lobo to stop to make sure she drank it. Nora shut her eyes and tried to numb her taste buds as she poured the blood into her mouth. She made a gagging noise as it hit the back of her mouth. The warm iron liquid rushed down her throat. She made a face as she showed Kip the empty bottle. Kip nodded to the Lobo, who pushed open the stairway door and chucked Asher down it.

"No!" Nora yelled, slamming her fist into Kip's chest.

"What? He's safe." Kip grinned.

"Now, let's go find your mate." Kip grinned as he motioned for the Lobo to grab her.

Chapter Seventy Seven
Almost There

Kip walked past the control center glancing at the monitors. He growled angrily, grabbing a hold of the desk and squeezing. The desk began to crack underneath his hands. He watched Jace's pack run past members of his. They kneeled down and bowed their heads as they ran past. No one was showing resistance. He growled loudly, beginning to huff and puff at the monitors. His eyes glowed red as he continued to glare at the monitors. His eyes glossed over as he attempted to command them.

"As your Alpha I command all pack members to stop the intruders now." He sent out a painful mind link.

Nora watched as the pack members of Kip's began to shake and shiver as they tried to resist the commands. She could tell they were in pain. Then suddenly it started from the left side, a calming reaction took over. The pack members began to relax and the painful shaking was gone. She watched Kip brace himself against the control panel as he looked like he was in pain. She was confused at how the pain was being transferred. As the pack members stood up from their positions she thought she saw their eyes glow amber as they began to walk out. They didn't want anything to do with what had been happening. They were no longer allied with Kip.

"They are breaking their bond with me." Kip groaned painfully.

Nora looked back at the screens, the pack members looked like they were relieved and free. She smiled looking down. She watched Kip straighten up, she wondered what he could possibly do now. He was a packless Alpha. He had no one to fight for him and nothing to back him up.

"Fine! They want to play that way. Then we will play. No mercy." He growled and slammed his fist into a bright red button on the table.

As his fist hit the button a siren went off in the building and a red light began to flash. Nora went to back up but couldn't move because the Lobo had one of its large paws pressed down into her shoulder.

"What did you do?" Nora asked as she looked around.

Then she heard it. The echoing of all the hospital rooms doors opening. The strange sliding clicking noise echoed louder than the sirens. She looked at him like he was crazy. They began to pile out of the rooms, the white floor were ones just turned or worse, still half human, half monster. The gray floor was all completely turned and ready to kill Lobos. Did he have more than just the two wings? What if she didn't know the whole extent of how many there were? Nora thought, panicking.

"Kill them all." Kip said into the intercom.

The Lobos seemed to nod and began to make their way to the exit. Nora watched horrified. She needed to warn them, they were running blindly to the pack house and they would be here any minute running into a swarm of Lobos. She shut her eyes and prayed that the mindlink she was hearing in her head was real and not something she was making up.

"Jace you're headed straight for a swarm of Lobos. "Nora sent out, she repeated it over and over again in her mind hoping he would hear it.

She thought of each member of his pack, Dante, Matt, Wyatt and even Logan. She didn't know if she could send it to any of them but if there was a chance she tried. She thought of the image of all the Lobo's piling out of their rooms and hoped they could see it.

Kip grabbed her by the back of the neck and forced her up to the monitors.

"First, we are going to watch them slaughter a few of them, and then we will go into the battlefield. Then I will turn you in front of Jace and let him watch helplessly as you do. Then I will laugh as you shred him to pieces." Kip said, forcing Nora's face closer to the monitors.

Cole braced himself as he heard Nora's voice. He was prepared for anything weird this time. An image flashed through his mind like a memory. He watched Kip hit a red button and Lobos began pouring out of the hospital rooms. He knew that they were located beneath the pack house.

"You're headed straight for a swarm of Lobos." *Nora's voice echoed into his head.*

Noah, running on the side of his legs, buckled beneath him and rolled into the ground.

" Dante?" Jace's mind linked him as Cole slowed down to see what was wrong.

"I swore I heard Nora, and then I started seeing things." Dante's mind linked back as Lilliana helped Noah up.

"I don't know what is going on but I've heard her twice. I think we're heading straight for a large number of those monsters. We need to check and see where Wyatt is in making his progress with Grayson. Wyatt update.' Jace's mind linked him.

"We are almost through the tunnel to the pack house, Alpha are you ok? Can Nora mindlink? I just heard her and then saw hundreds of those monsters coming out of the pack house?" Wyatt mind link back.

"Alpha?" Matt's voice chimed in his head.

Jace was shocked, Nora somehow sent out a warning to everyone she thought she could reach.

"I don't know if she can mindlink but she found a way to reach us. Dante and I are headed straight for them. We need to continue forward to not throw Kip off but we need Wyatt and Matt to get your teams here quickly. I don't know how many of these things there are." Jace said mindlink all three of them.

"We're close, Alpha ten minutes out. We had a delay. Logan almost crashed, Nora somehow messaged him." Matt responded.

"We are about to enter the pack house basement." Wyatt said.

"We will figure out what's going on with Nora after we have her back. We will continue forward. The pack house is in our sights." Jace's mind linked them all.

Wyatt shifted from his wolf form into human form as he reached the door in the tunnel it was made out of steel. He turned the handle part of him afraid it was locked. The goddess was on their side as the door handle turned and Wyatt pushed the door open. He stared into a gray hallway. Stepping inside he noticed several doors to rooms left wide opened.

"Be careful and be ready for anything." Wyatt whispered to the wolves behind him as they followed him in.

They walked by several hospital rooms that were left wide open. Blood seemed to cover the floor in each room. He paused seeing a nurse on the floor covered in blood. He knew he was too late but the nurse in him wanted to double check, wanted to make sure. He told himself no.

"We are in." Wyatt sent to Jace as he shifted back into Everette.

"See you soon." Jace sent back. As the mindlink finished, Lobos began to pile out of the pack house through the front door.

A garage door rolled up, exposing more. They stepped out onto the lawn of the pack house, forming a line. They towered over them and formed a line of attack. They were waiting, but Jace didn't know what they were waiting for. Jace felt the tension of his pack. They were afraid they didn't know what was going to happen. Jace shut his eyes, trying to block their fear from entering him. He thought about Nora, and Cole stepped forward. Noah let out a howl and moved next to him. Lillianna did the same, matching their howl.

Soon, a howl went up around them, and the rest of the pack moved forward.

"Oh, how touching." Kip chuckled while watching it.

Nora watched as the howl seemed to unite them more and give them strength they needed to stand against the Lobos. Nora smiled and glanced at Kip.

"I think you should be afraid." Nora said, taunting him.

"I think you should shut up." Kip growled.

"Let's see what happens when they are all out there." Kip growled, hitting the button a second time, and the sound of more doors opening echoed.

"Attack!" Kip yelled, and as if he had some magic button,

Nora watched on the screen as Lobo charged Jace and his pack. Nora moved toward the screen, and the Lobo holding her pulled her back. She struggled to shake his arm off of her. Kip nodded, letting Lobo know to let her go. She rushed to the screen, watching fearfully. The wolves ran at the Lobos, who were also in full force, racing to get to Jace's pack. They collided, and Nora flinched, trying to find the wolves she knew.

Chapter Seventy Eight
Battle

Cole collided into one of the Lobo using his body to take out his legs. They stood tall like people on their back legs. The Lobo fell over, Cole jumped on its throat trying to end it quickly. To his left he saw Noah doing battle with another one. A whimper echoed around them and he saw Noah become distracted. A Lobo flung Lilliana into a tree. The Lobo Noah was fighting went to chomp down on his throat. Cole lunged at the Lobo he was attacking and hit the Lobo going after Noah. The Lobo fell off to the side on impact as Cole saved Noah. Noah watched Cole tackle the Lobo, his eyes flickering to Lilliana who still hasn't gotten up off the ground and the Lobo who threw her was approaching her. Cole nodded to Noah telling him to go. Noah nodded back and rushed to Lilliana, skidding in front of her he stared the Lobo down growling showing his teeth. The Lobo smiled before starting to run at him. Lilliana got to her feet and stood next to Noah waiting for the attack. Two more Lobo joined the one running at them. Noah stepped forward more to block what he could from Lilliana. Noah stood hackles up ready. The first Lobo slammed into Noah; Lilliana lunged at it as it did, going for its throat. Her eyes watched the two that were fast approaching. She didn't know how she was going to fight all of them all at once; it took two wolves to bring down one.

She watched Cole going through the crowd, taking down who he could. Lobos and wolves scattered about the ground. She realized there were more wolves injured than Lobos. She sank her teeth into the Lobo's neck, ripping and tugging, trying to kill it as it slashed and clawed at Noah. A loud noise like a car came zooming from the left. Sarah's eyes flickered to the noise seeing the hunters lead by a dark red brown wolf enter. She watched a girl with blond hair stand tall on the ATV and as the driver slid the ATV to the side to take out the two Lobo's running at them The girl pulled out daggers and flipped off of it. She landed neatly on one of the Lobo's neck wrapping her legs around its throat, squeezing as she slammed her daggers over and over into it. The Lobo crashed to its knees, blood spraying everywhere as she continued to stab it. The blond male got off the ATV pulling a crossbow out from his back. He stepped on the third Lobo who was flapping on the ground beneath the ATV. He pulled out an arrow and plunged it into it's heart.

The thing let out a loud growl as he pushed downward and through it. The Lobo faded out. He ripped the arrow out of it and then fired it into the Lobo's shoulder that was fighting Liliana and Noah. As the arrow pierced its shoulder the Lobo let out a loud scream. The skin around the arrow turned black.

"They are just like regular wolves. Wolfbane affects them." Logan shouted to the others.

The hunters nodded, took out their weapons, and headed into the crowd. Logan watched Matt flank

Lilly's side, and the two of them began taking down another Lobo. His eyes scanned the battlefield, reloading his crossbow. He watched Cole taking down a Lobo by himself. He was the only one doing battle on his own. The rest had paired up, taking down one or two wolves at a time. Logan aimed his arrow at a Lobo approaching Cole from behind. Firing it, it sailed towards the Lobo.

On the way across the battlefield, the arrow sliced through another Lobo's arm. The Lobo grasped its arm and yelled. It crossed the way and plunged into the one trying to sneak up on Cole. It hit the ground as the wolfbane spread over its skin. The arrow pierces its heart, and the poison enters its bloodstream. Cole ripped the throat out of the Lobo and then turned to see the dead one behind him. Cole's eyes looked from the dead Lobo to the arrow and traced it back to Logan. He nodded to Logan before moving onto the next Lobo.

"Hunters!" Kip screamed, slamming his fist into the control desk.

Nora smirked, seeing his reaction. He thought he had killed all of her kind; he knew nothing about the ones left.

"He's working with hunters!!" Kip screamed, his eyes flickering to Nora.

She smiled at him, and his anger grew. He stepped to her, grabbed her by the hair, and wrapped it around his hand. He slammed her face into the desk. Her brow bone took the impact. She felt her skin split, and blood began to leak out of it. He pulled her back up, and she laughed in his face.

"Did you really think you got rid of all of them?" Nora laughed in his face.

He wanted to hit her again, but something caught his eye on the camera. Moving up through the stairwell were more wolves. He growled, yanking on her hair. They wouldn't be able to take on the coming wolves. He pulled her forward by her hair, yanking her down the hall. Nora grabbed a hold of her hair, trying to fight back. Kip looked at one of the Lobos and motioned for her to pick her up. The Lobo flung her up over its back. They reached the steel door, and Kip punched the code in.

As the steel door opened, Wyatt's wolf, Everett, skidded onto the white floor. He locked eyes with Nora as the Lobo as it began to carry her out of the floor.

"1493!" She yelled as the door slammed between them.

"Fucking Asher." Kip growled as they began to climb the stairs; he knew Asher was the one to give her the code.

Jace, he's moving her up to the main part of the pack house; he's got two Lobos with him." Wyatt *mind linked with Jace as Everett stopped short in front of the steel door.*

He shifted from his wolf form into a human as the rest of the pack piled up in the hall.

"I have not seen Chadwick Grayson; search the cameras. There's also a weird door towards this side that isn't open yet. Grayson's packs stay with him. The rest of you are with me." Wyatt yelled as he punched in 1493 into the keypad.

Cole's eyes flickered to the pack house, hearing Wyatt's mindlink. He needed to get there. He could feel Cole's strength starting to fade. He thought of Nora, and it pushed him forward. Logan was suddenly by his side.

"Let's do this, wolf." Logan said, seeing Cole was the only one without a teammate, Cole huffed at him, but they began to advance towards the house together.

Logan's wolfbane stained arrows were the thing making the kills go faster. A Lobo came up behind Logan, sinking its teeth into his forearm. He let out a yell as he slammed an arrow into its head. Cole grabbed hold of its throat, and as the arrow stabbed him and the Lobo let go, he pulled it away from Logan. Blood poured down Logan's arm; Cole looked at his arm with concern. Logan shook his head and motioned for Cole to keep going. A Lobo came up behind Cole.

"Jace!" Logan yelled, going to fire an arrow, but the Lobo sank its teeth into Cole's back, picking him up as he did.

Cole's body was blocking his shot. Ryker raced towards them, seeing Cole in trouble. Lilly ran alongside them. Lilly jumped up, lunging her daggers into its back, Ryker sinking its teeth into the Lobo's leg at the same time. The Lobo yelled, letting Cole's body drop out of its mouth. The Lobo kicked Ryker away, his body skidding into a tree. It began thrashing around, trying to get Lilly off of it.

"Logan!" Lilly yelled, needing him to fire.

"I can't! It won't hold still, I could hit you!" He yelled angrily.

Cole got up off the ground and lunged at it's leg. He locked his jaws around his calf, keeping it in place. Logan released the arrow, and it impaled the Lobo's heart. Lilly flipped off the back of it, landing on her feet on the ground. She looked around for Ryker. She went to his side to make sure he was okay. Kneeling next to him, Ryker whimpered slightly when she touched his ribs.

"Come on, wolf, I need you to get up and be okay." Lilly said to him as she ran her fingers through his fur.

Ryker got up slowly, some of his ribs broken. He nodded to Lilly and rubbed against her hand, telling her to let go. Their eyes flickered over to Logan and Cole. Cole was in bad shape; he was limping and looked drained. There were still so many Lobos left. Their eyes scanned the battlefield. Noah and Lilliana were still going strong, but most of the pack looked wiped out. Drake and Mina were fighting side by side, taking on a Lobo. Lilly's eyes found Kat and Phill. They were ruthless, hacking one to pieces. Lilly looked down at her red-brown wolf.

"This has to end soon. I don't know how much more your friends got in them." Lilly said, running her hand down his snout.

Cole approached another Lobo, teeth showing as he growled. Logan was guarding his side as they walked towards it together. Logan looked down at Cole and the blood spilling out of his wounds.

"Jace, we need to come up with a better strategy for you, and you just keep attacking. This method is going to kill you." Logan whispered down to him as they waited for the Lobo to approach them.

Cole snarled at him in response as he dropped lower to the ground; the Lobo would have to lean over to get him before it could attack him. Just as the Lobo approached him, the pack house's front door slammed open. Kip stepped out, and as if a silent command was given, the Lobos shifted back.

"Jace! Look what I have!" He laughed hysterically as he had the Lobo toss Nora on the ground.

Chapter Seventy Nine
Enough

Cole went into overdrive seeing Nora and began trying to push through the Lobos. He was fierce, growling, snapping, and biting, trying to get through. The pause didn't last long; as soon as Cole lost it, the pack picked up his anger and went into a fierce attack mode. Logan began firing arrows into the Lobos that were blocking Cole's way. Kip was grinning, watching as if he had something manically waiting for him. The Lobos were falling over from the wolf's bane. Cole was getting close. Nora watched her friends fighting. She locked eyes with Cole; he was so injured that his black fur looked wet from the blood coming from his wounds. Her heart ached to see his pain. She felt a Lobo come up and grab her shoulders, forcing her to her knees. She could feel her power building; she needed this to stop. She needed to save her friends. She watched a Lobo pin down Noah; he didn't do anything, just restrained him. Another snatched up to Ryker, holding him in the air but not doing anything. Ryker fought hard, clawing and biting the Lobo, but nothing worked. Something was about to happen; she could feel her body vibrating, her skin crawling, and her mind shouting danger. She started freaking out what was going to happen, how could she stop it.

Cole was still struggling to get through. Logan was firing arrow after arrow, trying to make a passage for Cole. A Lobo reached down and wrapped his arms around Logan. She heard Kip's laughter as it got close behind her. She could feel him hovering. She went to move, but the Lobo held her in place.

"Move, let him have a good view." Kip yelled as he grabbed a hold of Nora's hair.

He yanked her head to the side; she could feel his mouth hovering over her neck. She panicked that he was going to bite her. She heard Cole fight, and his growl became louder and angry. It sounded like a demon was coming towards them. The pain that echoed in Cole's growl shook her to the core. She felt Kip was ready himself. Where are you? Nora thought, wanting to send him flying backwards away from her, but her powers were not working. She felt him come towards her; this was it she was going to be bitten and then turned. She was angry that he was going to bite her in the spot Jace would mark her. If she couldn't stop him from biting her, she was not going to let him take what should have been Jace's. She threw her arm up at the last minute and felt his fangs pierce her forearm.

Nora let out a loud scream as she felt her skin be punctured. Blood poured down her arm. She heard Kip growl,seeing he had missed her, but he still had bitten her. He shrugged his eyes, looking at Cole. In his panic, Cole tripped, hitting the ground. The wolf skeeted forward, and as he landed feet from Nora, he shifted back into Jace. His body is not strong enough to stay in wolf form. A Lobo stepped forward, reaching down and grabbing him with his long claws. The Lobo pulled him up to his knees.

"I am going to fucking kill you!!" Jace screamed, his eyes locking with Nora, pain, and rage flashing in them.

"I don't think so. She's going to kill you." Kip laughed.

She watched the blood flow down her arm, and her eyes rolled back into her skull. She crashed into Kip.

"Oh look, she fainted." Kip chuckled, holding her to his chest and looking at Jace.

"You know it's too bad she is so very pretty." Kip said, touching her cheek.

"Touch her again!" Jace yelled, lunging forward, trying to get to Kip.

Nora. Nora, you must act quickly. The darkness called to her. You can stop this. You can drain energy for others to use and make yourself strong enough. Make your power strong enough. Nora's eyes shot open, her body registering what was happening.

Jace went to lunge forward again, but the Lobo pulled him back, its long claws slicing through the skin of his shoulder.

Nora felt a change starting to happen in her. She would not become one of them. She would not kill Jace or hurt her friends. She was not going to allow herself to do this. Her eyes scanned the crowd, seeing each one of them in danger. Ryker shifted back to Matt, allowing himself to get away. He raced forward towards the Lobo holding Jace. Jumping on its back, he locked his arms around its throat, trying to get Jace free. Another Lobo came up behind Matt, its jaws widening as he aimed for Matt's throat. He was going to kill Matt. Nora's heart jumped as her mind screamed no! They were all going to die because of her.

Nora, you can steal others' energy and use it. The voice seemed to whisper in her ear again.

She didn't know how she knew what to do, but she reached back and grabbed ahold of Kip's face. She focused everything she had; she could feel herself drawing off of Kip.

"Stop! What are you doing?" Kip yelled as he felt himself become weaker.

She didn't stop; she drained him, using it to feed the growing force inside of her. Nora's eyes began to glow amber as she looked out over her friends. The world turned into slow motion, allowing her the time she needed to save them. She shut her eyes, her body vibrating, and she imagined all the Lobos in the positions they were. She thought of Kip and his placement. This was enough! She let the feeling build and build until she felt like she was going to explode within herself, and then she released it. A wave of energy was shot out around her. Kip was thrown back away from her. The two Lobos on either side of her crashed to the ground, shaking. The Lobos on the battlefield began dropping, each one simply falling over dead. Nora watched a smile forming on her face as she saw her friends safe. Her eyes locked with Jace before she collapsed forward on the ground.

"No!" Jace yelled, rushing forward.

He collapsed on his knees in front of her, pulling her into him.

"Nora. Nora. Open your eyes." Jace said, his eyes glowing ice blue as Cole pushed forward.

Logan rushed up next to Jace; he, too, fell to the side of her. He looked at her. He was confused about what just happened. She had no wounds. Why was she hurt? He knew that it was because of her the Lobos died, but he didn't understand. He watched a bloody, bruised, and beaten Jace. Who was normally calm and collected, started to lose it as he saw Nora not responding. The door behind them opened up as Wyatt, and that section of the pack rushed out.

"Nora!" Jace shouted at her; if she had just waited a few minutes longer, backup would have been there.

"Jace, stop being so grumpy." Nora smiled, but she was so weak.

"Damn it, Nora, you should have waited." Jace said, pressing his forehead to hers.

"I couldn't. You all would have died." Nora said, her voice starting to fade.

"Don't you dare! Don't you dare fucking leave me!" Jace tried commanding her.

"You wolves always think you can command everything." Nora said, her eyes still shut.

She brushed his cheek lightly with her fingertips. Nora felt her body wanting to drain energy from Jace, but she wouldn't let it. She knew he was covered in wounds. She would kill him if she did. She touched his lips one last time with the tips of her fingertips. Her hand fell away from Jace, hitting the ground.

"Wyatt!" Jace screamed as he wrapped Nora tighter in his arms.

Wyatt nearly crashed into Logan as he reached them. He grabbed her hand, checking her pulse. No pulse.

"Jace, lay her flat now!" Wyatt yelled at Jace for the first time ever.

Jace placed her flat on her back. Wyatt began pressing on her chest, starting CPR. Logan stepped back, wanting to help but not knowing what to do.

"Breathe into her mouth." Wyatt orders Jace.

Jace opened her mouth, clamped off her nose, and blew into her mouth. He watched her chest rise; he gave another breath. Again, her chest raised and fell. Wyatt started doing chest compression again. Jace watched Wyatt press on her chest. Nora is not responding; her body is moving just because of the pressure.

"Come on, Nora." Jace whispered, touching her cheek, waiting for Wyatt to tell him to give another breath.

After several rounds of CPR, Wyatt glanced at Jace, sadness, and heartbreak on his face as he shook his head. Her heart had stopped, and nothing they were doing was pulling her back.

"No, Wyatt." Jace growled.

"Jace, she's been too long without a heartbeat or oxygen. I can't -" Wyatt tried to explain but Logan pushed Wyatt aside and began compressions.

Wyatt let him as he watched Jace. This was breaking him. He watches him look frantically over Nora. He needed to do something. She needed to come back to him. She was not leaving him. He looked to her neck, where he would have marked her. She had wanted him to. He could feel his chest collapsing inward. He placed a hand on Logan's arm, telling him to stop. Logan stepped back, unsure of what Jace was planning. Jace pulled her into his lap, cradling her. He brushed her soft jet-black hair aside and brought his mouth to her neck. His fangs emerged, and he bit down, marking her.

Chapter Eighty
Choose

It was warm, the kind of warmth that you want to curl up into. It was like the warmth from the sun as it kissed your skin. Nora opened her eyes. The world around her was golden. She stood up, looking around. She accepted the normal lost in the dark setting, but this was different.

"Nora." The same voice as always spoke to her.

"Hello?" Nora asked, turning around.

"You did it. You saved your friends and your mate." The voice said.

A shimmering, sparkling light foamed in the distance as a being emerged from it. A woman with the softest-looking silver hair stepped out from it. Her eyes glowed like embers from a fire. She walked like she was floating in the air.

"Who are you?" Nora whispered.

"I have many names and many things, but what you need to decide now is who you are?" The woman said.

"Who am I?" Nora asked, confused.

"Yes, Nora. Are you a hunter or wolf?" The voice said with a smile.

"Wolf?" Nora reacted, confused.

A sharp pain hit her neck, it sent chills throughout her body and caused her to fall to her knees.

She touched her neck and could feel a raised mark foaming. The woman smiled as she watched Nora touch the mark.

"Your Mate is trying to save you. That was actually quite clever." The woman smiled.

"What do you mean, wolf?" Nora said, ignoring the rush of pleasure she got from the mark.

The woman stepped to the side, and an almost gold-colored wolf stepped out behind her. The wolf rushed to Nora as if it had been waiting for her. The wolf's eyes matched Nora's. They were the color of the purest golden honey. Nora touched her fur and felt a spark. Something triggered deep within herself, and she felt like this wolf was part of her.

"Nora, this is Zara. She was buried so deep in your mind that even I couldn't reach her." the woman explained.

"Your family were once wolves cursed to become hunters. Each hunter from your bloodline wolves was locked away only until you. You broke the curse. You saw past the hate and were able to control the rage. The nagging pain that wanted you to kill your mate. You made the ultimate sacrifice to save both hunters and wolves. You are the bridge to both worlds. Now you must choose what world you stay in." The woman continued.

Nora petted Zara as she listened. Choose. The word echoed in her head. How can she choose?

She was just discovering she was a wolf but felt so strongly connected to Zara like she was her missing piece. Choose wolf? She thought about how she felt being a hunter with every part of herself. She found herself being a hunter. She clenched her jaw, debating. She couldn't.

"I can't." Nora whispered.

"Excuse me?" The woman asked.

"I can't choose," Nora said, looking from Zara to the woman.

"Explain." The woman asked, intrigued.

"I am just as much a hunter as I am a wolf. I found myself as a hunter. It saved my life. I was about to go off the deep end after my family was killed, but being a hunter saved me. It called to me and everything about it; I felt it deep within myself. But I am not just a hunter; Zara is my missing piece. I can't explain it, but seeing her. She is me. I can't choose." Nora said quietly.

"You are truly remarkable." The woman said as she seemed to debate with herself.

Nora watched her as she seemed to be trying to work things out. Zara pushed into her side, leaning against her. She smiled down at the wolf. She was like a big dog. She chuckled, petting her.

"Oh, alright. Come with me." The woman said as she turned, going towards the shimmer she came out.

"With you?" Nora asked, confused.

"Yes, Dear." The woman said, shaking her head at the question.

Nora hesitated but followed her. She watched the woman disappear to the shimmer. She reached out slowly with her hand touching it. Trying to see if it was dangerous. She paused. Zara huffed at her as she brushed against her, walking into the shimmer as well. Nora made a face at the wolf before following her. Nora crossed through the shimmer. A rush of warmth hit her, sending another shiver through her. A blinding light made her shield her eyes as she came out the other side.

As the light faded, she found the woman sitting on the ledge of a fountain. She was looking down into it. She had a small frown on her face. She was studying the water. Every so often, she would reach in and push the water side to side. Her brows would frown, and she would sigh. Nora was curious and wandered over to the fountain. She looked into it over her shoulder, and besides seeing the water glow different colors, she didn't see anything.

"What are you looking at?" Nora asked, sitting next to her.

"These are the waters of fate. I am creating one I like." She smiled, her smile was playful but proud, as she stuck her hand downward into the fountain again and swirled it around once more.

Nora watched the water swirl colors of dark blue, turquoise, and a shimmer of gold. The woman smiled happily and then glanced at Nora. She nodded to her like she had accomplished what she wanted. She motioned Nora to lean towards her. Nora did and waited to see what she would do next. The woman placed her hands on each side of Nora's head and placed her forehead against her.

"Nora, my little hunter, my child of the moon, I bless you." She said as she closed her eyes.

She pulled her forehead away from hers and placed a kiss on it. Nora looked at her, confused.

"You will be blessed to remain both hunter and wolf. Be warned, this will not be an easy life. If others find out that you are both, you will be in danger if they discover your abilities. I can only do so much." She said, touching Nora's face.

"Thank you." Nora whispered, feeling grateful to her.

"You must be sure this is something you want." She said studying Nora.

"I want to be both." Nora said firmly.

"Then it is done." She smiled proudly

"You need to go before your mate is completely lost." She chuckled.

"How do I-."

With a quick shove, the woman pushed Nora into the fountain. Nora crashed into the water, falling. She felt like she was falling forever, and then she hit the ground and felt the air rush out of her lungs as blackness took over.

"Nora, don't leave me."

It was the faintest plea; it was a broken one.

The kind that made your heart hurt hearing it. It was whispered into her ear. I don't want to. I'm not, she thought. She couldn't breathe. She fought to get air back into her lungs. She inhaled deeply and then began coughing. Air flooded her lungs as she felt like she had swallowed fire. She continued coughing, trying to sit up as she was pressed against something.

"Nora!" Jace yelled, seeing her begin to struggle against him.

"Nora?" Wyatt whispered, confused.

Nora's eyes shot open, and she found herself staring into Jace's, his eyes glowing ice blue as he looked down at her. She reached up, her hand going to the side of his face. She touched him like she didn't believe he was there. He leaned into her touch, just as shocked as she was.

"Hi." She smiled at him.

"Thank god." he said, pulling her into him, his lips crashing into hers.

He kissed her fiercely and deeply like it was the last kiss he was ever going to get from her. She kissed him back, her mind melting into the kiss. She was grateful to be back in his arms. Thankful he was safe. She pulled back slightly, remembering the battle they were in. Was everyone safe?

"The Lobos? Kip?" Nora asked as she tried to look around Jace.

"Dead." Jace said quietly, pressing his forehead to hers.

"How?' Nora asked.

"You tell me." Jace said to her, kissing her forehead.

"Don't ever, ever do that again. Don't you dare ever try to leave me?" Jace growled into her ear.

"You wolves." Nora laughed, and then her eyes began to glow.

Jace looked at her, not sure what was going on. Cole pressed forward, and Jace allowed him. There was something going on with him. He sensed something, and he needed to know what it was. Cole howled inside of him, communicating with something.

Nice to meet you, Cole, my mate. Zara spoke to Cole, showing herself to him.

Mate. Cole howled excitedly.

"How?" Jace asked, cupping the side of her cheek.

"I have always been a wolf but also a hunter. I didn't know about Zara. She was locked away inside of me." Nora whispered to him.

"I'll explain more later. Is everyone ok? Everyone safe?" Nora said, pulling away from Jace and starting to stand.

Jace helped her stand up; she leaned into him and looked around. The crowd around them dropped to their knees as she stood and bared their necks. The hunters bowed their heads graciously.

"Jace, don't make them do that right-" Nora started to say, but she became confused when she saw the hunters bowing their heads.

She looked over to Jace and then to Logan. Dante stepped forward, his head bowed in respect.

"My Luna," Dante said, bowing his head more.

"They are showing respect to their new Luna. They saw what you did and sacrificed." Jace whispered to her.

"Ok, but they don't need to do that." She said to Jace, shrinking into him.

"Logan, what's up with you guys?" Nora asked quietly, talking about the hunters.

"Nora, you are the hunter we have been waiting for. One that would show us the way and have the strength to do all that was needed. We just didn't expect you to build a bridge between hunters and wolves. We see now that an alliance can work, and we can work together." Logan said, lowering his head.

"Ok, that's enough." Nora said, waving her hands as she did. No one moved.

She sighed, annoyed. "Jace, can we go home?"

"Always." he said to her quietly.

Chapter Eighty One
Alpha

"Wait, we can't leave yet." Nora sighed, leaning into Jace; she was exhausted.

"The hospital, we need to get rid of it. We don't need anyone following in his footsteps. Also, I need to know how a man named Asher is; he helped me almost get out..... Kip's pack, we need to do something about them. They were innocently bound to follow his order, and if they didn't, he would hurt people close to them so that they would." Nora began rambling, thinking of everything that needed to be done.

Just as Jace was about to answer her and tell her to stop, Grayson walked through the pack house door. He was carrying his Alpha, and Asher was limping out behind him. The rest of the Black Sands pack walked out, their heads hanging low. Nora scanned the group quickly; Asher was the only one who seemed to be hurt. Her eyes landed on the man being carried. She knew in an instant he was gone. Jace frowned deeply as Grayson carried Chadwick towards them.

"They used every last bit of his blood." Grayson said, his voice a combination of hurt and anger.

"I'm so sorry," Nora whispered, reaching out and touching Grayson's arm.

"If everything is good here, I would like to take my pack home and lay our Alpha to rest." Grayson said quietly to Jace.

"I am sorry we didn't get here in time," Jace nodded to him, telling him he could go.

"Thank you." Grayson said, but it was a different Thank you, not just for Jace's comment but a Thank you as if he had saved them.

"Luna, we look forward to seeing more of you. I am glad we made it in time." Grayson smiled at her before his eyes glossed over, giving silent commands to his pack.

Asher limped over to them, relief spread over his face as he saw Nora. Reaching her, he smiled.

"I am so glad you're ok." He said quietly to her, his eyes flickered almost nervously to Jace.

Nora could feel Jace pushing back a growl. She leaned into him more, knowing her touch would comfort him. She glanced up at him; his eyes glowed as she looked down into hers.

"What is it?" She mind linked him. It was her first mind link done without effort.

The side of his lip curled up as her voice entered his head clear and perfect.

"Jace." Asher said with a small head nod.

"Asher, Nora mentioned that you helped her escape. As it pains me to say I owe you one." Jace said through gritted teeth.

Nora looked at him strangely. It was clear these two had a past; she was confused by the tension. She looked to Asher about to ask, but he spoke first.

"No, you freed my pack. You don't owe me anything." Asher said quietly.

"What is going to happen to Kip's pack?" Nora asked.

As she said the words, Kip's pack approached the pack house cautiously. Some were already there. Jace shoved Nora behind him protectively. Jace's pack was ready, waiting for them to make a move. Kip's pack looked to Asher, who kneeled. He didn't kneel in front of Jace, but he was kneeling in front of Nora. Nora's eyes glowed amber, and Asher's mimicked her color. The rest of Kip's pack followed suit as they kneeled, their eyes matching Nora's.

"Jace." Nora said nervously. He looked around, confused; Kip's pack was pledging themself to Nora.

Nora felt a surge of power rush into her. Jace noticed it, and the tension he felt eased up a bit. Kip's pack had now technically made Nora an Alpha. Jace looked down, studying her; to his knowledge, there had not been a female Alpha before. Nora was overwhelmed and looked at Jace, panicked.

"What's going on?" Nora asked both Asher and Jace.

"I, Asher of the Red Wood pack, pledged myself to you and bound myself to your command." Asher said, his head lowered.

Before Nora could respond, the rest followed in what sounded almost like a chant. Nora's eyes glowed brighter as each person pledged themself to her. She reached down and squeezed Jace's hand as she felt anxiety creeping up into her chest.

"Jace. I…I-" He pulled Nora against him; his scent invaded her nose, and she inhaled deeply.

Being close to him immediately calmed her down. She moved closer to him, just needing to be next to him. We don't need to figure all this out right now. Jace's mind liked her, and she nodded. The stress, anxiety, and the fact that she was now linked to everyone there was overwhelming. She could feel each pack member's feelings as well as Jace's pack. She felt drained. She looked up at Jace and sighed.

"Asher stand." Nora commanded.

Jace glanced at her curiously but didn't interfere. Asher slowly got to his feet and looked at her.

"Yes, my Alpha?" Asher asked her, his eyes still on the ground.

"Look at me." Nora said, annoyed with the submissiveness of his actions.

Asher looked up, locking eyes with her, his mood shifting slightly. Nora made up her mind quickly.

"I, Nora, Alpha of the Red Wood pack, appointed you, Asher, my Beta." Nora said, her eyes locked on Asher as she said it.

She watched a small force go through Asher as he became her Beta.

"Thank you, Alpha; I will not let you down." Asher said, going to lower his head again.

He caught himself when Nora cleared her throat, and he started to do it again. Jace pulled Nora closer to him; he could feel her starting to wobble.

"Dismantle the hospital. I want all research done by Kip destroyed. After that, you all go back to your families and settle in. I will return tomorrow to sort the rest of things out. Beta Asher will be in charge in my place while I am gone." Nora commanded.

She watched her pack nod and then start to complete her orders. Asher nodded to her before leaving and walking to the pack house.

"Home now?" Jace whispered to her.

"Please." Nora replied.

She was suddenly scooped up into Jace's arms, and he began carrying her. He walked toward one of the ATVs. He set her down before finding the Keys and turning it on.

"Why Asher?" Jace asked her quietly as he started up the ATV.

"He reminds me of you. He was willing to die to do the right thing for his pack. He will be a good Beta, maybe even Alpha." Nora yawned, leaning against him.

"Alpha?" Jace questioned her as he slipped his arm around her.

"Yeah, unless you want us to run both packs," Nora said, closing her eyes as she spoke.

"How do you know Asher?" Nora said, yawning again.

"That's a little complicated. We'll talk later after you just." Jace said, leaning down and kissing her on the top of her head.

She sighed happily as his lips brushed the top of her head. She felt so weak she didn't know if she was going to be able to stay awake much longer. The feeling of relief rushed over him; he felt like he could finally breathe, having her back tucked under his arm. He almost lost himself when he thought she was gone. He never wanted to feel that again. He watched her start sleeping against him, and a small smile ran over his face. He couldn't wait to be home with her. He honestly just wanted to curl up in bed with her and sleep. Nora was sound asleep leaning into him, her head resting against his chest as they reached the pack house. He switched off the ATV and moved his arm slightly so she fell gently into his lap.

He pulled her into his chest and began carrying her to the house. As he started walking up the steps, Nora jolted up. Her eyes were wide with panic and fear. She tapped Jace To put her down. She could feel a strong force of power; she couldn't make out where it was coming from or who. She struggled in Jace's arms. She went down in case she needed to defend them. She tried focusing on how far or close this thing was. She was too weak to focus her power. She couldn't handle any more today, but she was not going to let whatever it was ruin what they barely started.

"Nora? What's wrong? Are you okay?" Jace said, holding onto her tighter.

"Something is coming." She whispered, looking across the yard.

"Something?" Jace said, setting Nora down and standing in front of her, Cole pushing just under his surface.

He didn't pick up anything; what was she sensing? He squinted, trying to focus his eyes. He couldn't hear anything either.

"Yes. Something strong." Nora whispered, her eyes glowing amber; Zara was ready to fight.

Chapter Eighty Two
Visitors

As if she summoned them, a car pulled into the driveway of the pack house. Nora looked at Jace, who was bloody and still very much naked. The long black town car stopped, its tires scratching across the gravel. The doors opened, and Nora felt Jace stiffen beside her. She could feel the tension rolling off of him. A low growl rumbled from his chest as the doors of the black town car opened. The first thing she noticed was they were all wearing bright white shoes as they stepped out of the car. They had black suits on as they walked towards them. Nora reached out and ran her hand down Jace's forearm, trying to calm him.

"Who are they?" Nora asked through mindlink.

"The council." Jace replied.

"Jace!" The man with short brown hair that was combed to the side called to him as he walked towards them.

"Bruce." Jace said, nodding to him, Bruce stopped just in front of the stairs, two others following behind him.

Nora studied them; it was the three of them together that she had sensed. Their aura wasn't too much stronger than Jace's alone, but together, it was powerful. One man had spikey blonde hair and bright green eyes, and the other was bald with chocolate brown eyes.

"I didn't know you had taken a mate! Congratulations! What's your name-

"Are you an Alpha?" The one with the spiked blonde hair asked as the attention turned to Nora. She felt Jace trying to decide what to say. Nora cleared her throat as the three men gawked at her.

"Yes and No," Nora said, hoping Jace wouldn't be upset with her.

"Jace, what does she mean?" The spiky blond-haired man asked; the bald one shifted, trying to get a better look at Nora.

"What she says, Lance." Jace said shortly. Nora watched Lance grit his teeth and flex.

Nora could tell these men were not used to being talked to like this.

"I am an acting Alpha of the Red Woods pack." Nora answered quickly.

"Interesting. And Kip?" The Bald one said, crossing his arms across his chest.

"He's dead." Jace said, a growl coming through as his eyes glowed.

"Dead?" Bruce said quietly.

"Yes, he kidnapped my mate and was going to use her to help create more of his monsters." Jace said, leaving out the part that he was going to turn her so the council might not know she was human at one point.

'Monsters?" Lance said quietly.

"Yeah, the ones I called and told you about while you sat ideally by and let him cause havoc and chaos," Jace said, growling more.

Lance stepped towards Jace, his eyes glowing purple in color. Nora thought the color strange but stepped in between Jace and Lance.

"Gentlemen, my mate is tired, naked, and wounded. Would it be all right to continue this conversation in the morning? You are welcome to stay." Nora said, trying to smooth the tension.

Lance stepped closer to Nora; it was half curiosity, half a threat. Jace growled, going to pull Nora out of the way and take on Lance. Nora wouldn't move; her eyes glowed a bright amber, daring Lance to challenge her.

"Lance, that is enough. The female Alpha is right. We could all use some rest. I also don't want any more emotions out and about. Jace did just go to war over his mate. So let's not continue rocking the boat." Bruce smiled.

Lance stared at her steadily.

"You are very pretty." He said, a smirk across his face.

Jace began growling fiercely again, going to tug Nora aside. Nora's eyes glowed brighter as she stepped to Lance.

"I suggest you listen to your friend before I move aside and you meet your fate." Nora said, her eyes vicious.

Lance's eyes flickered to Jace, who was one breath away from shifting. Lance went to move towards Jace, and Nora placed her hand on his chest, stopping him.

"Choose your response wisely. I would listen to your friend." Nora said and let a wave of power roll off of her.

It wasn't just an aura of an alpha but something more. Lance stepped back, feeling it. Jace felt it, too, but acted like he didn't. He didn't want anyone to know how powerful Nora could be.

"Lance." Bruce warned.

"Jace and ?" Bruce continued but stopped asking Nora her name.

"Nora." She said shortly her eyes were not moving off of Lance.

"Lovely. Jace and Nora, we all need rest. We can hash everything out in the morning. May we stay at your pack house?" Bruce asked with a polite smile, but it was more of a command.

Jace growled at the questions. Nora reached behind her and entwined her fingers into his. She didn't know who they were, but she knew they were powerful. She smiled sweetly at Bruce, who seemed to be the leader.

"We would love for you to stay here." Nora smiled back.

"Excellent." Bruce smiled.

"We weren't expecting company, so you will have to do with what we have." Nora smiled and motioned for Jace to walk inside.

"You'll stay on the third floor. Last three rooms." Jace said before walking in.

Nora followed behind Jace. She felt movement close behind her. She glanced over her shoulder to see Lance following too closely to her. She stepped upwards and into Jace. He placed her arm around her and pulled her into him.

"This is the kitchen. Lori will be here shortly. If you need anything, she will get it to you or make it for you." He said, not even pausing as he walked to the stairs.

Nora walked up the stairs with Jace. Lance, Bruce, and the other man followed them up the stairs. Nora could feel Lance's eyes burning into her. She felt Zara becoming angry inside of her. Jace stopped short and turned suddenly as they reached the second-floor landing. He almost made Nora fall as quickly as he did. He turned and was face to face with Lance.

"If you keep disrespecting my mate with your eyes. My wolf will remove them for you. I don't care if you're a council member or not." Jace said, his eyes glowing, his voice cold and deadly.

Lance stepped into Jace, bowing up at him. Nora began to panic. Jace was wounded, and Zara could feel Cole, and he wasn't in the best shape either. Nora gritted her teeth as the two men stared him down. Bruce was watching with a smirk, waiting for someone to make a move. Nora was done with this.

"Bruce, could you rail in your man," Nora said, her voice was calm but holding authority.

Lance's eyes flickered to her as if no one had ever spoken to them like that. Giving them an order. Jace was in his own category; he was one of the few who didn't mind standing up. The rest all fell in line. Who was this girl? Lance wondered. Bruce smiled politely and placed a hand on Lance's shoulder.

"Lance, let's not do this just yet." Bruce said, a threat in his voice as he made sure to word his sentence just right.

"Jace, you need to remember who we are and your place." Bruce warned him.

Nora watched Bruce's eyes glow purple. She didn't feel anything, but she looked at Jace, and she saw him wince. Bruce sent his aura out there, trying to make Jace buckle. He was fighting hard against it. She watched sweat bead across his forehead, and his hands began to twitch. Nora took a deep breath and stepped between Bruce and Jace, trying to shield him.

"Mr. Bruce, if you go up this flight of stairs, the first three rooms are yours. If you don't mind, I am going to go take care of my mate. We hope everything is to your liking." Nora said, taking Jace by the hand.

She called us her mate… Again, Cole said excitedly to Jace, pointing it out but still having his guard up as he felt Bruce's aura leave him.

Bruce looked at her dumbfounded. How? Echoed in his brain. How did she act like she didn't feel what he was doing? How did she not buckle and submit? He knew why Jace was the way he was. He was strong, and his father was one of the strongest Alpha's. His blood ran through Jace, and in order for Jace to stand up to him, he had trained himself against the aura.

Nora smiled pleasantly at him before walking up the stairs with Jace. Nora felt them watching them as they continued up to the third floor. She was grateful when they finally made it into their room, and she shut the door.

"Who the hell are they?" She asked Jace, still looking at the door.

"The council." Jace growled.

"The council?" Nora asked, confused.

"Yes, three waste of space men appointed to uphold laws and ensure all packs were run fair. They let it go to their heads and do whatever they want." Jace growled as he began to pace.

"Lance, Bruce, and what's the third one's name?" Nora asked.

"Douglas." Jace said, his eyes glossing over as he answered her.

" *Council is here. Be cautious.*" Jace sent out to his pack.

Nora looked surprised when she heard his voice in her mind. She smiled a little bit, feeling included. He raised an eyebrow at her as his eyes went back to normal, asking about her smile. She shook her head slightly.

"I need to get you fixed up. Do all wolves just travel naked?" Nora said, pointing to the bathroom.

A smirk appeared across his lips, and mischief flashed in his eyes as he began to stalk her. Nora's playful smile appears as she tries to remain firm. She narrowed her eyes at him but stepped back against the wall.

"Bathroom. You have wounds." She tried to order him.

He pinned her against the wall, his arms on either side of her head. Her eyes glowed dimly at him as Zara pushed forward excitedly. In return, Cole pushed outwards as well, Jace's eyes glowing bright blue.

"Say it again." He said his voice was seductive.

"Go to the bathroom." Nora said, a small laugh escaping her.

"No. What am I to you?" He said, his voice deep and made Nora's heart race.

"My mate." She said, her eyes locked on his. Jace pressed his forehead against hers as he closed his eyes.

"Again." Jace said his voice was soft but demanding.

"My mate," Nora said. No matter how she said it, it sent chills through him.

His mouth crashed down on hers, claiming it. His kiss was hungry, wanting, and demanding. His arm pulled her against him as he scooped her into his arms. He, with one swift motion, carried her to the bed. Nora let out a small protest noise but was quickly subdued by his tongue invading her mouth as she crashed onto the bed.

"I want her." Lance mind linked Bruce as they *began making their way to their rooms.*

"She's marked by Jace." Bruce linked back.

"And I will mark it over." Lance's mind linked back.

"You know it doesn't work that way. Wolf law says you are not to mark an already marked mate. You cannot lay claim to another who is already claimed." Bruce linked back.

"It doesn't matter. We are the council. We should be able to take who we want and when we want. We are supposed to be all-powerful." Lance linked him back.

"Did you not just hear what happened? Jace went to war over his mate. Kip is dead." Bruce linked back.

"And." Lance said, making a face as he looked at Bruce.

"And nothing. We do not need any more trouble right now." Bruce said, turning and locking eyes with Lance.

Lance made a face and walked into his room.

"What was that now?' Douglas asked Bruce.

"Lance being Lace." Bruce said, but his voice had anger in it.

"He wants the Alpha's mate, doesn't he?" Douglas said his voice had no emotions to it.

"Yes. " Bruce sighed.

"This might cause trouble." Douglas said.

"Yes. You're very observant." Bruce said sarcastically.

Douglas grunted and went to his room. He was the outsider among the three of them. The one who had joined and was elected due to his ability to uphold the law. Unlike Bruce, who managed his way to the top, and Lance, whose dad paved his path. Douglas was here originally for the right reasons. He sighed as he walked into the room. Jace just might be the Alpha who could turn things around, he thought as he sat on the bed. He would have to play his cards carefully if he decided he wanted to push for this movement.

Lance slammed the door to his room, anger sitting in him. He walked to the bathroom, throwing water on his face. That She-wolf and her honey-colored eyes dancing in his hand. She had a power about her, an aura he couldn't resist. He wanted her. He wanted her in every way. It is like he found some new toy or trophy he needed to keep and put on his shelf. He was obsessing over her. He would get her, just wait. He told himself as he stared in the mirror.

Note from the author:
Thank you so much for reading! Jace and Nora's story does not end here! See what lies ahead for Jace and Nora. Book Two Coming 2024!
Breaking the Alpha Council

www.ingramcontent.com/pod-product-compliance
Lightning Source LLC
Chambersburg PA
CBHW062058290726
48975CB00001B/22